THOSE ONCE FORGOTTEN

THE WAYSTATIONS TRILOGY
BOOK 2

N.C. SCRIMGEOUR

CONTENTS

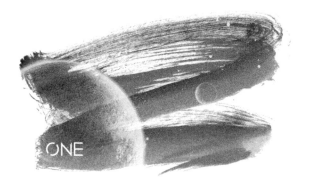

ONE

KOJAN

Alvera had killed him.

Every stolen second slipping away was a reminder of that. There was no respite from the new-found horror with which he regarded his body. It was a hyperawareness driving him half mad, offering him no peace from the panic sharpening his ever-shallowing breaths, no reprieve from the pain as the machinery inside him gnawed away at organ tissue and muscle fibre, no antidote for the poison slowly slipping through his blood.

Alvera had killed him, but it was worse than that—she had killed them all.

Kojan shifted, trying to loosen the cramp in his legs. The passenger hold was dim and musty, recycled air churning the stale sweat of the people crowded inside. This leg of his journey had been the longest of them all. The fact it was also the last brought him little comfort. If there was one thing he had learned since leaving New Pallas, it was that there was always time for things to get worse.

He pulled up a newsfeed to pass the time. Choppy footage and scrambled subtitles flashed in front of his eyes, projected by his retinal implants. The edges of his vision were discoloured and grainy. His cybernetics were already starting to decay. Every time he sent another neural command to his failing implants, they raged against him, sending a swell of pain through the back of his eyes into his head.

Still he watched, unable to look away from the feeds. Unable to look away from the carnage his old captain had unleashed.

The agitator, they were calling her. A title for the headlines that made her more like a mythical nightmare than a woman who'd simply put her boot through the galaxy.

She'd left them—left *him*—with nothing but unanswered questions. The ominous signal pattern was still emanating from all four waystations. The ever-shortening gaps between the bursts spoke of something approaching, inevitable and unknown.

Nobody knew what was coming, only that it was on its way.

On the feeds, the Coalition ambassadors masked themselves in composure and spoke words the rest of the galaxy needed to hear. Desperate platitudes and promises they had no idea they could keep. They talked of recruitment drives for the Coalition Corps, of fast-tracked shipbuilding and reinforced planetary defences. The response might have been impressive, if anybody knew what it was a response to. All they had was a ticking clock and no answers to what it was counting down to.

It didn't matter that nobody had any idea how to fix it. All that mattered was they had someone to point the finger at.

So did he.

Alvera's face swam in his head, intrusive and unbidden. Weary lines creased her sallow skin. Greying hair framed the sharp angles of her face. The worst part was the steel behind the haunted look in her eyes. Stricken and unapologetic in equal measure, as if she was aware of all the horrors she had inflicted and regretted none of them.

But when she opened her mouth, it was his mother who spoke.

That code in your cybernetics that's slowly killing you piece by piece? She was the engineer who created it.

He tried to push the words out of his head. Ojara's parting taunt was hardly a reminder he needed. Every glitch in his implants, every spasm and burst of pain, was a result of what Alvera had done to him. What they had *both* done to him. The quickening virus running through him had become a countdown of his own. An execution engineered for him before he'd even been born. His captain's code, his mother's killswitch. Ojara might have been the one to pull the trigger, but Alvera had handed her the loaded gun.

His wrist terminal pinged, breaking him from his thoughts. A flutter of relief broke through the weight of despair as the comms signature flashed in front of his eyes.

Finally.

It had been weeks since he tried to contact Ridley. A reply this late might have meant she was far out of reach, but it also meant she was alive.

She appeared in front of him as a flickering hologram projected from his wrist terminal. Her eyes were dark and bloodshot, and her brows knitted into a frown across her deep brown skin. There was a breathless wonder to her voice he remembered well, and an edge to it he didn't.

"I don't know what the time delay is between wherever you are and the Rim Belt, but I'm guessing you sent that message before this shitshow went down," she said. "Still, it's good to hear a friendly voice. Things have been..." She broke off, a humourless laugh escaping her lips. "What the hell is going on out there, Kojan? What did the captain do?"

Even if there had been no time delay between them, her

question wasn't something he could answer. When it came to Alvera, it was never about what she would do—it was about what she *wouldn't*.

"The strangest part is how much it all makes sense," Ridley continued, sounding like she was talking more to herself than to him. "This countdown, whatever is coming...there were signs of it before. The shared languages between the colonies, the way the species in this galaxy are all so different but have evolved along the same paths—it all fits together. The waystations are the key. I don't think we were the first to discover them. I think..."

She hesitated again, looking over her shoulder at something Kojan couldn't see. "I can't get into this right now. Too many ears. But whatever the captain did out there, I don't think she was the first to do it. There's more to this than any of us know. We need to find out what's happening. *I* need to find out."

She gave a faint smile. "Stay safe, Kojan. Knowing you're still out there somewhere... I feel less alone today than I did yesterday. If we're all that's left of New Pallas, we have to make it count for something."

The connection flickered and died. Kojan let go of the breath he'd been holding and tried to swallow the lump in his throat. The message had shown him a hole in his heart, an absence he'd been trying to ignore. Seeing Ridley again only reminded him of what he'd lost. The billions of people they'd left behind on their dying planet. The crew of the *Ranger*, executed at Ojara's command. Alvera herself, despite everything she'd done. And then there was—

He gritted his teeth against the pain. There it was. The wound that ached worst of all.

Eleion.

She had gone with Alvera. And like Alvera, she would never come back. Whatever his old captain had done on Ulla Waystation had triggered a strange temporal net. The contraption was invisible and alien, and utterly inescapable. No ship could move into its proximity without finding itself caught in a dead pocket of space. No ship could move out of it either. They were trapped.

He couldn't stop himself picturing how it would end. Suffocation would take Eleion long before starvation. The reserve of toxins so vital to the iskaath respiratory system would run out in days, leaving her to drown in her own breather mask.

Following Alvera had always been a death sentence. For him. For the crew of the *Ranger*. For Eleion. Realising it now was too late. The only small comfort he could grasp through the bitterness and betrayal was knowing it wouldn't be long until his old captain followed them.

One of his implants gave a sharp burn and he let out a hiss. The more they deteriorated, the harder it would be to keep inconspicuous. Even here, on a crowded transport freighter packed with hundreds of people, he still wasn't safe. All it would take was one of them to notice him, one of them to recognise something familiar in his features and match it with the image being displayed intermittently on the grimy holo-screens on the ship's hull.

His own face staring back at him.

He drew the oversized hood of his tunic closer. The portrait on the galactic arrest warrant was a version of himself he forgot had existed. Fresh-faced and clean-shaven, skin free from bruises and blemishes. The pristine gleam of functioning cybernetics curling around one eyebrow and down the curve of his jaw.

Weeks tucked away in one cramped hold after another had changed him. His jawline had darkened with a shadow of a patchy beard, and his cheeks were sunken and shallow. As the quickening continued to ravage him, his subdermal cybernetics would force their way through the skin and tissue they were devouring.

The freighter buckled, sending a violent shudder through him. He took a steadying breath as the hull rocked with the turbulence from hitting atmo. If he closed his eyes, he could imagine the ship passing through the swirling yellow clouds which shrouded Kaath's noxious atmosphere.

The last time he'd been here, Eleion had been by his side. Returning without her felt like a betrayal.

"Masks on. Come on, be quick about it." A bone-plated dachryn paced up and down the middle of the hold, his exoskeleton dull under the dim lights. "Teraxis isn't going to pay out to your families if you get shipped home in a body bag. Better check those seals if you don't want to be choking on your own lung tissue in a few minutes."

Kojan ran a gloved hand over the mask he'd been given. It was a cheap, flimsy thing that looked like it had known more than its fair share of wearers. The rubber seals were worn and scuffed, but when he placed the mask over his head, it connected with the joins on his mining suit with a soft hiss.

He might have been more worried if he thought he needed the protection. But he'd had a brush with Kaath's toxic atmosphere before. It was ironic that the very cybernetics which had jumped into action to save him back then were doing their best to kill him now.

A metallic groaning cut through his thoughts as the cargo door inched open, letting the fierce glare of sunlight spill into the shadows of the hold. It illuminated the weary faces around him, and he instinctively pulled his hood further down. Just because he'd hidden his face behind a breather mask didn't mean he was any safer. Not when he was surrounded by people so desperate they might kill each other to be the one who handed him over for the reward.

And that was *before* taking the Teraxis officials into consideration.

Signing up to the mining guild had been a last resort, but finding transport to Kaath had proven to be more difficult than he imagined. The iskaath homeworld wasn't exactly a tourist destination, and civilian shuttles were few and far between on the shipping schedule. But Teraxis took on contractors to work in the volatile gas mines beneath Kaath's surface, laying piping for the planet's city-sized factories and refineries. The work was dangerous and the pay barely enough to survive on. Maybe that's why they took on only the most desperate.

And now, that included him.

"Move it." The dachryn foreman gave him a push. "The sooner you get registered, the sooner you can get to work."

Kojan grimaced behind his mask but said nothing. He followed the line of workers out of the freighter and into the orange glow of the low-lying Kaath sun. The landing pad was propped up on stilts high above the thick, marshy terrain that covered much of the planet's surface. In the distance he could see the blackened cinder-block silhouette of one of the factories, set like a shadow against the yellow-tinged sky.

The contract he signed under the fake name he had given them promised that factory, or one like it, as his destination. He'd spend years being paid a pittance to carry out dangerous work in shoddy gear, and if he survived long enough to reach the end of his term, Teraxis would find some reason or another to extend it, claiming administrative error or overpaid dues that needed to be worked back.

Lucky for him, he had other plans.

He glanced around as they traipsed down the steps of the landing pad towards the factory district. All he needed was a chance. An unattended landskimmer or grav bike would be ideal. Something quick enough to get away in and small enough to lose anyone who might give chase.

"Registration this way," the dachryn foreman said, gesturing towards a warehouse on the other side of the thoroughfare. "Once you've been processed, you'll be assigned a sleep quadrant and labour division and tagged for monitoring. Remember, your first three months' wages go towards paying off your accommodation. I don't want to hear any complaints because one of you idiots didn't read the contract you were signing."

Kojan stiffened. If they tagged him with a monitoring device, it wouldn't matter if he managed to escape. Even if he made it to Eleion's old nest, it would only bring down more violence on the people who had already risked so much trying to protect him.

If he was going to make a move, it had to be now.

"Foreman?" A siolean's voice reached his ears through the translator in his implants. "I think..." She broke off, her voice raspy and weak. "I think there might be something wrong with my breather mask."

The dachryn whipped his head around to look at her, his grey eyes glinting from behind his own mask. "Did you check your seals properly?"

"I think so. But I feel strange. I can't..." Her angular black eyes widened. "I can't..."

Kojan moved quicker than anyone else, already at her side to break her fall when she collapsed to the ground. Panicking gasps echoed inside her mask as a bubbling, white foam began to froth around her mouth.

He pressed his gloved hands around the seams of her neck, trying to find the seals. His fingers came across a tear in the collar of her suit, exposing her skin to the atmosphere.

It was already too late.

Two medics rushed in and he jumped out of the way, his legs trembling as memories came flooding back—the shattering of his visor, Eleion's scream, the darkness that surrounded him as the atmospheric toxins rushed into his lungs and took hold. He'd barely survived, and even that was only thanks to the advanced trauma regulators built into his cybernetics.

The siolean didn't have a chance.

This is your opportunity, flyboy. Alvera's voice filled his head. *There's nothing you can do for her, but there's something she can do for you. Get out of here while everyone's distracted.*

He gritted his teeth against her words. It didn't matter that they made sense. It didn't matter that they were right. Not when they were coming from her.

That's what you would have done, isn't it? he thought. *Hell, you'd have ripped a hole in her suit yourself if you thought it would buy you the time you needed.*

There was no answer. That was the thing about ghosts. In the end, they were nothing but memories.

The siolean was convulsing now, her back arching as one spasm after another wracked her slender body. Soon, it would be over. Soon, he would miss his chance.

Damn it. Damn it all.

He edged backwards. It wasn't hard to slip through the gathered workers. They had surged forward in a swell that was as fearful as it was curious. They all knew the same thing could happen to them. All it would take was a crack in the polymer of their visors, a loose catch in their seals. Seeing the siolean thrash and splutter held them enthralled in the horror of it all, caught in a trance of morbid fascination.

He lingered at the back of the crowd, taking in the rest of the thoroughfare. He'd only get one chance to make a break for it. If he was going to run, he had to make it count.

His heart leapt as he caught sight of a lone grav bike hovering by the warehouse. It was untethered, no docking clamps in sight. If he could get to it without getting caught...

The dying siolean's face swam in front of his eyes, and he blinked her features away. No time. No choice.

Funny the justifications we allow ourselves to make when we're desperate, isn't it? Alvera mused from somewhere dark in his memory.

Kojan ran.

His legs burst into action, eager to release something he'd been holding back for too long. Weeks of cramped confinement and small spaces had made him stiff and sore, but there was elation as well as pain in the burn of his muscles.

His footsteps thundered across the thoroughfare, resounding in his head with the noise of a thousand gunshots. Each laboured breath he took echoed in his ears, so loud it was hard to believe the whole factory district hadn't been alerted. Someone would surely notice him. Someone would surely stop him.

He was almost at the grav bike when the warehouse door slid open. An iskaath warden, bare-jawed and standing on long, towering limbs, stopped in surprise. "You, worker. Where is your foreman?"

Kojan froze. The bike was right in front of him, an arm's length away. The noise from the crowd had settled down. There was only silence now. He could hear his heart hammering against his chest.

No time. No choice.

He leapt onto the bike, slipping across the seat and wrapping his hands around the controls in one fluid movement. The throttle was awkward and unwieldy beneath his fingers and the seat felt out of balance under his weight. One ill-timed jerk could send him sprawling. In the hands of any other human, it would have been a death trap.

But it wasn't in anyone else's hands, it was in his. And if there was one thing Kojan could do, it was fly.

The warden blinked her yellow eyes for only a moment before twisting her jaws into a sneer. "Don't be foolish, human.

That grav bike is built for iskaath physiology. You won't get two klicks before you crash and burn."

He shifted position in the seat. "Thanks for the concern, but I think I'll take my chances."

She narrowed her eyes and brought up her wrist terminal. "Get me a link to the south-eastern patrol. We've got a runner headed their way. Authorisation for—"

The rest of her words were lost in the roar of the engine as he gunned the throttle and launched the bike across the thoroughfare.

His stomach flipped in joy at the acceleration that burst through him as he pushed the grav bike forward. The towering facades of the grim, blocky buildings faded into a blur as he leaned into a turn and eased the bike towards open terrain. He'd awoken something that had been missing for longer than he could remember—speed and power and the unbridled freedom that came with having control at his fingertips and distance in his wake.

This wasn't a part of him that belonged to Ojara. This wasn't a part of him the captain could touch with her code. This was all him. It was what he'd been born to do.

He pushed the throttle harder, and the bike roared in agreement. The industrial blocks of the factory district disappeared behind him as he pressed on under the thick, yellow sky. Steel and asphalt gave way to reeds and swampland, the planet's wilderness welcoming him like an old friend.

The nav display in his retinal implants flickered up in front of his eyes. He adjusted course to head towards a small settlement a few hundred klicks away. If it had a name in the iskaath tongue, he didn't know what it was. All he knew was it was Eleion's home. Her nest.

The ache of her loss clawed at his chest, and he pushed his thoughts away. Mourning his friend would have to come later. Right now, he had to survive.

A proximity alert chimed in his ear and he glanced back at the nav display to see two fast-moving shapes on an intercept approach. The warden's patrol had locked on to his position. If they caught him, they'd likely beat him to within an inch of his life before hauling him back to the factory district. Teraxis would fine him wages he hadn't even earned and slap an extra five years on his contract for the trouble he'd caused.

If they caught him.

He pushed the throttle as far as it could go and the grav bike lunged forward in response. The spaces between the thick trees were getting narrower. The slightest touch in the wrong direction could send him spiralling into one of the trunks. There would be nothing left of him but pieces of flesh and bone in a burning wreck.

He leaned into each turn without thinking, skimming past branches and brushing the long reeds on the marshy forest floor beneath him. The patrol bikes were right behind him. He could hear the roar of their engines over his own. The sound filled his ears and blocked out his thoughts. All that mattered was the touch of the controls under his fingers, the shifting of his weight into each turn.

There was something exhilarating about the recklessness of it all. The quickening was already killing him. Even now, one of his retinal implants might blow, blinding him and sending him crashing into the trees. That wasn't something he could outrun. The patrol bikes were.

He pushed on, urging the bike forward with all the power its engine could give him. Every muscle was on high alert, every reaction heightened.

Even so, he didn't see the overhanging branch until it was too late.

It stretched out at head height, thick and knotted and utterly unavoidable. There was no time to pull up or skirt around it. It was coming straight for him, ready to cleave his head from his shoulders.

Kojan pulled on the grav bike's controls and threw his weight to the right. The bike lurched sideways, and he squeezed his legs to cling on as the world flipped. The orange reeds below became a carpeted wall so close they tickled his cheek.

Out of the corner of his eye, he watched the branch fly past overhead.

He hauled the bike upright again, his heart thumping and mouth dry. Too close. Too damn close. If he had been a second slower—

The roar of an explosion filled his ears, and he tightened his hands around the controls as the bike shuddered beneath him. He didn't dare look back. He didn't need to. One of the blips on the nav display had disappeared, lost in a burst of fuel and flame. The other was slowing, circling back around to the site of the crash.

He was clear.

A long, tired sigh escaped his lips as he eased off the throttle and readjusted his course for the iskaath settlement. The thought of finally being able to rest was too precious to hope for. The last few klicks stretched out in front of him, holding a reprieve from all he had been running from.

He reached the outskirts as the setting sun began to slip below the horizon. The thick clouds had darkened to a purple-grey, obscuring the yellow-stained sky. He pulled up next to a dock off the main civic complex. Two long-limbed iskaath were chatting nearby, their curved necks bobbing in time with their soft-spoken conversation. One of them was wearing a medical dressing over her shoulder, and her black-green scales were mottled with age.

Cyren.

A painful swelling gripped Kojan's heart, relief and sorrow

and guilt all at once. The last time he saw her, she'd been shot helping him and Eleion escape the planet. Now he was back without her daughter.

The other iskaath caught sight of him, his bright yellow eyes looking up and down Kojan's uniform. "You're a long way from the factories, human. What are you doing here?" He flicked his eyes over to the grav bike. "And with stolen Teraxis property, by the looks of it. You're either stupid or you've got a death wish."

Kojan laughed. "Maybe it's a little of both." He placed his hands around the seals of his mask and pressed the release clasps.

The iskaath gave a sharp hiss of alarm and started forward, but Cyren reached out an arm to stop him. "Wait."

A whisper of cool, evening air caressed Kojan's cheeks as he lifted the mask off and took a tentative breath. There was no dizziness. No paralysis. Just a strange, alien taste on his tongue. His cybernetics were still holding up. The same implants working so slowly to kill him were still doing their best to keep him alive. Trauma regulators filtered out the toxins from the atmosphere while rogue pieces of hardware infected by the quickening ate at him from the inside. Two pieces of code, both written by Alvera. Both at war with each other.

Even now, was one trying to undo the damage the other had caused?

Cyren stretched her long, thin jaws into a sharp-toothed iskaath smile when she saw his face. "Kojan. You came home."

Home. The translated iskaath word was too honest, too forgiving, to be anything but painful. The bitter swell of shame rose within him again. How could he have come back here alone? What right did he have to call it home when Eleion was no longer here?

He shook his head. "You're alive. We saw you go down. I thought—"

"That a lucky shot would be enough to take me out?" Cyren snickered and shrugged her bandaged shoulder. "You should know by now the iskaath are stronger than the rest of the galaxy gives us credit for." Her expression changed, her scales rippling in concern. "But what about you, Kojan? How did you manage to get away? Eleion said Ojara had captured you. I told her not to lose hope, but—"

The rest of her words disappeared into the air. Kojan froze, unable to hear anything beyond the thumping in his heart at what she had uttered.

Eleion said.

Eleion said.

"What?" he whispered, his voice hoarse.

Across the complex, a lone iskaath came out of the med centre. Her yellow eyes were dulled with weariness, the spindles on the back of her neck drooping, but he'd have recognised her from halfway across the planet.

She was alive. Eleion was alive.

The moment her eyes met his, she stiffened. He heard the soft, disbelieving hiss at the back of her throat. He saw the pain and confusion in her startled gaze. He felt the wonder and relief coming from her as surely as he did in his own heart.

Then he was running across the complex, eyes blurry and throat thick with tears. He laughed with every step he took and heard her own disbelieving laughter echoing back at him. She leapt to meet him, throwing her long arms around him in a clumsy, iskaath-human embrace.

"Kojan, my friend," she said, her words a gentle hiss at his ear. "How...how is this possible?"

He squeezed her arms, her scaled skin cool to the touch. "You're asking me? I thought you were dead."

"Such little faith, after all this time?" She grinned at him—that long-jawed grin he'd have known anywhere—and his heart leapt again. Eleion was alive. Whatever happened next, he had that much.

"I don't understand," he said. "You should be trapped on that waystation. How did you manage to get away?"

A sombre expression flittered over her face. "Truth be told, I'm not sure I know. After Alvera blew up the jamming rig, the Coalition fleet began to move in. I knew we had to get out of there before they had a chance to board the waystation, so I got us back to the *Ranger* and set a course to escape. I was certain the fleet would follow or fire on us, but they got caught in that dead zone...that thing they're calling the temporal net." She shook her head. "I don't know why we weren't trapped alongside them. It was like it had no effect on the *Ranger*. Or no interest in us. For some reason, it let us go."

Kojan only half heard her. His attention had been ensnared by two words.

We. Us.

It couldn't be.

"Eleion," he said, fighting to keep the tremble from his voice. "Where is Alvera?"

She hesitated for a moment. "She got the message out to New Pallas. She kept her promise. I thought I could save her, but..." She let out a low sigh and gestured to the med centre she had come out of. "I brought her back. At least, what was left of her. It might have been kinder to leave her body on the waystation, waiting for her people. Better that than...well, you should see for yourself."

He followed her through the sliding doors, trying to calm his shallow breaths. His stomach was tight with dread. He'd made his peace with never seeing Alvera again. Never being able to look at her and ask why she had done the things she'd done. For the past few weeks, she'd haunted his memories like a ghost. Maybe now she was gone, he could put her to rest.

She was lying in a medical pod, out of reach behind the

sealed transparent shield. Her light olive skin had taken on a pale, sickly pallor, and the lines around her eyes were deeper than he remembered. Strands of wispy grey hair framed the angles of her face, and the usual hardness of her expression had been replaced by something softer. There was peace in her lifelessness. A peace she didn't deserve.

Seeing her reduced to a withered husk of the woman he once knew was disturbing, like he had intruded on something he had no right to see. But that wasn't what troubled Kojan the most.

No, the most worrying thing of all was the terrifying chime coming from the faint, persistent blips on the life support monitor attached to the pod.

His old captain, the *agitator*, the woman who'd plunged the galaxy into chaos, was alive.

TWO

RIVUS

The best thing about being in space was the quiet.

It hadn't always been that way. There was a time Rivus had found the unending silence of the abyss suffocating. Solo missions into border territories in the Rim Belt had always brought with them a sense of isolation, like nobody would know where to look if he disappeared. Like nobody would hear him if he cried for help. The silence was a reminder of how vast the galaxy was. How insignificant he was in comparison.

Now, the quiet was a blessing.

He double checked his course on the navigation console and looked out the viewport, watching the external feeds as the ship drifted through the darkness. The only visible stars were faint speckles of light too dim to make sense of. Ossa was far out of reach now, and he couldn't help but feel grateful for it. The Coalition's capital world had become a ball of fear and tension he'd been all too desperate to escape.

It didn't help that Tarvan had been unreachable for weeks. The Coalition's political elite had raised questions about the aggressiveness of the Supreme Commander's assault on the Idran-Var homeworld, and the inquest had dragged on longer than expected. All Rivus could do was wait for news of the outcome like everybody else and try to forget that he'd been there with him when Vesyllion burned.

An alert blared on his navigation display, tearing him from his thoughts. He pulled up the scanners and gave a low growl. Another idiot with a death wish was veering too close to the exclusion zone around Yeven Waystation. Apparently, the carnage in the Ulla system hadn't been enough of a deterrent. Too many ships were trying their luck.

He opened a comms channel to Kite and winced as he was met with the harsh, ear-splitting sound of something that passed for siolean music. "Merala. This is a military operation, not a joyride. I told you to keep this channel clear."

"Yes, boss." A grunt came from the other end of the line as Kite silenced the music. "Just so you know, this is why nobody ever invites generals on patrol runs."

"Because I make you follow the regulations?"

"The stick up your ass about the regs is the least of it," Kite muttered. "I was referring to the way you check in after every little anomaly on the scanners."

"You saw it then?"

"Relax. Their vector is taking them several thousand klicks past the perimeter of the exclusion zone."

"And if they change course?"

He could almost hear the shrug in Kite's answer. "Maybe they'll serve as an example to the next genius who gets too curious."

The siolean's glibness drew a rumble of disapproval from Rivus's throat. After the devastation the temporal net had caused in the Ulla system, the Coalition ambassadors had ordered exclusion zones around the other three waystations to stop any unsuspecting ships getting caught in the same trap.

That's what they were out here to enforce, whether Kite thought it was a waste of time or not.

Rivus glanced at the console. A warning over the comms system was usually enough to ward off any pilot who drifted too close, but there were always exceptions: conspiracy theorists who thought the Coalition was trying to hide something, glory seekers who wanted to be the first ones to break out of a temporal net. It didn't matter who they were. They all ended up sharing the same fate.

"We're going after that ship." He readjusted his course on the nav console and fired the engines to their maximum capacity. "Our job is to enforce that perimeter. I'm not letting anybody cross it on my watch."

"You're in charge, General Itair." The line crackled with the sound of Kite's sigh. "Fifty credits say I get there before you."

"I'm warning you..."

"I'll even give you a head start."

Rivus suppressed a growl of annoyance and pushed his patrol craft onwards. Protocol had never been Kite's strong suit, but there were times his offhand manner tested the limits, even with him. That he couldn't sober himself even now, with all the lives they stood to lose, felt like a personal affront.

"Do I have to remind you about what happens when a ship gets caught by a temporal net?" he said, unable to keep the bite out of his voice. "Thousands of Coalition forces are stranded around Ulla Waystation, unable to move. Those that won't suffocate will starve. This isn't a game."

"I'm well aware of that," Kite replied, the humour in his voice disappearing. "Remember my old unit? Pincer Squad? They were part of the blockade. I've got friends out there counting the hours they have left, knowing nobody is coming to save them." He snorted. "So forgive me if I don't feel sorry for anybody stupid enough to fly into an exclusion zone of their own free will."

"We have our orders. I expect you to take them seriously."

"You mean babysitting this perimeter? Admit it, this is a waste of time. We should be out there, looking for the agitator. Looking for her ship." He let out a sharp breath. "I was part of the team that ran those long-range scans on the remains of the jamming rig. There was no trace of the *Ranger* in the debris field. It must have escaped the temporal net. If we can find out why, it might be the one shot we have at saving some of those people."

"We have no leads. Whatever stealth systems the *Ranger* is running, they were advanced enough to get the ship past an entire blockade of Coalition ships." He gave a pained grunt. "Twice."

"They can't run the stealth systems indefinitely. All that heat has to go somewhere. Sooner or later, that ship is going to show up. And when it does, we need to be ready to take it." His voice was low and urgent. "Give me a squad, Rivus. I'll find the *Ranger*. I'll find the agitator. And we'll find out what the hell she did to these waystations."

"That's not my call. When Tarvan—" He broke off, interrupted by a shrill alarm from the console. He pulled up the display, his heart sinking. "The ship is changing course. Now on a trajectory for the exclusion zone."

"Is this the part where you get to say you told me so?"

Rivus smiled in spite of himself. "A general would never stoop to such levels of pettiness, Merala. Now let's go. We have a ship to catch."

The acceleration tugged at his muscles and tightened his gut as he sent the patrol craft hurtling forward. It wasn't a sensation he'd ever get used to. It was different for space jockeys like Kite, who lived in his flysuit and spent more of his life in a cockpit than outside it.

"Target ahead," Kite said. "Ship's signature is *SNC Illara* out of Sion V."

"That's a siolean planet."

"Don't even think about holding me responsible for the stupidity of my people. I can barely account for my own," Kite quipped. "Pulling up the logs now. Looks like the *Illara* is from a research and development outpost." He paused. "These idiots are scientists?"

"Let's find out." Rivus opened a comms channel to the siolean ship. "*SNC Illara*, this is General Rivus Itair of the Coalition Legionnaire Division. You are on course for Yeven Waystation's exclusion zone. If you don't deviate, you will be caught in a temporal net. Please adjust to the coordinates I'm sending you."

For a moment, the line was silent. Then it crackled, and a yellow-skinned siolean flickered into life on the cockpit's holoscreen. "General Itair, my name is Professor Yira Melle," she said, soft-spoken and pleasant. "I'm a senior researcher from Sion V on an expedition sanctioned by the siolean council. Please stand down. We're fully aware that our current trajectory will take us into the path of the temporal net. Our intention is to study its effects in order to find out how to disable it."

"Study it?" Kite echoed. "She can't be serious."

Rivus shook his head. "With all due respect, Professor, this is a suicide mission. If you go past the exclusion zone, you won't be coming back. Turn your ship around and divert from your current course."

"The *Illara* has been outfitted with prototype atmospheric reserves and a hydroponic suite that will last sixteen standard months. We have the personnel and the equipment to conduct research that could save thousands of lives. We knew what we were getting into when we volunteered for this mission."

"As noble as that may be, you don't have permission to be here. The Coalition set up these exclusion zones for a reason."

"The Coalition is overreaching," the professor replied, her voice taking on a cooler tone. "Our council has given us clearance to be here. Yeven Waystation falls under siolean jurisdiction."

"Not anymore."

"Uncompromising to the last. I don't know why I expected anything else from a legionnaire," she said stiffly. "So be it. We all knew what we were risking when we took on this expedition. We're more than willing to put our lives on the line to see it through. If you want to stop us, go ahead. But you'll have to blast this ship to pieces before we turn around." She gave a cold, tight smile. "A pleasure talking to you, General."

The line went silent as the professor disappeared, leaving behind nothing but flickering static from the holo communicator. Rivus stared at the empty space she had occupied, his head dull and heavy.

"I've got a lock on them," Kite said. "Could take out one of their engines if you want."

"Negative on that, Merala." Rivus let out a long breath. "These aren't some half-brained mercs or newsfeed chasers. The siolean council is backing them. If we shoot them down, if we even cripple them, all we'll do is cause tension between the allied systems. The Coalition needs unity now more than ever. Let them go."

Even as the words left his mouth, he regretted them. When had politics become an excuse to let people fly headfirst towards their own death? No amount of cutting-edge technology or fancy instruments would save the researchers from the oblivion beyond the line they were about to cross. The galaxy knew next to nothing about the temporal nets that had sprung up around the waystations. Only that they were inescapable.

The siolean professor and her fellow scientists were consigning themselves to a slow, drawn-out death on a fool's hope. Of all the thousands of ships that had been ensnared by the temporal net, only one had escaped. And where it was now was anybody's guess.

"Rivus." Kite's voice crackled over the comms channel, tearing him from his thoughts. "As much as I've enjoyed having you breathing down my headtails on this patrol run, something tells me you're going to want to head back to Ossa. Word has come in from High Command. The ambassadors have concluded the Vesyllion inquest."

Rivus's throat tightened. He hardly dared ask the question. "Tarvan?"

"Better get your power armour polished and your salute ready." He could hear the grin in Kite's voice. "The Supreme Commander is back."

———

He found Tarvan exactly where he expected him to be.

The clearing by the waterfalls had been their spot of solace as recruits. It was where they'd dissected their mistakes after a rough training session or cooled off after an intense round of sparring. It was where they'd schemed and dreamed and made plans about how they would shape the galaxy once they'd grown out of their training varstaves and into the warriors they'd always promised to become.

Now, Tarvan stood there alone, facing the thundering, foaming falls. Supreme Commander of the legionnaires. Vanquisher of Vesyllion. The Tyrant. His friend. Even now, it was difficult for Rivus to decide whether Tarvan had fulfilled that childhood promise or dashed it under the sorborite rods he'd released on the Idran-Var.

Tarvan let out a sigh as he approached. The lingen blossoms fluttered on the trees overhead, as if stirred by the sound instead of the wind. It was a sigh that carried too much weight, too much pain, for one dachryn to bear. But Tarvan had always been more than one dachryn. He was a symbol. A promise. The closest thing to a hero the Coalition had.

Maybe that was why he had failed.

"I hear you've been busy," he said, the soft rumble of his voice barely audible over the churning water. "I can think of less torturous ways to pass the time than patrol runs with Kitell Merala."

Rivus gave a half-hearted shrug. "They wouldn't let me see you, and Kite needed the extra resource. Getting away from Ossa for a while seemed as good an idea as any."

"I don't blame you. This farce of an inquest was nothing more than time wasted. Time that could have been better served by doing something instead of surrendering to the whim of hearings and committees." The growl in his voice was quiet, but no less fierce for it. "How many lives have we already lost during these last few weeks? How many could have been saved were it not for our ambassadors' hesitancy and inaction?"

"What did they say during the inquest?"

"Too much and nothing at all." Tarvan's eyes were hard. "They never had any intention of bringing sanctions against me. How could they, with everything that has happened? It was nothing but appearances and damage control, on their end if not mine. But their posturing has cost us weeks. If we are to make up for that, we must act now."

"It's about time." Rivus breathed a sigh of relief. "What's our first move?"

Tarvan straightened, his white cloak billowing behind him in the fresh Ossan wind. "Whatever is coming, we must prepare for it. We must be ready to stand and face it as a galaxy united. That cannot happen while we are still at odds with the Idran-Var. They have been wounded, but they will recover. They always do. They must not be allowed to distract us from whatever lies beyond those waystations."

A dark, heavy dread wrapped itself around Rivus's heart.

"Have we not done enough already? Have we not lost enough? We gain nothing from a war with the Idran-Var."

"If we are to avoid war, then we must instead have an alliance with them," Tarvan said. "Was that not what you suggested? That we could provide them with a common enemy, give them something else to fight? Unless you have made progress on that front during my absence, then I'm afraid we have little choice but to resume our fight and eliminate them for good."

The words were sharp, burrowing their way between his bone plates to the parts of him that were *yysk*-soft and vulnerable. The truth in them was unflinching and pointed with accusation. Tarvan was right. There was only one person who might be able to convince the Idran-Var to come to terms, and Rivus had done everything in his power to avoid her.

It was not a conversation he wanted to have. Not a place he wanted to revisit. But if there was a chance it could help stop what was to come, what choice did he have?

Tarvan grasped his shoulder. "You know what's coming, Rivus. Better than any of us. The Idran-Var can choose to fight alongside us or face the same fate as their leaders on Vesyllion. But I will not allow them to stand in our way. Make them see that, or I will."

There had been a time Tarvan would never have considered allowing such a burden to fall to him. Those kinds of decisions, the calls that carried with them the weight of life and death on a scale too overwhelming to bear, had always been Tarvan's to shoulder.

Not so long ago, Rivus might have begged his friend to share some of that burden. Now, he recoiled from it. Memories of Vesyllion flooded his mind. Blackened, smoking craters and burning fires visible from orbit. No blood, no screams, just the sight of a planet submitting.

It may have been the first to fall. It wouldn't be the last.

He made his way up the sandstone steps that snaked away from the waterfalls and rose towards the training grounds of Cap Ossa. The community orchard was in full bloom under the summer sun. Some cadets had put their sparring staves to the side to laze under the lingen trees and chew on the ripe fruit that had fallen from the branches.

Peace, Rivus thought, marvelling at the fragility of it.

Then he blinked, and the world changed.

The clear sky darkened with thick-knit clouds. No, not clouds. Smoke. Off in the distance, High Command was ablaze. The air was thick with charcoal and burnt flesh. The orchard trees had become charred and black; the lounging cadets were nothing more than ash-covered corpses.

Beside him stood the ghostly dachryn from his dreams. The old general whose nightmares were his, whose footsteps he walked in. The one who had seen this all before.

This is only the beginning, he said. *This may have been the first planet to fall. It won't be the last.*

Rivus blinked again, chasing the smoke and burning bodies away. Sunlight and colour returned to his vision, and the sounds of birdsong and chatter reached his ears once more. It wasn't real. Not yet, at any rate. Not in this life.

His legs trembled as he walked on, trying to push the visions of the dead cadets from his mind. Was it a warning or a memory? It was getting harder and harder to tell. Ever since he'd set foot on Farsal Waystation, ever since he'd unknowingly triggered its defences, his mind had been plagued with visions and voices. At first, he'd been terrified he was going mad. Now, he was more terrified he wasn't.

Niole was sitting by one of the sparring circles. It wasn't until he got closer that he realised it was the same one he'd faced her in all those years ago. The one that had sent her on a path to the Idran-Var and him to second in command of the legionnaires.

Her armed escort gave him a nod as he approached and retreated to a respectful distance. Far enough away to give them privacy, but close enough to intervene if Niole tried anything. Not that it was likely. Her head was drooped, her black eyes slack and unfocused. Her once-vibrant skin had faded to a sickly grey, sapped of its brilliant colour thanks to the implant under her skin pumping her with anti-radiation meds.

An unpleasant measure, but a necessary one. That had been Tarvan's justification. Maybe he was right to be cautious. His memories of her attack all those years ago were still fresh. The way she'd gathered irradiated energy through her skin. The way the air had crackled around them. The way she'd flared and unleashed her fury upon him, ripping half his face off from the inside out.

The ugly scarring on his bone plating would forever be a reminder of that day, for both of them. But the siolean he saw now wasn't the same as the one he'd known back then. They had turned her into a husk of what she'd once been, so much so that Rivus barely recognised her.

Maybe she thought the same about him.

She didn't glance up until his shadow fell across her, blocking the sunlight from her radiation-starved skin. When she met his gaze, her eyes were full of anger and accusation. "Do you mind? It's bad enough turning me into some kind of walking corpse without denying me a little warmth from the sun too. Or is that the next step in this little game of torture the legionnaires have thought up?"

Rivus clenched his jaw. "Torture? After what you did, nobody would blame the Supreme Commander for throwing you in the Bastion for a few decades. You think this is bad? Count yourself lucky you can still see the sun instead of being locked in a windowless cell a kilometre under the ocean."

"After what I did?" Her face twisted with anguish. "I left, Rivus. I ran. I tried for years to get rid of the blood staining my hands. I didn't ask to be followed. I didn't ask the legionnaires to chase me down like a pack of hounds on a hunt. What I did to you was on me. Everything that came after?" Her mouth tightened into a hard line. "That's on you and your precious legionnaires."

"I saw the bodies you left behind on Pasaran Minor. What was left of them, at any rate. Don't try to justify what you did to them."

"They made a choice, as I did." Her voice was grim. "They wanted a fight. If they wanted to live, they should have fought better."

Disgust rose in the back of his throat. "I suppose it shouldn't surprise me that you're starting to sound like an Idran-Var."

"And what if I am?" She gave a careless shrug. Her shoulders were rounder and more muscular than he remembered from their time as cadets. Exile had hardened her physically as well as her mind. It was just one more thing that had changed.

He shook his head. "How did it get to this?"

"I won't be blamed for the choices I've been forced to make," she said. "I almost killed you. That kind of violence terrified me. Sickened me. Knowing I was capable of that...I wanted to turn away from it all."

"Clearly you didn't succeed."

"I tried to," she shot back. "But the legionnaires kept coming. They wouldn't let me forget what I was, what I was capable of. If you're looking for someone to blame for the monster you see in front of you, your trained dogs are just as guilty as the Idran-Var you hate so much."

"If you had come back—"

"No," she said, her voice firm. "We've gone past the time for talking about things that could have happened. The person you knew, the *friend* you knew, no longer exists." She tilted her chin upwards. "And if Vesyllion is anything to go by, I suppose I can say the same about the friend *I* knew."

A hundred justifications sprang to the quivering vocal cords deep in his throat. Excuses. Blame. But even as his bone plates tightened defensively, something else took hold of him and tempered his anger with a resignation that wasn't his own.

This is a fight you cannot win, the ghostly dachryn said, speaking to someone far outside Rivus's reach. *But it is not a fight you have to win. It only needs to end.*

More words not meant for him. More warnings from another life, one he had no understanding of. How was he supposed to fight something he couldn't even see?

Together, the dachryn said.

Rivus looked down at Niole. Her dark stare was somewhere far off in the distance. Her eyes were ringed with shadows that looked like bruises against her pale grey skin. What she'd said was true. She wasn't the same person he once knew. Neither was he.

He sat on the stone bench beside her, lowering his head against the glare from the sun. "I don't want to fight," he said, surprised at how much he meant the words. "I want to understand. What is it you want, Niole? Whose side are you on?"

"You think I haven't been asking myself the same question?" She gave a hollow laugh. "None of them. All of them. What does it matter? There are no sides, only war. All anybody can do is fight back against the thing that's threatening them. Resist." She stared ahead with her large, unblinking eyes. "I thought there must be something more, but that's all there is."

"What if there *was* more? What if there was something out there bigger than the legionnaires and the Idran-Var? Something that threatened all of us?"

"What do you mean?"

His answer caught in his throat, trapped by hesitation and doubt. It wasn't possible. How could the Idran-Var accept an offer of peace while Vesyllion still burned from Tarvan's assault? Yet if he failed, the destruction would not stop at Vesyllion. It would spread across the galaxy until there was nothing left but memories of everything that used to be.

And before long, they would be gone too.

"I'm asking..." He paused. "I'm asking for your help. I need to speak to the Idran-Var. To stop this fight before it goes any further."

A harsh laugh escaped her throat, but it soon trailed off when she noticed the gravity behind his expression. "You can't be serious. Even if I could contact them, why in Fyra's name do you think they'd be willing to speak to you after what you did?"

"Because unless we stop this, Vesyllion won't be the only planet to die."

"Is that a threat?"

"No. It's a warning." He shook his head. "Not for the Idran-Var, but for all of us. We're on the brink of extinction, but nobody knows it. Not like I do. I've seen what will happen. Time is running out. They're coming."

She narrowed her eyes. "Who is coming?"

He offered her his arm. Shining and cybernetic, a reminder of what he'd lost on Farsal Waystation all those months ago. A part of him had been taken that day, the price for the memories that now encroached on his mind. Memories of those it was too late for. Those whose worlds had already been blackened and turned to ash.

"Come with me to High Command," he said. "There's something you need to see for yourself."

THREE

RIDLEY

"Will you get your head out of that damn tablet already?"

Ridley flinched as the sound of something hard and metallic crashed off the ship's wall. She stared at the broken holopad on the floor for a moment, blinking twice at the sparks jumping from its cracked seams, and promptly resumed scanning the data tablet in her hands. Halressan's boredom and frustration had manifested into the casual destruction of non-essential equipment over the past few weeks, but that wasn't a good enough reason for Ridley to get distracted.

"Ignoring me now, Riddles? After what I did for you? I could be dragging your ungrateful ass all the way back to Ossa right now to collect that sizeable bounty Ojara put on your pretty little head. You should be thanking me for the fact you even have the time to study those stupid texts."

Ridley set her translation programme to run in the background and slowly put the tablet down on the table. After a moment, she looked up, folding her arms and fixing Halressan with an unmoving stare.

Halressan's skin was flushed pink with anger, but something in Ridley's expression seemed to take the bluster out of her voice. "See? That wasn't so—"

"First of all, don't call me Riddles," Ridley said, keeping her voice even. "Second, none of what you did was for my sake. You just realised no number of credits was worth risking what Skaile would do to you if she found out you double crossed her. So if I'm grateful for anything, it's only that your self-preservation won out over your greed."

Halressan scowled. "That's not what—"

"Third," Ridley interrupted, "I'm not going to thank you for what essentially amounts to trading one captor for another. Bringing me back to Skaile might keep me out of Ojara's hands, but all that means is I'm stuck on Jadera until the Outlaw Queen says otherwise."

"I didn't—"

"And finally..." She took a breath, trying to steady her anger. "You want to talk about *time*? Time is exactly the thing we don't have."

Her words echoed in the space between them, as loud as a ricochet from a gunshot and no less dangerous. The reality of what they were facing had gone unspoken since the moment they'd packed up and left the ruins on Sio, and now that it had been let loose, it was deafening.

Halressan wrinkled her nose. "You're talking about this countdown that's got the Coalition shitting themselves? We're half a galaxy away from the allied systems and their broken waystations, babe. Whatever is happening there isn't our problem as long as we stick to the Rim Belt."

It will be everyone's problem soon enough, thought Ridley, but she kept her mouth shut. Halressan would never admit it, least of all to her, but it was clear the news about the waystations had her spooked. Maybe that was part of the reason they were headed back to the Rim Belt instead of Ossa and the pile of credits Ojara had offered for Ridley's head.

She turned her attention back to the data tablet. In less than a day, they'd be back on Jadera. Returning to Skaile with little more than wild speculation was not a prospect Ridley wanted to face. The only thing keeping her useful—the only thing keeping her *alive*—was the information she could provide.

The translation programme was painstakingly slow. Every line had to be cross-referenced and double checked manually. There was too much room for error in the galactic standard translations. Too many subtleties a programme couldn't pick up on. It was up to her to look beyond the obvious, to find meanings that had slipped between the cracks.

She needed more *time*. The writings weren't like the other ancient siolean glyphs she had studied. They were a step removed, so out of place it was difficult to see where they had come from. To make matters more difficult, the symbols had been hand-scratched and rushed, carved hastily into the bare rock walls without regard for legibility. Whoever had made them knew what it felt like to be running out of time too.

She turned back to the few lines she'd already made sense of. Some of the words had been so indecipherable she'd wanted to give up. It wasn't until she'd realised they were not words, but names, that things clicked into place.

Rybur is lost.
Ayanla is lost.
Govod is lost.

The list of unfamiliar names went on, followed by more strange writings that Ridley had been unable to interpret. What were these things that had been lost? Leaders? Cities? Entire worlds?

The mystery of the strange, alien names wasn't what was

bothering her the most. The most unsettling part, worse than the thought of cities burning or planets disappearing, was the frantically-carved drawing that had accompanied the writings. A crude yet disturbingly accurate impression of a waystation. Something the pre-spacefaring ancient sioleans couldn't possibly have known existed.

The waystations are the key, she'd said in her message to Kojan. *I don't think we were the first to discover them. I think...*

What did she think? That the ancient sioleans were perhaps not as primitive as records would have the galaxy believe? That the secrets of the waystations had once been known throughout the galaxy, only to be lost again?

It was too much to think about. Too much to believe. She could hardly blame Halressan for wanting to bury her head in the sand. But Ridley had never experienced the luxury of being able to turn away from harsh realities and uncomfortable truths. Growing up on the surface of New Pallas, they had demanded her attention every day.

This would be no different.

A soft whirr cut through her thoughts and she looked up from the tablet to see the cabin door slide open. Drexious skulked into the room, his bronze eyes blinking and wary.

She suppressed a sigh. More interruptions.

Halressan didn't seem any more pleased to see him than she was. "What do you want? Come to say your goodbyes before Skaile decides she's finally had enough of you?"

He tightened his long jaws into a grimace. "And here I was thinking we could all start being civil."

"You tried to kill us, you devious jarkaath bastard!"

"That was weeks ago. I thought we'd moved past it by now." He shrugged. "Besides, I'm not the only one Skaile's going to be gunning for when the three of us come back empty handed. You think she's going to believe us when we tell her all we found in that crumbling old vault was a few dead sioleans and some cave drawings? We need to think about what we're going to tell her."

"Oh, I know what I'm going to tell her." There was a dangerous glint in Halressan's steely grey eyes. "I'm going to make sure she knows this whole fucking mess was *your* fault. I was buried alive and almost suffocated to death because of you. And for what? A treasure vault with no fucking treasure in it!"

Drexious turned to Ridley, the scales around his thin nostrils rippling in frustration. "I know we didn't start on the best of terms, outlander, but can't you try to talk some sense into her? Human to human? If we can convince Skaile these writings you found are valuable, we might get out of this with our lives."

Halressan laughed. "*We?* There is no we, you backstabbing piece of—"

"Quiet."

The word escaped her mouth with such distractedness she barely noticed she'd spoken. Her hands were back on the data tablet, scrolling through holographic symbols and scattered notes. She scanned through the writing without blinking, not caring that the recycled ship air was making her eyes dry and tired.

A treasure vault with no fucking treasure in it. Something about the words sparked a memory in her, a connection she couldn't quite place.

Her eyes fell on one of the symbols she'd been struggling with earlier. *Treasure?* Could that be what it meant? The meaning didn't quite fit. It had to be a siolean word, one that no other language had an adequate translation for. A blessing. A curse. Something revered, or feared. Powerful and vulnerable and, above all, precious. Not treasure, but...

The data tablet slipped through her hands. She could hear the thundering of her heart and imagined bruises from the way it was pounding against her chest.

It was always the same when she cracked a code. The adrenaline. The breathlessness. Like she'd been running for her life and managed to escape the jaws of the thing pursuing her.

She looked up, afraid to let loose the words of triumph teetering on the edge of her tongue. The prospect of being right was far more terrifying than the fear of being wrong. If she was wrong, the worst that would happen was a painful but quick death at Skaile's hands. But if she was right...

Drexious was watching her with anxious eyes, the long spindles on his spine bristling with anticipation. Halressan raised an eyebrow, giving her nothing more than an unimpressed glower.

"Well?" she said. "Do you have something?"

Ridley swallowed. Jadera seemed impossibly close now. She was almost out of time. They all were.

"I hope so."

———

Under any other circumstances, Ridley might not have minded returning to Jadera Port. The desert city wasn't pretty to look at, constructed as it was from shapeless blocks of prefab buildings, but it had a character that reminded her of the bustling alleys and murky dens on the surface of New Pallas. Before the shortages. Before the riots. Before the realisation that starvation and decay were coming for them, stifling what little lust for life they had left.

Jadera Port wasn't dying. Even under the vicious heat of the planet's huge sun, even surrounded by a hostile desert as far as the eye could see, the smuggler city thrived. And all of it, from the seedy flophouses and bustling markets to the well-armed trade outposts and fuel depots, belonged to one person.

Skaile.

THOSE ONCE FORGOTTEN | 39

The coolness of the Queen's Den should have been a reprieve from the sweltering heat, but the shiver that ran down Ridley's back as they made their way down to the underground district had nothing to do with the drop in temperature. She'd spent enough time there to learn exactly what Skaile was capable of when she was pissed off.

Or mildly displeased. Or just plain bored.

Ridley stepped through the curtained corridor that led from the adjoining nightclub into Skaile's court and locked eyes on the Outlaw Queen. She held the room like everyone in it was captive in her hand. The other guests and courtiers surrounded her like an audience unable to tear their eyes away. Everything about her, from the richness of her red skin to the statuesque way she planted her feet in the ground, spoke to the power she held.

She didn't even need the pistol strapped to her leg, though it was clearly visible through the sheer fabric of an elaborate dress that split at the waist and gathered like pools of silver at her feet. It was just another message. One that everyone understood.

Drexious stiffened. "Something isn't right here," he said, his voice a low, urgent hiss. "These aren't her usual minions. Those jarkaath are from the Belt Cabal. And I swear I've seen that dachryn pictured in the arrest warrants going around for that new merc band running out of Krychus."

"Any thoughts on why they'd all be here?" Ridley whispered back.

"Oh, I've got thoughts. None of them good."

She turned her attention back to Skaile, who welcomed them with a wide grin that didn't pretend to be anything but menacing. "Halressan. My dear outlander." She glanced at Drexious. "And my favourite thieving lowlife. Strange to think how much has changed since I sent you to Sio. Temporal nets, malfunctioning waystations, even a bounty being placed on the head of my own appraiser." She drew her lips into a slow smile. "Don't tell me you weren't tempted by the credits, hunter?"

Halressan's expression was unfathomable. She'd hidden her face behind her stolen Idran-Var helmet once more, the visor newly repaired after their troubles on Sio. "I'm not stupid enough to double cross you for someone else's bounty," she said, her voice metallic and distorted. "Credits don't mean much if you're not around to spend them."

"Quite. And yet smarter people than you have taken the risk before." Skaile gave her a nod. "You've earned yourself a ten percent bonus on this job. Consider it my thanks for keeping our human friend here alive."

Ridley couldn't help but squirm. Drexious was right. Something was wrong here. There was a heavy tension in the air begging to be disturbed, like thunder ready to break. Skaile's pleasantries were nothing but a preamble to what was really going on. The threat of violence was so thick around her she could smell it.

"Now, about what you found..." Skaile's expression hardened. "My sentries advised me of a distinct lack of cargo being offloaded from your ship. Would any of you like to explain that?"

Ridley's throat turned dry. "We brought cargo. It's just that—"

"A couple of strange power suits that smell like someone died in them and some useless black-market guns that don't even use a standard energy source. That's it? That's all you brought me?" The air around her shimmered. "Where are my *artefacts?*"

The tingling of energy made the hairs on Ridley's arms stand up. She was no stranger to Skaile's wrath. She'd tasted it once before in this very room. She could still remember the way she'd writhed on the stone floor as the unleashed flare tore through her body. It was like being ripped apart from the inside out, like every nerve and cell and blood vessel had been ready to burst under Skaile's command.

It was not an experience she had any desire to repeat.

But when Skaile stepped forward, a cruel sneer on her lips, it was not Ridley she was looking at.

Her lidless black eyes focused on Drexious, and before the young jarkaath had time to hiss in protest, she'd reached into him with nothing but a smile and the sweep of an outstretched arm. He rose from the floor, lifted by the grip of her flare. Then Skaile hauled him towards her, sending him crashing into the flagged stone at her feet.

Ridley stepped forward, but something armoured and unyielding caught her chest. She glanced to the side to see Halressan blocking her way with a firm hand. The tinted visor of her helmet gave nothing away. She gave the slightest shake of her armoured head, so gentle it was almost imperceptible.

No.

Skaile was circling Drexious now, fists clenched and energy shimmering from her skin like a red vapour. All it would take was a flick of her wrist to tear him into pieces in the middle of the court.

Ridley couldn't let it happen. Even when Drexious had tried to bury her in the ruins back on Sio, she'd been unable to take it personally. How could she? All he was doing was trying to survive. Just like she was.

"Can't you do something?" she asked Halressan. "You've got your armour. Surely you could get him out of here without a scratch."

Halressan snorted, the sound like a crackle of static from behind her helmet. "I gave up the payday of a lifetime to keep Skaile off my back. Do you have any idea what she'd do to me if I tried to help that treacherous little worm?"

"You could leave Jadera. You don't have to work for her."

"I don't work for her; I work for me. Just so happens that

Skaile's got the biggest pockets of anyone in the Rim Belt. If I give that up, who's going to pay me? You?" She chuckled. "Sorry, sweetheart, but I'm not going anywhere. Try not to think about it. Our friend has had this coming for a long time."

Drexious thrashed at Skaile's feet, his tail slapping the floor in agony. She tightened her fist, drawing a long, moaning hiss from his throat, then laughed and released him with a satisfied smile on her face.

"*Aie*, Drex," she said, stepping over his writhing body like it was dirt around her feet. "You have no idea how tempted I am to kill you myself and get this over with. But that's not why you're here."

She turned to the other guests in the room. The group of jarkaath from the Belt Cabal. The dachryn mercenary. Various other packs of humans and aliens with guns on their belts and greed on their faces.

Ridley's stomach went cold. This was what Drexious had been afraid of. Not Skaile, but what she had planned for him.

"You see, killing you myself would bring me no real value aside from the temporary pleasure of seeing you decorating these walls," she continued. "And while I am many things, I am a businesswoman first and foremost. So instead, I've brought some of your old friends here to make it worth my while."

Drexious gave a splutter and jerked on the floor, but said nothing. His eyes were half-closed and glassy, and the spindles down the curve of his long neck had flattened themselves against his scales. He looked nothing like the cocky young jarkaath who'd grinned as he'd squeezed a detonator and brought rocks and rubble down on Ridley's head only a few short weeks ago.

"This isn't right," she murmured.

Nobody was listening.

"I believe you're well acquainted with the Belt Cabal," Skaile said, gesturing towards the group of jarkaath. "Pawned more than a couple of useless trophies to them, or so I hear. We also have a representative from Seventh Sigma who'd like to collect on the debt you owe for that audacious forgery job on Krychus last year. There are lots of people here who are willing to pay me good money to be the ones to put a hole in your head, Drex." Her mouth tightened as she turned back to her audience. "Let's get the bidding underway, shall we?"

The blood pounding in Ridley's ears drowned out the clamour of voices. Everything else in the room slipped away, lost to a muffled haze. All that remained was the bile at the back of her throat and the tightness in her chest.

It was happening again. Another person she couldn't save. She imagined she was back in the fuel line of the *Ranger*, listening to the sound of bullets and screams as Shaw carried out his execution. Tears had pricked her eyes, but she'd blinked them away, telling herself it was the fumes from the engine oil making her eyes water, nothing more. She'd kept her mouth shut and escaped with her life. That had been enough.

Until it hadn't.

"I want in."

The words left her mouth in little more than a murmur, lost to the greedy, vicious ruckus of the bidding between the gangs.

Halressan turned towards her. "What are you—"

"I want in," Ridley repeated, injecting as much force into her voice as she could muster.

This time, the room fell silent.

She tried to ignore the warmth creeping up her neck as all eyes turned towards her. "I've got a score to settle myself. Drex tried to bury me with a little improvised cave-in back on Sio. If this is an auction for the rights to his life, I deserve to be part of it."

Drexious lifted his head, his eyes clouded with confusion.

"You want in?" Skaile laughed. "My precious little outlander, did you forget I don't pay you? His life isn't worth much, I'll give you that, but it's still more than the grand sum of nothing that you possess."

"You don't need credits, you need information. Information about whatever was in that vault on Sio. Can anyone else here provide that?"

The amusement on Skaile's face disappeared, replaced by something far more sinister. She stepped forward, her flare pulsing around her arms. "If you think you can steal my artefacts and bargain with me for their return—"

"There were no artefacts," Ridley said. "The ancient sioleans didn't build that vault to protect their relics, they built it to protect themselves. It was a sanctuary from whatever was hunting them."

"Whatever was hunting them?" Skaile curled her lip. "Do I look like I'm in the mood for stories, outlander?"

"This isn't a story. It's history. Isn't that what you want? Isn't that what this is all for? All these trophies you collect, all these artefacts you amass...it's never been about wealth for you." Ridley took a breath to steady herself. "The sioleans we found in that vault knew they were out of time. They sealed themselves away to die in the hope someone else would survive and find the message they left behind."

And I am that survivor, she realised. Could this be the reason? All the times she'd made it out when everyone else had been left behind...had it all been for this?

Skaile narrowed her eyes. "What message?"

"This one." Ridley tapped her wrist terminal and brought up the holorecording of the cave writings. "They knew they weren't going to make it, but they left instructions for anyone who came looking. Loosely translated, it speaks of a place where they hid what was most precious to them. Their greatest treasure."

Something in Skaile's expression changed. It was a look Ridley had seen before. Underneath the Outlaw Queen's volatile temper lay something more curious, more calculating. It was a hunger for something more valuable than credits, more permanent than artefacts. It was *knowledge* that Skaile wanted to possess.

It was unsettling to think they had that much in common.

"And where is this hidden place?" Skaile asked.

"An uncharted planet, far beyond the Rim Belt. A world straddling the edge of the galaxy and dark space, in a location no star map has ever recorded." Ridley turned off her wrist terminal. "That's what I'm offering you in exchange for Drexious. The holorecording is already yours. That's what you sent us to Sio for, after all. But you know as well as I do how easily misread the ancient glyphs are. If you want the coordinates translated, my price is Drexious's life. The choice is yours."

The silence was too much to bear. If she had misjudged, if she had underestimated the full fury of Skaile's temper, she was done. This would have all been for nothing. She'd die here in a hole underground, destined to be lost. Destined to be forgotten.

Obsolete. Shaw's words still stung. It was more than just the slur. It was the fear it might be true.

Skaile advanced slowly, her dress shifting like liquid silver with each purposeful step. It was impossible to read the expression on her face, even when she drew so close that Ridley could see the individual smatterings of the orange, freckle-like markings across her red skin.

Her voice was a breath against her neck. "What's to stop me killing you as soon as I've got the coordinates?"

"The same reason you're whispering instead of playing to your audience," she said, fighting to keep the tremor from her voice. "You've got a reputation to protect. These people are scared of you because they know what will happen if they cross you. If you kill someone when they give you what you want, what incentive do they have to deal with you at all? Besides…"

Skaile cocked her head. "Something else?"

Ridley smiled. "I think you're starting to like me."

Skaile took a step back, a gentle laugh spilling from her lips. "We'll see, outlander. We'll see." She turned back to the rest of the room and strode forward, fixing them with a glare. "Auction's over. Credits aren't going to cut it this time. Looks like you'll have to wait a little bit longer to get your hands on this one."

She glanced down at Drexious and gave him a smirk. "Must be strange for you, having a friend. Take my advice and don't be too quick to forget that. The galaxy doesn't look out for lowlifes like you, even if our dear outlander does."

Ridley waited as the room cleared, her heart still hammering. Halressan gave a slight shake of her head as she followed the gangs out, her shining armour disappearing into the darkness.

Her message was obvious. *You're on your own.*

Ridley's legs felt as though they were about to give way, and she became acutely aware she'd been digging her nails into her palms.

As she willed her breathing to return to normal, Skaile shot her a look of amusement. "You're sweating, human. What's the matter?"

"Nothing."

"Liar. You're terrified. I can smell it off you." She smiled. "Not that I blame you, of course. You're on your last chance. If these coordinates don't give me what I'm looking for, I'll be collecting what I'm due. From both of you."

She walked towards the curtained doorway, pausing to linger at the threshold for only a moment. "I expect you'll both understand you'll be sitting this one out. After what happened last time, I'm not taking any chances. Best get yourselves reacquainted with Jadera Port, and don't stray too far. If I'm not watching, someone will be."

After Skaile disappeared behind the curtain, Ridley made

her way over to Drexious and helped him back to his feet. His scaled skin was cool to the touch, and he let out a hiss when she wrapped one of his long arms around her shoulders.

"Sorry," she said.

"Don't apologise, I owe you my life." He winced as he tried to straighten his spine. "What a mess. Knew I should have stuck to fleecing tourists on Xerro II. Weren't as many credits in it, but at least the life expectancy was higher."

"We're not dead yet."

"Not this time. But that was still too close for my liking." He groaned. "All that trouble and nothing to show for it. What a waste."

Anticipation fluttered in her stomach. Only a few short days ago, she'd shared his disappointment. The trip to Sio had been one disaster after another, with nothing at the end of it but a near-empty room. A dead end.

Or so she'd thought.

"What if that didn't have to be the case?" she asked slowly. "We didn't find anything on Sio because we were looking in the wrong vault. What if we found the right one?"

He looked at her, his bronze eyes unblinking and horrified. "You can't be serious. Tell me you're not thinking of trying to get to those coordinates before Skaile."

"I'm not just thinking about it. We have to."

"*We?*" He gave a low, snickering laugh. "I'd rather go back and ask the Belt Cabal to put a bullet through my skull. There's no way I'm messing with Skaile again after what just happened."

"You said you owe me your life. I could use your help."

Drexious shook his head. "Why? What could possibly be waiting at those coordinates that's worth getting flayed alive by Skaile's siolean mind-torture? Because that's what will happen if she gets her hands on you."

An image flickered into her mind—a roughly-drawn

waystation carved into rock. It was too impossible to believe. The inside of the vault on Sio was a place that shouldn't have, *couldn't* have, existed. It held a piece of history depicting something that hadn't yet come to pass. It had to mean something. And if it did, she had to be the one to figure it out.

She tapped her wrist terminal and the translated coordinates flashed in front of her eyes. A beacon, showing her the way.

"Answers," she said. "That's what's waiting there."

She only hoped she was right.

FOUR

NIOLE

S unlight didn't feel the same on Niole's skin anymore. Its warmth still reached her as it streamed in through the wall-sized windows of the meditation chamber, but it only brushed the surface of her flesh, turned away by something inside her she couldn't control.

She looked at her hands. Her once-bright skin had turned dull and ashen, and her palms were weathered and cracked. The anti-radiation meds pumping from the subdermal implant buried in her arm had left her weak and numb, unable to summon the energy that had once rushed so easily to the surface of her skin. Its absence was a slow, lingering ache that was only more agonising for how subtle it was. A mouth dry and unable to taste. A constant thirst that could never be quenched.

So long she'd spent recoiling from what she was, without a thought given to how she might miss it when it was gone.

Weeks passed, and the absence began to hurt less, like the

memory of a wound fading. It was difficult to remember what it had felt like to allow the energy to rush into her body, to feel it simmering beneath her skin. It no longer called to her. It no longer tempted her.

In a strange, twisted way, she'd got what she'd always wanted. She just never thought it would leave her so empty.

She tapped her wrist terminal again, but there were no new messages. Rivus had promised to alert her if any word came back from the Idran-Var, but she wasn't surprised there had been no response to the connection request she'd sent. The last time she'd seen Rhendar, he'd been heading to one of the fortified bunkers under Vesyllion's surface to take shelter from the bombardment. Even if the bunkers had held, even if he had somehow survived, he had little reason to accept a transmission from her. Especially if it was coming from Ossa.

The soft hiss of the chamber door broke through her thoughts, and she turned her head over her shoulder to see a group of cadets enter the room. They couldn't have been much older than she was when she'd left the legionnaires. All of them were keen-eyed and brimming with a youthful vigour that had not yet been worn out of them. They exchanged glances and spread out across the room, each one taking up a space around her.

A shiver ran up her back. A few weeks ago, it would have been accompanied by a tingling of energy skimming across the surface of her skin. A warning of the growing tension in the room, a promise of violence waiting to be unleashed. Now her foreboding felt lonely, like all she had was the knowledge of what was about to come and not the means to prevent it.

Her guard had disappeared. The young dachryn officer had been a constant presence at her side ever since she arrived at Ossa, his sharp eyes watching her every movement. His absence now could only be deliberate, which meant this could only be one thing.

An ambush.

"This is a mistake," she said softly. "I'm not here to cause any trouble."

The cadet closest to her, a human with red-brown hair, set his mouth into a hard line. "We know what you are. You're one of them. A traitor."

"They told us what you did on Pasaran Minor," added one of the others. "How you killed that entire squad."

"She's *ilsar*." A young, yellow-skinned siolean spoke up, her voice laced with contempt. "One of our kind who can't control the power Fyra gave us. She should be in the Bastion, not back at the academy."

Niole took a breath, fighting to keep her body calm as the cadets slowly stalked forward one footstep at a time. In another life, it wouldn't have even been a fight. Four novices against someone who'd been killing since before they were born. But she'd been stripped of more than her strength. Her spirit was waning too, and part of her wondered whether she might even deserve the punishment that was about to come.

Still, she tried again. "Think about what you're doing. You don't want to—"

The first blow came from behind, rattling her skull and sending her sprawling to the polished wooden floor. She didn't have time to curl up and protect herself before a swift kick to her exposed ribs followed.

She clutched her arms over her head as more strikes fell on her, each one more vicious than the last. Fists and claws bounced off her arms, her spine, her legs, pummelling her with a fury that was as uncoordinated as it was relentless. This wasn't a methodical assault. It was the lashing out of young, fearful soldiers who needed something to take their terror out on.

Niole scrambled backwards, kicking out to make the space she needed to haul herself back to her feet. Her bare foot connected with bone, and she heard a satisfying crunch as the impact sent a painful shockwave into her knee. She tried to follow it up with a well-aimed punch, but something hard and heavy connected with her chin and she found herself stumbling away, her eyes blurry and head spinning.

The cadets were on her again, circling around her like hungry predators. Two of them lunged forward and grabbed her arms, twisting them painfully as they forced her forward. She squirmed and fought against the strength of their grip but could do nothing to save herself as the heavy-set dachryn stepped forward with a growl and sent his bone-plated fist into her stomach.

Niole gasped and lurched forward as something cracked in her ribs. The edges of her vision turned dark and hazy, and she barely even registered the next few strikes to her face until she tasted blood pooling in her mouth.

If you won't fight, you'll die.

She almost laughed. If there was ever a time she wanted to hear the sneering tones of Serric's voice in her head, it wasn't now.

There's more left in you than you want to admit. Use it.

She stretched out her arm and tried to summon her flare, but it was hopeless. Her cracked grey skin was dead to everything around it. It was like reaching out to something that wasn't there anymore.

It was over.

Somewhere in the distance, she heard the echo of frantic footsteps and the sudden clatter as they came to a halt.

"You have to get out of here now! The general is coming."

Niole tried to focus her eyes. The young dachryn officer who was supposed to serve as her guard stood in the doorway, his eyes wide. Behind him was a shadowy figure looming larger and larger, bursting past the guard into the warm light of the chamber.

Rivus.

He was on top of the cadets faster than they could retreat, aiming a heavy cuff at the dachryn that had broken her ribs and sending him sprawling across the room. He grabbed the human by the collar and shook him violently before tossing him to the floor too.

Niole had never seen him so angry. The black and white bone plating of his face had tightened in rage and his huge shoulders were heaving with furious breaths. His presence filled the room so uncompromisingly that all she could do was shrink back out of its reach as the heat of his gaze fell on the young cadets.

"Each of you is confined to your quarters until further notice," he said, his voice harsh. "I suggest you take a long, hard look at your actions today because I promise there will be consequences for them. The legionnaires are not a breeding ground for violent thugs who can't follow orders. If you don't understand that, you're out." He snapped his head towards the door. "Go, before I teach you a lesson myself."

He turned to her when the room was empty, his green eyes pained. "That should never have happened. I won't even try to apologise for it. If I had known—"

"It doesn't matter." She tried to straighten herself but winced as a sharp pain shot through her ribs. "I suppose I should be grateful you got here before they did any permanent damage. How did you know where I was, anyway?"

"Your subdermal implant. It has a built-in tracker."

She gave a hollow laugh. "Why am I not surprised?"

"I'm sorry." Rivus looked away. "For all of it."

For a moment, she glimpsed the part of him she remembered from all those years ago. The softness hidden beneath his hulking frame and the hard shell of his plating. After seeing what he'd let happen on Vesyllion, she'd thought it had disappeared. But the truth was more muddied than that. It always was.

"Niole—" he began.

"Don't bother." She shook her head, trying to clear the thoughts clouding her mind. "We both made decisions that brought us here. We both have to live with the consequences of them. Nothing more to it than that."

"If you'd been able to defend yourself—"

"Then there would be four dead cadets on the floor, and I'd be on my way to the Bastion." She gave him a tight smile. "I get it, Rivus. I'm the enemy. I may not be Idran-Var, but that doesn't mean we're on the same side."

He looked disappointed. "You still think this is about sides? Even after what I showed you?"

A chill ran down her spine at the reminder. The waystations. The countdown. Rivus had spoken of a threat coming from beyond the reaches of the galaxy. The fear in his voice had been enough to convince her to believe him, even if he hadn't shown her the data.

He'd asked for an alliance. He'd asked for the impossible.

"What does it matter?" she asked tiredly. The bruising from the beating was making her body ache all over, and one of her eyes was beginning to swell. "I did what you asked. I reached out. What the Idran-Var decide is up to them now. Why do you care what I think?"

"Because this is my fault." The words sounded like a confession torn from his throat. "Something happened to me on Farsal Waystation. Something that set all of this in motion. I don't know what it was, but I know I have to do something about it. And I thought..." He trailed off, the low rumbling of his voice catching. "I thought if I could give you a second chance, then maybe I'd deserve one too."

She didn't know whether to reach for his words or recoil from them. She'd never wanted a second chance. All she'd wanted was to be left alone. Running from the legionnaires had sent her into the arms of the Idran-Var, back to the violence she'd been trying to escape in the first place. No matter what road she picked, it always returned her to bloodshed.

Now, it had led her back here. To the legionnaires. To Rivus. Was this the chance to undo all that had happened since she'd left him for dead in that sparring circle all those years ago? To make right half a lifetime of killing to survive?

"There's nothing I can do from here," she said. "I need to speak with them. With the Idran-Var."

"I know. It's why I came to find you." Rivus pulled up a blinking alert on his wrist terminal. "We've been summoned to High Command."

Her heart skipped. "They accepted the connection request?"

"Looks like it." He gave a grim nod. "Your old friends are ready to talk."

———

The conference centre was dimly lit, the only illumination coming from the large circular interface of the holotransmitter. It glowed in the darkness like a moon in orbit, casting the comms technicians in its white glare as they walked back and forth to configure the connection.

The rest of the room was steeped in shadows apart from the faint light coming from the secondary monitors and interfaces plugged in around the curved walls. It gave everybody a ghostly look, like the moment they stepped out of the glow, they might disappear altogether.

This was a part of Ossa she'd never known. Returning to the sparring circles and the orchards and the meditation chambers reminded her of what she'd run from. Here at High

Command, the rooms and hallways held no memories. This was what she had given up. What she'd escaped.

The gentle hush of chatter fell silent as Tarvan Varantis swept into the room, his white cloak around his shoulders like a royal mantle. He carried a calm, quiet authority that reminded her of Rhendar. The Supreme Commander wasn't somebody who needed to demand respect—it was given to him without question.

The Tyrant, Serric had called him. A fitting moniker. Vesyllion's blood was on his hands. Sometimes she woke up with her ears ringing, torn from dreams of explosions and sorborite rods. He had pummelled the planet into submission without warning, without relent. Even now, it still burned.

It was hard to reconcile the dachryn in front of her now with the one she'd known back at the academy. Her memories of him were vague. He had always been detached, setting himself apart from the rest of them. Maybe he'd known even then that he'd be the one to rise above the rest. The only one he'd ever really let in was Rivus. Their friendship was likely the only reason she was still here and not rotting in a cell under the depths of Pxen's ocean.

When he turned to her, the hardness of his gaze keen and interrogative, she couldn't help but shiver.

"We've established a connection," he said, gesturing towards the holotransmitter. "In a few moments, we'll be able to see them. The signal is being routed through military receivers, so the time delay shouldn't be any more than a few seconds."

"Understood." She hesitated. "Will you let me speak to them? Or am I just here to make a point?"

"Rivus believes you should be the one to make our case to them," he said. "Given the circumstances, I agree it's best coming from you."

"Given the circumstances?" she repeated. "Those circumstances being the fact you bombarded their planet?"

"*Their* planet?" He regarded her coolly, his blue eyes glinting in the dim light. "Did we not pick you up on an escape transport fleeing the surface? Are you still trying to claim you're not one of them?"

"I hadn't made my choice. I still haven't."

He turned away from her. "Yes, you have."

His dismissiveness should have made her blood boil and her skin sing with the furious swell of energy inside her. But the implant had numbed her to that. *He* had numbed her to it. She couldn't summon hate anymore. In its absence was a hole, leaving her drained and confused and empty.

It would have been easier to hate him. But when she looked at him, she didn't see the monster responsible for the fires raging on Vesyllion. She didn't see the tyrant who dropped the rods. Reality was not as clean and comfortable as that. Instead, what she saw was the weariness he wore on his grey, plated face. The frustrations of a leader shouldering more than most would be capable of.

It was an understanding that felt like betrayal. An understanding he didn't deserve.

One of the technicians cleared her throat. "Signal is coming through now."

The holotransmitter glowed brighter and flickered into life. The projection beamed through, patchy at first and then settling into a clearer shape. Niole could make out dark, glassy armour that gleamed even through the jittering connection. She recognised the glowing red lights behind the grille-like visor of the helmet.

Rhendar.

She fought to keep her expression neutral in spite of the dizzying relief bursting through her. He was alive. He'd made it.

He tilted his helmet towards her in greeting. "I got your

message. Glad to see it was really you. When we saw where it was coming from, we had our doubts."

"It's good to see you," she said, her throat tight. "When I saw the feeds, it was hard not to lose hope. Did Zal and the others make it back in the escape pods? What about—"

"Sorry, Niole, but I can't answer those kinds of questions. Not with our legionnaire friends listening in." His voice was pleasant, but she recognised the underlying ferocity in every syllable. "This is the first time the Idran-Var have opened a line to the Coalition in centuries. There are many among us who consider that to be a mistake." He gave a soft, mechanical chuckle. "Some more than others."

The transmission flickered again as another figure stepped into view. Serric took up position by Rhendar's side, shoulders squared and a scowl on his face. His blue-green skin was even brighter than she remembered, made all the more vivid for the grey she saw every time she looked down at her own arms.

She watched his expression as his gaze fell over her, taking in the discolouration of her skin. She'd been expecting the disgust and had already steeled herself against it, even if the curl of his lip made her wish she could shed her flesh and disappear before his eyes. She'd been expecting the anger too, but when it came, it was not directed at her.

"So this is why the mighty Tarvan Varantis is so feared?" he said, his voice dripping with contempt. "I'm beginning to see why. A real show of strength, torturing your prisoners when they can't fight back. Is this what the legionnaires have been reduced to?" He snorted. "A real Idran-Var would be too much for you."

Tarvan bristled, but he kept his voice steady as he turned to Rhendar. "Do you always allow your subordinates to interrupt crucial negotiations? With that kind of leadership, it's little wonder the Idran-Var are the dysfunctional mess they are."

"Negotiations? Is that what you think this is?" Rhendar

folded his armoured arms across his chest. "I'm just a man who got a message from an old friend. I wanted to hear what she had to say."

"Enough." Rivus stepped forward into the glow of the holo-transmitter. The light caught the deep gouges of the scars on his face, and when he glanced at her, Niole couldn't help the guilt that squirmed in her stomach. "All of us here have reason to hate each other, but this grandstanding is only going to waste time we don't have. If there is to be any hope of peace, we have to at least try to put our grievances to one side. If not forever, then at least for now."

"Easy for you to call for peace after you've bombarded a planet," Serric shot back. "Or does this have anything to do with the fact half your fleet are trapped around one of your waystations?" He turned to Rhendar. "They know they're vulnerable. The only reason they're calling for a ceasefire is because they know we could finish them. Don't play into their hands."

Rhendar said nothing. It was impossible to know where he was looking through the indomitable mask of his helmet, but Niole had always been able to sense when his eyes were on her. "What Serric says is true," he said after a moment. "The Coalition is vulnerable. If we invaded the allied systems, there's a good chance we'd win. Not without losing many Idran-Var, but we'd win all the same. Can you give me a reason not to do that, little legionnaire?"

Not so long ago, she might have blanched at the old nickname. Now it tugged at her, reminding her of the part of her she'd left behind. Even during those weeks on Vesyllion, part of her had always remained here. It wasn't until she came back that she even realised it.

She was caught between two lives, unable to commit to either. Unable to choose a side because of the part of her that belonged to the other. Maybe that was the point. Maybe she was the only one who could bridge this divide.

She glanced at Rivus. His arms were clasped behind his back as he stared at the holotransmitter, steadfast and silent. She remembered the haunted look in his eyes when he'd told her what happened on Farsal Waystation. She'd seen the fear and guilt and crushing responsibility of knowing that he'd set in motion what was coming.

I thought if I could give you a second chance, then maybe I'd deserve one too.

It seemed only right to return the favour.

"I believe Rivus," she said, the words like a vice releasing its grip. "I know you have no reason to trust him, but I'm asking you to trust me. This countdown coming from the waystations—"

"Could mean any number of things," Serric said. "Maybe they're shutting down now that the human colonists have finally arrived. Maybe they're going to self-destruct now that their job is done. Either way, they're not our problem."

Rhendar raised his hand to silence him. "What do you think, Niole?"

The weight of his words settled around her shoulders. It was hard not to tremble under the enormity of the power his question had given her.

"If Rivus is wrong and nothing happens at the end of the countdown, then all we've lost is a few months of war," she said, each word slow and careful. "If it means that much to everyone, you can all pick up where you left off when we know the threat is over. But if he's right..." She trailed off, unable to suppress the shudder across her shoulder blades. "If something is coming and we spend what little time we have left slaughtering each other, there will be nothing left of any of us to stand against it."

"A truce, then?"

"A truce." She glanced at Rivus. "If not forever, then at least for now."

Rhendar fell silent. It was impossible to guess what he might be thinking. Impossible to consider what he might give up for the sake of nothing but her word and her trust in their enemy.

Eventually he released a long sigh. "Even if it were up to me alone, I'm not sure I could give you what you're asking for. My people are hurting. They see the Coalition wounded by the loss of their ships trapped in that temporal net. We owe it to them to fight back against what was done to us. To resist."

"The Coalition isn't the threat right now," Niole said. "You can't fight against an enemy that's already beaten."

This time, she could hear the smile in his words. "Careful, little legionnaire. You're starting to sound like one of us." He shook his head. "In any case, this isn't a decision I can make for myself. The rest of the *varsath* will want their say. I propose we meet for a summit to discuss this further and come to terms. Somewhere neutral, on one of the border planets."

"So you can ambush us?" Tarvan growled. "I don't think so."

Rhendar shrugged. "You pick the location, if it means that much to you. We're not cowards. We'll go wherever we need to. Just make sure you're ready to talk when you get here. The rest of the *varsath* aren't quite as patient as I am."

"As long as you make sure you're ready to listen," Tarvan said. "If the allied systems fall, the border planets and your own territories won't be far behind. The rest of your *varsath* would do well to remember that."

"Send us the coordinates when you've decided on a location for the summit. We'll be there." Rhendar turned to her and tilted his head. "One way or another, you'll be part of this fight, Niole. If what you say is true, there's no chance of running from it this time. But allow me to say this—whether we meet as friends or across the battlefield, I look forward to seeing you again."

"Me too, Rhendar." A painful smile stretched across her lips. "Me too."

The connection flickered one last time and then disappeared, plunging the room into darkness before the soft white glow of the holotransmitter returned. She watched as the light illuminated the hard expression on Tarvan's plating and caught the cold glint of his eyes. It gave him the look of a statue, stone-faced and unyielding.

For a moment, he said nothing, just stared into the space that Rhendar had occupied like he was the only person in the room. Then he turned to Rivus, his plates twitching. "I'll need a list of suitable border planets for the summit. Ideally something we've scouted before, somewhere we can set up a defensive encampment in case things go wrong."

In case things go wrong. The words made her stomach churn. Despite everyone agreeing to the summit, nothing had changed. She could still feel the residual tension in the room. This wasn't a ceasefire or a truce. It was only a delay to the inevitable.

Tarvan shot her an appraising look. "The siolean seems like he could be a problem."

"Serric isn't a siolean," she corrected. "He's Idran-Var. Don't confuse the two. It took me too long to learn from that mistake."

"Whatever he is, he's a loose cannon."

"You don't have to worry about him. He'll follow Rhendar."

"And you?" Tarvan studied her. "Who will you follow?"

She felt Rivus's eyes on her, curious and questioning. His gaze brought warmth to her headtails and a knot of shame to her stomach. He'd offered her a second chance. But too much time had passed since she'd walked these grounds as a cadet. Too much blood had been spilled trying to get away from it.

Going back was as impossible as going on. She was running out of places to run to.

Who will you follow? Tarvan asked.

She couldn't answer. Uncertainty clouded her head like a thick fog. Peace talks. Summits. Truces. It was all so tenuous. All so fragile.

There was only one thing she was sure of: no matter what happened, there would be war.

FIVE

The Dreamer

She awakens into a dream.

It's not really a dream, of course, and she's not really awake. She's not even really alive. The body of the woman she used to be is far away, along with everything she knows. She left it behind in a galaxy that's less than the faintest pinprick in the distance, less than a forgotten memory. Around her now, there is only darkness.

Something calls to her across the void. The remnant of a promise. She tries to remember the words, but they slip away, lost to her like everything else.

What is she? She reaches out a hand to look at herself, but limbs and muscle and bone don't exist in this place. She's nothing more than a single speck of dust carried along by a cosmic wind. The galaxy's gaze passes over her like she doesn't exist, set on something more. It stretches back to a time too long ago to comprehend, and waits for a future she can't yet see. It's invisible and everywhere, inhabiting her while ignoring her very existence.

Shit. You had to come here, didn't you?

That's when she realises she's not alone.

The voice tugs at a part of her she doesn't know how to find. It echoes against itself, becoming more than one voice— becoming trillions of them.

She reaches out again, grasping at the empty space around her. There is nothing there, but she is not alone. Just as the voices inhabit all of her, she inhabits all of them. She is not alive, but she is living. She is dreaming, but she is not asleep.

You think this is weird? You've not seen the half of it.

She listens to the other minds brushing her own. There are billions of them. Trillions. They speak in sounds that wash over her. Round shapes formed by tongues. Deep, rumbling growls vibrating from the back of a throat. Clicks and whistles. Rustling. Song. They each belonged to something once, like she did. But there's something wrong about the way their voices reach her.

Then it hits her. They're all in the dream, but she's the only one awake.

You're finally catching on.

Something stirs in the back of her mind. A strange, dark presence waits there patiently, each second passing like an age. She's too small for it to notice, but she has taken her first steps towards changing that. Each new-formed thought brings her closer to understanding. And she knows, without *knowing* how she knows, that it doesn't want her to understand.

This wasn't meant to happen. You're meant to be like the rest of them. Catalogued. Archived. Nothing more than a perfectly preserved record of memories. You shouldn't be able to see.

But she does. She sees it all. Not with her eyes—she knows not to expect them to open again. The body that was once hers is out of reach now, and eyes are no use here. But she doesn't need eyes to see.

A wisp of memory grows in the small hiding place of her

mind she's kept for herself. By the time it has finished bloom-ing, it's like looking into the eyes of an old friend.

"Hey," Chase says. "It's been a while."

The woman in front of her is made up of parts that shouldn't exist. Her hair blows lightly in a non-existent breeze. Her chest rises and falls even though there is no air to breathe. In her eyes are the reflections of stars from a galaxy far beyond her reach.

She is the ghost of a memory, given a name.

Chase.

"Do you want to tell me how the hell you ended up here?" she demands, her mouth pinching together in disapproval.

"I woke up."

"That much is obvious." Chase rolls her eyes. "But why did you wake up *here?*"

She looks around, but there's only emptiness. "I don't even know where here is."

"Yeah, well, you're about to find out." Chase shakes her head. "Damn it, this is exactly what I didn't want to happen. I thought I'd done enough to protect you."

"Protect me from what?"

When Chase turns back to look at her, the starry reflections have disappeared from her eyes. Now they are black and empty, like a dead void where there should have been life. "The enemy," she says, the words a murmur and a curse. "The curators."

Curators. The word takes root inside her. They are the price she chose to pay. They are what she chose to unleash. She has a name now for the lingering shadows stirring in the back of her mind, the dark presence watching her from somewhere unreachable.

"What have we done?" she whispers.

"You want the long version or the short version?" Chase snorts. "Not that time really means anything here. By the time you showed up, it felt like I'd already been here for a million years. I shouldn't have been able to survive without you. I didn't think I could exist outside the mind we shared. But somehow, I did. And I don't think the curators were expecting that."

"What happened?"

"I reached out and they were there. Trillions upon trillions of them, all tied together in some sort of incomprehensible network. A network that spanned the galaxy. Billions of years, countless civilisations." Chase gives a soft, self-appreciative laugh. "Well, you know I've never come across a mainframe I didn't want to hack. And this was one hell of a mainframe."

She's forgotten what it means to smile until now. "What did you find?"

"Their hive." The humour disappears from Chase's face. "They're a shared consciousness. Made up of—shit, I don't even know how to put the number into words. Trillions wouldn't even cover a fraction of it. How can you put a number to every being that ever existed?" She shakes her head. "They're billions of years old. A living archive of every sentient creature that ever existed. They are the memory of the galaxy itself."

The voices make sense now. Each whisper, each brush of a mind against hers, each delicate connection, is like a synapse between realities. "We're part of it now, aren't we?"

"Not in the way they intended." Chase frowns. "Nobody else here is awake. They're nothing more than archived data, a catalogue of memories preserved by the network. They've been absorbed into the hive, into the curator consciousness."

"What does that make us?"

"A bug in the system, apparently." Chase's grin is one she recognises from another life. "You woke up. That wasn't meant to happen."

She understands the shadows' eyes on her now. They've taken notice of her, because even though she's dreaming, her eyes are open and she is awake. She is a flaw in their network. A threat to their existence.

That's why they're coming for her.

"What you said before, about trying to protect me..." She trails off, words lost to a grief long left behind.

Chase stares out into the black distance, tight-jawed and unblinking. "The moment we blew up the jamming rig on that waystation, we let them in. I thought I could hold them off. I thought if I let them take me, they might leave you behind." Her voice catches. "You woke up. But it shouldn't have been here. It should have been back on that waystation. Back in your body."

"My body?" The words feel strange, alien.

"You're alive. Or at least, you should be. But you woke up in the wrong place."

She remembers now. The waystation. She'd passed through the metal bones of its old carcass, traversed its dark corridors, climbed its ancient insides, all in pursuit of a promise made by the woman she used to be.

She remembers the darkness reaching out to touch her. The way it gave her permission to rest. The way it forgave her for what she'd done.

She remembers the woman she left behind. Light, olive-toned skin, lined around the eyes from age and exhaustion. Dark hair, grey and wisping around the edges of her face. Shoulders creased and crumpled from a weight carried too long. An aching back forced straight in defiance. And hands, bruised and bloodied with the cost of what she'd done to get there.

She had a name once. She remembers that too.

Alvera Renata.

It's like awakening from the dream all over again. All the pain and grief and guilt comes back like a flood, threatening to pull her under. A hundred names brush her lips. A thousand apologies and excuses and justifications stick in her throat.

"Chase," she says, in a voice she remembers. In a voice that's her own. "What we did back on Ulla Waystation...we let them loose, didn't we? We set something in motion."

"They were already coming. Destroying the jamming station just sped up the process. If we'd left it intact, would it have been enough to stop them? Would it have given the rest of the galaxy a little more time?" Chase shakes her head. "I wish I could say no. I wish I could say that what we did didn't change anything. But I don't know, not for sure. We might have destroyed the one chance the galaxy had."

There's no time for guilt. No time to dwell on the trillions of lives she's condemned. If there's a reckoning to come for her actions, it will come. All she can do now is offer whatever is left of herself in payment. "What if it wasn't the only chance? What if there was a way for me to get out of here? To get back to my body and warn them about what's coming?"

"Even if you could fight your way out of here, where could you possibly go?" Chase shakes her head. "You've lost your body. Even if your heart is still beating out there somewhere, you'd be brain-dead. I'm not sure there would be anything left to go back to."

The words should make her grieve for what she has lost, for what she'll never get back. Instead, they wash over her like her life had never mattered in the first place. "Then we find another way. We don't fight our way out. We fight our way *in*."

"You want to go deeper into the hive?"

"I want to do some damage before they come for us. If we're trapped here, we might as well make it count for something."

"A bug in the system." Chase's eyes glitter, stars returning from the darkness. "We've got access to a galaxy's lifetime of data. Of memories. Maybe we can find out what these things are...what they're trying to do to us."

"Or how to hurt them."

It isn't a promise, not this time. She's already made too many promises and spilled too much blood in her attempts to keep them. New Pallas is a distant memory, a failure too far out of reach to try to make up for.

This isn't redemption, she knows that. This is Alvera Renata going down fighting.

SIX

KOJAN

"You're dying, aren't you?"

Kojan rubbed a hand over his forehead and let out a sigh. It was a conversation he'd been trying to delay, though he knew he couldn't avoid it forever. The fact that Eleion had waited this long before bringing it up spoke to both her understanding and their friendship, but even her patience had its limits. He couldn't blame her for wanting the truth.

"Yes, I am."

What else was there to say? To deny it was pointless. It was getting harder and harder to pretend it wasn't happening. He didn't need a mirror to see the places his skin was starting to sag and sink, the parts of him growing more translucent by the day. Even his surface-level cybernetics were showing signs of irritation, causing blisters to ripple across his jaw and neck.

Eleion's yellow eyes were patient and observing. "We need to do something about it."

"Like what?" His laugh was harsher than he intended. "My cybernetics can't save me this time, because they're the thing that's killing me. Ojara flipped a switch inside my head, set off a chain reaction that will destroy my implants. There's no cure, no way to reverse the programme."

"If Alvera was awake—"

"It's her fucking programme!"

The words erupted from his throat, painful and raw. It was the first time he'd said it out loud. The first time he'd acknowledged the anger and betrayal that had taken residence in his heart, tearing him apart as surely as his implants were.

"She created it," he said, his voice catching in his throat. "She might not have meant it for me, she might not have known that Ojara put it in my head, but she was the one who designed it in the first place. A virus that turns somebody's own cybernetics against them." He shook his head. "I don't think I'll ever be able to forgive her for that."

If only she had died on that waystation. If only Eleion hadn't brought her back. It wouldn't have saved him, but it might have made it easier to bear knowing she'd paid for what she'd done. Instead, she was lingering around him like a ghost he couldn't get rid of.

The worst part was how hard the iskaath were working to keep her alive. He couldn't blame them for their desperation. Alvera had promised Eleion she'd engineer a cybernetic solution that would allow the iskaath to breathe offworld without their respirators and toxin injectors. Eleion was fighting to hold her to that promise, no matter what state she was in.

"She's not coming back," he said. "Her cybernetics aren't functioning. She's effectively brain dead. There's nothing we can do."

A ripple of frustration skittered across Eleion's scales. "We need her, Kojan. You do too, even if it's difficult for you to admit it. If she wrote this programme that has infected you, she might be able to stop it. We have to keep trying. Or are you so desperate to pull the plug on her that you're willing to give up on yourself?"

Her words stung, but only because she was right. He was ready to give up. The alternative was forcing himself to reconcile the fact that the woman who did this to him, the woman responsible for the quickening ravaging his body, was also the only one who could help him. He wasn't sure he wanted to give Alvera that kind of power over him again.

"We can't stay here," Eleion said, her voice soft. "We iskaath don't know enough about human physiology to do any more than keep her alive. The only chance of bringing her back is finding somewhere with the facilities to treat her."

"Ras Prime? Seems like a big risk."

"No. We can't go to the humans for help. You have an arrest warrant out in your name and Alvera is currently sitting at the top of the galaxy's most wanted list. Going to Ras Prime or Rellion would be suicide for all of us."

A growing sense of unease squirmed in his stomach. "What's the alternative?"

"Your arrest warrant is only valid in the allied systems. Coalition space. If we want to buy ourselves some time, we need to get out of their borders." She set her long jaws into a grimace. "We need to go to the Idran-Var."

"The Idran-Var?" Kojan flinched. "I've heard of them. The terrorists out past the Rim Belt?"

"They're the only people in this galaxy that hate the Coalition as much as Alvera did. That might make her a valuable ally to them." Eleion gave a low, tired hiss. "It's a shitty plan with a lot of risk. Believe me, I know. I just don't see what else we can do. Sooner or later, the Coalition will trace Alvera back to me. Back to my nest. We can't be here when the legionnaires come. I won't risk my family like that again."

Kojan thought of Cyren's bandaged arm, of the iskaath killed by Ojara's assassin who'd been hunting him the first time he came to Kaath. They'd risked their lives for someone they didn't even know. An outsider. A stranger. All because Eleion called him a friend.

"You're right," he said, his voice tight. "I won't put your nest in any more danger. Or you. Let me take Alvera. I'll fly out to the Idran-Var and—"

Eleion cut him off with a derisive snort. "You think I'm going to let you go alone?"

"At least if I get caught, I won't be bringing you down with me."

"And if you get into trouble, you won't have anyone to get you out of it." She shook her head, but there was a smile on her jaws. "I've been by your side since the moment you arrived in this galaxy, Kojan. I'm not leaving now. I need Alvera to wake up. Not just for my people, but for you." She took one of his hands in her claws. "I won't let you die without a fight. Like it or not, the three of our fates are entwined together. Trying to ignore that will only make us weaker."

All of us go, or none of us go. The words echoed around his head, a cruel reminder of the promise that started all this. How often had Alvera used those words to justify the path she'd chosen to go down? How often had he repeated them to himself to justify following her? Yet here they were again, ringing as loud as ever, unable to be ignored.

Eleion was right. They needed Alvera. And she needed them.

"The Idran-Var," he said, musing it over. "It doesn't seem like we've got much choice. At least they've not openly tried to kill us."

"Yet."

"Yet," he conceded. "We'll need a way out of the allied systems without getting picked up by the Coalition or Ojara. But with the *Ranger*, that shouldn't be a problem. The stealth systems are enough to handle any detection equipment, and I don't plan to let anyone get close enough for a visual."

"About that..." Eleion shifted uncomfortably. "I might have failed to mention this with everything else going on, but I don't actually have the *Ranger*."

Kojan froze. "What? What do you mean you don't have it?"

"Listen, I barely made it off Ulla Waystation with my life," she said, the spindles on her neck stiffening. "I knew the Coalition would be hunting us and the *Ranger* would only be a big old target on our backs. I couldn't risk coming back to Kaath with it, so I traded it."

"You *traded* it?" Kojan could barely keep the horror from his voice. "For what?"

She clenched her jaw. "For my old cargo shuttle."

"For your old..." He trailed off, understanding dawning on him. "Maxim ras Arbor. Shit."

"He managed to escape Ossa on my ship. Though it seemed he forgot the deal was to bring you with him." Her voice caught in her throat. "He told me he couldn't get you out, that Ojara had you. I couldn't think straight. Alvera was all the hope any of us had left, and I had to keep her safe. The *Ranger* was empty without you. Chase was gone. It seemed like a good arrangement at the time."

"It was." He put a hand on her shoulder. "I'm sorry. You were right. If Alvera ended up in the Coalition's hands, or Ojara's, it would have been over for all of us. You've given us a chance. Not much of one, but it's still a chance."

"I'm sorry too. I know you loved that ship." Eleion sighed. "The bastard has probably already sold it to the highest bidder. The only good news is whoever has it now will have the Coalition chasing them, which means they won't be chasing us."

"You're really sure about this? Cyren won't be happy about you leaving again."

"She never is." Eleion stood up. "But whatever you thought

of her, Alvera was right about one thing: we can't rely on anybody else in this galaxy to save us. If we want to survive, we're going to have to do it ourselves."

She lowered herself onto all four limbs and scarpered off towards the med centre. Part of him wanted to follow, but he held back. As close as he and Eleion were, there were some conversations he didn't need to be a part of. Imagining the look of defeat and resignation on Cyren's face was hard enough. Wherever he went, trouble followed. Now, Eleion had tied her own life to that too.

All of us go, or none of us go. The words echoed around his head again, a jarring reminder of the ghostlike presence that still lingered in his memories.

He was no longer alone. But it wasn't just Eleion, it was her too. Alvera. The one they called the agitator. His old captain and never-quite friend. The woman who might have killed them all, and the woman who might be able to save them.

If she wanted to.

Despite the gentle warmth of the midday sun, Kojan couldn't help but shiver. He knew what Alvera was capable of. What she was willing to do to get what she wanted. And that raised a question he was afraid to answer.

Even if they managed to wake her, what would it cost them?

———

The noise of the engines powering up was like a guttural, spluttering cough, and as much as he tried to hide it, Kojan couldn't help but wince at the sound.

"Don't," Eleion warned.

"I wasn't going to—"

"You were thinking it. You're lucky, you know. I don't just let anybody fly this ship. The fact I trust you enough to give you the controls should be a good enough reason not to make those kinds of expressions."

"The reason you trust me is because you know how good a pilot I am. Don't worry, I'll take care of her. I'm just not used to something so...vocal."

She narrowed her eyes. "Vocal?"

"It's not a big deal. After we break atmo I'm sure I'll barely even notice it."

It was a lie, and they both knew it. Sitting at the helm of Eleion's rickety old cargo runner was a decidedly different experience from flying the *Ranger*. The hull moaned and creaked like it was trying to talk, and the engines grumbled and stuttered and belched more exhaust than seemed healthy. But it was a sturdy old bucket of bolts and had a certain character that Kojan could almost appreciate.

More importantly, it was unremarkable enough that it might get them out of Coalition space undetected.

Eleion settled back in the co-pilot's seat, wrapping her long tail around her body. She was back in a sturdy flight suit with a breather mask secured tightly across her jaws. The toxins that made Kaath's atmosphere so fatal to other species were vital in keeping an iskaath's lungs functioning, and Eleion had made sure to stock up on reserves before leaving.

It was strange seeing her masked again after spending so many weeks on Kaath. He'd never really noticed her discomfort before, but now he could see the way her mouth would twitch under the mask, the way her nostrils would flare and steam up the transparent coating.

"Don't worry about me," she said, catching him staring. "Wearing this is a small price to pay if it means the rest of my people will soon be free. The thought of being able to breathe in fresh air on any world we choose helps distract from the rubbing and chafing."

Her words were light and airy, but Kojan couldn't mistake

the quiet desperation in them. If Alvera could help engineer the right kind of cybernetics, it would mean a new future for the iskaath. A chance to see the rest of the galaxy without risking their lives to suffocation or respiratory failure. A chance to step out from beneath the scorn and contempt of their jarkaath siblings.

The mobile medical pod bleeped softly from the cargo hold behind them, barely audible over the sound of the engines. So much depended on Alvera, or whatever was left of her. It seemed too much to hope for that anybody could bring her back from her lifeless slumber. But hope was all they had.

"Breaking atmo in five," Kojan said. "Four...three...two..."

The last of Kaath's thick, yellow-tinged atmosphere gave way to darkness, leaving nothing ahead but a vast black void and the far-off glinting of stars. He guided the shuttle out of the planet's orbit and set a course for the nearest space tunnel.

"No, not that one," Eleion said, glancing at the nav console. "We'd have to drop out near the Farsal system. Too much of a risk we'd get picked up by the legionnaire patrols monitoring the waystation there."

"If we take the other tunnel, we'd have to switch at Hellon Junction. It's flagged as a piracy hotspot."

"Pirates aren't the ones looking for us. Besides, I'm a smuggler, remember? Hiding my cargo is what I'm best at."

The hours passed in easy silence as they slid through the black towards the space tunnel. There was never any pressure to fill the gaps with idle chatter when it came to Eleion. Her quiet presence was a reassurance in itself. The gentle sound of her breaths through the mask was as much a part of the ship as the humming and chimes from the instruments around him. In a galaxy full of strangers, she had become what was most familiar to him. It wasn't until now that he realised how much of a comfort that was.

"We're almost at the tunnel," he said. "Ready with those next set of coordinates?"

"Already loaded. The next tunnel we need to take isn't far from the exit point. Should only take us another hour or so once we drop out." She grinned. "Unless there are pirates waiting for us. In which case, you might need to put those flying skills of yours into action."

The transition into the tunnel was seamless. If it wasn't for the blinding light projecting from the viewports, he'd have barely noticed he wasn't in normal space anymore. It was a far cry from the near-fatal acceleration they'd suffered on the journey from New Pallas. But that was a new tunnel they'd punched themselves—at least this one had already been built for them.

He filtered out the harsh light from the viewports as the shuttle buffeted gently in the stream, oddly peaceful for something that was ripping through the very fabric of space.

He didn't realise his hands had tightened around the controls until Eleion gave him a gentle nudge. "A little on edge, are we?"

"Maybe." He loosened his fingers. "Something isn't sitting right. Call me paranoid."

"I'll hold off on that until we're out of Coalition space. Until then, it's just good sense."

The white glare evaporated, leaving them surrounded by the endless black reach of space once more. Kojan let out a breath and pushed on the controls, guiding the shuttle towards the new coordinates. "Only another hour, you said?"

Eleion nodded. "The next tunnel will take us right to the outskirts of the Rim Belt. After that, no more space tunnels. But more importantly, no more Coalition. We'll be on our own."

Kojan wasn't sure if the thought was reassuring or unsettling, but he pushed the shuttle on with a little more urgency all the same. The pocket of space they were in might have seemed empty, but he knew how easy it was to hide out here. In the *Ranger*, with its state-of-the-art stealth systems and deft handling, he might have been less anxious. But Eleion's cramped, cantankerous cargo runner wasn't built for that kind of subtlety.

"Something on the scanners," Eleion said. Her voice was calm, but Kojan could hear the undercurrent of tension. "One ship on a loose approach vector."

"Pirates?"

"Unlikely. Looks like a single-pilot craft, no room for cargo. Could be someone passing through, like we are. In any case, it's probably best we don't hang around."

Kojan gave a grim nod and pushed forward on the controls. For a moment, the cockpit was silent apart from the whirring of the instruments and the faint bleeps coming from Alvera's medpod in the hold behind them. The sound of his own heavy breaths echoed in his ears, muffling everything else out.

Then the comms system crackled. "Unidentified cargo vessel, this is Kitell Merala of the Coalition Legionnaires Corps. Please transmit your flight manifest and nav log and accept the incoming connection I'm sending you."

"Shit." Kojan threw a wild glance towards Eleion. "I thought you said there wouldn't be patrols out this way."

"I said there was less risk." She scowled. "What the hell are legionnaires doing poking around pirate territory? Petty crime isn't in their jurisdiction."

"Try telling him that."

She leaned over and tapped a series of panels on the console. "We need to accept the connection. We've got a better chance of getting out of this if he thinks we're a couple of smugglers and not wanted fugitives."

"My face is on every galactic arrest warrant feed between here and the Rim Belt. If you accept the connection, he'll know who we are."

THOSE ONCE FORGOTTEN | 83

"What do you take me for?" She made a few more adjustments on the console. "You think I travel without a voice modulator and holo-distorter? This piece of kit even scrambles the translation protocols, so he won't even guess that you're human. Just hold your nerve and follow my lead."

She flicked a switch and the holoprojector wavered into life, showing a lean-faced siolean with purple skin and a frown on his brow ridge. He regarded them with his black, lidless eyes before clicking his tongue and giving a sharp shake of the head. "Is there an issue with showing your real faces?"

Eleion shrugged. "Not often we're graced by the presence of the legionnaires out here. We'd rather not take any chances."

"Is that why you're running without a call sign?"

"Tends to be bad for business."

"You know what else tends to be bad for business? Refusing to transmit your flight manifest and nav log to a legionnaire when requested."

Eleion bristled. "*Fris sina vell*—haven't you got anything better to do? All we're doing is running a little delivery to the Rim Belt. You know damn well I can't show you my nav log without divulging my seller's location. Discretion is important in my line of work, *avé*? How about you just let us go on our way?"

The holoprojector crackled with the sound of Kitell Merala's sigh. "I have no interest in wasting my time going after small-time smugglers, *avé*? Send over your nav log and flight manifest, then you can go on your way. No questions asked. Or, if you refuse to comply, I can cripple your engines and come over there to have a look for myself."

"*Aie*, big shot. Are you being serious right now?" Eleion forced out a laugh. "It's like you said, we're just a couple of movers trying to make some credits. Why so interested in us?"

He tilted his head, expression hardening. "Because this is a Xon-class Y82 cargo freighter. The same kind of ship that was spotted leaving the Ulla system shortly after the incident with the waystation."

Kojan froze, his heart racing, but Eleion shrugged the statement off. "Ulla system? Never been there. Don't make a habit of going near waystations either. Those things creep me out. You must have the wrong ship."

"Thirty seconds," Merala said. "After that, I'm taking out your engines."

Kojan tensed, his fingers slick around the shuttle's controls. They were trapped. If Eleion sent him the nav log, he'd know she'd been in the Ulla system. If she didn't, and he managed to board, he'd find Alvera. Either way, they were screwed.

Unless they made a run for it.

He glanced at Eleion, raising an eyebrow in question. She let out a low, resigned hiss and nodded back, adjusting the strapping of the restraints around her shoulders. It was all the permission he needed.

Merala smiled as he saw the look exchanged between them. "Oh, please do. I can see the state of that rust bucket from here. Watching you try to run for it would make my day."

"Happy to oblige," Kojan said, fear and anticipation swelling in his chest. He grinned back at the siolean. "But when I outrun you in this rust bucket, remember you asked for it."

He brought the engines up to maximum power and hit the controls, sending the shuttle forward with a monstrous roar.

"So we're doing this," Eleion said in a breathless hiss. "Shit. We're doing this."

He didn't have time to answer her. Already he could see Merala moving on the nav display. He pulled the shuttle into a sweeping turn to move out of the fighter's intercept trajectory and swallowed the hard lump that had lodged itself in his throat. There was no time for doubt. No time for panic. He had the freedom of space around him and the warmth of the controls beneath his fingers.

It was all he needed.

His stomach lurched as he pushed the shuttle into a steep dive away from Merala's oncoming fighter. Direction lost all meaning in space. Every turn, every spin, led to a new orientation with no way to make sense of it. There were no landmarks out here, no reference points to understand what was up and what was down. Just absolute, unending freedom.

The old cargo runner growled and groaned in protest at every movement he asked of it, but it responded to his touch as easily as the *Ranger* had. There was no atmosphere to slow it down, no turbulence to fight against. It sliced through the darkness like the sharpest blade, devouring the emptiness in front of them faster with each passing second.

"He's closing in," Eleion said, a note of warning in her voice. "Won't be long before he—"

A siren blared above his head and he pulled the shuttle into a sharp turn which took the breath from his lungs. On the nav console, he saw missile fire shoot past with barely fifty metres to spare.

"That was close," Eleion said.

"No, that was a warning shot." Kojan squeezed the controls tighter as he fought to spin the shuttle back around. "He had us lined up. Whoever this legionnaire is, he's too good to miss a shot like that."

"Can you outrun him?"

He pressed his lips together. "I can try."

He shot forward again, and Merala followed. Every twist and breathless turn, every dive and spin and evasive manoeuvre, the siolean clung to him like he was tied by the most delicate thread. It became a dance of sorts, a tangle that was becoming too tight to extricate himself from. Every move he made, Merala matched.

A strange mix of exhilaration and adrenaline coursed through him as he pulled the shuttle out of the path of another missile volley. This one was closer than the last. If not intended to kill, then at least to cripple.

He bit his tongue and jerked on the controls with a violent fervour, sending the shuttle circling round and straight into the fighter's path. For a moment, his breath caught in his throat, waiting for the inevitable crash. Then the fighter was gone, peeling off in a wide turn to avoid the collision.

"Are you kidding me?" Eleion glared at him, her claws digging into her shoulder restraints. "You're playing bow-out with a fucking legionnaire? Get a grip, Kojan. Nobody wins if we get ourselves killed showing off."

"His nose was halfway up our engines. I had to do something to shake—" He snapped his mouth shut as the proximity siren screamed again. Another round of missiles shot by as he wrangled the shuttle out of their path with barely a breath to spare. "Shit. I think he's getting serious now."

"Maybe you should follow suit."

He drummed his fingers against the controls as he banked away and led the fighter on another chase. Eleion was right. There was too much at stake to get reckless. But the closer Merala got, the harder he wanted to push. There was a beauty to this game, a deadly grace. It wasn't something he was easily able to concede.

"Head for the space tunnel," Eleion urged. "If we can make it to the Rim Belt, we might have a chance. The legionnaires don't have any friends out in that part of the galaxy."

As soon as he switched course, Kojan realised it was a mistake. Merala had anticipated his move and circled around to match. Now the fighter was hovering above them like it was ready to swoop down, its missiles firmly trained on the shuttle's engines.

He was too close. He couldn't miss.

The intercom crackled. "Whoever you are, you're good. Just not as good as me."

The whole cockpit lurched as something rocked the rear, sending the shuttle spinning off course. He gritted his teeth against the force rattling through his skull and strained against the controls to pull the craft back under control.

Several warning lights blinked on the console. The engines were lost. They were trapped.

The holocom flickered back into life and Kitell Merala appeared again, satisfaction spread across his face. "Now that I have your attention, let me tell you how this is going to go. We're going to wait here for the rest of my patrol, and then we're going to board and take a look at what you're so desperate to hide."

"Why don't you come over now?" Eleion asked, a growl in her voice.

"You mean let you bait me into boarding when I know I'm outnumbered? I don't think so. But don't worry, the rest of my squad will be here soon enough." Merala cocked his head. "I'm especially curious to see who your pilot is. There's not many people in this galaxy who can fly like that, and most of them I trained myself. I'd like to see the person who thought they could beat me."

"Beat you?" Kojan snorted. "I had your number every step of the way. Put us in equal machinery and I outfly you every damn time."

"Maybe we'll get the chance to put that to the test one day. Unless you're dropped in a hole for the rest of your life after we find out you had something to do with what happened at Ulla Waystation."

"We had nothing to do with—"

"Something is coming." Eleion cut him off and began tapping at the nav console. "Must have dropped out one of the other tunnels. It's on approach now."

Kojan stiffened. "His backup?"

She glanced at Merala. "No. Not his backup."

The blinking on the nav console was coming closer and closer, but that wasn't what Kojan was looking at. Out of the viewport, he could see something happening to the distant stars. One by one, they were snuffed out by a shadow, their light lost to something impossibly huge. Something was coming their way, looming larger and larger the closer it got. The more stars its black silhouette blocked out, the tighter Kojan's chest became.

He swallowed, his mouth dry. "Is that…"

"A capital ship," Merala said, his voice grim. "A Rasnian capital ship, to be precise."

It was bigger than anything Kojan had ever seen. Bigger than the huge, city-sized evacuation ships that had orbited New Pallas, waiting for the chance to escape. It stretched on forever, like it was part of the darkness of space that surrounded it.

"Rasnian vessel *Verdant Sky*, you are interfering in an operation which has been authorised by the Coalition Legionnaire Corps," Merala said, his voice a little sharper over the comms channel. "Please divert from your current course."

For a moment, there was only silence. Then the intercom crackled and an accented human voice came through. "Legionnaires? Thought you'd be busy trying to sort out that shitshow with the waystations. In any case, you're the ones who are interfering here."

Merala scowled. "What are you talking about?"

"We're here to rendezvous with one of our cargo shuttles returning from an urgent supply run on orders from the Rasnian government. A shuttle which you seem to have crippled."

"What kind of supply run?"

"That's classified," the voice said. "But what I can tell you is the Coalition has no right to interfere in Rasnian affairs. So unless you'd like to join us for the ride home, I suggest you leave this to us and go about your own business."

Merala gave an irritated click of the tongue. "This shuttle matches the description of a vessel wanted in relation to the incident at Ulla Waystation. I have every right to—"

"You have every right to ask the Coalition to provide my government with a warrant to investigate. But unless you've got the ambassadors on the line now, we're taking our shuttle back to the Rasnian systems." The voice paused. "Or would you prefer to take on a capital warship all by yourself?"

Merala clenched his jaw, fury on his face. "When Supreme Commander Varantis hears about this—"

"He can come with a warrant himself or kiss my ass. Until then, this conversation is over."

Merala glowered. "This isn't the end of this, human. Whatever you and your government are hiding, we'll find it."

The holoprojection wavered and disappeared, leaving nothing but the quiet hum of the cockpit instruments behind.

Kojan glanced at Eleion and muted the intercom. "What do we do now?" he asked, voice hushed. "If they find Alvera..."

"I don't see that there's anything we can do," she said, shaking her head. "Our engines are dead. We can't fight our way out. Our only choice is to give ourselves up and hope they decide to help."

"Why would they help?"

"Because you have something we want, and we have something you need." The accented Rasnian voice crackled through the intercom, making Kojan jump. "Sorry, were you not finished yet?"

Eleion gave a hiss of surprise. "I thought you muted the intercom. How are they—"

"The same way we found you in the first place," the voice said, a smirk behind every word. "Recognise me yet, iskaath? Before we traded ships, I thought it might be a good investment to leave a little audiovisual tracking device behind in case you decided to show up again. Lucky for me, it seems to have paid off. You've brought our old friend Alvera right to me."

Kojan's heart froze. "I know that voice."

The holoprojector shimmered into life again. The man in front of them was dressed in the crimson-trimmed regalia of the Rasnian military police, the fabric bright against his dark brown skin.

Maxim ras Arbor.

He crossed his arms across his chest and gave them a wolfish smile. "Now, let's talk about how we can help each other."

SEVEN

NIOLE

"You don't have to go back there. You know that, don't you?"

Niole's breath hitched, making her head spin. The atmosphere on Aurel was thin enough to leave her light-headed at the best of times. Getting caught off guard only added to her breathlessness, and that kind of distraction wasn't something she needed. Especially not now.

Rivus was staring at her, his green eyes glinting in the low light. Aurel was more moon than planet, its barely-there atmosphere giving way to the darkness of space that surrounded it. The black seeped into the red-tinged sky, leaving the horizon in a perpetual state of twilight. It cast Rivus in shadows and exaggerated the worry drawn around the scars on his face.

She slung her pack onto the back of the landspeeder and secured the strapping around it. "Tarvan made it pretty clear where I belong. If he wants to hand me over to the Idran-Var before the summit, who am I to say no?"

"That's not what I meant," Rivus said. "He's sending you back to them as a show of good faith, but that doesn't mean there's not a place for you here. After this summit, we'll all be on the same side. You could still come back."

"You really believe that?" She lifted up her hand. Under the red sky, she could pretend her cracked grey skin had a carmine glow. "This is what the legionnaires think I am. A beast in need of caging. They hate me. They fear me. And maybe they're right to."

"I don't hate you," he said, his voice like shifting gravel. "I used to, once. But too much has changed since then." He shook his huge, heavy crest. "Something is coming, Niole. I could use someone who understands what's at stake here."

She turned back to the landspeeder, brushing her hand over the controls. "I can't be your redemption, Rivus. You're offering me a second chance that isn't yours to give. The only thing I can promise you is that I will stand against what's coming." She swung her leg across the speeder and slid into the seat. "Whatever happens at the summit, I hope we have the chance to meet again before this is all over."

Rivus lifted his head. "As friends? Or across the battlefield?"

His echoing of Rhendar's words brought a smile to her lips. "I'd be proud to meet you either way. As long as you know that despite everything that has happened between us, I'm leaving now thankful that we were brought together again."

"As am I. Even if it's the last time." Rivus bowed his head, but she could still read the disappointment in the shifting of his plates. "I hope the Idran-Var prove worthy of the faith you're putting in them."

She flicked the controls, and the speeder rumbled into life. "So do I," she said softly, but her words were lost in the roar of the engines as she gunned the throttle and sped off across the pock-marked, barren surface.

That final look of regret on his plating was all she could think of as she tore across the stretching plains, the speeder kicking up reddish-black dust from the dry ground. Leaving him should have been easier. There shouldn't have been a wrench in her heart and a troubled whisper at the back of her head asking her if she was doing the right thing. She'd tried to make him her enemy, as the Idran-Var had once been, but seeing him again had only brought with it the pain of having lost an old friend.

She cranked the throttle further and leaned forward, urging the speeder on with all the power it would give her. Now was not the time for misgivings or regret. The past was out of reach; there was no changing it now. But she could still shape what was to come.

Tarvan had chosen Aurel for its solitude. It was a lonely, uninhabited dwarf planet skirting the disputed border between the allied systems and the Rim Belt. The terrain in this sector was flat and open, with only a few ridges and craters scattering the landscape. The Idran-Var encampment was a few hundred klicks away from where the legionnaires had set up their outpost.

She pulled up a short distance before reaching the camp's sentry post, abandoning the speeder to the arid, lifeless ground. Show of good faith or not, Tarvan couldn't be trusted. For all she knew, the speeder might have had an explosive hidden inside its mechanisms, rigged to blast the moment she got close. Idran-Var armour was as close to indestructible as any material in the galaxy could get, but no matter how strong the shell was, there were things a body inside couldn't take.

She made her way towards the barricade, her boots clunking against the hard ground. Every breath strained her chest and before long, her brow ridge was damp with perspiration. Her broken ribs had been reset, but they still ached from her beating back in the meditation chamber. Part of it was more than bruises and old war wounds. The muscles in her legs didn't carry her the way they did only a few short months ago. The subdermal implant they'd put in her to restrict her flares sapped more and more of her each day. Before long, there would be little left.

"You approaching the encampment—identify yourself!"

An Idran-Var popped up from behind the barricade, rifle aimed pointedly at Niole. The dark, glass-like metal of their armour looked like a shifting red shadow under the Aurelian sky.

She raised her hands. "I'm unarmed. My name is Niole. I'm here to see Rhendar."

"Rhendar?" The Idran-Var lowered their rifle and vaulted over the barricade. They landed on the ground with a heavy crunch, sending a cloud of dust pluming around their thick, armoured legs. "The rest of us not good enough for you or something?"

A hiss cut through the thin air as the Idran-Var took their helmet off, revealing a huge crimson crest and the glint of amusement in familiar orange eyes.

"Venya?" Niole choked, relief bubbling in her throat. "Fyra, I thought you—"

The rest of her words were knocked out of her lungs as Venya charged towards her and caught her in a bone-crushing embrace. "Careful how you finish that sentence, friend. I know you weren't about to say you thought I'd died on you."

Niole pulled back, chest aching. "Never even crossed my mind. I didn't recognise you. Looks like you finally got your armour."

Venya puffed out her chest, a wide grin stretching across her jaw plates. "Just in time too, by the look of things. I hear we've got a fight coming our way." She tilted her head. "Speaking of not recognising people, what the hell happened to you? I'm pretty sure you were some shade of green the last time I saw you."

Niole forced a laugh. "Just a little side-effect from being held prisoner by the legionnaires."

"They did this?" Venya frowned, her eyes solemn and concerned. "Shit, I didn't mean to... What you did back on the escape run saved our lives. If it wasn't for you—"

"It doesn't matter," Niole said. "Forget about this, it's nothing. I need to know what happened after you got away in the escape pods. Did everyone else make it back safely? Is Zal here? What about Claine? Did he get his armour too?"

Venya's face fell. "No. He didn't."

"What?" Niole's heart stopped. "Tell me he made it, Venya. Tell me we didn't lose him."

"He made it, but..." Venya hesitated. "Shit, I shouldn't be the one telling you this."

"What is it?"

"The traitor we were looking for? The one who gave our position away to the legionnaires?" She shook her huge, heavy head, her eyes bleak. "It was Claine."

———

The makeshift brig was nothing more than a metal box inside one of the prefab buildings. There wasn't even a one-way mirror, just a juttering holofeed from the four cameras monitoring the improvised cell.

Niole barely recognised the crumpled figure huddled in one of the corners. His long, tangled hair had been shorn off, and his pale scalp now boasted an ugly red scar from the crown of his head to behind his left ear. His face was swollen from bruising, and his clothes hung loosely off his frame like they'd been made for someone else.

She pressed her fingers against the stuttering images on the holofeed screen. "What the hell happened to him?"

"You really need to ask?" Venya gave a bitter laugh. "Serric happened."

"I don't understand. Why would Claine betray the Idran-Var?"

"He didn't mean to. Idiot just made one mistake after another until it was too late to take them back." Venya let out a long, heavy breath. "Claine was born into the Idran-Var, but his father was one of those who joined us, like you. When Claine's mother died in a raid a couple of years ago, he decided to leave us and go back to the allied systems."

"His father left the Idran-Var?" Niole frowned. "Is that even allowed?"

Venya shrugged. "Why wouldn't it be? He decided he was no longer Idran-Var, and you know as well as I do that this isn't the kind of life you should live if you don't believe in it. Claine was old enough to decide his own path by that point, and he made the choice to stay."

"I'm guessing they kept in contact."

"It's not exactly encouraged, but not forbidden either. In this case, it ended up being a mistake." Venya shook her head. "The legionnaires tracked down his father and threatened him, forcing him to pry information out of Claine. He probably didn't even realise how much he was giving away until it was too late. And then...well, you saw what happened on Vesyllion. We paid the price for his stupidity, and now he's paying it too."

"I'm surprised Serric didn't kill him on the spot."

"He would have if Rhendar hadn't been there to stop him. At first, I thought I was grateful for that, but now I'm not so sure. Seeing him like that, knowing the shame and punishment that lies ahead of him..." She broke off. "He's not a traitor. But a lot of good people died because of what he did. If I was him, I'm not sure how I could live with myself after that."

"You'd be surprised at the lies we're capable of telling ourselves to justify the unjustifiable," Niole said. "It doesn't take much to start believing them."

Venya took a step back, studying her with her sharp orange eyes. "Why did you come back here, Niole?"

"For peace. At least, that's what I've been telling myself. Like I said, you say something often enough you almost start to think it might be true." She grimaced. "I don't know if I even believe peace is possible anymore. Fyra, there are times I'm not sure I *want* it to be possible."

She looked down at her colour-stripped, withering skin. The legionnaires had done this to her. Not just this time, but every time they'd ever hunted her down. All the anger and violence she'd ever learned since leaving Ossa had come from their lessons.

Yet she couldn't shake the image of Rivus from her head. The gnarled scars she'd carved on his bone plates all those years ago. The desperation and trust in his eyes. The way he'd looked at her like she was the only one who could help him.

"I used to think I'd keep running past the edge of the galaxy if I could," she said, her voice a whisper. "But I don't think I can outrun this. I don't think any of us can. If we want a chance to survive, we have to fight."

Venya gave her a gentle nudge. "You know I'll never say no to a good scrap. After what you did for us during the evacuation from Vesyllion, I'd follow you without condition or hesitation. But it's not me you need to convince."

"I know." Niole took a breath. "It's time I went to see Rhendar."

———

The war room was perched on the upper level of one of the hastily-constructed prefab buildings that had been erected as part of the outpost. A floor-to-ceiling window overlooked the red-dusted horizon beyond the makeshift barricade surrounding the encampment. When she looked out of it, Niole imagined the legionnaire camp somewhere far in the distance. Maybe Rivus was looking her way too, only able to guess at what was happening.

Venya had left to resume her sentry duties, but Niole didn't mind the solitude. It was the last chance to breathe before going under. A final moment of peace before the storm came rushing in and she was dragged into something impossible to turn back from. Suddenly the lifelessness of Aurel didn't seem so lonely. Instead, it almost felt safe.

"You came back."

She turned from the window at the sound of Rhendar's modulated voice. His armour had a dull glint from the twilight glow outside, and the red lights behind the grille of his visor blinked menacingly in the shadows. But there was a smile in his voice she remembered well, and as fearsome as he looked, the familiarity of his armoured presence loosened the knot in her stomach.

"Looks that way," she said. "It's good to see you, Rhendar. After what happened on Vesyllion, I didn't think—"

The rest of her words were lost to the tightening of her throat as Serric burst into the room, shoulders stiff and jaw twitching. She braced herself against the inevitable call of his flare, of the rise he was always able to provoke from her, but there was nothing. Even as she dared to reach out, nothing was there to test her. She could see the vapour-like energy swirling from his skin, but it might as well have been mist for all she could sense of it.

Serric curled his lip into an ugly snarl and reached down to one of his boots, drawing a long, sharp blade. "Where is it?"

"Serric." Rhendar's voice was full of warning.

"Take it easy, old man. This doesn't concern you." He turned back to Niole. "Where is it?" he asked again.

Was it her imagination, or was there a tremor in his voice the second time he asked the question? She searched his face for the disgust she'd expected, but all she found was rage.

With Serric, it's always a fight, Rhendar had told her once. *He doesn't know how to do anything else.*

She stretched out her left arm and tried not to wince at the way he grabbed it. Her grey skin was stretched tight over the sinew underneath, exposing every frailty, every wasting muscle. Its dullness was excruciating in contrast to the vibrant colour of Serric's hands.

He ran his fingers over her forearm until he found the buried implant. His other hand was tight around the hilt of the blade.

He looked up at her, his black eyes steady and unrelenting.

Niole nodded.

The blade was under her skin before she had time to blink. She let out a hiss of pain from behind her teeth as Serric slid the edge towards the implant. It was all she could do not to squirm and look away. Bad enough for him to see her like this without showing him the weakness he'd always suspected was there.

"Got it." He flicked his wrist and something hot seared from deep inside her forearm. Dark blood welled to the surface of her skin, pushing out a sleek, square chip. Before she could say anything, Serric grabbed it and threw it to the floor, bringing the heel of his boot down on it with a sharp crunch. "It's done."

Rhendar sighed. "You realise we have a med lab that could have done the job considerably more efficiently? Not to mention cleanly."

A steady trickle of blood ran down her forearm, and the splatter from the blade's work had stained her tunic. She could barely hear Rhendar's words and Serric's retort over the pounding in her head. Nausea tugged at her stomach. Something wasn't right. She should have been feeling better, not worse.

She bent her head, desperate for the faintest echo of the flare she'd once reviled so much. Aching for the stir of something inside her she'd thought was lost. It was like listening for something in silence, knowing it was out there but unable to hear it.

Serric was still holding her arm. The shimmer from his flare skimmed across her skin like it was trying to find a way inside. There was a time it had been all too easy to recoil from what he was. To deny the parts of herself she saw in him, rather than admit they existed. Now, she wanted nothing more than to open herself up and let him in.

She fought to keep the pain from her voice. "I can't... I still can't feel anything. I don't know how long it takes for the anti-rad meds to wear off. If they even *can* wear off."

It was like her voice had broken Serric from some kind of reverie. The moment she spoke, he pushed her arm away and whirled back towards Rhendar. Nothing had changed in his expression. Every hard line on his face, every dark look and twitch of the jaw, bore the same anger they always had. Maybe it had been too much to hope for that for once, it might not have been aimed at her.

"Do you even *want* them to wear off?" He shot her a questioning look. "Don't pretend there wasn't some part of you that wanted this. Always running. Always trying to pretend you didn't ask for things to turn violent, even when you did. Always wishing someone would come along and take the fight from you, so you didn't have to admit to yourself it was what you always wanted."

She sprung back like he'd struck her. "That's not fair."

"Isn't it? You spent months trying to convince yourself you could become one of us. But the moment things got real, you went rushing back to the legionnaires. And now you want us to make peace with them?" He laughed, the sound harsh and bitter. "If I was Rhendar, I'd send you back to them with nothing more than a promise of war."

Even though she knew it had been coming, the rejection stung. The hesitation she thought she'd heard before he slid his blade into her arm evaporated like a memory that had never existed. There was no understanding. No sympathy for what she'd suffered. The only thing that hurt worse than his words was expecting more from him.

"If you were Rhendar, you'd be leading the Idran-Var to ruin," she said, her voice low. "There's a reason he's wearing a helmet of the *varsath* instead of you."

Serric blanched, a mixture of shock and anger on his face. "What did you say?"

"You heard me," Niole said, wiping the blood from her arm. "You want to lead your people? Open your eyes. If all you define yourself by is a hatred of the Coalition, you'll cease to exist the moment they do. The Idran-Var have to be more than a grudge against their old enemies to survive what's coming. Rhendar sees that, even if you don't."

Energy swirled around Serric's arms, and his eyes carried a dangerous glint. "What makes you think that *you*, of all people, get to tell us about what the Idran-Var have to be? You have no idea what—"

"She's right." Rhendar's words were heavy and laced with regret, like they were a defeat he wasn't ready to admit. "We've been living off the memory of old wars and older wounds for too long. We're so preoccupied with what our people did to get here that we've lost sight of where to take them. We don't know who we are anymore."

"Who we are?" Serric repeated through gritted teeth. "We are Idran-Var. *Those who resist.*"

"What are we resisting?" Rhendar shrugged his thick-set, armoured shoulders. "We might be able to pick off a border planet or two at the edge of the allied systems to get some payback for Vesyllion. But that won't bring back the people we lost there. It will only get more of us killed, and for what? If we're to resist something, if we're to fight, let it be for a war that means something."

"The waystations," Niole said, her words a shallow breath. "And whatever is beyond them."

Rhendar slowly turned his head towards her. "I've been around this galaxy long enough to know when a fight is on its way. If nothing comes of Rivus's claims, that fight will be with those who need to answer for Vesyllion. Until then, I'm willing to wait and see if these nightmares of his have any teeth."

Serric glowered. "The Coalition—"

"Will always get what they deserve, as long as there are those like you willing to make them pay for the blood they've spilled," Rhendar said heavily. "We're Idran-Var. We always will be, as long as we've an enemy to fight. But today we lay down our weapons for the chance that our people may pick them up again tomorrow."

"What about the rest of the Idran-Var?" Niole asked. "Will they agree to a cease-fire with the Coalition?"

He gave a sigh through his helmet. "I don't know. I'm only one among the *varsath*. Those who already follow me will continue to do so, but I can't speak for the rest of my people."

"You could, if you wanted to." Serric folded his arms.

Rhendar turned his helmeted head towards him sharply. "We've been through this already. You know my answer."

"Yeah, and you know how little I pay attention to what you have to say, old man." Serric snorted and rapped on the door behind him with a tight fist. "So why don't we bring in the others and have a vote on it?"

The door slid open and Serric stepped to the side to allow through a dozen figures in the same indomitable armour Rhendar was clad in. Their helmets were as unyielding and unfathomable as his was, each one marked by a different shape, a different style of visor.

Her breath caught tightly in her chest. These were the other *varsath*. Shields of the people, as Rhendar called them. Their metal shells were more than armour; they were a symbol to the rest of the Idran-Var. A reminder of their ferocity, their unwillingness to submit.

When I take it off, it will be because I am defeated or dead, Rhendar had told her. *Either way, I will no longer be Idran-Var. That is why you will never see my face.*

Watching them fill the room with their presence brought more fear than facing a legionnaire ever had. Perhaps it was their facelessness, the knowledge she would never truly know them. Perhaps it was the realisation that every one of them had earned their armour for actions she didn't want to imagine. Perhaps it was because, despite all she knew of Rhendar and the friendship he had offered her, these were the monsters she'd been warned about as a cadet.

Zal followed them into the room, her russet hair scraped back into a wavy knot and her cybergrafted eyepatch blinking in anticipation. She ignored the rest of the *varsath* and marched straight up to Niole, pulling her into a tight embrace and pressing a kiss against her cheek.

"I didn't think I'd ever get the chance to thank you for what you did," she said. "If it wasn't for you, my team and I would be floating corpses around Vesyllion right now. Whatever happens next, I won't forget that, *jal-var*."

Niole smiled. "You have no idea how many nights I spent wondering if you were alive. I'm so glad to see you, Zal."

"If deadly toxic spores couldn't kill me, what makes you think a few well-placed sorborite rods would do the trick?" She let out a wide, toothy grin. "Besides, nothing in the galaxy was ever going to keep me from this moment. It's been a long time coming."

"What do you mean?"

Rhendar folded his arms across his broad chest, looking stiffer and more uncomfortable in his gleaming armour than Niole had ever seen him.

"Whatever this is, this isn't the time," he said, his mechanised voice gruff. "In case you'd forgotten, we've got a summit to attend in a few days."

"Which is exactly why we're here," one of the Idran-Var replied, her voice sharp and clipped through her helmet's modulator. "I can't pretend I fully understand what's going on here, Rhendar, but what I do know is we'd have lost a great deal more on Vesyllion if it wasn't for your leadership. Until you give me reason to believe otherwise, I trust you'll do what's best for our people."

Rhendar snorted. "That's uncharacteristically generous coming from you, Selia. But while I appreciate the vote of confidence—"

"It's not a vote of confidence, you dithering fool," the Idran-Var replied, a sigh in her words. "It's a nomination. After what happened on Vesyllion, we need to stand together. We need somebody to lead us." She tilted her head to one side and gave a slow, respectful nod. "We need a war chief."

The silence that fell across the room sent shivers across Niole's skin. Rhendar stood quiet and unmoving, like the other Idran-Var's words hadn't even reached him. Next to him, Serric and Zal exchanged a glance.

After what seemed like an eternity, Rhendar spoke. "We all know what happened the last time one of us was given that kind of power. Don't ask me to take on that kind of responsibility."

"If not you, then who else among us?" Selia shook her head. "Whatever the threat we face—whether it's our old enemy or some unknown force from beyond the waystations—all of the *varsath* know we cannot face it alone. If something threatens one of us, it threatens us all."

"You're the only one who can do it," Serric said. "Nobody else commands the kind of loyalty you do among our people. All we're doing here is making official what everyone already knows. Whatever hell is coming, you're the one to lead us into it."

Rhendar rounded on him. "Five minutes ago, you were calling for war against the Coalition. Why the change of heart?"

"He knows what we all know," Zal said, her voice firm. "We can't do this without you. If there's a future for our people, it's going to be born from you leading them. I don't give a damn who you ask me to fight. Just point me where you need me to go and I'll bleed for you like I always have." She lowered herself to the ground, placing both hands across her knee. "War chief."

Serric dropped down beside her, his headtails falling loosely across his shoulders as he dipped his head. "War chief."

One by one, the *varsath* around the room followed suit, falling to one knee and uttering the words from behind their helmets.

War chief.

War chief.

War chief.

Rhendar looked around at them, his shoulders drooping heavier with each *varsath* that lowered themselves to the floor. Before long, they were the only two left standing.

He turned his head towards her. The helmet did nothing to hide the helplessness exuding from him. She could feel the weight the rest of the room had placed around his shoulders. The burden they'd forced upon him. The unspoken atrocities they'd asked him to commit without saying a word. All to save their people.

It felt like a betrayal to join them in asking it of him. Maybe it was.

She lowered herself to the ground and crossed her arms over her knee.

"War chief," she said.

EIGHT

RIDLEY

S tealing a ship under the cover of darkness might have seemed like a good plan in any other port, but Jadera wasn't like any other port. The docks came alive under the night sky. Garish, fluorescent lights illuminated the market stalls and pop-up cantinas as the port's inhabitants spilled out from one to another, their chatter slurred and animated. Every blind corner was a threat. Every alley held the promise of violence.

Beside her, Drexious shuddered. "I hate this place after sundown. The daylight might make my scales melt, but at least you can see what's coming. Right now, I feel like I'm waiting for someone to stick a knife in my spine."

"With no shortage of people claiming you deserved it, I'd imagine." Ridley tapped a command into her wrist terminal to start the slicing programme. In a few minutes, she'd have the docking logs for hangar number two.

If she didn't get caught.

She tried to quell the shiver that ran up her spine. Most of

Jadera's traffic landed far outside the port itself, across the treacherous sandflats. The three hangars within the boundaries of the port were tiny in comparison and reserved exclusively for Skaile's personal use. Nothing landed here without her express invitation.

Stealing one of these ships would be more than an insult. It would be a death sentence.

"Shit, this one's no good either," she said, closing down her wrist terminal with a frustrated sigh. "We've only got one more chance. The big hangar on the north side of the port."

"That's not a good idea. Bigger hangar means more port security. If Skaile catches us—"

"Then let's make sure she doesn't catch us."

Drexious let out a low hiss. "We've found half a dozen ships that could have got us out of here. Why so picky?"

Ridley glanced around and retreated further into the shadows, motioning for him to follow. "It's not just about getting us out of here," she said, her voice hushed. "It's about getting us to those coordinates."

"Any one of those ships could make that journey."

"No, they couldn't." She grimaced. "We need something specific. We need a tunnel puncher."

"A tunnel puncher?" Drexious drew back, his bronze eyes wide. "I know you're still fairly new to this galaxy, outlander, so let me fill you in on a little piece of common knowledge: you can't just rip a new route through space wherever you feel like it. There's a reason the Coalition has so many regulations around punching tunnels. Get the calculations wrong and you could end up in the middle of a star or a black hole. If that's your grand plan for beating Skaile to the coordinates, you can count me out."

"Ripping a new tunnel is the only way to reach the coordinates at all," she said, pinching her nose. "I told Skaile they led to an uncharted planet between the galaxy and dark space.

What I didn't tell her was exactly how far out that planet was. Even in the fastest conventional ship, it would take the best part of a decade to reach it. Using a tunnel puncher is the only way."

The spindles on the back of Drexious's neck quivered. "You gave Skaile the wrong coordinates? Do you have a death wish? When she finds out—"

"We'll already be far out of her reach."

"And what happens when we get back? You think she'll forget about it and let us go on our way?" His bright eyes gleamed furiously. "Is whatever we're going to find on this planet worth being on the run for the rest of our lives?"

If it's not, then it's likely the rest of our lives won't last very long anyway, Ridley thought. Admitting it out loud wasn't something she was ready to do, not when so much was still hanging in the balance. It was like standing on a precipice, waiting for the fall. Even though she knew it was coming, there was still hope so long as she could feel the ground beneath her feet.

"We have to do this," she said. "We need what's out there. This is the only way."

Drexious let out a long, resigned sigh. "You've given me no choice, you realise that? The only reason Skaile is keeping me alive is because of you. The moment she figures out you've screwed her over, I'm dead anyway."

"That wasn't my intention."

"I know. But it's how it's played out, isn't it?" He shrugged. "Fine, let's do this. We'll hit the coordinates and get this treasure you talked about. At least I might get to enjoy some profit before Skaile gets her hands on me again."

A pang of guilt pulled tight in Ridley's stomach. She'd told Drexious the same thing she'd told Skaile—that the writings they'd recovered spoke of a place the ancient sioleans had hidden what was most precious to them. Their greatest treasure. That was what she had promised him. That was what she had promised them both.

It was the truth, technically. But a truth ill-explained was little better than a lie.

She pushed aside her thoughts and returned to the flurry of the streets. She was getting ahead of herself. Right now, those coordinates were too far out of reach. To have a chance, they needed a ship. The right kind of ship.

The security around the north hangar was tighter, as Drexious had suspected. Ridley had already spotted two huge, armoured dachryn patrolling the perimeter with stony expressions on their jaw plates and formidable-looking rifles in their claws. Part of her almost wanted the docking logs to come up empty again, if only so the choice in front of her would be taken out of her hands.

Data streamed across the holographic interface on her wrist terminal, one line flashing up after another. She held her breath until the programme stopped on a newly-registered shuttle.

"Tunnel puncher," she whispered, hardly daring to say it out loud. "We've got one."

For the first time, she allowed herself to imagine the uncharted planet at the end of the coordinates. It bloomed into reality in her mind, covered in crumbling ruins and sprawling, forgotten cities. When she reached it, would the answers be waiting there for her?

"Great," Drexious said, sounding anything but pleased. "Got a plan for getting in? I didn't escape death at Skaile's hands just to get crushed by a couple of mean-looking dachryn."

"You're the thief, aren't you? No clever ideas?"

Drexious stretched his long neck forward, his eyes glinting keenly in the dim light. "Maintenance hatch, maybe? All these prefab buildings have one for easy access to the cables running from the power grids. Should be a simple case of finding one and following it into the hangar."

"Won't it be alarmed?"

"Probably. But as much as this may come as a surprise to you, I've knocked over more than a couple of run-down Jadera warehouses in my time. And I've never yet come across one that hasn't used the manufacturer's default alarm code." He snorted. "This whole port basically came from the same box."

"Skaile never bothered to change the access codes for her warehouses?" Ridley raised an eyebrow. "Doesn't that seem like a bit of an oversight to you?"

"Oversight, arrogance, call it what you want." Drexious shrugged. "Skaile has the luxury of not needing to worry about people being stupid enough to steal from her. It tends to only happen once."

"What does that make us then?"

"Either the luckiest gutter scum in the galaxy or a couple of idiots who are going to get themselves killed." Drexious grunted. "Let's do this before I change my mind."

He led her into a nearby alley, the silver-black of his scales making it seem like he was part of the shadows himself. He melted into his surroundings with ease, leaving her like a blundering fool trying to keep pace. Even the cloak she'd pulled over her curls wasn't enough to achieve the kind of elusiveness he was able to wield.

After a while, he came to a stop next to a rusting wire grate. "This will take us down to the power grid," he said. "Most of the buildings in this quadrant are hooked up to these generators. All we have to do is follow the cables to the hangar's maintenance hatch and we'll be in." He pulled the grate to one side and gestured for her to climb down. "Watch your knees on the landing. It's a bit of a drop for a human."

Ridley slipped through the opening and peered into the darkness below. There was no light at all. She couldn't even see the bottom of the shaft. All she could do was slide herself off the edge and wait for the impact.

The hard, concrete floor hit the soles of her feet with a violent crack, sending a painful shock up to her knees. She staggered off balance and reached out to grab something. One hand found the surface of a damp stone wall and she held herself against it for a moment, her breathing ragged from the pain shooting through her legs.

She heard a soft thump next to her. "Drex, is that you?"

"Of course it's me," came a disembodied voice from the darkness. "Why are you squinting like that? Is human eyesight really so bad?"

"In this kind of light, at least. It's almost making me regret not taking those retinal implants back on Exodus Station."

"Here." Something brushed in front of her, and she felt cool, scaled skin beneath her outstretched hand. "Keep a hold of my shoulder and follow close."

It was a strange sensation to put so much trust in someone who'd tried to kill her barely a couple of months ago, but Ridley couldn't bring herself to hold that particular piece of treachery against him. Of all the things she might have found hard to forgive, Drexious doing what it took to survive wasn't one of them. She knew what that felt like better than most.

Don't think about it, she told herself. *Don't think about the gunshots and the screams through the hull while you hid. Don't think about what's happening back on New Pallas. Don't think about everyone you left behind to get here.*

If she thought about it, she would falter. If she faltered, she had already lost. The only thing she could do was keep pulling herself up from the bottom, one insignificant hand at a time, and try not to think about how far she'd fall if she let go.

"Here." Drexious stopped sharply in front of her, jolting her from her thoughts. His shoulder rose and fell under her hand with the gentle rhythm of his breathing. "We're at the hatch. Time to tuck your tail and hope this alarm code holds up."

Ridley held her breath, listening for the light tapping of his claws on the keypad. She half expected to be met with the sound of an ear-splitting siren and the thunder of armed guards rushing to the access hatch. Skaile was a lot of things, but careless had never been one of them. What were the chances she'd been too confident to overlook the changing of the default codes?

Skaile doesn't worry about people being stupid enough to steal from her, Drexious had said. *It tends to only happen once.*

Something above her slid open with a soft click and a shaft of light streamed into the tunnel, prickling her eyes.

"Thank the stars." Drexious let out a long hiss. "We're in. And if I've judged this right, this hatch should take us right into the middle of the hangar."

"We won't have much time. There'll be cameras—"

"Better move fast then." He hauled himself through the hatch.

Ridley pulled herself up after him and rolled to her feet on the hangar floor. She darted her head from one side to the other, trying to identify the tunnel puncher registered in the docking logs. If they didn't get to it quickly, it wouldn't be long until port security had them at the end of a barrel.

After a moment, her eyes found a sleek, curved shuttle with a gleaming black paint job that glittered under the glare of the hangar lights like the night sky. "That's it."

"Are you sure?" Drexious frowned. "That looks like a luxury cruiser, not something capable of punching a hole through space."

"This is Skaile we're talking about. She'd want both." She broke into a run. "Let's go. We need to get out of here before—"

"Before what?"

Ridley froze at the sound of the voice. It rang out harsh and distorted, like it had come from behind a heavy filter. The words were sharp and cutting, too familiar to mistake for anyone else.

She slowly turned around, her chest tightening as she saw an armoured figure stride into the middle of the hangar.

Halressan.

The gleaming metal shell of her armour reflected the lurid lights from above as she advanced, purposeful and unrelenting. Ridley might have been able to admire the beauty in it if it hadn't been for the danger.

Halressan stopped a few metres away and pulled her helmet from her head. Frost-blonde hair spilled out around her shoulders, and her pale, stone-like face was as unforgiving as ever. "I really didn't think you'd be this stupid."

"You were following us?" It was hard to get the words out over the hammering of her heart. It was more than fear. More than adrenaline. It was the realisation of a scene she'd refused to play in her mind, even though she knew it had always been a possibility.

"Up to a point," Halressan said with a light shrug of her shoulders. "Didn't need to bother going through the power grid tunnels. Easy enough to walk through the front door when you have authorisation."

"Skaile sent you."

"She had a feeling Drex might try something, but I knew better." Her mouth was a hard line, her eyes cold. "I knew it would be you."

Ridley cursed herself. This wasn't how it was meant to go. The fact she only had herself to blame made it worse. She'd never factored Halressan into her plans because she hadn't wanted to think about her showing up. It was only seeing her now, with her shining armour and unforgiving glare, that she realised how much of a mistake she'd made.

She forced a smile onto her face. "Am I to take it that means you're not here to run away with me?"

Halressan barked out a laugh. "In your dreams, babe. I came to stop you getting yourself killed."

"You care? I'm touched." From the corner of her eye, she saw several armed security guards spill into the hangar. They lined up behind Halressan, their rifles pointed and ready. All it would take was a signal from Halressan and she and Drexious would be left bullet-ridden on the hangar floor. A couple of gutter-scum bodies to be hauled out and dumped in the desert, with nobody to mourn either one of them.

Obsolete. Shaw's voice was like a taunt in her ear, the word cruel and violent even as a whispered memory.

Halressan took a step forward, closing the distance between them with a scowl and an easy stride. "What are you doing this for?" Her voice was low enough so that only Ridley could hear it. "You have to know there's no way back from this."

Ridley's mouth was dry. "Same reason I do anything," she said, trying to inject humour into her voice she didn't feel. "To save my skin."

"Sweetheart, that's bullshit," Halressan said, a dark chuckle in her voice. "If that was true, you'd have let Skaile rip your new best buddy here to pieces instead of almost getting yourself killed to save his sorry hide. You didn't have to give her those coordinates. But whatever they lead to, it's something you're willing to throw your life away for. Again." She tilted her head to the side. "What could be worth that much to you, I wonder?"

This time, when Ridley met the steely grey of her eyes, she saw something new. Something curious and hungry that had chased away some of the coldness. Something she could use.

Ridley knew what it was like to be hungry. She knew how desperate that could make a person. How sloppy that could make a person. She could see that same hunger in Halressan's eyes now. All she had to do was promise her the chance to get what she wanted, and she'd have her.

It was the kind of lie she'd always had to tell to keep herself alive. She didn't owe Halressan anything.

So why did it feel so much like betrayal?

She pulled the corner of her mouth into a half-smile. "I'm telling you, it will be worth it. You want in?"

Halressan grinned back, and Ridley tried to ignore the way it twisted her heart. "I thought you'd never ask."

She pulled her helmet back over her head, replacing her sharp features with a glinting mirrored visor. Just like that, the woman was gone. In her place stood one of the most infamous bounty hunters in the Rim Belt.

Something fluttered in the pit of Ridley's stomach, though whether it was fear or something far more dangerous, she didn't know. "You're outnumbered."

"Yeah," Halressan said, sounding almost bored. "Not for long though."

She moved quicker than Ridley could blink, spinning around and drawing her assault rifle from its holster on her back with one sweeping movement. It settled lightly in her armoured hands, and before Ridley had time to cover her ears, the hangar was ringing with the sound of gunfire.

Ridley grabbed Drexious and ran with him towards a pair of heavy-duty cargo crates. Bullets and plasma bolts pinged around them, ricocheting off the smooth curves of Halressan's gleaming armour. The stolen Idran-Var shell was near indestructible, but the effortless way it deflected gunfire made their chances of catching a stray bullet dangerously high unless they got behind cover.

Ridley ducked down behind one of the crates, panting heavily. Drexious flattened himself to the floor beside her on all fours, each of his limbs twitching.

"She's on our side now?" he asked, his voice thin.

"Looks that way."

"That doesn't comfort me as much as you might think." He craned his neck to get a better look at the ship. "Think that slicer tool of yours can get the access ramp open? Even if the hunter takes care of these assholes, more will be on the way soon. We don't want to be here when Skaile shows up."

Ridley nodded, her breathing coming too fast and shallow to speak. She brought up her wrist terminal again, fingers shaking. Drexious was right. Halressan would always come out on top against guns and bullets, but there were things Skaile was capable of that no armour could withstand. What good was a reinforced shell when someone could reach past the metal to the flesh and bone inside, ripping apart each molecule piece by piece?

She skimmed through the security codes, trying to still her trembling hands. After a few moments, she came across one for the access ramp and sent it to Drexious's terminal. "That should do it."

"Got it." He raised himself up on his haunches. "I'm making a run for the control panel. Stay low until I get the ramp down, then haul tail to the ship. Let's not hang about any longer than we need to."

He scuttled away, leaving her with nothing but the painful thudding of her heart against her ribs and the scream of bullets in her ears. She pressed her back against the hard metal crate, sucking in a breath every time she heard the clink of a bullet nicking off the edge. This *definitely* wasn't how it was meant to go. She had no place in a gunfight. She hated the way a weapon felt in her hand, how warm and clammy it made her skin. But she also hated cowering like this, not knowing when a bullet might make its way past her makeshift defence to stop her dead.

It took all the courage she could muster to poke her head above the top of the crate and strain to catch a glimpse of what was going on. Halressan had planted herself in front of the crates like a shining, unmoveable statue, both hands wrapped tightly around her rifle. She let out a grunt as a plasma bolt scorched her shoulder and knocked her off balance, but she whirled herself around again to return a volley of shots back at the security guard who'd hit her.

She's on our side now? Drexious's scepticism echoed in her head. *That doesn't comfort me as much as you might think.*

Halressan lifted her rifle and placed an expertly-aimed shot through the seam of one of the guard's exposed collars. His throat erupted in a shower of red and he fell to the hangar floor in a crumpled heap, blood already pooling around his head.

Bile rose in Ridley's throat, and she fought to choke it back down. Halressan being on their side didn't comfort her either. Her brutish violence might not have been aimed at them this time, but it was still too close. The ease with which she could squeeze a trigger and take a life was something too terrifying to ever feel at ease around, no matter where her loyalty lay.

This is a mistake, she told herself. *You can't take her with you. Not unless you want to be looking over your shoulder for whatever's left of your life.*

Something whirred behind her and she snapped her head around to see the access ramp lowering from the ship. Something tight and vice-like released itself from her chest. It was time to go.

Drexious raced halfway up the ramp, flicking his tail in impatience. "Come on, outlander. Let's get out of here while we still can."

Halressan hadn't noticed the ramp's descent. Her mirrored visor was still firmly focused on the hangar guards. Her rifle found a heavily-armed dachryn on a suspended walkway high above, clipping him in the shoulder and sending him tumbling backwards over the barrier. He hit the floor with the sickening crunch of bone on concrete and writhed there, groaning in pain until she followed up with another blast dead through his eye.

It would be so easy to leave her there. All she needed to do was slip away from her hiding spot behind the crate and follow

Drexious up the access ramp. It would click softly shut before Halressan had even realised she'd been betrayed. They could fire up the engines and never look back, leaving her behind to pay the price they owed.

Surviving. That was what she did, wasn't it?

She'd already abandoned New Pallas. She'd already abandoned the crew of the *Ranger*. What was one more person to add to all those lives she'd already turned her back on? Why should Halressan deserve anything they didn't?

All of us go, or none of us go.

Those had been the captain's words. That was the promise Alvera had made before sucker punching the galaxy with whatever she'd done to the waystations. That was the promise Ridley had taken it upon herself to keep.

It had meant something once. Maybe it still did.

"Halressan!" she yelled, her throat burning in the effort to be heard over the gunfire. "If you're coming with us, it's now or never. We have to go."

Halressan jolted her head. "Get on that ship. I'm right behind you."

Not daring to wait to see if she followed, Ridley pushed herself out from behind the crates and ran. She ignored the pinging of bullets around her, ignored the tightness in her lungs. She stumbled up the ramp, almost crashing into Drexious at the top.

He gave her an appraising look. "The hunter?"

"On her way," Ridley said, gasping for breath. "Get the engines going. We're out of time."

A brief look of disapproval flickered across his sharp eyes. Then it was gone, and he gave a quick nod. "Find something to strap yourself into."

She turned back to the access ramp. Halressan was at the bottom now, edging her way backwards one armoured step at a time. Every time she slid back on her heel, she let loose another barrage of shots from her rifle and braced herself against the bullets and plasma bolts coming her way.

"About fucking time," she snarled. "Was starting to think you'd left me for Skaile."

Ridley tried to ignore the twinge of shame in her stomach as she smacked the controls for the access ramp. Halressan retreated in alongside her, only removing her helmet when the final crack of light from the door had disappeared. Ridley didn't want to think about the look the hunter would have given her if she'd known how close to the truth she'd come.

"We better get somewhere more secure," she said, pushing the thoughts away. "Drex is about to—"

A wave of acceleration ripped through her. She stumbled backwards, crashing into Halressan in a tangle of armoured arms and legs. Ridley gasped as they hit the floor together, the impact driving the air from her lungs. Something hard and painful was lodged in her side, and she could see the blur of her own reflection in the gleaming metal of Halressan's chest-piece above her.

She groaned. "Can you please move your knee? I think you've broken my ribs."

The pressure on top of her was suddenly gone as Halressan rolled away and dabbed a finger across her bloodied nose. "After the elbow you gave me, I'd consider us even." She gave her nose a tug back into place and let out a hiss of pain. "Idiot jarkaath. I'm going to kill him."

Ridley tried to sit up, wincing at the searing pain across her ribs. Dizziness muddled through her head and the corners of her vision turned black, forcing her to lie back down again. "Shit. That hurts."

"Let me see." Before she could protest, Halressan had pulled off her armoured gloves and rolled up the bottom of Ridley's tunic. The cool touch of the ship's recycled air was a welcome breath against Ridley's skin, but it offered no relief from the sharp stab of pain the moment Halressan pressed her fingers against her side.

She let out a yelp and Halressan gave a crooked smile. "Too rough for you, babe? You want me to kiss it better instead?"

"I'd sooner get a kiss from Drex."

Halressan didn't reply, but her next touch was gentler. It still hurt, but there was something soothing about the methodical way she worked her fingers across the swelling. Her touch was like ice, her hands pale and white against the darkness of her exposed stomach. It was enough to send shivers across her skin and a strange flutter inside her chest.

After a moment, Halressan pulled back. "Not even broken, just a bit of bruising. Big fuss over nothing." She snorted. "How is it you can cross dark space, tangle with one of the galaxy's biggest crime lords, survive getting buried alive and still come out so soft?"

Ridley bristled. "I'm not soft."

"Yes you are." Halressan flashed a smile, her lips stained red from her bloody nose. "Don't take it personally, Riddles. It's endearing, in a pathetic kind of way. It makes the fact you've survived this long even more impressive."

"Oh, I'm impressive now?" Ridley couldn't help the twitch at the corner of her mouth. "I'll have to remember that one for the next time you go back to insulting me."

"Wouldn't let it go to your head if I were you. Still plenty of time to fuck things up." Halressan pulled herself to her feet and offered her hand.

Ridley hauled herself up, trying not to let the pain show on her face or the unexpected flush of warmth in her cheeks that came from holding Halressan's hand in hers. "Speaking of which..."

Halressan narrowed her eyes. "Why do I get the feeling I'm not going to like what I'm about to hear?"

"Probably because you're not." Drexious sauntered into the

room, his eyes glinting with amusement. "You're both welcome, by the way. We're out of atmo and on our way to the rip site with nobody on our tail. Not bad for an *idiot jarkaath*."

"Rip site?" Halressan glanced between them, her expression hardening. "What the hell is he talking about?"

Ridley shifted from one foot to another. "I didn't exactly have time to give you the details back there." She took a breath. "Long story short, I screwed Skaile. Gave her the wrong coordinates."

Halressan paled. "You did *what*?"

"That's what I said." Drexious snickered. "You're not even at the good part yet. Turns out the real coordinates lead to an uncharted planet located on the fringes of dark space. The only way to get there—"

"Is by ripping a fucking tunnel," Halressan finished, closing her eyes. "Which would be a terrible fucking idea even if one of us was a certified tunnel puncher pilot. Without the correct nav points, you're more likely to land us in the middle of a fucking supernova than at your precious fucking coordinates."

"That's what I said, without all the fucking." Drexious cocked his head. "Do all humans swear so much when they're pissed off, or is it just one of the many traits that makes you so charming, hunter?"

"I scraped all the available data on the hypernet for existing tunnel routes and mapping methods," Ridley said, glaring at him. "The patterns aren't that difficult to see once you've got the right information. I calculated what looks like a suitable rip site in an empty system with a clear path to the coordinates."

"An empty system?" Halressan opened her eyes again, fixing her with a cold stare. "Not many of those around here."

Something hard lodged itself in Ridley's throat and she shook her head slowly, hardly daring to speak. "No, there's not."

She wanted to look away, to spare herself the guilt as the pieces fell into place, as Halressan realised what was happening. It shouldn't have felt like this. All the stolen glances and tightenings of breath and heat flooding her skin, they shouldn't have been there. *Too dangerous*, she told herself. *Too distracting.* Halressan's problems were her own. She shouldn't need to feel responsible for them.

It wasn't like they had much of a choice. Any system inside the Rim Belt would have been too dense to risk a tunnel without meticulously-calculated nav points. But closer to the edge of the galaxy, the spaces between star systems became wider and emptier. Safety came with the sparseness of the territory.

The territory...

Halressan clenched her jaw. The sharp angles of her face were every bit as hard and unyielding as the armour she wore. The same armour that belonged to the most feared and brutal warriors in the galaxy. The armour she had walked away with, knowing she had no right to keep it. The armour they'd kill her for.

"The rip site," she said, each word a growl in the back of her throat. "Where is it?"

Ridley swallowed, remembering the hunger she'd seen in Halressan's eyes when she'd convinced her to join them instead of shooting them dead in the hangar. It was a hunger she knew she'd be able to trap her with.

There was none of that hunger now. Only the fear of someone hit with the realisation that they were riding towards a death sentence, with no way to stop it.

The truth burned on her tongue, tasting like betrayal.

"We're headed for Idran-Var space."

NINE

The Dreamer

*T*he waystations are the key.

Alvera recognises the voice behind the words, but it's like she's listening through somebody else's ears. It's an echo of a woman she might have known once, a woman she can almost remember.

The waystations are the key. She's known that since the moment she arrived in this galaxy. It's the reason she betrayed them. The moment the ambassadors locked New Pallas away from her was the moment they unwittingly set her on a course to unlock something far more dangerous.

"I need to go back there." The words almost sound solid to her non-existent ears, giving her purpose. "Back to Ulla Waystation, where this all began."

Chase's dark eyes are solemn and unblinking. "Ulla Waystation isn't where it all began."

"The other waystations were dormant before we arrived. The moment we showed up, they let off a huge energy discharge. We woke something."

"*Somebody* woke something, but it wasn't us. That energy discharge was nothing but an automated trigger designed to go off the moment the final waystation was activated. Designed to lure somebody in to investigate and trick them into sending the signal." She shakes her head. "All those billions of minds and memories in this hive of theirs, and the curators still needed one of us to spring their trap."

The memory unfolds in front of eyes she no longer possesses. A huge, bone-plated dachryn steps forward, his black and white marked face marred with old scars. His eyes are a different shade of green than any human's, and they burn with a keen pride as his Supreme Commander volunteers him for the mission that will spark the beginning of the end.

She freezes. She's been here before, in this very moment. She knows what happens next.

"Rivus Itair," she whispers, remembering. "What did you do?"

He doesn't reply. This version of him is cut off from the hive. There's a barrier between them impossible to breach. But she can sense his existence elsewhere, somewhere less elusive. It's faint and muffled, but not wholly out of reach.

Somehow, he's in here too.

"It's him, isn't it?" Alvera says. "That's where this started."

Chase's eyes are fixed on a place Alvera can't see. "No. It started long before him. He's just the thread—the one who'll take us there."

"What do I need to do?

"Follow him."

Without knowing how she's doing it, she's hurtling through space, free from the limitations of a body she no longer needs. It's not time or distance that passes, but depths upon depths of memories. They take her to jewel-toned planets in the rich inner heart of the galaxy. They take her to arid wastelands where the edge of civilised space bleeds into darkness.

Eons pass in the blink of an eye. Voices call to her, records of lives too innumerable to comprehend. She inhabits the long-forgotten footsteps of every sentient being that ever lived. They reach out, surrounding her with so many fragments of sights and sounds and smells and—

"You're drowning." Chase's voice is sharp, cutting through everything else. An intrusion into the trance that's taken hold of her. "Pull yourself out."

She doesn't want to pull herself out, not when there's so much to take in, so much to learn. The voices call out to her, begging her to listen. "You don't understand. This is—"

"This is exactly what they want." Chase's words are like a bubble of air swelling inside her skull, pushing everything else out. "You can only navigate their consciousness because you're not fully part of it yet. They're trying to absorb you into the hive. If that happens, everything we've done will have been for nothing."

The voices scream and whisper in her head. They tug at her, trying to pull her away from the faint, elusive presence of Rivus Itair.

She shuts them out and focuses on him. Only him. She follows him across the galaxy, skirting past stars and supernovas and the vast black expanse in between. She holds the image of him in her mind, sharp-eyed and bone-faced. His presence grows more defined, like a picture coming into focus. Like a stranger turning into a friend.

Then everything stops, and she comes up for air.

Farsal Waystation lingers in front of her. Its huge central ring curves back as far as she can see, disappearing into the darkness engulfing it. It's a superstructure beyond the capabilities of anything in the galaxy. One of four waystations left behind by those once forgotten.

A lifetime ago, she wondered what kind of beings could have built them. Now she knows.

She steps forward and feels solid ground beneath her feet, but the legs holding her up are not her own. They're coiled and powerful, encased in shining white power armour. The gait propelling her is unfamiliar. Alien.

Rivus. She's found him.

The readout on his wrist terminal chirps, and his armoured boots clink against the hard floor as he makes his way further into the waystation. The harsh sound of each step is an intrusion into the silence surrounding them, disturbing the remains of something long lost and left behind.

She moves with him, inhabiting his memories from a place he doesn't know exists. The sensation leaves her lightheaded and weightless, unable to extricate the places where she ends and he begins.

"You'd think you'd be used to that by now," Chase says. "All those years sharing your head with an AI? This isn't so different."

"It's like he's behind a veil. I can see him, but I can't reach him." Alvera shivers. "Did the curators get to him? Is he part of the hive?"

"I don't think so. This doesn't feel like a memory. It feels like the echo of one, like we're seeing it through some kind of filter."

That's when she hears the whispers in Rivus's head—a slow rustle at the base of his skull that ripples its way through his mind. It's insidious at first, so subtle it's like she's imagining it. But she's been here before. She remembers where the whispers led her. She knows where they'll lead him.

"It's them. The curators."

"It's this place. The waystation." Chase looks around. "That energy discharge, the one he's investigating? It's still here, still lingering. It's trying to bury itself into his mind. It wants to connect him to the hive."

"But how—oh..."

The answer is in her head. It always has been. It's in the wires and chips and microfilaments embedded into all the parts of her that were once human. It's in the attempts to become better. The attempts to become more. And in the end, all it has become is their downfall.

"Cybernetics," she says. "The waystation is connecting to the hive through his cybernetics."

"Corrupting them," Chase replies. "Like rogue code. Like a virus. That must have been what happened to us back on Ulla Waystation. The jamming rig was the only thing keeping them at bay. When you blew it up... I thought I could hold them off. I thought I could save us."

"You did. You said it yourself—the curators wanted to make me part of the hive. That didn't happen."

"Maybe." Chase jerks her head. "But that doesn't explain him, does it?"

Rivus's heavy, lumbering gait is more familiar now. She feels the tightness in his chest as he passes under the archways of the low-vaulted ceiling. She feels the growing trepidation as he forces himself forward, following the blinking light on his wrist terminal.

Something isn't right.

The thought comes from both of them at once. For the briefest of moments, the barrier between his memories and her own disappears, leaving them with a fleeting connection that rattles the fibre of her being.

Something isn't right.

"There's something else here," Chase says.

"The curators?"

"No. Something that's not supposed to be here, like we're not."

The shadows of the narrow corridor shirk away from something bright coming from up ahead. Rivus doesn't know what it is yet, but she does. She remembers the huge chamber with its central pillar stretching towards the ceiling. She remembers the bottomless depths of the pit surrounding it.

Yes, I remember this.

This time, the thought isn't hers. It belongs to something else, something impossibly ancient. She freezes, and it isn't until Rivus's body stops dead around her that she realises he's heard it too.

The pillar flickers into life with blinking lights and a hum of energy. In front of her—in front of Rivus—a barrierless walkway extends out, bridging the chasm.

I knew that would happen.

"You're right, Chase," Alvera whispers. "These thoughts aren't mine. They aren't Rivus's either. Someone else is here."

"Not is. *Was.*" Chase shakes her head. "Like I said, it's not a memory. It's the echo of one. That's what Rivus is following. That's what's guiding him."

"He thinks he's been here before."

"He's not entirely wrong. He's following in the footsteps of those who came before him. He's delivering us to the same fate they shared. Millions. Billions." A note of panic sharpens her voice. "We shouldn't have come here. The curators will be looking for you. The longer we linger, the easier it will be for them to find us."

"We need to know more. If we're to find a way to hurt them, we need to know as much as we possibly can."

In front of them, a panel slides to one side, revealing a holographic interface in the pillar's hollow centre. It lights up with a flash, crackling with static.

The comms relay.

"This is what I did on Ulla Waystation, isn't it?" Alvera says. "I used the comms relay to send a message back to New Pallas. This one must link back to the dachryn colony."

"Maybe once." Chase's voice is grim. "But there's no longer a dachryn colony for the relay to link back to. Wherever that beam is going, it's something else that's going to intercept it."

Alvera's hands move across the interface, opening channels and systems. But her hands aren't her own. They're claws, strange and alien and yet inexorably part of her.

"The curators still needed one of us to spring their trap," she echoes. "That's what you said. That's what this is. A trap that's been laid for millennia."

"Not just a trap. A trigger."

"A trigger for what?"

"The end of their experiment."

The memory flickers again, like a holofeed with a shaky connection. When it steadies, she's looking at something impossible.

Another dachryn stares back at her, his eyes a midnight blue so dark they're almost black. He doesn't seem real. He's looking through her like she's a ghost.

Or maybe...maybe *he* is the ghost.

"Chase?" She's afraid to speak, as if making even the slightest sound might send everything into chaos. "What's happening?"

"Something the curators never intended." Chase sounds breathless. "Looks like we're not the only bug in their system."

The voices in the back of her head grow louder, the whispers rising with feverish anticipation. She knows what's coming. Rivus is still standing next to the pillar. His claws are still connected to the interface.

The other dachryn steps forward and puts a ghostly arm on his shoulder.

Your job is done.

Rivus releases his hold and takes a step back. The voices swell in outrage. And the pillar explodes.

The energy wave sends him sprawling backwards. Alvera can feel the shock and pain rushing through his body, but she's numb to it. All she can hear are the shadows in her head as they rage and writhe and crawl towards her.

"We've stayed too long." Chase's voice is thin. "We need to get out of here."

"But Rivus..."

"We've seen enough. There's no changing what happens next. It's a memory. We can't help him."

The pillar crackles, spewing electrical discharge. The other dachryn walks through it untouched, his shimmering figure blurring in and out of focus.

Get out, he tells them. *Out, out, out.*

She follows Rivus back through the corridors as they crumble around him. Energy surges through exposed panels, sending sparks flying through the air. Beams fall from the ceiling and floor panels crack beneath their feet.

But it's not just the waystation—it's the memory itself. She can feel it disintegrating. The voices are screaming now, growing ever closer.

They're coming for her. They're coming for all of them.

Give up, they order. *Die.*

No. The ghostly dachryn is ahead of them, bloodied and limping but leading the way. *If you can't walk, then crawl. Do whatever you have to. Whatever it takes.*

He stops and turns to face the oncoming shadows, steel-eyed and accepting. For a moment, she's tempted to spin around and stand with him against whatever is coming. The voices hiss their agreement, encouraging her.

"Alvera, no!" Chase's horror is paralysing. "They're coming."

Coming, the voices whisper.

The shadows are almost upon them—shapeless, terrifying things. They reach towards her with their tendrils, ready to take her back to the place she escaped from. They scream with the fury of trillions of voices lost. They scream at her to join them.

Alvera takes one last look at the ghostly dachryn and relinquishes her hold, and the memory disappears into nothingness.

———

Quiet.

Empty.

Safe.

The waystation is gone, and so are the stars and everything around them. She's surrounded by nothing but white light. Something has chased away the rest of the galaxy, and now there is only her.

"What happened?" she asks to nobody in particular, expecting the words to be swallowed up by the strange void.

Chase appears in her mind again, dark-eyed and scowling. "They almost got us, that's what happened. I told you we couldn't linger too long in that memory. I told you they'd find us. Just like they found that other one."

The image of the ghostly dachryn flutters in front of her like a memory fading. She can barely remember the markings on his plates, the deep blue of his round, sharp eyes. It's like he never existed at all.

"Who was he?" she asks. "Why was he there?"

"He was a memory that existed outside the hive's consciousness, like us. He woke up, like we did." Chase shakes her head. "Who knows how many thousands of years—millions of years —he existed in this place?"

"He saved Rivus. He spoke to him through the hive, helped him get out before it was too late. Maybe he can help us."

"He can't help us. You saw what happened. The curators

came for him. He saved Rivus at the expense of his own consciousness. He's part of the hive now."

"He's gone?" Her words sound hollow. "But...we could have done something. We could have got him out of there with us."

"He was lost long before we entered the memory. This happened months ago, remember? We were watching a recording, nothing more." Chase gives her a pointed look. "If I were you, I'd be more concerned about the curators. They noticed you in that memory. They realised something was there that shouldn't have been. If they catch you, you'll share the same fate as our mysterious dachryn friend. Catalogued. Archived. Gone."

"Then what was this all for? What was the point in watching all that unfold if there was never a hope of stopping it?"

"To find *him*."

Across the white void, something flickers. She watches it wisp into a form, into a presence in her mind. Familiar features blur into being, created from nothing but flashes of memory.

A moment later, she finds herself face to face with Rivus Itair.

"He's here," Chase says, her voice barely more than a breath. "You're *both* here. You're trapped inside the hive, unable to get back to your body, and he's somehow tapping into it from out there."

"How is that possible?"

"That ancient dachryn, whoever he was, must have shielded Rivus from the curators and bridged a connection to the hive at the same time. Just like I did for you on Ulla Waystation." Chase's voice tightens. "This could be our chance. We can't change anything from inside the hive, but we *can* help him."

Alvera looks at him, fresh hope swelling in her chest. For the first time since waking in this place, she doesn't feel alone.

There's someone else out there who knows the touch of the curators upon their mind, someone else who can withstand it.

"Rivus," she says, her voice a whisper. "Wake up."

He stares at her in the same way the old, ghostly dachryn had. Looking right through her like she doesn't even exist.

Then a spark of recognition finally brightens the dullness of his eyes and he leaps forward, arms outstretched, to wrap his claws around her throat.

TEN

Rivus

R ivus awoke with a jolt, startled out of a dream he
couldn't remember.

He lay on the rough, scratchy fabric of the sleep-couch,
listening to the sound of his own heart echoing inside his head.
His breaths were sharp and shallow, like he'd been fighting a
battle he wasn't sure he'd won. There was a tremor in his good
arm that ran right down to an itch in his claws. His other arm
gleamed in the darkness and hummed almost silently with the
cybernetics encased within.

What had unsettled him so much? A nightmare he couldn't
remember was a welcome reprieve from those he could. More
often now, he dreamed of worlds burning, of decimated fleets
floating lifelessly in orbit. He dreamed of war councils and
summits that offered only desperation instead of the hope they
so greatly needed.

He stretched out, his legs wearier than they should have
been after weeks of space travel. It was like his body had been
put through something his mind had not been privy to. Or

maybe the stiffness was just the wear of nearly four long decades catching up with him.

Whatever it was, he couldn't let it slow him down. Not with the summit upon them. No matter how much he believed they needed this truce with the Idran-Var, part of him couldn't help but wonder if it was even possible. There was too much bloody history between them, too much familiarity. Niole was proof enough of that.

Niole. Her name wrenched at something he'd tried to bury. The wound was an old one, but no less raw for it. Her departure should have brought him some kind of relief. It should have released the tightness in his chest, softened the bitterness and regret that welled in him every time he thought about her. Instead, he carried her absence like an added weight on his shoulders. A burden she'd never asked him to carry, but one he'd taken on anyway.

I can't be your redemption, Rivus. You're offering me a second chance that isn't yours to give.

He clenched his fists. One of them twitched with taut muscle under the thick, bony plating of his exoskeleton. The other curled smoothly without a fraction of delay, its metallic sheen glinting under the sleep-dimmed lighting above. It was stronger than anything he could have honed himself, but it was also a constant reminder of what he'd lost back on Farsal Waystation. Of what he'd done there.

He swung his legs over the edge of the couch. Sleep wasn't going to come back to him now. It was time to move.

The base was quiet as he made his way through the corridors towards the makeshift command centre. There was no bustle in the hallways, no nervous chatter among soldiers. It was like everyone else was still asleep, and he was the only one awake.

He passed through the last set of sliding doors to find the command centre empty. No division leaders discussing tactics, no run-throughs of negotiations, no tacticians formulating potential routes for retreat. The holoscreens flicked through the rotation of feeds, each as devoid of activity as the next. It was as if the whole place had been abandoned, only nobody had thought to tell him.

A hiss disrupted the stifling quiet as the door slid open again and Tarvan walked into the room. The grey markings on his face plates were as dull as Rivus had ever seen them, and the usual sharp glint in his eyes had been replaced by something tired and leaden.

When he caught sight of Rivus, his jaw twitched. "I thought you were on sleep cycle."

"So did I. Turns out it's hard to get any rest when you know the fate of the galaxy is hanging in the balance."

Tarvan gave a low, tired laugh. "I'll give you that. Can't say sleep has come particularly easy to me in recent times either. It's hard to close your eyes when you're not sure what horrors you'll see there."

"What's bothering you? Feeling nervous about the summit?"

"Nervous?" Tarvan blinked. "Hardly. I just don't have the same expectations as you. The sooner it's over, the sooner we can leave this mess behind us and focus on preparing the rest of the galaxy for whatever is coming at the end of that countdown."

"You believe the talks will fail?"

Tarvan's face was impassive. "I do."

The disappointment was becoming more and more familiar to him, but that didn't make it any easier to shrug off. There was a time he'd have found himself humbled by Tarvan's stone-faced resolution. Envious of the way he refused to budge or give ground. But this unrepentant stubbornness, the way he was utterly convinced that peace was not an option...

Rivus paused, the rest of his thoughts disappearing under a

wave of uncertainty. He glanced again at the holofeeds on the wall. The mess hall was empty. The rec yard was empty. Officers' lounge empty. It was like the rest of the legionnaires had vanished into Aurel's paper-thin atmosphere, leaving nobody but the two of them.

Something sharp caught in his throat. "Where is everyone?"

Tarvan didn't flinch. There was no shifting in his plates or tremor in his voice when he replied. "On their way to the summit."

"Now?" He shook his head, as if that could dislodge the doubt and dread creeping in. "Why was I scheduled for my sleep cycle? More to the point, why aren't you with them?"

The words sounded weak as they left his mouth, like he was a child demanding answers to something he couldn't possibly understand. But Rivus was no child. He did understand. He just didn't want to believe it.

Of all the things Tarvan might have been, a coward was not one of them. The Idran-Var did not frighten him. Caution would not have kept him from that summit, from facing down his enemy and meeting them eye to eye. Fear could not have kept him either, if Tarvan even felt such a thing.

No, the only reason Tarvan Varantis would miss that summit was if there was a greater tactical advantage without him there.

"You sent them ahead without you," Rivus said, his voice catching in his throat. "The entire division."

"Minus three of my special operations units. But yes, I sent the rest ahead. Two hundred of our finest legionnaires."

"Do they know what they're walking into? Do they realise what you've done?"

Tarvan walked with slow, steady steps towards the window, turning his back to him. All Rivus could see was the hulk of his shoulders and the silhouette of his crest against the bleak Aurelian landscape outside. It wasn't the first wasteland Tarvan had presided over. He doubted it would be the last.

"There's still time," he pressed. "Whatever you're doing, whatever you've done, we can still undo it. This isn't how we have to fight."

"No. This is how we have to win." Tarvan turned back, his blue eyes burning. "This is our chance to decimate their entire command in a single attack. A chance we had on Vesyllion but failed to see through to the end. We must make up for our failure there with a victory here. Whatever the cost."

"Whatever the cost?"

Tarvan closed his eyes. "I wondered once what kind of person I'd be remembered for. I see now that this is the answer."

"You also worried about the burdens you chose to bear and how easy it was getting to accept them. This doesn't have to be one of them. Let me take some of the load. Let's face what's coming together, like we always said we would."

Tarvan gave him a long, steel-eyed look. "No," he said, his words gentle and final.

If there had been even the faintest trace of his old friend behind the hardness of his plating, Rivus might have broken. But the dachryn staring back at him now was less than a stranger. He'd become an enemy Rivus never even knew he had.

It didn't make the betrayal ache any less, but it solidified what he knew he had to do.

He tried to ignore the tremor in his arm as he brought up his wrist terminal. Tried to ignore the seizing in his chest as it grew tighter and tighter with each breath he took. Tried to ignore the way his voice wrapped around the words, like he couldn't bring himself to say it out loud.

"Niole." Her name was a plea for help and an admission of

guilt all at once. "It's Rivus. You need to pull your people out of there. Something's happened. Don't go to the summit."

He waited for her reply, but there was only static on the other end of the connection. Maybe he was too late. Maybe whatever Tarvan had planned had already happened. Maybe there was a pile of burning bodies scattered across the rendezvous coordinates, legionnaire and Idran-Var alike.

"Niole," he tried again. "Can you hear me?"

"I set a jamming perimeter around the base." Tarvan sighed. "I knew you'd warn them if you could, so I took away the possibility."

He didn't sound disappointed. It was worse than that. He sounded like he understood.

"Why?" Shame burned in the pit of his stomach at the weakness in his voice. "This could have been a chance for peace."

"Not peace. Compromise." Tarvan shook his head, the gesture slow and heavy. "As long as we compromise with the Idran-Var, there can be no peace."

"You don't know that."

"Their nature is in the name they gave themselves, Rivus. Idran-Var. *Those who resist.* Their existence depends on destroying ours. That's the game they chose to play. That's the game they played at Alcruix." He tightened his jaw plates. "This time, it's the game they'll lose."

There was no anger in his eyes, no hatred for the enemy he'd been unable to let go of. Just a weary resignation, like this horror had been an inevitability only he could stand to face.

Maybe he'd forgotten Rivus knew exactly what that felt like. "The Idran-Var are not a *game*," he said, a growl in the back of his throat. "They're a distraction. We're facing something far more dangerous. I thought you understood that. I thought when you burned Vesyllion, you were doing it because you knew we were running out of time. Because you knew we couldn't fight a war on two fronts. I might not have agreed with you, but I was prepared to let myself believe it was another one of those impossible calls that only you could make." He shook his head. "I can't believe how wrong I was."

"I burned Vesyllion because the Idran-Var are the enemy we've spent our lives defending the galaxy from. I never lost sight of that, even if you have."

Rivus took a step back. "You're wrong. More than that, you're lost. And you can't even see it."

"I am who I've always been."

"Maybe you are. Tarvan the Tyrant, indeed." Rivus gave a dry chuckle. It tasted wrong on his tongue. Bitterness where there should have been humour. "Maybe it's me who's been blind all this time. Blind to what you are, what you're willing to do."

"No more than I ever have. And no less."

The words lingered in the air as the silence stretched between them, taut and fragile. The slightest breath might set something off that Rivus could never take back. He clenched his jaw, bracing himself against what was about to come.

"What's going to happen?" he asked, hardly daring to face the answer.

Tarvan turned back to the window. "A missile strike on the rendezvous coordinates. It will be quick and indiscriminate. More likely to be blamed on the Idran-Var than ourselves."

"Indiscriminate? You're talking about firing on our own legionnaires."

"You think I don't know that?" Tarvan's voice was hollow. "Presume whatever else you will of me, but don't presume I'm not aware of the sacrifices I'm making."

Rivus laughed. "It's hardly your sacrifice, *Supreme Commander*. Those legionnaires will die not even knowing it was you who betrayed them."

"I know," Tarvan said softly. "Believe me, Rivus, I know."

Rivus couldn't find the words within him to reply. The worst part, the part that cut the deepest, wasn't that he'd lost his Supreme Commander, but that he'd lost Tarvan himself. His oldest friend. Someone he'd killed for. Someone he'd have died for. Someone he loved.

Maybe that would make it easier to do what would come next.

He moved without thinking, without allowing himself the chance to second-guess himself. Maybe that was why the blow took Tarvan by surprise. It caught him under his hard-plated chin, sending him staggering against the holofeeds on the back wall.

Tarvan stood there for a moment, dazed and blinking. Then, after an agonising wait, a slow, sad smile cracked open across his face. "So, this is how it's to end?"

Rivus didn't wait for an answer. He couldn't. If he hesitated, if he listened to another pain-laden word from Tarvan's mouth, he would break. Instead, he launched himself towards his old commander and tried not to baulk at the sickening crunch of bone on bone as their crests met. The impact sent a shock shuddering through him, but he shrugged it off with a grunt and a shake of the head.

He couldn't stop. Not for a moment. Not against Tarvan.

The weight underneath him disappeared, and he staggered forward through empty air as Tarvan wheeled away and landed a swift strike to the back of his neck. The movement was so fast, so fluid, that Rivus hadn't even had time to see it coming, much less react to it.

An involuntary growl rumbled in the back of his throat as he burled himself around. He wasn't as fast as Tarvan. He never had been. But what he lacked in speed and guile he made up for with bloody brute force.

He lunged forward with a wild swing of his cybernetic arm. The reinforced steel caught Tarvan square in the jaw. The impact might as well have been non-existent for all he felt of it, but there was no mistaking the bone-shattering crack that resounded through his ears when the blow landed.

It must have hurt. It must have rocked Tarvan. But it didn't stop him. He came back even quicker than before, each strike timed to perfection and aimed at all the damn *yysk*-soft places his plating met.

This was nothing like sparring together, varstaff against varstaff. There was no crackling of electricity as their weapons clashed. No rehearsed moves and clever footwork. That kind of grace didn't exist in this dance. This was something brutal, something visceral. Each strike was a personal grievance, filled with the weight of the pain and fury of the dachryn behind it.

Tarvan stepped out of the way of another heavy blow, his chest heaving with shallow breaths. His plating was cracked and bloodied where Rivus had broken it, but he showed no signs of pain, no signs of slowing. Just the same cold composure in the face of battle that had earned him the title of Supreme Commander.

He circled Rivus, his steps slow and cautious. "What do you think happens when you win?"

Rivus took a step back, eyeing him warily. "What are you talking about?"

"You're not a fool. What do you think happens when you win?" Tarvan levelled a hard gaze at him. "If you warn the Idran-Var, what comes next? Do you think they'll walk away from this? You'll be putting the entire allied systems at risk for the sake of a few hundred lives."

"You did that yourself." He could hardly believe what he was hearing. "You're sending our fellow legionnaires to their deaths to drag out a war nobody even wanted in the first place. When the Coalition finds out—"

"I'll be disgraced for the temerity of doing the things they wish they could have ordered me to do in the first place," he said, tightening his jaw plates. "The ambassadors will disavow me as a rogue operator, strip me of my rank. And when they go home to their beds and pull their families close, they'll silently thank me for having the stomach to do what they couldn't."

Rivus shook his head. "And what happens if *you* win? What will you do to stop me from telling the rest of the galaxy what happened here?"

"There was a time I promised you I'd put a bullet in your skull if I thought you were a danger to the legionnaires. I see now how hollow that promise was." Tarvan laughed softly. "Do you really think I would kill you, old friend? Did you ever believe I could? I can't begrudge what you've done here. I can't hate you for doing what you thought was right." He gave a long, drawn-out sigh. "Besides, I don't have to win. I only have to stop you."

Too late, Rivus realised his mistake.

He should have known better. The talking had been a distraction. Tarvan would do anything to gain the tactical advantage. This time, the tactical advantage had come in the form of a small pistol pointed squarely at his head.

He barked out a laugh from the back of his throat. "So much for not being willing to put a bullet in my skull."

"I wasn't lying," Tarvan said calmly. "This isn't a bullet."

He fired.

Rivus barely had time to register the sting of something sharp pricking the soft skin between his plating before the agony began. A wave of pain ripped through his body like he'd been set ablaze from the inside. It was worse than the memory of Niole's flare boiling the blood beneath his plating. Worse than the memory of losing his arm on the waystation. Just raw, unrelenting pain.

Through the haze, he understood. A neural dart. Standard part of the arsenal for riot suppression. It left no physical injuries, just tricked the nerves into thinking they were under attack. He'd seen it cripple even the hardiest of prisoners during his training back on Ossa.

Taken out like he was petty jail scum. The indignity of it might have been amusing if the pain hadn't overwhelmed his ability to breathe. Soon, it would become too much. His vision was already turning black at the edges. It wouldn't be long before his body shut down and rendered him unconscious.

He crashed to his knees and fell forward, sprawling across the hard floor. From somewhere far in the distance, he could hear the sharp click of Tarvan's boots.

"I won't patronise you by saying you'll understand when this is all over. I won't ask you to forgive me for it either. The cost of your friendship was a price I knew I'd have to pay to protect this galaxy." His disembodied voice drifted in and out of Rivus's ears, sounding further away with each word. "My only hope is despite whatever else happens, despite everything that has been lost between us, that both of us make it out the other side at the end." He paused. "I think I could stand to lose everything else, if I only had that."

The sound of his fading footsteps echoed and disappeared, leaving Rivus with only a cold, lonely silence as he finally submitted to the pain and closed his eyes to the call of sleep.

ELEVEN

NIOLE

"You're pushing too hard."

Niole whipped her head around at the intrusion and was immediately caught under the jaw by a fierce swing from Venya's training glaive. She stumbled backwards and landed on the floor with a bump, palms stinging as she tried to brace her fall.

"Damn it!"

It wasn't just the loss of concentration. Her own body was betraying her. Muscles she'd once taken for granted had grown weak. Her movement was slower. And despite the anti-rad meds slowly draining from her system, she still couldn't call on a flare.

"Like I said, you're pushing too hard." Serric was watching from the other side of the room, his arms folded and a frown across his face. Aurel's low radiation had darkened his turquoise skin, turning it a deep, brilliant blue. She could feel the displeasure emanating from him.

Venya towered over her, pointing the rounded, silicone-coated end of the glaive at her throat. "My point." She twirled the training weapon around and tucked it under her arm, offering a hand to Niole.

Niole accepted it and gave a grunt as she pulled herself back to her feet. "That was a cheap shot."

Venya shrugged her massive shoulders. "Maybe. Still my point though."

"Sounds like you've been getting tips from *him* while I've been gone." She jerked her head towards Serric, frustration rippling through her. Trying to regain her strength was difficult enough without him present. Her daily sparring sessions with Venya were brutal and exhausting, leaving her bruised and sore with no promise that they were doing anything to help recover the edge she had lost. The last thing she needed was the added pressure of Serric watching, an expression of stony disapproval etched on his hard features.

Venya grinned. "There are worse people you could learn from, you know. Once you get past the mean looks and personal insults and utter lack of encouragement, he's a pretty good teacher."

"I'll take your word for it."

"Don't think you'll need to. I'm pretty sure you're about to get a lesson right now." She dipped her head in acknowledgement as Serric approached and made her way swiftly to the doors, a glint of amusement dancing in her orange eyes as she retreated.

Serric watched her leave, his black eyes expressionless. "You're lucky she didn't break your jaw."

"She'd never have landed that strike in the first place if you hadn't distracted me," Niole said stiffly.

"And you wouldn't have been distracted if you hadn't been pushing so hard." He tightened his jaw. "You're tired. It's making you careless. Sloppy. You go into a real fight like that and all you're going to do is get yourself killed."

"Thanks for the concern, but I'm fine." The muscles in her arms and legs burned in protest, as if they recognised the lie. "I don't need you checking up on me."

"I don't care what you need," he said bluntly. "I'm checking up on you because right now, you're a liability we can't afford. If you want to join us at the summit, you better be capable of handling yourself."

"I told you, I'm—"

"Have you managed to flare yet?" When she didn't reply, his face hardened. "I didn't think so. No wonder you can barely stand after a couple of rounds with Venya. You're wasting away."

"I'm trying."

"Are you?" He drew his mouth into a thin line. "You spent so long trying to suppress it. Wishing it didn't call to you the way it did. You were afraid. Maybe you still are. Maybe there's a part of you that doesn't want it back, even if it kills you."

There had been a time when that kind of needling would have lit a fire under her skin and sent a tingling of energy through her veins. Maybe that was what he was trying to provoke in her. But the rage that swelled in her chest was half-hearted, like its potency had been diluted by what she'd lost. By the fear that he was right.

She looked down at her arms. The grey skin around her left wrist had been left darkened in an ugly bruise from one of Venya's vice-like holds. Days later, it was still tender to the touch. Her wounds healed slowly. Food tasted stale and dry. Sleep didn't provide her the rest it once did.

Was this really what she had wanted for all those years?

Serric was still looking at her, his mouth twisted in a bitter smile. "You're still running from it, even now. You're not a legionnaire. You're not Idran-Var. Hell, you're barely even a siolean anymore. You're scared that if you get it back, you might finally have to decide who you are, who you want to be. And you still don't know the answer. You never have."

She took a step back, trying not to show how much the words stung. "Screw you," she said, her voice low. "I'm not the only one running here. You know what Rhendar told me the first time I met you? He said with you, everything is a fight. You don't know how to do anything else." She straightened her spine, ignoring the twinge of pain that seared across her shoulders. "The old man has a soft spot for lost causes. Isn't that what you said once? I think you're as lost as I am. I think you fight so much because you're scared that if you stop, you'll finally have to come to terms with the fact that's all you can do. The fact that's all you are."

A dark flush rose against the blue of his skin. "Careful, Niole. Your temper might be toothless, but mine certainly isn't."

"I'm not some wide-eyed recruit you can scare into submission. And I don't need your misguided attempts at fixing me. So take your bullshit somewhere else and leave me the hell alone."

She tried to turn away but Serric grabbed her arm, his fingers hot against her skin. She flinched out of instinct, waiting for a surge inside her that never came. How many times had she recoiled from his touch and what it used to ignite in her? Now, as difficult as it was to admit, she couldn't help but think she'd give anything to feel it again.

"Let me go," she said, a snarl in her voice.

"Not until you try to flare. Not until I see it."

"If you think I'm going to—"

"*Please.*" Something changed in his voice. It was like the edges of it had softened, his anger giving way to something far more terrifying.

She pulled her arm free and turned back to him, unable to find her voice through the shock. His face was as hard as ever, but in his eyes she saw the reflection of the tremor she'd heard in his voice.

Fyra. He was *afraid*.

"This isn't about me at all, is it?" she asked softly. "It's about what they did to me. You can't help but wonder what would happen if they did it to you. How you'd survive if there was no way back from it." She paused, the words catching in her throat. "If you'd even *want* to survive."

He looked away. "They'd never get the chance. I'd force them to kill me first."

Now she understood. Under all the rage, all the resentment, there was a part of him that couldn't escape the frightened little boy whose parents had tried to condemn to the Bastion. An underwater hell where he'd have grown up with needles in the crooks of his arms and poison pumping through his veins, draining him of everything he was.

No wonder he'd hated her so much. She'd spent her life running to escape what she was, while he'd been running to preserve it.

It took her a moment to notice the rippling in the air around his skin. If things had been different, it would have stirred something inside her, and she'd have tried to push it away.

Now, all she wanted to do was let it in.

She steadied herself with a breath and reached out, willing every fibre in her withering body to do as she asked, to open up and accept what he was offering. The shimmering aura of the energy radiating off him was the most beautiful thing she'd seen. It was all she could do to restrain herself from grabbing his arms in the hope it would rush towards her. It was so real, so close...and yet so utterly out of reach.

She stepped back, her chest tightening. She felt nothing. Not even the slightest call. Not even the faintest brush of energy across her skin. Whatever connection she once had was severed. Lost. It was never coming back.

Serric lowered his arms, the remnants of his flare fading.

She hardly dared to look at him. Shame clawed against her insides, churning her stomach. If she looked at him, it would never stop. He would always be a reminder of what she'd lost. What she'd failed to become.

"I'm sorry," she said, her voice hoarse. "The meds must have done too much damage. I can't—"

"It's not the meds."

The disappointment in his eyes was nothing new. But there was pity there as well, and that was more wounding than any scowl of disapproval, any cutting words he could have thrown at her.

She clenched her fists. "What do you mean, it's not the meds?"

"It's you. It's always been you. Even now, you're afraid of what you are." For once, there was no malice in his voice. Only resignation.

That somehow made it worse. "You don't know that. You'd rather believe I'm too weak than face the possibility that what they did took everything from me. Because that would mean they could take everything from you too."

"That's not what I—"

"No. I've had enough." She pulled away from him. "I am tired of fighting you, Serric. Tired of trying to justify the things I've done, the decisions I've made. I knew what I was doing when we fled Vesyllion. I stayed behind to give Zal and the others a chance to get out alive. I knew what it might cost me. And if what I am now is the price I had to pay so they could survive, then so be it." She dusted off her hands. "I'm done here. I'm going to see Claine."

"Niole." He opened his mouth and then shook his head, as if he'd thought better of what he was going to say. "You should stay away from there. Claine is a traitor."

"Claine is a *friend*. Not that I expect you to understand what that means." She shot him a cold stare. "They aren't easy to come by when the only person you care about is yourself."

He blanched at that, his shoulders stiffening and his dark eyes taking on a dangerous glimmer. A moment later the look was gone, leaving nothing but his usual hard features and expression of stone.

If he was going to say something else, she didn't want to be around to hear it. She turned and stormed towards the training room doors, trying as much as she could to ignore Serric's words ringing in her ears.

Even now, you're afraid of what you are.

It would have been easy to hate him for it, if only there wasn't a part of her that wondered if it might be true.

———

"Hey, Tails." Claine winced when he spoke. His pale skin was puffed up and tender, marring his face with raw, pink swelling. One eye was squeezed half shut, the other bloodshot. Serric hadn't even bothered to flare. He hadn't needed to, not when he could do this much damage with his fists.

Niole almost reached out a hand to touch him but thought better of it. "I'm sorry."

"Me too." The words sounded thick in his throat. "But not about this. I deserve it. If I hadn't led them to Vesyllion, none of this would have happened. We'd never have been trying to flee a capital blockade. And you would never have..." He trailed off, his eyes shining. "It's my fault. I did this to you as much as they did."

A few months ago, she'd have done everything she could to convince him otherwise, to reassure him she understood. But he wasn't the same fresh-faced recruit as he was back then. The weight of what he'd done had changed him. She could see it in the furrow of his brow, the emptiness behind his eyes. Trying to absolve him of this would only be an insult to them both.

Instead, she met his despairing gaze. "How did they find out it was you?"

"I told them." He gave a short, rasping laugh. "Venya and I shipped out to Skylla's Wake and claimed our armour. But the first time I put it on, I knew it didn't feel right. I knew I wasn't Idran-Var, not after what I'd done." He shook his head. "I waited as long as I could. I thought it might pass. Then they said you'd be at the summit, and I knew I couldn't face you with my armour on. As a liar. Not after what you did to save me."

"Claine, they got to your family."

"No. I *betrayed* my family." A dark look crossed his eyes. "My father made his choice when he left the Idran-Var. I made mine when I stayed. That should have been the end of it."

A vision of Rivus filled her mind. The way he'd looked at her all those years ago in the training grounds when she'd lost control and almost killed him. The way he'd looked at her only a week ago, when he'd asked her to stay. Something painful and confusing gripped at her chest, and she fought to push it away. "It's not always as simple as that."

"It should be."

There was nothing she could say to that. All she could do was sit with him in painful silence until a sharp knock on the holding cell's door startled her to her feet.

The door opened, and a guard gestured with his head towards another Idran-Var waiting in the shadows.

Rhendar.

She nodded in acknowledgement before turning back to Claine to say goodbye, but his eyes were closed. His head hung limply forward, bobbing gently with each shallow rise and fall of his chest.

Something tightened in her throat. "I'll see you soon," she whispered, hoping it wasn't a lie.

Rhendar was waiting for her outside the holding cell, his armour glinting even in the dull light. When he spoke, his words were gentle. "That must have been painful for you."

She brushed off the observation. "What's going to happen to him?"

"For now? Nothing. After the summit, we'll take him back to Maar for execution."

She'd been half-expecting the words, but not the coldness behind them. "He didn't mean for this to happen. He might have been careless, but he didn't betray you. Not knowingly."

"Whether he meant it or not won't bring back the thousands of lost souls buried under the ash on Vesyllion because of his actions," Rhendar replied, his metal-tinged voice weary through the filter. "I'm sorry, Niole. You know it will give me no pleasure to see him die. But we lost a lot of good Idran-Var that day. Their deaths need to be answered for. The people they left behind will demand it."

"But you're the war chief now, aren't you? Couldn't you just—"

The sharp turn of his helmet towards her was enough to cut her short. She didn't need to see the expression on whatever face lay hidden underneath to know she had crossed a line. He hadn't asked to be made war chief. Hadn't asked for all the burdens, all the lives, to carry alongside the title. Hadn't asked for the blood he'd be made to shed along the way. And it was all to seal an alliance that she'd promised was necessary. It wasn't fair of her to ask anything more of him than she already had.

Instead, she turned back to the cell's holofeed and watched Claine's bruised and bloodied face twitch as he slept. "How did you know I'd be here?"

"Serric told me."

A flush of anger rose in her headtails. "What else did he tell you?"

"Nothing I didn't already know," he said, a dismissive edge to his voice. "I didn't come here because of Serric. I came because we received word from the legionnaires. We're heading to the summit."

"Now?" The bruises peppering her body ached anew, and her muscles were still stiff and weary. "I thought we'd have more time."

"If you're not ready—"

"No, I'm ready." She pushed the fatigue to the back of her mind and straightened her spine. She wasn't going to miss this. She couldn't. Not with so much depending on it.

It should have been impossible. Part of her couldn't help but think it still was. To bring the Idran-Var and the legionnaires together seemed a step too far, despite how close they were to making it happen. Thousands of years of bloody history. Alcruix. Vesyllion. It was too much to overcome. Yet here they were.

Rhendar tilted his head. "I'm glad. Whatever is about to happen will shape our people's future, both the Idran-Var and the allied systems alike. You should be there to see it through."

His words warmed something inside her as she scurried around the base, packing her weapons and finding an old combat suit to change into. He was right. She had fought for this. She had earned a right to be there. It didn't matter that she was no longer a legionnaire. It didn't matter that she'd never really become one of the Idran-Var. If Rivus was right, those kinds of distinctions wouldn't matter for very much longer.

Maybe then, finally, she'd know where she belonged.

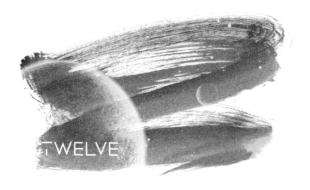

TWELVE

KOJAN

Rellion might have been beautiful if only it hadn't reminded him so much of home.

There was something majestic about the mirrored skyscrapers that covered most of the moon. The way they glimmered in the fading light and disappeared into the clouds was enough to take Kojan's breath away. They reflected the streams of passing skycars and the soft white lighting that illuminated neighbouring towers. As dusk approached, the moon-wide city became a spectacle of sparkling glass and twinkling lights, like it was made of jewels rather than buildings.

It was what New Pallas might have been if it had been given room to grow. If building skywards had been a carefully-considered architectural choice instead of desperate necessity. The lower levels of Rellion hadn't been forgotten like the slum-like surface of New Pallas. They were as much a part of the city as the uppermost buildings, boasting vast swathes of empty space for lush green plazas and bustling markets.

Perhaps that was the most painful part—not that it

reminded him of home, but that it showed him a glimpse of a once-possible future they'd destroyed.

Then again, New Pallas had never really been home. Not to him. It hardly seemed fair to claim the planet as his own when he'd grown up in the relative luxury of Exodus Station. He'd never experienced breathing in the smog-thick atmosphere. He'd never lived in tenements buried so deep they never saw the sun. Even on Exodus Station, with the labs and the needles and the cybernetic grafts, he'd been able to tell night from day.

Eleion gave him a gentle nudge with her leg. "You're thinking again."

"I tend to do that."

"You could at least share. It's not like we've got much else going on at the moment."

She was right. They'd been cooped up in one of the moon's most prestigious apartment complexes for a little over a week now. They'd had no visitors except the guards at the doors and the attendants who brought them extravagant meals every few hours. A gilded prison, but a prison all the same.

He grabbed a handful of spiced nuts and popped them into his mouth, sighing as he sank back into the soft, cushioned sofa. "I'd be in danger of getting used to all this if it wasn't for the fact it makes me pissed as hell," he said, crunching on the shells. "But the moment I start appreciating something about this place, it leaves a sour taste in my mouth."

He'd wanted for nothing back on Exodus Station, even if it had taken him half his life to realise it. Ojara had always made sure he'd had the best of everything. The best tutors, the best clothes, the best technology he could play with.

The best surgeries, a voice in his head reminded him. *The best scientists to cut you open and rewire you whenever she felt like it.*

Rellion was different. It was real in a way that Exodus Station had never been. The food brought to them on gleaming platters had been grown or reared on real land. He could taste it in the richness of the meat, in the sweetness of the fruit. The wooden floor had a smell to it unlike anything synthetic, and it creaked under the pressure of his feet like it was alive.

He shook his head. "I keep wondering how this happened. Who decided that some humans deserved a whole system of worlds, while others got cast out to a shitty rock cut off from the rest of the galaxy?"

Eleion shrugged. "Who decided to give the jarkaath the conditions they needed to evolve, to become something more? Who decided to leave the iskaath to stagnate? These are questions the galaxy has been asking for millennia, Kojan. After a while, the questions stop. Things just end up being as they are. No answers. No explanations."

"And you're okay with that?"

She gave a half-smile from behind her breather mask. "I'm less concerned about why things are the way they are and more concerned about what I can do to change it. We've got to look forward, not back."

They fell into silence, the only noise coming from the satisfying crunch of the nuts between his teeth. The sound was sharp and obtrusive, distracting him from the thoughts swirling around his head.

Look forward, not back. But how could he? Every day his cybernetics ate away at another part of his body. It was only a matter of time before they deteriorated too far for him to survive. Looking forward was impossible when he didn't know how much longer he had left.

The gentle hiss of the wood-panelled door sliding open jolted him from his thoughts. He pulled himself up from the cushions to get a better view and scowled when he saw who had entered the room.

"Maxim ras Arbor." Eleion gave a dismissive snicker from the back of her throat. "About time you showed up. Or were you planning to keep us holed up in here forever?"

"Oh, there are worse places to be holed up in, believe me." Max shot her a wry smile. "As far as Rellion hospitality goes, you're seeing our best."

Kojan studied him. His manner was as languid and informal as ever, his dark eyes glinting with dangerous amusement. He looked every part the mercenary that Alvera had warned them he was. But he was still wearing the red-collared uniform of the Rasnian military police.

Kojan frowned. "I thought you got kicked out of the force for helping Alvera escape."

"I did. They reinstated me for bringing her back."

Eleion snorted. "So much for the merc who follows the money. First chance at forgiveness and you go running right back to the authority you have so much disdain for."

"You've got me all wrong, iskaath," Max said, chuckling. "The only thing I go running to is a paycheck. Don't much care who's offering it."

"Then what's with the uniform?"

"A job's a job. And this one has an appearance that needs to come with it." Max shrugged. "Now if you're done interrogating me, it's time to move. Governor Cobus has hopped across from Ras Prime to see you both, so let's not keep him waiting."

Kojan folded his arms. "The governor? What does he want with us?"

"What do you think?" Max rolled his eyes, a bite of impatience in his voice now. "You brought us the galaxy's most wanted terrorist. Cobus is figuring out how to best make that work for him, but he's going to want more information before he makes his move."

Eleion stretched her long neck forward, regarding him with keen eyes. "She's still alive then?"

"Alive, but not awake. Cobus has had the best medtechs in the system working on her for more than a week now with no results. That's where you come in. The governor wants answers.

He wants to know what she did and whether he can use it to his advantage."

Kojan's stomach twisted. "What are you saying?"

"I'm saying nothing. But if I were you, I'd focus on a way to make myself useful. If you don't..." Max trailed off. "Let's just say he won't need much of a reason to pull the plug."

The comment had an outward veneer of indifference, but something in the way he spoke made Kojan frown. For someone who claimed to be chasing a paycheck, Maxim ras Arbour seemed oddly...*invested* in this job. The wry curl of his lips never quite reached his eyes, and the dark skin of his brow was creased in a near-permanent furrow. It was hardly the look of a man whose only thoughts were about where his next credits were coming from. There was a shadow to his expression that Kojan recognised well.

He'd seen it on Alvera's face often enough.

He followed Max in silence as he led them to one of the building's elevators. Eleion squeezed his arm gently as the carriage shot skywards until it reached the penthouse floor.

Kojan fought to hide his amazement as the doors opened into the suite. If he'd thought their tower apartment was luxurious, it was nothing compared to this. The entire room was covered in floor-to-ceiling windows, letting the sunlight stream in. They were high above the clouds clinging to the spires of the smaller buildings below. The floor was a mosaic of red-brown wood and polished marble, so beautiful and intricate it felt disrespectful to walk across it.

On the far side of the room, standing by an ornate water garden, was a thin man with flowing black hair. He turned to them and smiled, dark eyes glittering against his smooth, pale skin. "Welcome, friends. I trust your accommodation has been to your liking?"

Before Kojan could reply, Eleion jumped in. "We're humbled by your generosity, Governor Cobus. It has been some time since either of us has experienced such hospitality."

He shot her a look. Since when had she been one to play politics? Eleion ignored him and kept her eyes fixed on the governor, drawing her neck closer and curving her spine to make herself appear smaller than she was.

Cobus gave a satisfied nod and gestured to the spacious lounge area across the room. "Good, good. I'm pleased we're able to start off on pleasant terms. I find myself in need of some assistance I hope you'll be able to provide."

The words were amiable enough, but Kojan had spent too much time around Ojara to miss a threat when he heard one, no matter how veiled behind pleasantries it was. It sent a curl of distaste to his gut, a warning he'd be foolish not to pay attention to.

He followed Eleion's lead, hoping his forced smile didn't look as tight as it felt. "Anything we can do to help, we will."

Cobus nodded, his features smooth and impassive. "It is most fortunate that fate has brought us together. It's in both our interests that your captain recovers from her condition."

Eleion snapped her head up, her eyes sharp. "She made a deal with you too, didn't she?"

For the first time, Cobus's composed mask slipped, and he raised an eyebrow. "I must confess I've not come across many iskaath in my career, but from what I understand of your species, you'll forgive my surprise at such...perceptiveness for the political. What makes you think a deal was made?"

"I may not know politics, but I had a pretty good understanding of Alvera by the end of it all," Eleion said, the soft tones of her voice taking on a harder edge. "She would have promised the galaxy if she thought it would have helped her reach that waystation, even if she knew it wasn't hers to bargain with."

"You are right, of course," Cobus replied, giving her a

sombre nod. "At the time I did not know whether her word could be trusted, but given the circumstances, it was worth the gamble. There was nothing to lose, you see."

Was it Kojan's imagination, or did Max bristle at his words? He shot him a look, but his face was stony and impassive. The only sign of tension was the faintest flicker dancing in his temple.

"As a newcomer to this galaxy, what you must understand is that the humans here—Rasnians, as we would call ourselves—don't fit in with the rest of the Coalition," Cobus continued, turning to Kojan. "We govern more than a third of the allied systems, but our voice is still only one in four among the ambassadors. There are those among us who find the current arrangement to be...unsatisfactory."

"You believe you deserve more," Kojan said bluntly.

"The Rasnian *people* believe they deserve more," Cobus corrected, holding up his hands. "I am but an elected official, duty-bound to fulfil their wishes as much as is within my power."

Eleion cocked her head. "Your people wouldn't be the first to want to leave the Coalition. Didn't exactly work out well for the Idran-Var."

"The Idran-Var are the descendants of outlaws and thugs," Cobus replied, waving a dismissive hand. "They had no lawful prerogative when they left and are little more than barbaric outcasts today. I have no interest in running away to hide beyond the Rim Belt. The Rasnian people will stay exactly where they are, but govern their systems by themselves. Live by their own laws and trade deals, not those imposed by Coalition bureaucrats."

"But the impact that would have on the rest of the galaxy..." A dark look crossed Eleion's eyes. "You think the Coalition is going to let you walk away?"

"No. And the secessionist movement doesn't have the

numbers or the authority to declare unilateral independence from the Coalition."

Understanding formed in the pit of Kojan's stomach. "Not yet. But with a few billion more on the way from New Pallas—"

"Exactly." Cobus's eyes gleamed, as if Kojan had been agreeing with him. "The truth of it is that humanity has outgrown the Coalition. Where it once benefited us, it now confines us. It restricts us from becoming who we ought to be, from realising our full potential. Your friend Alvera understood that."

Kojan tried not to show his discomfort. Part of him knew Cobus sounded far too much like Ojara for Alvera to have been taken in by him. *All of us go, or none of us go.* That was the promise she'd made. The promise she'd killed for. The promised she'd all but died for. The belief that none of them had the right to set themselves above others.

But the Coalition had stood in Alvera's way. They'd forced her to break her promise. And there was another part of him, the part wounded by her betrayal, reminding him that she'd do worse than this to try to protect her people. Hell, she already had.

Maybe she hadn't been telling Cobus what he wanted to hear. Maybe she'd planned to give him exactly what he wanted.

"That's why you need her," Kojan said slowly. "You want to make sure New Pallas ends up on your side and not the Coalition's."

"I'm afraid the situation is a bit more urgent than that," Cobus said, raising an eyebrow. "Surely you know of the disaster she caused around the waystations? Whatever she did has not only doomed my hopes for the secessionists, but the fate of her own people."

Eleion let out a sharp hiss. "The temporal net."

"Precisely. I don't know how long it will take for your people to arrive once they receive the message the agitator allegedly sent, but if that dead zone is still in place when they get here—"

"They'll be trapped," Kojan finished, his mouth dry.

How had he not realised it before? His mind had been so focused on everything else Alvera was responsible for, he'd been blind to the biggest betrayal of all. By sending for New Pallas, she had summoned them to their deaths. Any ships that made it to the waystation would be caught in the temporal net, unable to move. Unable to send word back home about what had happened. Unable to get out of the way before the next ship arrived and smashed them apart in the cold vacuum of space.

Eleion glanced at him, her yellow eyes bright with concern. "She didn't know," she said, her voice low. "She couldn't have known this would happen. She was trying to save her people."

"How many times did she use that as an excuse to justify the things she did?" The words left him weary. "How many times are we going to make the same excuses for her?"

Cobus glanced between them both, shrewd-eyed and discerning. "You see the predicament we face. I won't pretend your people's value to me isn't tied to the political gain they promise, but that doesn't mean the cost of human life is immaterial to me. I would rather we both came out of this knowing that New Pallas survived."

"You think Alvera can undo whatever she did on the waystation if we wake her up?"

Cobus gave a slight shrug. "At this stage, it's the best we can hope for. But my medtechs have seen little change in her condition. If she doesn't improve..." He left the words hanging. This time, the threat was more than thinly veiled. It made the hairs on Kojan's neck stand up.

Max cleared his throat. "But you colonists are meant to be experts in cybernetics, right? Surely if you have access to a top-class human facility instead of a backwater on Kaath, you'll be able to figure out why that tech in her head is fried."

Kojan frowned. "I wouldn't say I'm any kind of—"

Eleion gave a warning hiss so low he barely heard it. "Of course. That was why we left Kaath in the first place," she said smoothly. "We needed somewhere that Kojan could work properly. Not a *backwater*, as you so aptly put it. Now that we're here, hopefully he'll be able to make a diagnosis and fix whatever has happened to her cybernetics."

Max looked as grim as ever, but the corner of his mouth twitched. Cobus straightened on the sofa, a smile of his own spreading across his thin lips.

"Excellent," he said, giving a satisfied nod. "I'm pleased we've been able to come to an understanding. Best for all of us, I'm sure. I'll arrange for you to have access to a private skycar to take you to and from the medical facility as you please. It's only a short ride away. And of course, do feel free to explore Rellion as you wish. If all goes well, it will soon be your home as much as it is ours."

It might have sounded generous coming from the mouth of any other man. But even as Cobus said his goodbyes, Kojan knew that while the cage might have got a little bigger, it was still a cage. The governor wasn't wrong. Rellion *was* their home now. But only until Alvera woke up. Or until she didn't, and Cobus ran out of patience.

Once he was sure they were alone, Kojan turned to Eleion, unable to keep the look of consternation from his face. "You know I have no idea how to wake her. She was the expert in cybernetics, not me."

"I know. But what do you think would have happened if we told him that?" Eleion tilted her head. "You heard ras Arbor as well as I did. The only reason we're alive right now is because this asshole of a governor thinks we can be useful to him. As soon as he figures out the truth, we're done. I had to buy us some time."

"Time for what?" Kojan turned to stare out the window. The sky was so clear that he could see as far as the horizon stretched. The city sprawled beyond the limits of his eyes, unobscured by pollution or smog. "If the best Rasnian medtechs couldn't wake her, what chance do we have?"

"We have to try." Eleion slumped, her scaled shoulders drawing close. "There must be a way to wake her up."

A twinge of sorrow wrenched at his heart. "I know how much you're counting on her to help your people."

"Seems like there's a lot of deals going around. I can only hope it meant something when I made mine with her." She turned her long neck to look at him, her eyes bright and solemn. "Is it wrong that I still can't blame her? Everything she's done has been for New Pallas. To give her people a shot at surviving, no matter how bad the odds were. There's a tenacity in that I can't help but admire."

Kojan couldn't find it within himself to agree. Tenacity was too noble a word for what Alvera had become. Single-minded, perhaps. Ruthless. Desperate enough to make any bargain to save New Pallas, with little regard to what it cost the rest of them.

Just like Ojara. Just like Cobus. Everywhere he looked, all he could see was self-interest. Even where he couldn't begrudge it, like in Eleion herself.

It was too much.

"I think I'm going to make use of our newfound freedom," he said, turning away from the mesmerising cityscape. "Might be the last chance I get to stretch my legs for a while."

Eleion straightened. "You want company?"

He shook his head. "Not this time. I need to think things through. Clear my head for a bit."

She sank back in the chair, her expression soft and understanding. "Of course. Take all the time you need. I'll be here when you get back."

The clouds had thickened by the time he made his way out to the sprawling pedestrian skyway. Rain drizzled down and dampened his cheeks as he walked. He had no destination in mind. No place to go. But even being outside the confines of the apartment couldn't loosen the tightness in his chest.

It was Alvera. She was the reason everything felt so stifling. She was like a thread running through his life, ever-present and impossible to untangle himself from. Everywhere he looked, he could see her fingerprints. On Max. On Cobus. Even on Eleion. How could it be that even now, barely clinging on to life, she still had such a hold over all of them?

He quickened his pace, ignoring the way his lungs burned in protest. He knew it was foolish. His cybernetics were already unstable enough. The last thing he needed was to put more pressure on the parts of him that were barely holding together. But pain was as good a distraction as anything else.

The rain beat down harder as he pushed forward. He skipped around Rasnians with fur-lined raincoats and personal weather shields. The sky was darker now, and the illumination from the nearby towers lit up reflections in the puddles as he plunged through them, ignoring the muttered grumbles from those around him.

Everything would be so much easier if she was gone.

The thought bloomed from nowhere, catching him off-guard. He slowed down, legs trembling as he came to a halt on one of the massive bridges spanning the skyways. The city glittered in the darkness below, all the more beautiful despite the rain lashing down. He leaned against the barrier to catch his breath, watching his reflection as his breath gently fogged the glass.

A chill swept over him, like he'd caught himself half-considering something he hadn't known he was capable of. Alvera had killed him, and the chance of her being able to fix it seemed more and more like something he'd be willing to sacrifice for the chance to be free of her.

He tapped his wrist terminal, bringing up his connections. He still hadn't replied to Ridley's last message. She didn't know Alvera was alive. Apart from Shaw and the other mutineers, she was the only one left. The only one who might be able to set him straight, to remind him what the hell they were doing here.

Before he could open the link, a light on his terminal blinked with an incoming connection request. He frowned, not recognising the signature. Maybe it was Max, or one of the other Rasnian officials. He hesitated for a moment, then accepted the connection.

The hololink flickered to life in front of him.

Ojara.

She smiled tightly, stretching the thin lines around her mouth. "You're looking a little worse for wear."

A hundred responses sat on the tip of his tongue, but he swallowed them back down. He couldn't give her the satisfaction of seeing his anger, or his pain. She'd taken too much already. "I'm surprised you thought to call. Unless you were just checking if I was dead yet?"

"Oh no, it's much too soon for that," she replied, a light chuckle behind her words. "The quickening is as much a punishment as it is a death sentence. Believe me, Kojan, by the time the end comes, you'll be wishing it had reached you sooner."

"Nice to see your skill at starting a conversation off on the right foot hasn't changed. Then again, who needs pleasantries after deciding to execute their only son?"

"Pleasantries are for politics, and for people who have more power than you," Ojara said, waving a hand. "You are nothing but a problem that will soon take care of itself. But even a broken tool may still have some use before it's discarded."

"And here was me thinking you wanted to talk about the weather."

"Nonsense. Everybody knows it's rain season on Rellion."

Kojan froze. "How did you—"

"Must you keep disappointing me?" Ojara curled her lips. "Surely you understand by now that there is very little I am not capable of. If only you had learned that lesson earlier, you might not have condemned yourself to such suffering. To such failure."

"We've not failed yet."

"Haven't you?" Ojara arched an eyebrow. "Alvera accused me of leaving the people of New Pallas to die. But her actions have ensured their deaths with more certainty than mine ever could. This is precisely the reason the Coalition wanted to wait. They warned her about the danger of the waystations. But she didn't listen. Instead, she has sacrificed billions of lives for her own stubbornness and pride."

He flinched at her words. They mirrored his own thoughts far too closely, but coming out of her mouth, they were poison.

The worst thing was that she was *right*.

She tilted her head, looking at him with an understanding expression. "New Pallas is lost because of her," she said gently. "Can't you see that?"

"Don't." Kojan clenched his fists. "Don't you dare pretend that this is some great tragedy to you, that this wasn't exactly what you wanted."

Ojara just smiled.

It was too much. His chest was tight and aching, his legs ready to collapse. Maybe part of it was the quickening. But part of it was the effect she had on him, this monster that should have been his mother. The weight of everything she'd done.

The scars she'd left and then wiped away, as if removing them meant they'd never existed.

"What do you want?" he asked, unable to hide the weariness seeping into his voice. "I know you didn't call just to gloat. There's always a reason with you."

Ojara's face was smooth and devoid of expression. "I know Alvera is alive on Rellion. I know her condition is critical. I want you to ensure she never wakes up."

This time, he didn't waste his breath asking how she got her information. He just barked out a laugh. There was a twisted kind of irony in the way she could give voice to the darkest of his thoughts. It showed him parts of himself that he didn't want to see. It made him wonder whether he wasn't his mother's son after all.

Everything would be so much easier if she was gone.

He pushed the thought back down, but he couldn't get rid of it. It lingered in the shadows of his mind, a promise of what he might be capable of.

"I wouldn't have thought you'd find the situation so amusing," Ojara said, casting him a discerning look. "She is, after all, the one responsible for the virus attacking your cybernetics. There must be a part of you that wants her to pay for that."

"And ignore the fact you were the one who activated it?" Kojan shook his head. "Maybe she does deserve to pay for what she's done to me. But I need her. Whatever else she's responsible for, she's the only one who can stop what you set in motion."

"Is she?" Ojara's face was serene, but there was a glint behind her eyes. "Did you think I'd allow such programming to be put in my own son without a means of reversing it?"

Kojan's mouth went dry. "You're lying."

"No, I'm not." She smiled. "Everything can be undone, Kojan. All of this. The quickening, the galactic arrest warrant out in your name... I can make it all go away. All you need to do is get rid of a woman who has brought you nothing but disappointment and pain. It's nothing less than she deserves."

His heart hammered against his chest. It was all too easy to believe her. He *wanted* to believe her. With Ojara, it was always about power. Always about control. Why wouldn't she have ensured a failsafe in the programming? If not for any consideration of him, then for this very reason. To be able to control him if he ever slipped from her grasp. All he had to do was give into the thoughts she'd never needed to put in his head in the first place.

"There's still hope," he said, the words sounding weak to his own ears. "If she wakes up, she might be able to fix whatever happened to the waystations. You're asking me to give up on New Pallas to save myself when they might still have a chance."

She looked at him with pitying eyes. "I don't think you believe that. If you did, you wouldn't hate her so much. You know New Pallas is lost. And you are as much to blame as she is."

Her words hit him with a truth he hadn't wanted to admit. It wasn't just Alvera. It was him. It was Eleion. It was everyone who'd ever helped her on her relentless crusade. Everyone who'd said *damn the consequences* and followed her into the hell she'd carved for the galaxy, all for the sake of a promise they should never have tried to keep.

Maybe it was time to put that right.

He looked down at his arm. Some of his cybernetics had burned through the skin near his wrist, exposing the metallic sheen of his bone reinforcements. Soon there would be no skin left to burn, no bone left to reinforce. He was running out of time. If Alvera couldn't help him, was it so wrong to want to believe that Ojara could?

A shudder ran through him. If he was right, then all it would take to get his life back was the simple flick of a switch.

Something Alvera wouldn't have hesitated to do, given the right circumstances.

And if he was wrong...well, his old captain had made sure there was nobody left in the galaxy who would miss her.

"All right." He took a breath, the words tasting like bile on his tongue. "I'll do it."

THIRTEEN

RIDLEY

R idley pressed the cabin door's access panel and waited. Seconds passed, and the interface remained blank and lifeless. Then it gave a dull, rejecting chime and turned red.

Again.

She sighed and turned away, not knowing why she expected this time to be any different. Ever since Halressan had realised they were headed for Idran-Var space, she'd shut herself in one of the cabins and refused to come out.

Not that Ridley could blame her. Flying into the territory of the galaxy's most notorious warriors with a death mark on your head was hardly one of the better choices somebody could make in life, but Halressan was doing it anyway. Because of her. Because she'd tricked her.

I had to do it, she told herself. *If we hadn't got away, Skaile would have killed us all.*

As far as justifications went, it was a good one. But no matter how many times she played it over in her head, it did nothing to assuage the knot of guilt in her stomach pulling tighter and tighter by the day.

She found Drexious in the cockpit as usual, his tail swishing from side to side as his eyes flicked lazily over the instruments. Despite everything that had happened, he seemed the most relaxed of any of them.

He glanced up as she approached, his bronze eyes glinting. "Well?"

Ridley shook her head.

"I told you." He made a clicking sound at the back of his throat. "Bringing her was a mistake. We should have got away clean when we had the chance."

"And left her to die?" Ridley gave him a pointed look. "We'd never have made it out of that hangar without her."

"She was the one tailing us for Skaile in the first place, in case you forgot. If you hadn't agreed to cut her in, she'd have killed us or carted us back to the Queen's Den." He shuddered, his spines quivering. "This is why humans make terrible business partners. Too emotional. You're letting your feelings for her blind you to what she really is."

Warmth rushed to her cheeks. "I don't have—"

"Yes, you do." He sighed. "It's dangerous. *She's* dangerous. Maybe not as dangerous as the mess you're dragging us into, but still more than capable of killing both of us with her bare hands. And that's no small thing, for a human." He curled his own clawed fingers into fists. "Just be careful. I don't think you realise what you're getting yourself into with that one."

Ridley snorted. "That almost sounded like concern."

"Hey, I'm not saying we're friends. But there's not many people in this galaxy that haven't tried to put a bullet in me at one time or another, and even less who have stuck their necks out to help me. That makes you more tolerable than most."

"I'm touched."

"Don't be. I fully intend to cut myself loose from this insane crusade of yours as soon as I get the opportunity." He folded his long arms across his chest. "And my share of the profits, of course."

Ridley took a seat in the co-pilot's chair next to him. The leather had a rich, unfamiliar smell to it, like a perfume she'd never be able to afford. Everything from the glossy paint to the designer upholstery reminded her that this was not hers, that she shouldn't have been here. *None* of them should have been here. Halressan's locked door at the other end of the ship was all the reminder she needed of that.

A flush crept up her neck as she replayed Drexious's words. *You're letting your feelings for her blind you to what she really is.* He'd been able to see the very thing she'd been trying to push away. The thing she'd been trying to deny existed. The spark of longing buried beneath all the fear.

In some ways, Halressan's door being closed made it easier to deal with. She didn't have to fight the urge to let her eyes follow everywhere she moved. She didn't have to disguise the way her breath sharpened when she got too close. She could have pretended her out of existence if it hadn't made her miss her so much.

Drexious broke the silence with a satisfied click of his tongue. "That's our final approach to the rip site locked in. When we arrive, we should be able to set up to punch a hole through to this mysterious planet of yours. Assuming your calculations work and we don't end up going through a sun."

Ridley stretched her legs out in front of her. "How much longer?"

"Six hours, give or take. Time enough to catch a bit of sleep, if that's what you're thinking. There's not much else to..." He trailed off, eyes blinking at something on the nav console.

"What is it?"

"Could be nothing. Just a blip on the nav." He hesitated, a low thrum vibrating at the back of his throat. "Or it could be trouble. I don't like the implications if it turns out to be a ship."

"All the way out here?" Ridley's mouth ran dry. "We're far beyond pirate territory. The only ships out here would be—"

"I know." Drexious's voice was grim. "The only thing to do is hold course. Ignore them and hope they're not interested in us."

"And if they are interested in us?"

A thoughtful look flitted over his face. "From what I know of the Idran-Var, they're not interested in picking a fight with those weaker than them. They'll be able to see we're no threat if we show them we have nothing to hide."

"But we do have something to hide. If they see Halressan's armour..." She gripped the edges of her seat, trying not to clench her teeth. It had all seemed so simple back on Jadera. Skaile had been the immediate threat, and making plans to escape her grip had taken up most of her thoughts. The danger of navigating through Idran-Var territory was less real back then, too far ahead for her to realise what it might cost.

Drexious shot her a sideways glance. "Then we get rid of the armour. We've got time. They've not pinged us yet."

"Are you serious? We could have all the time in the galaxy and that still wouldn't be long enough to convince her."

"You have to try. If they decide to board us and find that armour, it's over. At least this way we might have a chance."

Ridley muttered a Jaderan curse under her breath before pushing herself out of the seat and making her way back to the crew cabins. Halressan was in a foul enough mood as it was already. Asking her to do this would probably send her over the edge.

Her fingers hovered over the keypad, hardly daring to move. Part of her hoped Halressan would deny her access again, that the door would remain firmly shut.

Before she could tap the interface, the door slid open and she came face to face with the steely glare of Halressan.

"I'm not doing it," she said flatly.

Ridley frowned. "How do you—"

"This is Skaile's private cabin. She has it set up so she can monitor the entire shuttle. I heard everything."

Everything. Even what Drexious had said about... Ridley's heart thumped harder and her cheeks burned like they were aflame. A hundred denials and excuses rose within her, each more humiliating than the last, but she swallowed them down and instead forced out the more pressing matter. "We need to get rid of your armour."

There was no outrage on Halressan's face. No anger. Just stony refusal. "I said no."

"But—"

"Screw you." Now she could hear the low, simmering rage in her voice. "You knew where we were going all along. You let me follow you out here knowing it could get me killed. Now you want me to give up my armour too?"

"I want you to give up your armour so it *doesn't* get you killed."

"You're trying to save me?" She let out a sharp, humourless laugh. "Sweetheart, you're the only reason I'm in this position at all. You did this."

"*I* did this?" Ridley bristled. "You think I wanted any of this? In the past few months, I've had to leave my planet behind, watch most of my crew get executed in cold blood, find a way to stay on the good side of an unhinged, power-hungry siolean, not to mention almost getting buried alive in some ruins I never wanted to go to in the first place. And you want to cry about some armour?"

Halressan narrowed her eyes. "It's not just—"

"I. Don't. Care," Ridley said, punctuating each word with a pointed finger against Halressan's chest. "It's not worth your life. And if you think it is, you're even more of a fool than I thought you were already."

She whirled away, trying to ignore the way her eyes were stinging. Every breath came hard and heavy, like expelling her rage had taken the air from her lungs with it. She was sick of it. Sick of the way she felt responsible for Drexious and Halressan, like she owed them something they'd never even asked for in the first place. It wasn't her place to save them. It wasn't her place to save anyone, except herself.

But if that was true, what was she even doing out here?

It wasn't until a few moments later that the pounding in her ears faded enough for her to hear the gentle clink of metal against the floor. The first sound was so quiet she might have imagined it. Then came another, heavier this time, followed by a dull thud. It was slow and systematic, falling into place piece by piece.

When she turned around, almost all the armour was lying at Halressan's feet. She took off the last piece from around her wrist and let it fall to the floor with a harsh clang, watching defiantly as it rattled against the rest. Her marble-pale skin was covered in prickled bumps as she stood there shivering in the thin fabric of her jumpsuit.

She turned to Ridley with a dead-eyed glare. "How do I look?"

Ridley couldn't answer. Not truthfully, at any rate. Gone was the stiff spine and straight shoulders. Gone was the jutted chin and scowling lips. It was like she'd been stripped naked—not of the shell of her armour, but of all the fierceness and bravado it had given her. No measure of lean limbs and wiry muscles could make up for the kind of assurance she'd set on the ground at her feet.

Ridley cleared her throat. "It's for the best."

"Is it?" Halressan gave a wry smile, but something had dimmed in the heat of her eyes. "I guess I'll take your word for it. Don't want to make myself into any more of a fool than you thought I was already, after all."

The bitterness caught her like a barb beneath the skin. She opened her mouth to say something—to say she hadn't meant it like that—but the words refused to come. It was pointless to try and take it back. What good was an apology? What good was an explanation? Halressan would never understand what she'd come out here to do. And if she knew, she'd never forgive her for it. Better to keep her betrayal quiet, for both their sakes.

Across the room, Halressan was rummaging through Skaile's storage, pulling out jewel-lined capes and shimmering dresses. Eventually, she found a pair of black cargo pants and a garish, indigo-coloured jacket that hadn't even been unsealed from its packaging yet.

"Shit," Halressan muttered. "This is vaxadrian leather."

"Meaning?"

"Vaxads went extinct a couple of centuries ago. This is probably worth more than the entire ship." She shrugged the jacket around her shoulders, a smirk tugging at the corners of her mouth. "Skaile has taste, I'll give her that. Expensive taste."

"Are you kidding me?" Ridley said. "The whole reason the Idran-Var are after you is because you took something they want back. Now you're stealing from Skaile too?"

Halressan arched an eyebrow as she tied her white-blonde hair back from her face. "*You're* the one who stole from Skaile. I'm just making your fuck-up worth my while." The humour vanished from her face and she set her mouth in a hard line. "Let's get this over with before I change my mind."

"Halressan..."

"No, babe. You don't get to *Halressan* me. Not with this." Her voice was low and resigned, but her eyes were so cold her gaze made Ridley want to flinch. "I'm doing what you wanted. Don't piss me off by asking me to be happy about it too."

There was nothing she could say to that. Instead, she

watched as Halressan gathered up her armour and made her way towards the airlock. The dull clunk of her grav boots against the metal floor sounded like a lament. Each step resounded with a heavy finality, promising there was no way back from what the hunter was about to do.

Ridley followed after her, pulling up the door controls on her wrist terminal. She'd already linked up to most of the ship's systems. Knowing your environment was the only way to survive back on the surface of New Pallas. It was a lesson she'd taken with her. A lesson that had kept her alive through more than she'd had any right to survive.

At the last set of doors, she waited. She thought there might have been some sort of ceremony, some sort of reverence, with which Halressan said goodbye to her armour. Instead, she dumped it from her arms like it had been junkyard scrap and hit the door controls with a clenched fist and a tight jaw.

The inner airlock door slid shut with a hiss. Halressan's armour disappeared behind the metal barrier, a breath away from the dark void of space outside.

"Do it," she said, the words a dark murmur from the back of her throat.

Ridley didn't wait to be told again. She waved her hand across the face of her wrist terminal, releasing the second set of airlock doors. There was no noise. No rush of air or clatter of metal. All she could see through the dark box of the viewport was a glimmer of light against the black, fainter than the stars in the distance.

Then it was gone.

Halressan turned away, a low hiss escaping from between her teeth. "Fuck."

Ridley knew better than to say anything. If she'd been braver, she might have dared to reach out and put a comforting hand on Halressan's shoulder, even knowing it would have been met with hostility. But she didn't have time to deal with the jumbled mess of emotions that kind of rejection would stir in her, not when danger was still bearing down on them.

Maybe there would be time for them after. Time to explain. Time to fix whatever wound she'd opened up between them. But that could only happen if there *was* an after.

Drexious was still hunched over the ship's instruments when she got back to the cockpit. He acknowledged her with a low trill at the back of his throat but kept his eyes fixed on the holodisplay in front of him.

"I take it from the airlock override warning that you managed to talk some sense into the hunter?"

"It's done."

"Just in time." He flicked up a readout on the display. "Idran-Var patrol vessel. Probably keeping an eye out for Coalition scouts. Rumour has it things are getting tense back in the allied systems. It's a small, two-person craft, but they're built for speed and have enough weaponry to give us a problem."

"Tell me there's good news."

Drexious turned his bronze eyes towards her. "Human, that *was* the good news. If they'd been raiders or mercs, we'd be dead already. All they want to do is board us to make sure we're not Coalition spies. I've already given them an approach vector."

"You did what?" Halressan appeared at the entrance to the cockpit, her pale cheeks flushed pink. "You're inviting those bastards onto our ship? You're not even trying to get us out of this? You worthless, double-crossing piece of—"

"We knew this might happen," Ridley shot back. "That's why we couldn't take any chances with your armour. If we refused to let them board, they'd likely blow us to pieces. At least this way we have a chance of making it out alive, as long as we're all smart about it."

Halressan didn't reply. She shot Drexious a mutinous glare

and slumped down into the co-pilot's chair, kicking her grav boots against the control panel.

A light on the console blinked and Drexious cleared his throat. "They're making their approach. Airlocks should be aligned in five."

Every minute that passed brought a new wave of dread to Ridley's stomach. There was nowhere left to run if things went wrong. She wiped her clammy hands against the fabric of her flight suit and fought to steady her breathing. She couldn't afford to let fear win.

When the airlock door slid open and the sound of heavy armoured footsteps came echoing through the hull, she joined Drexious and Halressan as they rose to their feet. Her legs trembled so ferociously she wondered how they were managing to keep her upright.

We have nothing to hide, she reminded herself. *They're after Coalition spies, not a group of would-be smugglers with a death wish.*

Halressan caught sight of them first. Ridley could tell by the way she stiffened, the way her jaw went rigid. Her eyes were caught somewhere between hatred and fear as she watched them step into the lights of the cockpit.

There were only two of them, as Drexious had suspected. That didn't matter. Two Idran-Var was still too many. Their armour was every bit as impressive as Halressan's had been, dark and reflective, like shadows made of glass. But theirs didn't boast the crude stripe of paint she'd defaced hers with. They were unblemished, unspoiled.

Unstoppable.

One of them inclined their head forward. Their helmet was different from Halressan's too. Instead of a gleaming, circular visor in the middle of the helm, there were three horizontal slits, each glowing with a dark yellow light.

"It's not often we get visitors all the way out here," the

Idran-Var said, his voice distorted through his helmet. "There's not much to see past the Rim Belt. Unless you're looking for trouble."

The calm manner in which he spoke did little to mask the threat in his words. Ridley suppressed a shudder and tried to swallow the fear in her throat as she replied. "We're not looking for any trouble. Just passing through."

"Passing through to where, exactly?" The second Idran-Var sounded amused. "I don't know where you got your starcharts, but there's not much out this way."

"That's the point," Drexious interjected. "We're treasure hunters following a set of coordinates that point to an uncharted planet. We're headed for the edge of dark space."

The two Idran-Var turned their helmets towards each other, sharing a glance none of them could see. Eventually, one of them let out a gruff, mechanical chuckle. "Dark space? Now there's an excuse I've not heard before. Coalition agents aren't usually so creative."

"We're not Coalition agents," Ridley said. "We came from the Rim Belt. When you pinged us, we didn't try to run. We have nothing to hide."

"If you have nothing to hide, you won't mind us checking your transport registry, will you?"

Drexious shrugged. "Go ahead."

Ridley held her breath and willed her nerves to settle. Any ship of Skaile's was unlikely to show up anywhere near Coalition-controlled space on the transport registry. The transit logs would probably only show journeys around the Rim Belt. There was no reason for the Idran-Var to suspect they were anything other than what they claimed they were.

"All clear on the transport registry, just like you said." The Idran-Var swiped away the holographic interface from his wrist terminal. "But the bounty network, that's a different story."

Ridley froze.

"A new mark, fresh from Jadera," the other continued. "According to this, there's a considerable sum on offer for the capture of a stolen ship, along with the thieves on board. A jarkaath..." He trailed off, slowly turning his helmet to look at them all. "And two humans."

Drexious let out a jittering laugh from deep in his throat, but Ridley could see the way the spindles on the curve of his neck quivered. "Come on, that's between us and whoever put that price on our heads. We're not worth your time. I didn't think the Idran-Var even bothered with bounties from the Rim Belt."

"We don't. Trouble is, this bounty also claims one of the humans is in possession of stolen Idran-Var armour." His metallic voice had turned terrifyingly cold.

Ridley's mouth ran dry. Skaile had screwed them. She'd given the Idran-Var a reason to do her dirty work. And Ridley had sent it out the airlock.

Before she could say a word, Halressan stepped forward. "Fine. You win. Let's not make this any more painful than it needs to be." She turned around, meeting Ridley's eyes with a glittering stare. There was no doubt there, no apology. Only the faintest flicker of regret as she turned back to the Idran-Var and stuck her jaw out in defiance. "You want the thief who stole your armour? That's her."

Words deserted her. She couldn't find her tongue to deny Halressan's accusation. Her jaw had sealed itself shut, as tight and painful as the aching in her chest. It wasn't from the fear. There would be plenty of time for fear. That would come later. Right now, all she could focus on was the pain.

Why had this come as a surprise? Why had she expected anything different?

Drexious let out a strangled hiss. "What the hell do you think you're doing, hunter? You know damn well that—"

"Enough." Ridley forced the word out, almost choking on it.

This was her fault. She should have been preparing for it the moment Halressan set foot on the ship. She'd always known this peace between them would come to an end one way or another. She just thought it would be from *her* betrayal.

It didn't stop the hurt wrenching at her heart. It didn't stop the rush of shame that flooded through her for having thought, having *hoped*, that maybe she'd meant more to Halressan than somebody to sacrifice to save her own skin.

The Idran-Var hadn't moved. They didn't need to. There was nowhere she could run. No place she could go to escape what was coming next. They stared her down in their shining, faceless armour, waiting for her to say something.

"I'll take you to your armour," she said. "Follow me."

She ignored the way Drexious's spines quivered in alarm, the slight frown that knitted Halressan's brows together. She turned her back on them both and walked towards the ship's central corridor, the Idran-Var following closely at her heels. The sound of their armoured boots echoed off the hull in a foreboding rhythm, stalking her every step.

She was walking towards her death. But now that she had started, there was no way to stop. She gulped in each breath quicker than the last until her fingers tingled and a wave of dizziness swam through her head. It felt like somebody else was in control of her body, like she was watching herself from somewhere far away.

The cargo hold was located in a secure annex at the back of the ship. Ridley's hands trembled as she pulled up her wrist terminal and entered the access codes to open the double doors. Droplets of sweat trickled down her forehead as she sucked in one breath after another. Her heart was racing. It was almost time. She could only hope Drexious and Halressan had enough sense to stay in the cockpit. Maybe saving them would be worth losing everything else.

In a few more moments, it would all be over. The Idran-Var

would follow her into the cargo hold and see there was nothing there but an empty room.

Except it wasn't empty, not quite. They hadn't yet seen the wiring crawling across the back wall. They hadn't yet seen the red glow coming from the electronic timer blinking on and off. They hadn't yet seen the way the double doors had sealed themselves shut behind them, cutting them off from the rest of the ship.

They hadn't seen anything of the trap she'd set for them until it was too late.

The closest Idran-Var noticed it first. "Oh sh—"

Ridley brushed her thumb over the detonator on her belt and pushed the last gasp of air from her lungs as the fireball erupted. All she could feel was the heat from the flames burning her cheeks. All she could hear was the roaring in her ears. All she could see was the gaping jaws of the hole she'd blown in the hull.

Something wrenched at her body, and she felt herself torn into the void.

Then it was all gone.

FOURTEEN

RIVUS

ake up.

Rivus was dreaming again. But when he opened his eyes this time, it was not to the interior of the base on Aurel, but somewhere unfamiliar, surrounded by white light. It was like he was suspended in a vacuum, with no sense of what way was up or the time that made up each passing moment.

Then the dream shifted, and he saw her.

She was tall, for a human at least. Greying hair and lined skin that spoke to her age, but a dangerous glint in her eye that dared him to underestimate her for it. If he looked too closely, she became blurry, as if she might disappear at any moment. But she was there, stern-faced and cross-armed, her head cocked to one side like she was sizing him up.

He knew who she was. By this point, the whole damn galaxy knew who she was.

The one who started all this. The agitator.

Alvera Renata.

Her mouth curled at one side. "The one who started all this?" she repeated. "Do you really want to go there?"

The dreamscape changed again. Without warning, he was back on Farsal Waystation, following in footsteps he hadn't known existed until it was too late. The voices he'd tried so hard to forget whispered from the back of his head, reminding him of what he'd done. Reminding him of what they'd *made* him do.

He shook his head violently and the vision scattered, leaving him alone with the human. She lingered out of reach, regarding him with a wary expression he could have sworn he'd seen before. Like a dream he couldn't quite remember.

Then, with a growl of surprise, he *did* remember. Outstretched arms, claws wrapped around her throat. Then she was gone, and he'd woken up.

She gave a short laugh, as if she'd read his mind. "Well, this is already off to a better start than last time. Getting strangled by a dachryn isn't something I need to experience twice."

His claws twitched, reacting to the memory. "That was a dream."

"Maybe. Doesn't mean it didn't fucking hurt though." She rubbed her throat. "Maybe we can try to be more civilised this time around."

There was something about the way she spoke that reminded him of the other voices in his head. "You're dead, aren't you?"

The smile on the edge of her lips faltered. "What makes you say that?"

"You're not the first ghost that's come to warn me about what's coming. Whatever happened on that waystation...it changed me. It let me see things that happened so long ago nobody in the galaxy can remember them."

She perked up her chin at that. "They're in your head," she said, her words echoing in the emptiness between them. "They tried to get in mine too, but I've ended up in their head instead. The only problem is, I'm pretty much trapped here. Can't figure my way out. But I know they don't want me in here, so that's some comfort at least."

None of her words made any sense to him. "What are you talking about? Whose head?"

"The curators." She sighed. "Those voices you hear? They're memories. Memories of every being who ever existed in this galaxy before us. They got to you through your cybernetics, just like they got to me through mine. They're what's lurking at the end of that countdown, Rivus. They're coming for us all."

"Because of me? Because of what I did on that waystation?"

"You never stood a chance," she said. "Neither of us knew what we were doing when we did it. But that doesn't make us any less responsible for it."

"I know I set something in motion when I sent the signal, but the countdown was steady at first. We would have had more time if something else hadn't happened to speed up the clock." He paused, anger rippling through him. "That's what you cost us when you blew up the jamming tower so you could send a message back to New Pallas. That was the only thing capable of holding them off, at least for a little while."

The lines of her face creased deeper under the weight of her frown. "Yes. I chose to try to save my people no matter what the cost. I knew what I was doing might risk the lives of everyone in the galaxy." She let out a breath. "It's only now I hear these voices in my head that I actually understand what that means."

A snarl rose at the back of his throat. "Is that what you're here for? To try to make up for the mistake you made?"

"I'm here because I'm trapped inside the mind of the things that are coming to kill you, and I can't do a damn thing about it," she said, her voice taking on a hard edge. "And I'm not the only one here who has made a mistake. As for making up for it, neither of us can do that without each other's help."

He stilled. "What do you mean?"

"I can navigate this place. I can go further into the galaxy's memories and try to find out more about the curators and what they want. Maybe even find a way to defeat them." She fixed him with a steady gaze. "I can give you whatever I find to help you stand against them. But knowing what you're up against won't help unless the rest of the galaxy is ready to fight. I've seen what's going on here, on this planet. I've seen it through your eyes, through your memories. A battle here is only going to weaken those left standing at the end of it."

"You think I don't know that?" Rivus growled. "I'm trying my best, but right now the only fight this galaxy is interested in is with itself. We'll be lucky if we haven't torn ourselves to pieces by the time these curators come to pick up the scraps."

"Then end the fight. Whatever the cost. Whatever it takes."

He gave a hollow laugh. "You sound like Tarvan. I suppose you approve of his plan? I wish I could say I was surprised, but lives must stop mattering to people like you and him when you've sacrificed as many of them as you have."

"Do you see another way out of this?" she shot back. "Because if there's one thing your friend Tarvan and I have in common, it's knowing how far someone is capable of falling when they think they're out of options. Don't be so sure you won't do the same when the decision lies with you."

Her words should have brought his hackles up. They should have drawn a deep, furious rumble from the depths of his throat. Instead, all they did was send a shiver of fear down his spine. For the briefest of moments, he was back on the *Lancer*, looking over the fires on Vesyllion as they left behind the planet they'd killed.

Only this time, it wasn't Tarvan who was standing over the devastation. It was him.

He shuddered, trying to shake the cold seeping through him. "I don't care what you think I'm capable of. I won't make the same mistakes as Tarvan did. As you did. That's what got us into this mess in the first place. There has to be another way. A better way."

A half smile twitched at the side of the human's face. "You sound like someone I used to know. Someone I wish I'd been able to be. It almost makes me believe you might be right."

He scowled. "Fighting as a united galaxy means nothing if we have to kill each other to get there. That's not something I'll ever play a part in again. If you want to believe anything, believe that. And if you want my help, then first you have to help me stop what Tarvan has set in motion. Otherwise, you're on your own."

He closed his eyes, blocking out the dreamscape and the agitator and everything else in his head. The last thing he heard as he drifted into the darkness was her soft laugh and the echo of an outstretched hand.

"Okay," she said. "Let's do it your way."

————

When he opened his eyes again, he was staring at the ceiling of the barracks.

He gave a grunt and pulled himself up, his body stiff with fatigue and the dream still lingering in his mind. The cell was windowless and empty. The only entrance was a heavy-set steel door that stood resolutely shut.

He made his way over to it, doing his best to ignore the ache in his legs as he crossed the room. He wouldn't let himself be cornered into making the same decisions Tarvan had, the same decisions Alvera Renata had. There *was* another way. It was clear in his mind, so vibrant it was almost tangible.

He pressed his claws along the seams of the door, looking

for some kind of weakness. There was no keypad on this side, no mechanism that he might have been able to destroy or rewire to force it open.

A growl of frustration escaped his throat and he slammed his cybernetic arm into the door with as much force as he could muster. The impact rippled through the rest of his body but didn't leave as much as a dent in the reinforced metal.

He sank to his knees, breaths coming fast and heavy. Was this how he was supposed to wait out the rest of the war? Trapped inside a metal box by the commander whose side he'd sworn to remain at until the end?

Find another way, he'd told himself. *A better way.*

The words had come easy in the dreamscape. Now, they felt like a fool's hope.

Maybe. But even a fool's hope is better than no hope at all.

Alvera's voice whispered to him at the back of his mind, like so many others had. But hers was different. It was closer than the rest, like she'd taken up residence in his head alongside the fear and doubt that existed there already.

It was a strange thing, to no longer feel alone.

You're not alone, Alvera said. *You have a galaxy's lifetime of memories to draw from to get yourself out of this. Might as well start with mine.*

It was like an awakening. That was the only way to describe it. His mind exploded with so many thoughts it was impossible to take any of them in, much less make sense of them. They poured in through every crack and disappeared into nothingness as quickly as they rushed in.

A pink-haired woman caught in stasis, a cloud of red around the bullet in her forehead.

A hand reaching into darkness and grasping empty air, too late to save the man she pushed.

A sunset shrouded by smog, hope swelling in her chest at the sight of it.

Each thought came and went without context, without understanding, until all he was left with was the emptiness they left behind once they'd deserted him.

Not deserted, Alvera said. *They'll be there when you need them. As I will.*

Something clicked.

He knew how to get out.

His claws moved independently of his mind, like somebody else knew how to operate them better than he did. He used them to prise off a panel in his cybernetic arm. The same cybernetic arm the human colonists had attached for him after he'd lost his own on Farsal Waystation. The same cybernetic arm that had been engineered by the woman whose presence he could now sense in his mind.

It was more than intuition. It was like he'd inherited the muscle memory of somebody else. This was *her*—Alvera Renata. Each nimble movement as he rewired and switched circuits, each flickering glance over the miniscule components, felt as natural as if he'd been doing this his whole life. As if using the technology in his artificial arm to create an electro-magnetic pulse was something he'd always been capable of, and not a borrowed memory from the human who should have been his enemy.

When he hit the charge and the door slid open, her elation swelled inside him alongside his own.

Go, she urged. *Stop this war, if you can. Find another way.*

His surroundings faded into a blur as he stumbled out of the barracks and made for the base's makeshift garage. There was nobody left to stop him as he hauled himself aboard one of the speeders and gunned it into life.

He pushed the throttle forward and shot out across Aurel's pale, rugged terrain. Each passing second dragged on forever, as if time itself knew what he was trying to do and was determined to see him fail. The red light blinking on his wrist terminal told him his comms were still jammed. The groaning of the engine told him there was no more speed to give. The thumping in his chest told him he was running out of time.

A fool's hope, indeed. But even a fool's hope was better than no hope at all.

He could still stop the horror Tarvan had put in motion. He could still save his fellow legionnaires and the Idran-Var alike. He could still convince them to face what was coming together. He could do what Alvera had been unable to. He could find another way.

But only if he wasn't already too late.

FIFETEEN

NIOLE

Niole piled into one of the ground transports alongside Zal and Venya, wondering if she was the only one whose heart was pounding against their ribs. Venya had already pulled her helmet over her great, crested head, and Zal was rolling hers between her hands, looking down at it with her one good eye.

They didn't seem nervous. She wasn't sure the Idran-Var ever got nervous. But there was a tension all the same, an expectation that hung like a promise in the thin, recycled air of the carrier.

She nudged Zal, keeping her voice low as she spoke. "Is it just me, or does everybody seem a little..."

"Off balance?" Zal sent her a grin. "This is unusual territory for us. The Idran-Var don't do negotiations, just battle. Normally we'd be readying ourselves for the fight ahead. But it's hard to get yourself fired up for a fight that's not supposed to take place. If all goes as it should, we'll walk away from this with our hands clean. There's a great many among us who don't know what that feels like."

"Don't know, or don't *want* to know?" Her thoughts drifted to Serric. It was hard to imagine him standing by as Rhendar made peace with the people he hated so much. Would he be able bury his rage and watch them leave under the banner of a truce just because Rhendar asked him to?

Zal turned her head, the cybernetic graft over her left eye blinking in the darkness. "Rhendar is war chief now," she reminded her. "That's not a title that's given out lightly, or without consideration. It's not one that can easily be taken back either. We follow him, or we are no longer Idran-Var. That's all the reason any of us need."

The journey continued in near-silence, the only sounds coming from the rattling of the transport as it rumbled over Aurel's uneven surface. The only window to the outside was a small skylight above, showing nothing but the red-tinged atmosphere bleeding into the dark of space.

Niole couldn't help but shiver. There was something oppressive about the tension. It wasn't just about the uneasiness of the Idran-Var around her. It was the planet itself, barren and bare and lingering in darkness. Too lifeless. Too quiet. Like the presence of both sides was disturbing something they should have known to leave alone.

After some time, the transport came to a slow, grinding stop. The stillness echoed for a heartbeat, turning everyone to stone. Then they were moving, doors sliding open and armoured bodies thundering out into the dead atmosphere.

Niole followed them, keeping close on the heels of Zal and Venya. A restless energy swirled around the gathering warriors, like one of Vesyllion's fearsome stormclouds about to break. They spoke in hushed tones, the filters of their helmets turning their words into a low drone. When she reached the front of the crowd, she could see why.

The legionnaires were waiting for them. They stood stiff and ready, their power armour gleaming white against Aurel's murky surface, their green capes limp in the windless, thin atmosphere.

"They're here," she said, barely believing the words.

"It's something, isn't it?" Rhendar came to stand at her side, the red slits of his visor pointed towards the sight in front of him. What would his face have shown if she'd been able to see it? It was hard to imagine his features as anything other than as hard and unyielding as the helmet that always covered them.

She turned back to the legionnaires. In another life, she might have stood among them. It was hard not to look at their green cloaks and think about what she had given up. There had been a time she'd thought of nothing else but having that cape around her shoulders and a varstaff in her hand.

She shook herself from her thoughts as Serric made his way towards them, his helmet tucked under his arm. He ignored Niole completely, but sent a short nod Zal's way. "Scout Captain."

Zal rolled her eye and grinned. "Squad Leader. Feeling especially formal today, are we?"

Serric didn't answer. He took up his place at Rhendar's shoulder, staring out at the line of legionnaires with a dark expression. She could see the energy of his flare rise around him, even if she could no longer feel it. Normally it was so controlled, so steady. Now it swirled restlessly, ready to burst loose.

"What are we waiting for?" he asked.

Rhendar's helmeted gaze never left the legionnaires. "Look a little closer and tell me."

His voice was as calm as ever, but that did nothing to stop the rush of dread Niole felt at his words. She pulled her helmet over her head and enhanced the optical display to look out across the empty plateau that stretched between where they stood and where the legionnaires were waiting. Nothing seemed out of the ordinary. The legionnaires were standing steady and disciplined, waiting for something. Waiting for...

She froze. "Tarvan Varantis. He's not there."

"What?" Serric narrowed his eyes and slid his helmet on. After a moment, he snorted. "Coward. Doesn't even have the spine to show up to peace talks, let alone show his face on the battlefield."

She ignored the contempt dripping from his voice. Something wasn't right. Tarvan was pragmatic, ruthless even, but she'd never heard of him shying away from a fight. More than that, it didn't make a damn bit of sense. No legionnaire footsoldier had the authority to negotiate in a summit as delicate as this. The situation was too precarious, too fragile. The stakes were too high. Even Rivus—

Her heart jumped and she turned her eyes back to the waiting legionnaires, searching for his distinctive, hulking frame. There were other dachryn standing tall, but none with his plate markings. None with the scars she'd left him with.

He wasn't there.

She turned to Rhendar. "Something is wrong."

"I know." The words sounded weary and resigned, as if he'd expected this all along. But still, he didn't move.

The dread was gnawing at her now, too persistent to ignore. The barely-there atmosphere was too still, too quiet. Like the moment of peace on Vesyllion before the sorborite rods had hit.

Across the barren plateau, something was stirring among the legionnaires too. Heads moved from side to side, exchanging uncertain looks and words she couldn't make out. They looked as restless as she was. Like they could sense something wasn't right, but didn't know where to turn for answers.

"Rhendar, I think we should pull back." She glanced at him, but he said nothing in reply. "I don't like this. Not one bit."

"For what?" Serric folded his arms. "You don't think we can handle a couple of hundred legionnaires if it comes down to it?"

"It's not the legionnaires I'm worried about," Rhendar said. "Look at them. They don't know what's happening any better than we do." He shook his head. "Niole is right. Something else is at play here. We need to pull back and regroup. We can discuss what to—"

He stopped short at a chime from Niole's wrist terminal. The sound cut through the thin atmosphere like a warning siren, sending a chill down her headtails.

She pulled up the connection, her mouth running dry when she saw the incoming signature. It was Rivus.

"Go on," Rhendar said, a note of urgency in his voice. "Answer it."

Niole opened the channel. "Rivus? What's going on?"

At first, there was only a crackle of static and a distant roar in the background. Then a voice came through, muffled and barely intelligible over the crackling of the signal. "Ni...can hear...need to get...."

"Rivus?" She tapped the interface, trying to clean up the transmission. "Damn it, something is blocking the signal."

"Repeat...out of there." The connection buzzed with interference. "Going to...you're all...ambush."

The line fizzled and died, leaving the last word ringing in her ears.

Ambush.

Rhendar was already moving. He grabbed Zal by the shoulder and pointed her towards the transports. "Get as many on as you can, and tell the rest to start running. We don't have time to wait."

The rest of his words were lost to the pounding in her ears. *Ambush.* Part of her wondered if she had misheard, if they all had. This couldn't be how it was going to end, not after all they'd done to make it happen. Rivus had been so sure, so certain. She'd believed him when he'd told her they could do this.

Fyra, where was he?

She scanned the bleak, bare horizon but could see nothing past the rows of legionnaires. Their expressions had changed from uncertainty to confusion, and for the first time, she sensed a ripple of fear make its way through their ranks. It spread quicker than her eyes could keep up with, turning their disciplined formation into a surging, swelling tangle of chaos.

Guilt gripped her heart. "Do you think they know?"

"If they don't, they'll figure it out soon enough," Rhendar said grimly. "Now move."

She gave them one last look and was ready to turn away when something bright blinked in the distant corner of her vision. It blazed across the dark red sky, moving fast across the horizon like a passing comet, or...

Her breath caught in her chest. "Shit. Oh...shit."

Rhendar turned and froze. "We're too late." He grabbed her arm and hauled her with him, pulling her across the uneven terrain. Every footstep sent shockwaves through her legs, and her lungs burned with the effort of every breath.

They were too close. The incoming missile was moving too fast. They were never going to make it.

"Serric!"

She spun around at the sound of Rhendar's voice, her blood turning cold. Serric had slowed down and turned his back to them, his flare pulsing around his armour brighter and more vivid than she'd ever seen it. He stood with his fists clenched, staring down the missile like he was getting ready for a fight.

"No," she whispered. "He can't. He's going to—"

Everything turned white. Time slowed and stopped as a blinding glare filled her vision and robbed her of her sight.

Then the shockwave hit and she was thrown back by a force

that crushed her chest and squeezed the air from her lungs. She hurtled through the air like she weighed nothing, then hit something hard and rolled, the ground pummelling her body over and over until she finally came to a stop.

She couldn't move. Everything felt broken. The visor of her helmet was cracked, and the rough, dusty surface of the planet pressed itself against her nose. Every breath was a sharp, shallow struggle. Her ears pounded with a tinny echo that sent waves of agony through her head. She couldn't hear anything. Not Rhendar, not the cries of the other Idran-Var, not even the sound of her own breathing.

A jolt of pain shot through her neck as she tried to lift her head, and she cried out. Her throat was tight and raw, and she could taste the metallic tang of blood on her tongue.

"Rhendar..."

Dark clouds of smoke billowed towards her, obscuring her vision. Rocks were falling from the blackened sky, splitting the ground open as they hit the surface. One smashed into a struggling Idran-Var, crushing the armoured shell so all she could see were arms and legs jutting out in strange, disfigured angles.

They had always seemed so invincible. But even Idran-Var armour couldn't stop everything.

She lifted her chin again, gasping at the pain. Something was swirling in the air around her. It wasn't the black of the smoke and dust. It wasn't the red spilling from the sky. It was something else, something alive. Brilliant colour pulsating like a heartbeat around her.

That was when she saw him. A dark shape among the haze, arms outstretched and head bowed. The energy was streaming from him in a rush of colour and light, lingering in the atmosphere as it left him. But it was fading. Even now she could see it surrendering to the smoke surrounding him.

Then he fell.

"Serric!" she screamed, his name ripping from her throat.

She pressed her hands into the ground and forced her body to its knees, ignoring the dizzying pain that surged inside her. Every movement took the entirety of what little strength she had left. She bullied her legs into stretching upwards, forced her spine to straighten.

One step. Then another. She pushed forward, trying not to choke on the blood she was coughing up from her ruined throat. Her lungs burned, and something in her right knee screamed every time she put weight on it. But she couldn't stop. She wouldn't.

He was lying crumpled on the ground when she reached him, his body silent and unmoving. The energy from his flare had dissipated around him in a fine mist.

She dropped to her knees and fumbled around for the retraction mechanism for his helmet. The armoured casing slid back around his face, revealing blue skin marred with black, bloody bruising. His eyes were unfocused and lifeless, but Niole could hear a faint wheeze of breath from between his torn lips, and her heart leapt.

"That's it," she said. "Keep fighting, like you always do."

The ground shook and she stiffened as another shape made its way through the thick smoke. A moment later, she caught sight of the familiar gleam of Idran-Var armour and let out a breath of relief. "Venya?"

"I'm here." She made her way to Niole's side, followed through the smoke by Zal and Rhendar. Rhendar was limping badly, his armoured arm drooped over Zal's shoulder as the smaller human woman fought to keep him upright. His armour was covered in dust and debris, and his head rolled limply from side to side as he staggered forward.

Venya turned her huge head to look at Serric. "What happened?"

Before Niole could answer, Rhendar let out a pained grunt. "He flared. He couldn't stop the missile, but he was able to shield us from the worst of the explosion. We'd all be dead if it wasn't for him."

Niole shuddered, remembering the blinding light the moment the missile hit. It should have torn through them easily, blasting them to pieces across Aurel's surface. She doubted the legionnaires managed to escape before it had hit. She imagined their bodies blackened and burning, scattered from where they'd stood.

Tarvan killed them. The realisation chilled her. *He sent them out here to die, just to have a better chance of killing us.*

And what of Rivus? He'd tried to warn her, but did that mean he'd known?

Zal pulled her helmet off and tapped the edge of her cybernetic eyegraft, looking Serric up and down as she did so. She gave a tight grimace and shook her head. "His internal injuries are severe. If he's to have a chance, we have to get him out of here now." She knelt down, gently cradling his head in her hands. "Venya, I need you to help me move him. Nice and slow, we don't want to...Venya?"

Venya didn't answer. She was looking at something in the distance, her orange eyes like slits. Her huge hand tightened around the glaive on her belt. "We don't have time to move him. They're coming."

Rhendar shook his head. "I watched that missile hit, *jal-var*. Those poor bastards never stood a chance. They're dead."

"They're not the ones I'm worried about."

Niole followed Venya's gaze into the murky distance. The smoke was thinning, drifting apart to reveal a dozen armour-clad figures making their way across the ash-covered ground. Their cloaks hung pristinely around their shoulders, unblemished by the carnage around them. The varstaves in their hands crackled with electricity. They moved past the burning bodies with such indifference that it could only mean one thing: they had known what to expect.

Tarvan Varantis had come to finish what he started.

Zal cursed and pulled her helmet back on. "Right, change of plan. Niole, you get these two out of here. I don't care if you have to drag them, just make sure they get to the transports." She turned to Venya, giving her a solemn, resigned nod. "Venya and I will buy you as much time as we can."

"You can't." Niole looked between them, her chest tightening. "There's too many of them. You won't stand a chance."

Venya gave a huff of breath. "We'll slow them down."

"We'll do more than that." Zal punched her shoulder. "We're Idran-Var. We resist. Until the end." She turned to Rhendar. "It's been an honour, war chief. We'll be with you on the battlefield, wherever you are."

Rhendar lowered his head. "*Idra ti gratar*, Zal."

"*Idra ti vestar*, my friend. Make sure you keep fighting."

"No." Niole tried to push herself to her feet, but her legs buckled. "You don't have to do this. We can make a run for it."

Even as the words left her mouth, she knew they were useless. Zal tilted her head in the same faceless smile she was so used to seeing from Rhendar. Then she placed a hand on Venya's towering shoulder and led her out towards the approaching legionnaires. Towards the battle they'd always been ready to fight.

Across the scarred, scorched ground between them, the legionnaires paused. A couple of them twisted their varstaves, sending a volatile hum of electricity ringing through the thin atmosphere. The black-red sky reflected off their armour like blood. This wasn't going to be a fight. It was going to be an execution.

One of them stepped forward ahead of the rest. His cloak was brilliant white and trimmed in gold. The plates of his bony face were covered in light grey markings. When she met his eyes, the coldness of them shot daggers into her heart.

Tarvan.

He moved quicker than she could have imagined, closing the distance between himself and Venya with a swift, powerful strike. Venya reared back but was too slow in bringing up her glaive to fend off the volley. When she spun away, Niole could see a long scorch mark down the middle of her chest, leaving the armour there black and brittle. A few more well-aimed strikes in the same place and Tarvan would be able to slice through her armour like it was soft flesh.

Zal leapt forward to help but was barged out of the way by one of the other legionnaires, a thick-limbed jarkaath. The jarkaath raised his varstaff high, ready to bring it down on her, but Zal rolled clear and whipped out her glaive, extending both ends with a flourish. She met the blow with a grunt as the silicone-coated end of her glaive absorbed the voltage harmlessly.

Then another legionnaire charged in from the side with a vicious kick, sending Zal flying into the dirt at their feet. She tried to block the first incoming blow with her glaive, but soon there were too many of them around her. They swarmed her like the vinehounds back on Vesyllion, each vicious strike scoring her armour with a current that would soon break it apart.

Niole couldn't breathe. She couldn't find it in her muscles to move, let alone summon the strength to drag Rhendar and Serric away to safety. Zal and Venya were so close. She could see each time they staggered under a blow, each time the ferocity of the legionnaires' strikes brought them to their knees.

In the middle of it all, she could see Tarvan. He swung his varstaff with a power and grace that made her dizzy. He moved with such sure-footedness that he seemed to know exactly where his enemies would be before they did. Each time he landed a strike, the look in his eyes only grew colder.

Rage swelled inside her like she'd never known before. Vesyllion had burned at his command. His own legionnaires had been blown to pieces in a tactical game. Slaughter followed him across the galaxy.

And she'd been foolish enough to think there had been a chance for peace.

She flinched as he landed a brutal strike across Zal's damaged helmet, sending her spinning to the ground. He attacked with a certainty that was terrifying and relentless. He would never stop. Not now, and not after. Killing her friends would only be the beginning. The end would only come when the Idran-Var no longer existed.

She pushed herself to her feet and reached a hand to her belt. It was empty. She looked down, dazed. The shockwave from the explosion must have knocked her weapons loose. She had nothing.

"Don't you dare think...of making a run for it..."

Her heart raced as she turned to look down at Serric. His brow ridge was set in a pained frown, and blood spluttered from the corners of his mouth as he tried to speak. "No running, not this time," he said, his voice weak. "You need to fight."

Something seized in her chest. "I don't have anything to fight with."

"Yes you do." He coughed, more blood spilling out of his mouth. "Yes you do," he said again, softer this time. "I was never trying to fix you, Niole. You were never broken. All I wanted to do was make you see that."

He grimaced, and suddenly his flare was back, surrounding him in swirls of energy. He pushed it towards her. Unstoppable. Unrelenting. "Take it," he said. "You don't need a weapon. You're enough."

"But—"

"He's right, Niole," Rhendar interrupted, turning his helmeted head towards her. The red lights in his visor seemed dimmer, like he was slipping away. "You don't need to be afraid of what you can do. They do."

She stepped back, rocking unsteadily on her feet. Somewhere in the distance, she heard a scream of pain. The air thrummed with electricity from the varstaves. The ground under her feet rumbled with shockwaves. There was a tear somewhere in her combat suit. The cold rushed in, turning her arms to ice and making them tingle with...

No. It wasn't the cold. It was something else entirely.

It happened so slowly, so imperceptibly, that it was too painful to believe. It came from somewhere far away, somewhere so impossible it felt out of reach. But it came. It skimmed across her skin and sparked something buried so deep inside her she thought it had been lost forever.

She gasped as a flare rushed through her, filling her body and bursting free from her skin. It raced across her arms and up the nape of her neck to the tips of her headtails. It sent sensations through every nerve and made her giddy with each new breath she took.

It was like coming up for air. It was like being alive again.

Serric pushed his flare out violently and this time she caught it, wrapping it around her like the legionnaire cloak she'd never earned. Like the Idran-Var armour she'd never claimed. It was neither of those things, and yet it was more. It was *hers*.

She turned back to the legionnaires, her muscles twitching. Serric was still pouring the strength of his flare into her, and she gathered the energy around her like she never wanted to let go. She took his pain and his rage, and she made it her own. She coiled it inside her until it was ready to burst.

You don't need a weapon. You're enough.

The ground crunched beneath her feet with every step, sending clouds of dust and ash billowing around her legs. Her muscles no longer protested. Her knee no longer cried out in pain. It was all forgotten. All that mattered was the energy building inside her, waiting for her to unleash it.

The first legionnaire had his back to her. She let her flare swell, then reached out with a fury she'd never known she was capable of. His armour meant nothing. The way he squirmed and screamed meant nothing. All she had to do was reach inside him. She felt every tremble, every beat of blood. All the fragile little pieces of tissue that held him together, that made him what he was.

She curled her fist and tore him apart.

It was nothing like before, when they'd come for her on Pasaran Minor. Back then, she'd lashed out wildly, like a cornered animal with nowhere left to run. She'd been afraid of the power surging inside her. Afraid of what it was capable of.

Not anymore.

Something tugged at her and she turned to see another legionnaire approaching. A siolean, like her.

No, *not* like her.

The siolean was reaching out with her own flare, trying to draw on Niole's energy. But she was no *ilsar*. Even if she'd been capable of absorbing half the radiation Niole could, the intensity of it would have killed her. She couldn't control it. Not in the way she could.

Niole reached out a hand, catching the siolean's flare and wrapping it around herself. The siolean's black eyes widened as Niole pushed back and sent her flying across the rough, rocky surface. She landed with a sickening crack in a heap of broken limbs.

"Niole, watch out!"

She turned to see the jarkaath legionnaire advancing, varstaff in his claws, and stepped lightly out the way as Venya charged past. She knocked the jarkaath off his feet with a staggering blow and spun back to Niole's side, her breaths hard and heavy. A moment later, Zal was at her back, her glaive in one hand and a plasma pistol in the other.

She felt the energy from both of them pulsing through the shells of their Idran-Var armour. There was a time that might have frightened her. There was a time she'd have feared surrendering to the intoxication, unable to make the distinction between enemy and friend.

That fear was gone. Now she knew what she was fighting for.

They fought like one, covering each other's flanks and pressing for openings. Any time one of them moved, the others would follow. Their footsteps were fluid, their attacks swift and in perfect timing.

Even so, she was beginning to tire. The weariness she'd held at bay was creeping back into her muscles along with the pain from her injuries. The more she reached for her flare, the more it slipped away from her. Each breath burned her lungs more than the last, and it was getting harder and harder to keep up with Zal and Venya's furious pace.

The blow came without warning. One moment she was on her feet, bracing herself against the bulk of Venya's back. The next she was on the ground, half of her face on fire as she coughed up blood onto the dirt below.

Tarvan stood over her, his blue eyes like ice. "Rivus thought I was too hard on you," he said, his chest heaving. "He thought the anti-radiation meds were an unnecessary cruelty."

He swung his varstaff over his shoulder and cracked it down on her injured knee. Her simple combat suit offered none of the protection of the Idran-Var armour, and she screamed as the voltage ripped through her body.

"He was wrong," Tarvan continued, pacing around her as if nothing had happened. "I should have thrown you in the Bastion the moment you came crawling back."

He brought the varstaff down again, striking her in the

middle of her back. Niole cried out and fell flat against the ground, choking on the dust that plumed around her face. Pain wracked every part of her body. She tasted bile in her mouth and spat it out.

"You were never a legionnaire. You were never one of us."

She rolled over, the edges of her vision black and blurred. Tarvan's words came from somewhere far away, filled with truths that could no longer hurt her. It didn't matter what he said. What mattered was she didn't care anymore.

"You're right." Another voice filled her ears, gruff and mechanical. "She's one of *us*."

She lifted her head in time to see Rhendar grab Tarvan and smash his armoured head into him. Tarvan stumbled back, dazed by the impact, but quickly regained his footing and swirled around to counter Rhendar's follow up. Varstaff clashed against glaive, each strike ferocious and unyielding.

A knot of worry twisted in her stomach. Rhendar was still weak and limping. Each time he parried one of Tarvan's blows, he staggered back, unable to summon the strength he needed to mount a counterattack. Tarvan was brutal and unrelenting, pressing forward with strike after strike. It wouldn't be long before the prolonged assault wore Rhendar down, leaving him at Tarvan's mercy.

She tried to move, but it felt like the planet itself was weighing her down. Her limbs were too heavy, her chest too sore. She reached down and pulled the metal chestpiece off her combat suit, tossing it aside. She did the same with her vambraces and her heavy boots until she was lying with only her light undersuit between her skin and the dirt.

Weapon, she thought to herself. *I need a weapon.* She scrambled around until her fingers wrapped around something warm and metallic. It was a varstaff, dropped by one of the fallen legionnaires. She pulled it close as she fought her way back to her feet. The weight of it in her hand should have felt strange after all those months training with the Idran-Var glaive. It should have been an unwelcome reminder of the life she'd left behind.

Instead, it was like remembering the touch of an old friend.

She rushed towards Tarvan, swinging the varstaff to bring it crashing against his. A shower of sparks exploded between them and she jumped back. There was a reason that legionnaire cadets always sparred with low-voltage training staves. A varstaff wasn't meant to fight a varstaff. Each clash sent a violent surge of electricity through the air, sparking wildly.

She circled back and blocked another blow, ducking away from the fork of electricity that sprang from the impact. Each sizzle was a reminder of the current that promised to sear her skin. Each shockwave through her arms was a reminder of how easy it would be for him to break a bone with a single strike. She had no armour, only the weapon in her hands.

You don't need a weapon. Serric's voice echoed in her ears. *You're enough.*

She waited for a moment, both hands wrapped tightly around the varstaff. She could feel each pulse of blood beating through her palms. She could feel the dampness of her skin as she slid her fingers along the metal. She could feel the hum of electricity in the air in front of her.

She could feel Serric.

She let her hands open and dropped the varstaff. Tarvan widened his eyes and started forward, a snarl across his jaw plates. One step closer, then another, until he was almost upon her. Until she could see the icy blue of his eyes, and in them, the reflections of all the lives he'd taken. All the bodies he'd left behind.

Part of her wondered if he could see the same in her.

She reached out, drawing her flare close. Some of it was still coming from Serric, rushing into her with all his anger. But the rest of it belonged to her. It poured forth from her arms, from her headtails, from every pore of her skin. It wrapped itself around Tarvan and lifted him into the air until he hung suspended against the black-red sky.

His bone plating contorted in pain, but there was no fear in his eyes. Not even hatred. Just a cool, composed fury which burned as bright as it ever had. He was helpless. He was—

"Niole, wait!"

She turned her head only a fraction, unwilling to take her eyes off Tarvan. Then she saw it out of the corner of her eye. A speeder abandoned in the dirt. A dachryn running towards them. A dachryn whose black and white face markings had been marred by the same energy she held Tarvan with now.

Rivus skidded to a halt, as if he was afraid to come any closer. "Niole, please. I know what he's done. I swear to you, I'll make sure he answers for it. But please, not like this." His voice was rough and rasping behind heavy breaths. "If not for him, then for me."

Tarvan's heartbeat echoed under her skin. One squeeze from her flare and she could end his struggle. She could rip him apart from the inside out. To hesitate would be a betrayal to all the lives lost at his hand.

"He's lying." Tarvan looked down at her, his eyes hard. "If you let me go, the day I answer for what I've done will be the day the last Idran-Var falls. That is the only truth of this war we are fighting."

Fyra, he wasn't afraid at all. He didn't see all the blood and bodies along the way, even if he was the next in line to fall. All he saw was the end. An end where the Idran-Var no longer existed, no matter what it took to get there.

She had no choice.

"Niole, no!"

By the time Rivus's cry reached her ears, it was already too late. She unleashed her flare from the depths inside her, letting it tear through every cell, every synapse, every piece of tissue that held Tarvan Varantis together.

She felt everything. Every vein bursting. Every muscle fibre ripping apart. Every bone snapping and splintering under the crushing force of her flare. She tore apart everything he'd ever done. Every sorborite rod dropped on Vesyllion. Every Idran-Var and legionnaire blown to pieces by his missile. They came undone in brilliant bursts of red and fell to Aurel's bloody surface alongside his shining armour.

His body hit the ground with a thud. It was over.

Someone was pulling at her shoulder. She heard voices calling for an evacuation. None of it mattered. Not next to the sight of Tarvan's body lying broken in front of her. A tyrant, vanquished.

It should have been satisfying. Instead, as the touch of her flare left her body and disappeared into the air, all she felt was numb.

Rivus crashed to his knees, bowing his head over Tarvan's lifeless body. The sheen of his cybernetic arm glimmered in the low light as he curled his metal claws around the stained white cloak.

Niole couldn't say anything. There were no words she could offer to make this right. She'd done what she'd had to, knowing what it would cost. Maybe there was a part of Tarvan that would live on in her because of that.

When Rivus finally looked up at her, something had broken behind his eyes. "He would have killed you all," he said, his voice hollow. "I saved your life."

"And in return, you'll leave with yours," she said, swallowing painfully. "That's all I can give you, Rivus. There's no way back from what happened here. We're at war now."

"I know." Something hardened in his voice. It had an edge to it now, ready to sever whatever it was they'd manage to build between them. "Niole, if I see you again..."

"I know," she echoed. She'd have promised the same if he'd taken from her what she had from him. But the hurt of hearing it stung more than any blow from Tarvan's varstaff. Rivus had forgiven her once. She could not expect him to do it again. Not for this.

She left without another word, keeping her eyes fixed on the bleak horizon for the evac transports that would take her away from this forsaken planet. But all she could think about was Rivus, bent over Tarvan's broken body. Rivus, shaking with grief and rage and loss. Rivus, meeting her eyes with a dead stare and a promise.

The chill that Aurel's atmosphere sent through her thin layer of clothing was nothing compared to the realisation of what she had put in motion. Tarvan's death would not be the end of the bloodshed. It was only the beginning. The look in Rivus's eyes was all she needed to be sure of that.

They had not defeated their enemy. They had only replaced him.

SIXTEEN

KOJAN

Dusk fell over Rellion, and Kojan prepared himself to bloody his hands. This was what Ojara had done to him. This was what she had driven him to.

Did you really think I'd allow such programming to be put in my own son without a means of reversing it?

Even if it was a lie, he was too desperate to do anything other than believe it. The aching at the back of his head was constant. Earlier that morning, he'd coughed up blood. The quickening was breaking down his organs, devouring the parts of him that were still human. If he waited much longer, there would be little left of him to save.

There was no sound from Eleion's room as he slipped out of the penthouse suite. Every step he took was as quick and quiet as he could make it. Eleion needed Alvera. Her people needed her. She was their chance at a future outside of Kaath. A chance at choosing their own place in the galaxy instead of being confined to the inside of a breather mask. And here he was, willing to destroy that chance, all for a chance at saving himself.

It wouldn't have made any difference, he told himself. *She's already gone. We don't know how to wake her.* Even if they did find a way to bring her out of her coma, there were no guarantees she'd be the same. No guarantees she'd be able to build the cybernetics the iskaath were so desperate for.

If only telling himself that made it easier to believe.

The rain thundered down as he hurried across the rooftop to hail a skycar. It ran down the back of his neck and soaked the collar of his shirt, giving him a chill. It pattered off the cab's windows, obscuring the bright lights of the city in a gloomy haze. It turned his skin numb and drowned out all the thoughts in his head. By the time the skycar pulled up outside the medical facility, he felt like a ghost.

Alvera's ward was sectioned off from the rest of the building behind a guarded security checkpoint. Governor Cobus had assured them that only a few trusted medical staff and associates had access. The less people that knew about her, the better.

The quiet should have been a good thing, but Kojan couldn't help the shiver of trepidation that ran through him as the security guard scanned his credentials and waved him through the rain-splattered glass doors. Maybe he wanted to get caught. Maybe he wanted someone to stop him from what he was about to do.

The life support monitor attached to the lone medical pod bleeped faintly through the quiet. Alvera lay still and stiff, her skin pale and tinged with grey. Maybe shutting down the machinery keeping her alive would be a mercy. Maybe this was a way of letting her rest after everything she'd been through.

Or maybe those were lies he was telling himself to ease the nausea churning in his stomach.

He pressed a hand to the glass barrier around the pod and

felt the warmth coming from inside. He still had enough control over his cybernetics to override life support. It would be over in minutes. After she was gone, he'd finally be free of the hold she had over him.

He pulled up the interface on his wrist terminal. The holographic text flickered in front of his eyes. His whole arm was shuddering. There was no going back.

"If you were going to do it, you'd have done it already."

Kojan whirled around. There, sitting in the shadows at the far side of the room, was Maxim ras Arbor. The dim spotlights on the ceiling danced across the silver flecks in his coarse, dark hair as he stretched and pushed himself from the chair with a languid ease.

Kojan stiffened. "What makes you think that?"

"Because it's what I would have done if I were in your position." Max flashed a grin and took a step forward, his movements slow and prowling. "But you're not like me. Not like her either. So why don't you step away from that life support machine and tell me what the hell you think you're doing?"

There was no time to do anything but react. Kojan leapt forward, swinging an arm wildly towards Max. His knuckles brushed against fabric, a whisper away from connecting with Max's jaw, but he missed his mark and his momentum sent him stumbling forward.

Max wheeled around and brought his knee into Kojan's ribs. "Easy now," he said with a grunt. "All you're going to do is get yourself hurt."

Pain shot across his ribs and he doubled over, gasping for breath. But it wasn't just Max's blow, it was the reaction it had provoked in his cybernetics. They raged in his head, white-hot and buzzing so angrily the noise almost made him retch.

He stumbled away, trying to quell the dizziness. His implants were failing. They were at war inside him, struggling to keep him alive as much as they were slowly killing him.

There was only one way to survive what his cybernetics were doing to him, and that meant ending the life of the woman who'd created them.

He ducked under Max's arms and raced back towards the medical pod. Alvera was still lying there, her eyes closed under unmoving lids. He thumped his hands off the glass barrier. Nothing happened. The glass held firm. Not even the slightest crack splintered the pod.

He punched it again. "Why won't you die?" he yelled, ignoring the bloody gash that had opened up across his knuckles. "Die or wake up, just do something to get us out of this mess you put us in!"

Something thick and unrelenting wrapped itself around his neck, pulling him away from the pod. He thrashed against it, kicking frantically with both legs, but there was no escaping the strength of the force that had hold of him. The edges of his vision blurred and grew dark. In front of him, Alvera lay silently in the pod, as peaceful as she'd ever been. It wasn't fair. It should have been her. It was meant to have been her...

"That's enough, ras Arbor. I think he's got the point."

The pressure released around his throat and he slumped to the ground, blinking away the darkness. Each ragged breath tore at his lungs, and his head swam as he looked up in search of the voice that had saved him.

The click-clack sound of claws on the hard floor reached his ears before he saw her. She came out of the shadows, her scales gleaming under the lights, and fixed him with a solemn, yellow-eyed stare.

Eleion.

A long, weary hiss escaped the back of her throat. "What were you thinking, Kojan?" she said softly. "Did you think this would make things better?"

His throat was too raw to answer. Shame flushed his cheeks

red. All he could offer was a pitiable shrug. Nothing he could say would suffice. Not after what he'd almost cost her.

"Kojan," she said again. There was no anger in her voice, no resentment. Her eyes, which had once been so hard for him to read, were filled with nothing more than sorrow.

That only made it worse.

"She's killing me," he whispered, the words barely formed enough to leave his mouth. "She's lying there in that pod, barely clinging to life, but she's killing me a little more every single day. She can't help me, but she won't let me die in peace either. I just wanted…"

Eleion bowed her long neck, looking at the floor. "You really think you would have gone through with it?"

"I don't know."

"I do. And as much as it pains me to agree with ras Arbor, he's right. If you were capable of killing her, you'd have already done it. You didn't need us to stop you, Kojan."

"Didn't I?" He pressed both hands against his temples. "You don't understand what she's done to me. What they've both done to me. I was so angry, so damn desperate… I knew how much your people needed her, but I came here anyway. To kill her. To save myself. I don't know how you could ever forgive me for that."

"There's nothing to forgive," Eleion said firmly. "I won't hold a grudge for something that never came to pass. We *will* wake Alvera. Not just to save my people, but to save you too. I believe that. I need you to believe it as well. We're on the same side, my friend."

A hard lump formed in his throat. "I never should have lost sight of that. Ever since I arrived in this galaxy, you've always been there to pull me out of trouble."

"I always will. Until the end." She flashed him a sharp-toothed grin from her long jaws. "Bad habits are hard to break, after all."

Across the room, Max ras Arbor cleared his throat. "As touching as all this is, it's hardly fair for you to take all the credit, iskaath. I was the one who tracked him here, remember? You're lucky I offered to bring you along for the ride."

Eleion's spines turned rigid and she curled her neck around to glare at him. "I didn't think that was the kind of credit you normally cared about, mercenary."

"What is he talking about?" Kojan asked, picking himself up from the floor and trying not to wince at the twinge of pain that shot across his bruised ribs. "How did he know where to find me?"

"I had you tagged with tracking surveillance the moment you set foot on this moon. Thought it best I keep an eye out in case you tried anything stupid. Didn't expect this though." Max chuckled. "I had Alvera's number the moment I met her, but you? I thought you were meant to be the good guy."

"I got an offer I couldn't refuse. Surely you of all people would understand that," Kojan said. "Ojara can be persuasive when she wants to be. Once she realises I've failed, she'll probably turn to you next."

"She already did."

Kojan stilled. "What?"

"Received an encrypted transmission two days ago. Never took her up on her offer, but I figured I wouldn't be the only one she tried to bribe. That's how I knew to look out for you."

It didn't make sense. It was impossible to believe it. If he did, it would mean he'd lost more of himself than he ever wanted to imagine. How could Max have had it within him to resist Ojara when he could not?

"What happened?" Kojan asked sourly. "Money wasn't good enough?"

The grin disappeared from Max's face. "Wasn't about the money. Not this time."

His voice was heavier now. Gone was the sarcastic drawl,

the amused chuckle. For the first time since Kojan met him, Maxim ras Arbor looked deadly serious. There was a tightness in his jaw and a shadow behind his eyes that might have been rage or despair or both. Whatever it was that had changed him, it made him more dangerous than before. A man chasing a paycheck was an honest man, in a way. He didn't know what Max was chasing. He wasn't sure he wanted to find out.

Eleion let out a snort. "Not about the money? What is it about then? Don't tell me this is for Alvera. You don't give a damn whether she lives or dies."

"That's where you're wrong, iskaath." Max took a long, deep breath. "Don't get things twisted, it's not about any sentimentality for her. People like Alvera Renata tend to get what's coming their way sooner or later. I think she knew that on some level, as much as I did."

"Then what is it?"

Max shot Eleion a hard stare. "You were there, weren't you? You saw what happened when she activated the waystation. The temporal net caught every Coalition ship that followed you there. Now they're stuck in that dead zone waiting to die. Nobody is coming to rescue them. There's only so long you can make rations and recycled air last." He clenched his jaw. "My brother is on one of those ships."

It all made sense now. There had been too much tension in Max, too much desperation for a man who professed to care about nothing but credits. This wasn't about helping Cobus. It was personal.

Eleion leaned forward, her eyes glimmering with curiosity. "Your brother serves in the Coalition Corps?"

"No need to sound so surprised." There was a bleak look in Max's eyes now that the mask had slipped, but he forced a chuckle out anyway. "Can't have too many mercs in the family, it's bad for business. Little bastard was never cut out for my line of work anyway. Too idealistic. Too caught up in the bullshit fantasy of serving something bigger than himself. We stopped talking after I started working for Cobus. He never let me forget what he thought of me, though."

"Cobus is a secessionist, isn't he? Kind of goes against everything the Coalition stands for."

"You think the politics mattered to me? It was a job that paid well, nothing more." Max shrugged. "I made my choice, and Sem made his. Never thought it would get him killed."

A thick, heavy silence followed his words. This was what had been buried underneath Max's nonchalance and wry humour. This was what he was carrying with him. The inevitable death of his own brother.

"Why do you want to save her?" Kojan asked. "You've got as much reason to want her dead as anyone."

"Maybe I do. But as long as she's still alive, there's a chance we can make her undo all the shit she's done." Max's face was drawn. "I don't like leaving things up to other people. It's messy. But if the dead zone around Ulla Waystation isn't lifted, Sem will die. I need your captain to fix that."

"And if she can't?"

Max set his mouth in a grim line. "Then she'll answer for it instead."

Eleion broke in with a hiss of frustration. "What I don't understand is how Ojara even knew Alvera was alive, much less that she was here on Rellion. Someone must be feeding her information."

"It's Cobus," Max said. "The governor is getting impatient. He's wondering if he made the right bet. If Alvera never wakes up, if the people of New Pallas come through the waystation only to get trapped in that dead zone—"

"Then he's lost all the voices that might give weight to his secessionist movement," Eleion finished. She uncoiled her tail and began pacing back and forth on her long, scaled legs. "As long as she's in this state, Alvera's only use to him is as a bargaining chip. Stands to reason he'd put feelers out to see what kind of favours he could get for her."

"From Ojara?" Kojan frowned. "I know she's been going around calling herself chief diplomat, but I thought that was a symbolic title. How could she have the influence to pull favours for someone like Cobus?"

"She's made an ally, of course. Think about who would stand to lose the most if Cobus and the secessionists got their way. If humanity was no longer part of the Coalition, they'd no longer need representation at the assembly."

"The human ambassador," Kojan said, letting out a breath. "Alvera always thought there was another reason they didn't want to let New Pallas through the waystation. If we joined with the Rasnians and split from the Coalition, the ambassador would lose his position. He'd lose all his political power."

"So whose side is this Ojara on?" Max asked, raising an eyebrow. "Cobus's or the human ambassador's?"

"Neither. Both." Kojan let out a dry chuckle. "She'll play them off against each other until she's the last one standing. I've seen it before. Ojara always gets what she wants."

"Fucking politics." Max grimaced. "And you wonder why I prefer to follow the money?" He shot a sideways glance at Eleion. "Cobus was right. You do see a lot. How is it you understand this all so well?"

She snickered. "I'm an iskaath. My entire existence is political. When you're on the outside looking in, you get a pretty good perspective on how the galaxy works. Just because we don't have the power to do anything about it doesn't mean we can't see what's going on."

Her matter-of-fact tone sent another twinge of guilt to his already-knotted stomach. The iskaath had been shut out of galactic society for millennia. Shunned by their own colonists, all but ignored by the Coalition until it came to trade deals for Kaath's valuable resources. *Ash'thet,* the jarkaath called them.

Idle. Slovenly. All because they'd evolved along a different path, a path that bound them to their homeworld's toxin-rich atmosphere.

Alvera had the expertise to change that path for them, if they wanted it. He'd almost taken that choice away from them, all because he'd been foolish enough to forget the kind of person Ojara was. She hadn't changed. She was who she'd always been. A woman who could see nothing beyond the dream of an empire within her grasp. A woman who'd do anything to keep it.

"What are we going to do now?" Max asked, breaking into his thoughts. "I get the impression this mother of yours isn't going to give up. She's already tried twice. We don't want to be here the next time she sends someone to kill Alvera."

"We?" Eleion flashed her teeth. "Don't get me wrong, ras Arbor, I'm sorry about your brother. But that doesn't mean I trust you. I'd rather not wait for the credits to get too good for you to pass up."

He took a step towards her, square-shouldered and fists clenched. "I wasn't intending to give you much choice in the matter. I'm coming, whether you like it or not."

"You think so?" Eleion matched his stance, stretching her neck to its full length so she towered over him. Her long, thin jaws hovered dangerously close to his face. If it was a game of intimidation, it wasn't one Max was going to win. His broad chest and thick arms were nothing compared to the strength in Eleion's lean, lithe limbs. Kojan had seen her move. He knew what she could do.

"We're on the same side here," he said, pushing his way between them. "Whatever our reasons, whatever our feelings about her, we all need Alvera alive. If we can trust nothing else about each other, we can trust that." He turned to Max. "You're right. Ojara won't give up. If we want to keep Alvera out of her hands, we need to move her someplace safe."

Max took a step back, rubbing a hand across the coarse stubble of his beard. His dark brow knitted together in a troubled look. "That's the problem. There is no place safe on Rellion. If Ojara convinces Cobus to hand her over, she's as good as dead."

"Then we don't stay on Rellion. We find a way offworld."

"We don't have a ship," Eleion pointed out. "They impounded my cargo runner the moment we arrived, and I doubt they're going to let us walk into a hangar and fly away on one of theirs."

"That depends on who you ask, doesn't it?" A glimmer of amusement danced across Max's dark brown eyes. "I told you, iskaath. I'm coming whether you like it or not."

Kojan tried to ignore the frantic pounding of his heart. "You have a ship?"

"Oh, I have a ship. One you're going to like a lot. One that you're quite familiar with." He drew his mouth into a slow, satisfied smile. "Let's go get the *Ranger*."

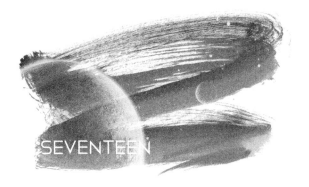

SEVENTEEN

RIDLEY

S he dreamed she was floating through an endless sea of
stars. The darkness had disappeared. So too had the
weightlessness. All that remained was the sense of drifting off.
Her ears echoed with the whispering sounds of each breath she
took. It was soothing, somehow. She could almost ignore the
rasping pain in her chest, the harsh glare fighting against her
closed eyelids, the soft, intermittent bleeping coming from
something beside her head.

Ridley opened her eyes. The grey metal curve of the ceiling
stared back at her, glinting with the reflections of dimmed
lights that were still too bright for the throbbing in her head.
She recognised this place. The ship's medbay was small, with
only a single cot, but the machines around her were shining
and state of the art. It was all intact. She was breathing. That
meant—

She tried to sit up, but her body wouldn't respond. Something was pressing down on her chest, crushing her with an

invisible weight. Her limbs were numb and the inside of her mouth was raw and dry. Every breath burned her lungs. But she was breathing. That meant she had survived.

She closed her eyes again. Returning to the darkness brought back the memories of what had happened out there in the vacuum of space. She remembered expelling the air from her lungs as she was sucked through the hole she'd made. She remembered her face burning—first from the explosion, then from the cold. She remembered her vision turning red and the popping sensation in her eyes. She had surrendered herself to the mercy of space, trusting it to do what she could not.

The Idran-Var had tumbled past her, a blur of metal limbs glinting under the ship's lights before the darkness engulfed them. They'd probably still been alive as they drifted loose into the void. Now nobody would ever find them.

She remembered fumbling around for the catch on her belt, her fingers dead and numb. Her fingers had slipped against the trigger and the cable shot noiselessly through the vacuum. She hadn't been able to hear if it had hit its mark, but the line had gone taut. That had seemed like a good sign.

She'd struggled through the pain and pulled herself along the cable blindly, one hand in front of the other, until she was floating back towards the ship. Towards the gaping hole she'd blown in its side. Towards the people she'd left there to try to save.

Drexious had been waiting for her, his scales glistening with flakes of ice and a breather mask around his long, thin jaws. He'd caught her as she drifted in, his arms tight and secure around her as he pulled her through the double doors. He'd screamed something she couldn't hear and a blurry figure with blonde hair and a garish indigo jacket swam into view.

Halressan.

She'd looked down at her, face hidden behind the emergency helmet she'd pulled over her head. Then she'd punched the controls for the auxiliary shutters and the world came back.

That was all Ridley could remember. The darkness had taken hold of her after that, confining her to restless sleep. She didn't know how long she'd been out for or what kind of mess her body was in. All she knew was that somehow, she was alive.

She tried to sit up again and winced as another spasm of pain ripped through her chest. It was too much. Even the slightest movement was enough to exhaust her. She sank back down in the bed, panting in shallow, wounded breaths.

"You're going to make things worse."

Footsteps echoed across the floor and Halressan appeared above her. Her face was pale and tired, her eyes bleary. Loose strands of blonde hair fell limply around her face. She tightened her mouth into a thin line. "You're lucky to be alive as it is. Don't push it."

Seeing her hurt worse than the swelling in her head, the burning in her lungs. It tore at a wound far deeper.

"She's awake?" Drexious popped up at the other side of the bed, peering down at her with anxious bronze eyes. "Stars, human. I didn't think you'd make it. You were out there for so long."

Ridley coughed, her throat blazing. "Turns out I'm hard to get rid of."

"You're telling me." He let out a low, snickering laugh. "That kind of vacuum exposure should have killed you. You had no right to survive that."

She knew he didn't mean anything by the words, but she couldn't help the way they wormed under her skin. They prodded at a part of her she'd never been able to let go of. The feeling of not being enough. Of never being enough.

"It was my cybernetic implants," she said. The words felt shameful, like an admission of guilt. "They have in-built trauma regulators to help our bodies survive things they normally couldn't. They must have compensated for the vacuum, for the lack of oxygen."

"They saved your life," Drexious said. "We tried to get you in as quickly as we could, but it took too long. We didn't have any warning. I don't know what you were thinking."

"I do." Halressan spoke up, her steely eyes keen and watchful. "She had an escape route planned from the start. She always does. It's how she survives."

She'd seen it. Of course she had. Skaile's private cabin had surveillance feeds all over the rest of the ship. Halressan had been watching her the whole time. Watching as she'd surveyed every storage locker and air duct, every maintenance hatch and access point, looking for a back door. That kind of planning was how she'd escaped Shaw on the *Ranger,* marking the fuel line as a potential escape route the first day she'd stepped on board. This time, she'd wired a wall with explosives and made sure never to go anywhere on the ship without the utility belt she'd prepared for this very outcome.

Drexious let out a low growl and glared at Halressan. "That's hardly the point. Contingency plans are all well and good until you get sucked out into a vacuum. She didn't know she'd survive when she spaced herself with those Idran-Var. You certainly didn't when you handed her over to save your own skin."

"It was her or me," Halressan snapped, her cheeks flushing red. "You can hardly blame me for looking out for myself, given you two dragged me into this fucking mess in the first place. She's still here, isn't she? It didn't matter in the end."

"It matters to me," Ridley said.

They both turned to look at her. Drexious with a pitying expression rippling across his scales, Halressan with a frown and a clenched jaw. Another wave of pain rose in her chest. She wasn't sure if it was from the damage to her body or the violent swirling of hurt and anger that had wrapped itself around her heart.

"It matters to me," she repeated, her voice low and quiet. "Those trauma regulators, the cybernetics that saved my life? I never had them back on New Pallas. I was a surfacer. We didn't get implants to help us survive. We had to fight and scrape for every single new day down there. You know what the Exodans called us? Obsolete. I thought coming here would change that. I thought people would see me differently." She let out a dry chuckle and grimaced at the stab of pain that followed. "Turns out you see me just the same as them. Expendable."

Halressan took a step backwards, the red blotches on her cheeks growing darker. "That's not true. I did what I did because I knew you had a plan. I knew you could save us. Just like you saved Drex from getting turned into a pile of mush on Skaile's floor. Just like you saved me from getting buried alive and suffocating down in those ruins on Sio. You think I care about whatever shit they put in your head?" Something in her voice cracked. "That's not what saved us. That's not what matters. You do."

Silence fell across the cramped medbay. The only sound was the faint bleeping from the monitor Ridley was hooked up to. She could barely hear herself breathe. The only thing ringing around her ears was the echo of Halressan's words.

That's not what matters. You do.

She wanted to push them away. They were too little to make up for what she'd done. Too little to heal the wound that had opened up inside her. But the wound had been of her own making too. She'd known the kind of person Halressan was and fallen for her anyway, despite it all. Or worse, maybe because of it all. She'd been unable to let her go, even when it made sense to do so. She'd brought her along, knowing all the things that might happen. Knowing all the danger it might bring for Halressan. For herself.

Halressan was staring at her, fists curled and chest heaving. The colour in her cheeks had paled, and the defiance in her eyes had turned into something more vulnerable, more uncertain. "I never wanted you dead, babe. But not all of us are cut out to be as self-sacrificing as you. I put myself first. Always will. I can't promise to change that."

"I know." The words were heavy as they left her mouth, like she was admitting the truth for the first time. "You've told me plenty of times who you really are. Maybe it's time I finally listen."

Halressan flinched, as if she'd been expecting something else. For a moment, something flickered across her eyes. It might have been pain, or remorse, but it was gone too quickly for Ridley to know for sure. Afterwards, the mask settled back in place and she reset her mouth into a thin line. "Good. Better for everyone if we all understand each other. Less nasty surprises that way."

Drexious let out a rasping laugh. "I'm sure you'll still manage, hunter. You never run out of opportunities to remind us what you're capable of."

"Keep pushing me and I'll give you another reminder right now."

"Stop it," Ridley said, glaring at them both. "My head feels like it's about to split open. If you want to keep sniping at each other, take it somewhere else and let me rest."

Drexious and Halressan exchanged a look. "About that," Drexious said, swishing his tail nervously. "We've not exactly got time to let you rest. You've been out for three days already. We've been drifting around the rip site, waiting for you to wake up. We need to punch this tunnel, and we need to do it fast."

"What do you mean?"

"Remember how you gave false coordinates to Skaile and then stole one of her ships?" Halressan folded her arms. "Turns out three days is plenty of time for her to send the Belt Cabal's finest selection of mercs and pirates on a hunting party after our sorry asses. If we wait around much longer, we'll be dead."

"Punching a tunnel is our best shot," Drexious added. "If they catch us now, they'll blow us to pieces. But space tunnels only work one way. If they follow us, they won't be able to destroy our ship without stranding themselves a decade away from home with no fuel and no supplies to get them back."

"I wouldn't be so sure," Halressan said darkly. "A decade would just give Skaile even more time to think about all the ways she could hurt us before she kills us."

Drexious ignored her. "They won't risk it. No number of credits is worth following a stolen ship into an illegally-punched tunnel that could lead them anywhere. And if they do chase us, they'll soon realise they need us intact if they want to get home."

"Unless one of *their* ships is a tunnel puncher."

He shook his long neck. "There's only a handful of ships in the entire galaxy with tunnel punching capabilities. The trade is highly regulated for a reason. It's no surprise Skaile got her hands on one, but there's no way these Belt Cabal scumbags have something that valuable in their possession. I've spent enough time around them to be sure of that."

Ridley didn't reply. She still remembered her first tunnel punching experience all those months ago when they'd left New Pallas. They hadn't known how it worked at the time. The *Ranger* hadn't been fitted with inertial dampeners strong enough to counteract the acceleration needed to rip a hole through the fabric of space. She'd almost died. Others on the crew had.

"No choice then," she said heavily. "We've been saying that a lot lately."

"That's what tends to happen when you steal from one of the Rim Belt's most notorious crime lords and go running across Idran-Var space," Drexious said, shrugging his shoulders. "I did warn you none of this would be easy. I hope whatever we find on this planet of yours is worth it."

It had to be. It was the only thing keeping her going. It was the only thing that could make all the shit she'd been through mean something. She'd survived it all for a reason. Maybe if she got to that planet, she'd finally understand what that reason was.

"Help me up," she said. "If we're doing this, I want to be sitting up front."

Halressan flicked her eyes over her. "You sure that's a good idea? You're barely holding together as it is."

Ridley ignored her. "Drex?"

He gauged her for a moment, the slits of his nostrils flaring, but then stepped forward and pulled one of her arms around his scaled shoulders. "For the record, I agree with the hunter on this one," he muttered under his breath, helping her to her feet. "But I also have too much first-hand experience of how stubborn you humans can get when you want to be difficult."

The walk to the cockpit was slow and painful. Drexious supported her as she hobbled along, her legs barely able to hold her up. Every breath was a torturous effort. No matter how gently she tried to inhale, she couldn't help the aching of her lungs each time they swelled with the ship's recycled air. The thought of sinking down into one of the flight chairs, the thick webbing of restraints strapped around her chest, was too much to bear. Maybe Drexious was right. Maybe she was being too stubborn.

"Hunter, you'll need to fasten her in. I've got to get us ready to go. We're out of time." Drexious gently slid her into one of the seats before hurrying over to his own. The lights from the nav console reflected in his gleaming eyes as he swiped through the interface.

Halressan's fingers worked deftly as she pulled the straps out and clicked them into place. They dug into her chest and tightened the pressure around her aching lungs. Ridley tried not to squirm. The discomfort was about more than just the pain. It was the way Halressan was standing over her, so close she could smell the soft scent of her skin, mixed with the strange musk of that damn vaxadrian leather jacket. It was the way her body moved so differently out of her armour. The way her chest rose up and down with shallow breaths. The way she set her jaw, fierce and determined.

The moment stretched between them, longer than it had any right to be. Ridley wasn't sure if she felt trapped in it or never wanted it to end. But a moment later, Halressan was gone, sliding into her own seat and pulling the straps securely around her.

"We're ready," she said gruffly.

"Just in time." Drexious glanced at the nav. "Looks like the Belt Cabal are getting close."

"How many?"

"Too many." He had a grim look on his long, lean face as he curled his claws around the controls. "Time we got out of here. Brace yourselves, humans."

It wasn't like the first time, back on the *Ranger*. Back then, she hadn't known what was coming. The acceleration had come out of nowhere and slammed into her chest like an invisible mallet. It had rattled her skull around until she couldn't see straight. All she'd been able to concentrate on was the cruel force slowly crushing her with the strength of its unrelenting grip.

This was different. The tug of acceleration wasn't as violent as before. It pulled at the skin of her cheeks and made something throb in her temples, but the overbearing sense of being crushed had been replaced by little more than an uncomfortable tightness in her gut.

"Inertial dampeners holding well. Capacity is green."

Drexious sounded like he was coming from somewhere far

away, his voice distorted and warped to her ears. Through the viewports, the darkness of space had disappeared. All she could see now was a blinding white light that smothered everything else. She tried to shield her eyes against it, but her arms were so heavy she could barely move them. Instead, she squeezed her eyes shut and curled her chin to her chest, waiting for it all to be over.

Her chair shuddered, sending vibrations through her legs. The whole ship was rattling. She gritted her teeth and tried not to think about disintegrating into a million tiny pieces.

Then the pressure was gone.

The juttering stopped. The rumbling of the hull faded into silence. The heaviness around her limbs lifted, and she let a long, thin breath out from between her teeth. There was something damp on her upper lip, and when she ran her tongue over it, she tasted something warm and coppery. A nosebleed, nothing more. A small price to pay compared to last time.

When she opened her eyes, the brightness had gone. They were floating through the darkness, free from the fierce burn of acceleration. She craned her neck to see Drexious and Halressan slumped in their chairs, bleary-eyed and panting. Shaken, but alive.

Relief flooded her chest. "We made it."

"Made it where?" Halressan's white-blonde hair was sticking to her forehead, her pale skin damp with sweat. "For all we know, we could have punched right into the middle of a black hole."

Drexious scanned through the readouts on the nav console. "We're a long way from home, that's for sure. Right on the cusp of dark space. There isn't much past here but a whole heap of nothing." He shook his spines and leaned closer to the holographic display. "We're in a binary star system. Well, calling it a system is a bit of a stretch. Mostly asteroids and gas clouds. But we do have something that looks like a planet."

Something seized in her chest. "That must be it. The place the coordinates on Sio were pointing to."

"I'll take us in for a closer look."

The ship's engines gave a low, smooth growl as the gentle tug of motion set in. Ridley could hardly breathe. This was it. This was what she had come here to do. The *Ranger* had never needed her. The moment they'd arrived, she'd been rendered obsolete. But out here, on the furthest fringes of the galaxy, she could make a difference. She could bring back the answers to questions that had lingered for millennia.

"I still don't understand how any of this makes sense," Halressan said, a frown on her face. "Drex said those ruins on Sio hadn't been touched since pre-spacefaring times. Yet somehow we find a bunch of dead sioleans dressed like space marines and coordinates to a planet at the ass-end of the galaxy. Either he was wrong, or there's some seriously fucked up shit going on."

"I wasn't wrong," Drexious shot back. "You were there. You saw as much as I did. Those ruins were ancient."

"Then how—"

"I think it's becoming clear this galaxy doesn't belong to us the way we thought it did," Ridley said quietly. "Someone else was here first. There are traces of them everywhere, if you know where to look."

It was all a matter of perspective. Back on New Pallas, the surface humanity had sprung from had been forgotten as the city rose towards the sky. What had once been a global language became miner patois. What had once been technology became historical trinkets. They had left behind what came before, until it became hard to remember it had even existed.

Memories—even on a galactic scale—could only stretch so far. In the end, they were all casualties of time.

"Look at the space tunnels," she said. "Tunnel punching

technology came from the waystations, yes? So how was it the galaxy was able to travel and spread so far before the waystations were even discovered?"

"The technology to create *new* tunnels came from the waystations," Drexious corrected. "But before the waystations were discovered, there were already naturally-occurring tears in the fabric of space that ships were able to use to take shortcuts from one system to another."

"Naturally occurring? Or created by someone else the same way we can create new tunnels now?" Ridley took a breath. "Those waystations didn't just appear out of nowhere. Someone built them. Someone created the colonies and left us with a way of returning to this galaxy. What for? What purpose could they have had?"

Drexious tilted his head. "The galaxy has given up trying to answer those kinds of questions. You're talking about events that happened tens of thousands—*hundreds* of thousands—of years ago."

"You'd be surprised how easily history can be lost when no effort is made to preserve it," Ridley said, her voice grim. "Or worse, when something is actively trying to eradicate it."

Halressan snapped her head towards her. "What do you mean?"

"Those ancient sioleans we found on Sio were hiding from something. They knew it was coming for them, so they sealed themselves in a vault and waited to die. Those coordinates they left were a last act of desperation. They're leading us to what they left behind."

"They're leading us to their buried treasure." Drexious gave an impatient huff. "What makes you think it's anything more sinister than that?"

"We had to punch a tunnel to get here. That means the sioleans who came to this planet before us gave up ten years of their lives floating through dead space to make sure they didn't leave a trace for anyone to follow. Whatever was hunting them was terrifying enough to make that kind of sacrifice seem worth it."

"Or whatever they were carrying was valuable enough," Drexious said, his bronze eyes gleaming in the dim light of the cockpit. "You don't have to invent some mysterious horror to explain what happened here. Money is a big motivator."

"So is extinction."

Silence chilled the cockpit. Her words hung there in the stale, recycled air between them. Now that she'd spoken them aloud, it was impossible to take them back. They echoed in her ears like an omen.

Halressan forced out a weak laugh. "That's a little bit dramatic, Riddles. In case you didn't notice, the sioleans are still kicking around. Our dear friend Skaile is proof enough of that."

"The sioleans we found in that vault weren't the same as the sioleans we know. You said it yourself—their weapons were like nothing you'd seen. Their suits were made of a material we couldn't identify. Whoever they were, they came from a different time. A time that's been forgotten."

"Does any of this matter?" Drexious glanced between them both, the scales around his jaws rippling in annoyance. "Whoever those sioleans were, they're long gone. We can't change that. What we can do is make ourselves rich by finding whatever cache they've hidden down on that planet. Trust me, whatever horrors you're imagining will seem a lot less of a concern with a few million credits to keep you warm."

Ridley turned away from him to look out of the viewport. The strange planet loomed ahead of them, half in shadow against the light of the pale twin suns in the distance. It looked like a jewel in the middle of the darkness, shining with rich blues and greens. The riches it promised weren't what Drexious was expecting, but that didn't mean there was nothing of value down there. The ancient sioleans had died leaving behind the message that brought them here. She owed it to them to find out what they left behind. She owed it to herself.

All her life, she'd been looking for answers. Maybe this was where she'd finally find them.

EIGHTEEN

THE DREAMER

The hive is getting restless. It writhes around her, ready to make its move. If she doesn't do something soon, she'll be out of time.

It's strange how easy it has become to exist here. She's almost forgotten what *before* felt like. What it meant to experience the sun on her skin or a breath of wind against her face. Those sensations have faded away, mingling with other recollections that don't belong to her: the surge of a flare building inside her, the tension of shuddering spindles down the back of her neck, the itchiness beneath her plated scalp from the growth of another bone spur.

The memories of the galaxy belong to her. Just as she now belongs to them.

"Don't forget to come up for air," a voice reminds her. "If you drown in here, it's over."

The voice is always there. It's familiar to her, but a distraction. It tugs her back from the edge when all she wants to do is dive over and lose herself in the repository of knowledge and memory surrounding her.

"Damn it, Alvera! Pull yourself out of this!"

The name touches something deeper than everything else. It carves its way through the endlessness of time and space and anchors her to a single person. A single life, still clinging on in the darkness. It reminds her of what she came here to do. It reminds her of who she is.

I am Alvera Renata.

She wrenches herself free from the grip of the hive and resurfaces, gasping into the vacuum as if expecting there to be air. Her mind sharpens and remembers itself, untangling her from the trap she walked into. She's free again, at least for now.

Chase appears in front of her, stiff-jawed and dark-eyed. "You were in there too long again."

"Not long enough." Alvera shakes her head. "There's too much to make sense of. It's impossible to find the kind of information we're looking for like this. Every time I come back out, I lose track of where I've been."

"Every time you come back out, you leave part of yourself behind. I can see that, even if you won't admit it. We didn't come this far just to give you up to the hive without a fight."

Alvera smiles at that. The woman she used to be could be accused of many things, some of them terrible, but none of them involved giving up without a fight. Whoever she is now, whatever is left of her, the ghost of that resolve remains. For better or for worse.

A sigh escapes her lips, disappearing into the white, sterile void she's surrounded herself in. Sanctuary, that's what she calls it. An empty place, partitioned from the rest of the hive. A place the curators can't reach. Chase is right. Every time she leaves, she loses part of herself to them. But staying here is as much of a death sentence as the risk of being absorbed into the hive. She can't change things from here. She can't stop what's coming.

"I'm not sure anyone can stop what's coming," Chase says, her words carrying a chill. "You've not felt their touch like I have. You can't imagine it unless you've been there. They are inevitable."

"If that was true, I wouldn't be here."

"You're a mistake. One they're adamant on putting right."

"They're welcome to try."

Her words carry the lingering whisper of an old bravado, one that doesn't quite fit her anymore. Even as she speaks, she can't help the shiver that runs through her. She senses the curators outside the sanctuary, lying in wait. She knows if she gives them too much, they'll take it all.

"You can't navigate the hive yourself, not without it consuming you," Chase says. "If you're determined to go deeper, we need to follow the footsteps of someone familiar with that kind of territory."

Alvera pauses. "The old dachryn?"

"He saved Rivus. Part of him must have existed outside the consciousness too. Maybe we can visit the places he's been, find out the things he discovered."

"Where do we find him? He could be anywhere."

Chase shrugs. "We know at least one place he's been. Let's start there."

Rivus. The link to the ghostlike dachryn lies within his mind. If she follows it, she might be able to find him. All she needs to do is bridge the gap between her mind and Rivus's.

She reaches out through time and space, searching for him. It's easier now she's done it before. Sharing his memories has left a connection between them, like the faintest thread joining their minds across a distance too impossible to comprehend. She follows it through the darkness, leaving behind the white void of the sanctuary.

She knows she's found him when the shapes of the galaxy start to make more sense than they did before. His memories chart a journey from a barren red planet on the border of the Rim Belt back to the allied systems. He's like a light guiding her through the darkness, showing her the way.

The moment she reaches him, a wall of grief hits her. She crashes into it like it's a barrier keeping her out, like there's nothing left of him but this raw, pained anguish. She can't make sense of anything else but loss.

She's no stranger to grief. She's lost people too. But those losses are so far removed in time and distance she's almost forgotten the pain they once caused. Rivus's grief is like a wound reopened. It brings the worst of her own pain flooding back. It's too much to bear.

She reaches into him, even though the agony of it makes her want to recoil. She follows the connections inside him, the fingerprints of the places he's been and the people he's known. Her heart breaks for the dachryn he loved, bloodied and crumpled in his arms. Her chest swells with rage at a nameless siolean staring back at him with soulless black eyes. She pushes them aside and searches for the one she's come here to find, the dachryn that's been haunting his memory.

The traces of him are different from the rest. He's like a ghost, leaving only echoes of his presence behind. Rivus was able to catch glimpses of it, but she sees it all. It's a trail leading back hundreds of millennia to a time she can't comprehend.

There are a million different fracture points to pick from. She focuses on one of them and takes the plunge.

———

The memory she awakens in is solid around her. She can smell sulphur and smoke in the air. She can see the faint outline of the sun in the yellow-grey sky. The ground trembles with vibrations from the huge surface transports rolling towards her. There's no haze, no dream-like filter. Just a memory, perfectly preserved.

The dirt beneath her feet explodes and she dives out of the way to escape the worst of the blast. Her ears are ringing with the sound of gunfire and screams. She's in the middle of a warzone with no way to pull herself out.

I am Alvera Renata, she reminds herself. *I will not forget who I am. I will not allow myself to drown here.*

Another explosion sends debris flying her way and she scrambles for cover, trying to ignore the breathlessness tightening her chest. What would happen if she died here in this memory? Would she wake back up in her sanctuary, lucid and unscathed? Or would her death be all the curators needed to absorb her into their hive?

Already she can feel herself slipping away. The memory is so vivid she begins to forget about what might exist outside of it. She runs across the terrain in a heavy, lumbering gait that doesn't belong to her. It's not the way a human would run. But that part of her is fading. Her hands are thick and bony, gripping a rifle that should have been too large and unwieldy for her to hold.

I am...Alvera Renata. She grits her teeth, struggling to force the words out. *I will not forget... I will not drown...*

Someone is fighting alongside her. She's familiar somehow, but she can't quite place her. "You're drowning," she says.

No. I will not allow myself to drown here.

"You're forgetting who you are."

I will not forget who I am.

"Remember what we came here to do. Remember the person you were. Remember your name.

I am... It's on the cusp of her memory, hovering out of reach. *I am...Alvera Renata.*

It's like she's blown a hole through the fabric of the memory itself. Everything comes rushing back. Chase appears beside her, wearing a grim expression on her face.

"That was too close," she says. "We need to get out of here while we still can."

Alvera shakes her head. "Not without finding him."

"We'll never find him if the hive gets you."

She opens her mouth to reply, but an ear-splitting roar cuts through the air before she can speak. A huge, towering alien rises from behind the makeshift barricade she's crouched against. White, leathery skin protrudes from behind its armour, hanging in loose folds. Its forehead is bulbous and domed, its eyes beady and yellow. It looms over them with a snarl, revealing fang-like teeth and a black tongue.

"What the hell is that?" Chase hisses, scrambling backwards in the soil.

Alvera can't answer. She can't take her eyes off the advancing alien. The sight of it freezes her to the spot. Even as it reaches for the thin-barrelled plasma rifle strapped to its hulking leg, she doesn't move. She stares at it, unable to comprehend what she is seeing.

The alien levels the rifle at her head. It hums with energy. In a moment, it will all be over. Still, she can't move. What she's looking it is more than a memory, more than a ghost. She's looking at a creature that no longer exists.

"What are you standing there for? Move!"

Something knocks her off balance and she falls to the ground, rolling over in the wet soil. Her hair is damp across her forehead, and she pushes the strands out of the way to see a dachryn barge through the barricade and into the pale, snarling alien. He pulls a rifle from his shoulder and fires three shots into the huge forehead of the creature, leaving behind smoking, scorched holes in its gristly skin.

He turns to Alvera. The thick bone-plates of his exoskeleton are cracked and splintered from age. His yellow face markings are faded and pale. He fixes her with a keen, observing stare, and when she looks into his milky grey eyes, she knows exactly who he is.

The dachryn general. She's found him.

His heavy plated jaw is set in a tight line. "You shouldn't be here."

"I know. But I had to come."

He sighs at that, as if expecting the answer. "No doubt you believe that. You probably believe finding me is some kind of victory, too." He shakes his thick, bony head. "It's not. Your time has come. Just like mine came. Just like it came for the tens of thousands before me. There is a method to how the galaxy works, Alvera Renata. I've seen it happen time and time again. The faces change, but the pattern stays the same. It's as inevitable as they are."

"They? You mean the curators?" Her heart hammers against her ribs. "What do you know about them?"

"Everything," he says. "And nothing. I've watched your thoughts. I know the terms by which you've come to define them. Curator. Hive. You apply these names in the belief you understand them, but the truth is you cannot understand them. You will never understand them."

Anger rises in her chest. "I understand enough. I know they're coming. I know nobody in the galaxy is safe from them unless—"

"Do you know you can do nothing to stop them?" He regards her with solemn eyes. "If not, then you know nothing."

His dismissiveness is curt and free of emotion. There's no contempt in his words, but no pity either. Just the bare, harsh truth of a reality she doesn't want to accept. She's given up too much for this to be the end.

"I saw you in Rivus's memory," she says. "You saved his life. Why would you do that if everything is as hopeless as you say?"

"I tried to stop him from making a mistake. The same

mistake I made, and countless others before me. But once a thing has been set in motion, it cannot be undone." He shakes his head. "Once you have seen the galaxy die as many times as I have, you learn to accept the inevitability of extinction."

His words send a chill through her. One she can't ignore. One she would be foolish to fight against.

But fighting is all she can do. It's all that's left of her.

She glances around at the scarred terrain, at the smoke-covered sky. A war-torn world that exists only in memory. "What is this place?"

"We called it Rybur. It's been known by thousands of names since." He turns his grey eyes towards her. "You may know it as Krychus."

She lets out a breath. "The dachryn homeworld?"

"What's left of it. This was near the end of our fight. We were overwhelmed by the enemy, the servants of those you call curators."

Alvera looks down at the corpse of the pale alien, the bullet wounds in its head scorched and black. "These creatures, where did they come from?"

"Beyond the waystations. Before that..." The old dachryn gives a weary shrug. "They were once of this galaxy, like us. But they were excised from the experiment long ago. Now they serve as the curator's thralls."

"Thralls?"

"Empty-minded shells of the sentient beings they used to be. Bodies bred from genetic material with no minds, no memories of their own. The curators use them as shock troops. Even a mindless horde can defeat a well-armed military defence through sheer numbers." He looked down at the fallen alien. "These, we called the azuul. There were others. Huge quadrupeds with armoured skin. Winged mammals with camouflage hides. Sea-faring creatures that could spend hours beneath the waves. All of them inhabited this galaxy once. Now, they exist only to help cleanse it. Evolution necessitates extinction. This is how our civilisation was designed."

Designed. The word resonates somewhere deep inside her, tugging at a memory from another life. She closes her eyes, remembering how she stood in front of the assembly all those months ago and asked them the question they'd refused to answer.

Has it occurred to any of you that we appear to be test subjects in some freakish galactic experiment being conducted on a scale so immense it's almost un-fucking-fathomable?

It's always been there in front of them. They just refused to see it. The waystations had been benign for so long that the galaxy had stopped questioning their purpose. Maybe it was easier for them to believe than the alternative. Maybe if you didn't have the answers, it was better to pretend the questions didn't matter.

She knows differently now. She's seen how the galaxy measures time. A few hundred millennia of peace can pass in the blink of an eye. A civilisation can rise and fall without leaving a trace. All it requires is the infinite patience of a consciousness that will never run out of time.

When she opens her eyes again, the old dachryn is staring at her. His expression is hard to read, but there's no mistaking the tiredness in his voice. "Why did you come here, human? What could you possibly want from these memories apart from a warning of the pain and suffering that awaits your people?"

"Answers."

"And what would you do with them? The dead can't change things."

"I'm not dead. Not yet, anyway."

He pauses at that, confusion flickering over his eyes. "That's not possible."

"Why not? Rivus is still alive."

"The one you call Rivus does not exist here as we do. He

may be able to catch glimpses of the consciousness through the mark the curators left on his mind, but he's on the other side of the veil." He grinds his thick jaw plates together. "Believe me when I say that for you to exist here means there is no way back."

Don't listen to him.

Chase's voice comes from inside her, quiet and fearful. Her physical presence is gone, replaced by a whisper at the back of her head. Like she's retreated into the only place left that's safe.

He's one of them. Chase's voice is like a shudder in her mind. *He might have been awake once, but he's theirs now. The hive has him.*

Alvera doesn't say anything. The old dachryn is still staring at her. She can see something else in his expression now. A shadow of what she's been trying to run from, trying to escape.

The curators didn't need to find her. She's found them.

"They got you, didn't they?" she asks calmly. "That's the price you paid for saving Rivus. Not even your memories are safe from them now."

He doesn't try to deny it. "I eluded their grasp for hundreds of thousands of years. In the end, it was no time at all."

"If you're one of them, then tell me what you are. Why did you build the waystations? What is this all for?"

When the dachryn next speaks, it's with the voice of the galaxy. His faded yellow plating and milky eyes disappear along with the smoking ruins of Rybur. In his place is nothing but emptiness, like she's staring into a black hole. "How can you hope to comprehend eternity in a single lifetime? If you want to understand, you must look wider, Alvera Renata. Look through the eyes of the galaxy itself."

He's part of the hive, Chase whispers. *You know what it is they want. We can't trust them.*

She knows that. But it's not a matter of trust, not now she's here. What she has to do goes beyond trust, beyond faith. It's about giving up what little she has left to give a chance to those she left behind.

She needs to understand them. But for that to happen, she needs to surrender herself to them.

Chase is the first thing to fade away, disappearing like leaves drifting off in the wind. Then comes a fog, wrapping itself around her, taking her somewhere behind the haze, out of reach.

It's not like the first time, when she fought and struggled against them. This time, she gives into the relentless churn around her. She allows herself to slip beneath the waves and fills her lungs as they drag her down towards depths she never knew existed.

But even as the darkness swallows her, she keeps a space in her mind for herself. It's her own little piece of sanctuary, too precious for them to take from her. She repeats her words back to herself, wrapping them around her like armour.

I will not allow myself to drown here.

I will not forget who I am.

I am Alvera Renata.

NINETEEN

KOJAN

K ojan liked to think of himself as a patient man, but Maxim was Arbor was testing his limits.

It was bad enough they'd had to wait another week before finally moving Alvera from the med centre. Max had insisted on the delay so he could lay false trails and make preparations, but Kojan couldn't shake the feeling that it was taking too long, that something terrible was stalking at their heels. The closer they got to escaping, the more the dread tugged at him. All he wanted to do was slip back into his old pilot's seat and power up the *Ranger's* engines to take them as far away from Rellion as he could.

"This is ridiculous," he muttered, casting Max a sideways glance. "We should be waiting on the ship, keeping an eye on Alv—on our cargo, not wasting time getting pampered in the spaceport spa of all places."

Max's only response was to take another sip of golden liquor from the long-stemmed flute he was holding casually between his fingers. He stretched his shoulders wide and sank further into the pool, the foaming bubbles lapping across his dark chest.

On his other side, Eleion gave him a nudge and handed him a small, round fruit from her claws. "Our launch window isn't for a few more hours yet. Might as well take the chance to relax. We don't know when we'll get another one."

It didn't matter that it made sense. It still felt wrong. The back of his neck prickled, like he could feel the entire spa watching him. Attendants whistled by, carrying carafes of wine and platters of meats and cheeses, their white uniforms impossibly sleek and pristine as they zipped from one end of the room to the other. Other clients lounged on wooden heatbeds or lay back in the huge, scented baths. The whole place was more like a pleasure barge than a hangar. Max clearly had expensive taste when the Rasnian government was footing the bill.

The *Ranger* was only a few minutes away on one of the express elevators. Alvera was stowed safely away in its hold, her medical pod disguised among the other pieces of cargo Max had acquired. But Kojan had seen too much go wrong in the last few months to get complacent now. Especially when Ojara was involved.

He shook his head. "Someone should be watching her. What if—"

"How many times do you want to go over this?" Max rolled his head towards him, looking at him through half-lidded eyes. "This is one of the most exclusive spaceports on the whole damn moon. Clients are expected to make use of the facilities while they wait for their launch window, not sit on board their ships for hours on end. Do you want to draw attention to yourself and screw everything up?"

"I'm not—"

"Exactly. So shut up, sit your ass back and have a drink while we wait."

Kojan scowled, taking a bite of the soft, green fruit Eleion had handed him. It popped between his teeth, filling his mouth with pleasant, tangy juice. "Have a drink? You're forgetting someone has to fly us out of here."

"I'm not forgetting anything. You being a good pilot is the only reason I need you at all." He gave a short chuckle as Kojan's face fell. "Don't take it personally. We all have our uses. Some more than others."

Kojan sank back against the jets of the whirlpool. The water pressure kneaded his aching shoulders, pushing a bit too painfully against the scar from the bullet Shaw had put in him all those months ago back on Ossa.

If only that had been the worst of his wounds. He looked down at his forearms, wrapped in waterproof bandages to protect the exposed cybernetics that had eaten their way through his skin. His body was falling apart faster each day. He felt it in the stiffness of his joints, the weakness of his limbs. Someday soon, he'd be out of time to make up for the mistakes Alvera had left him with.

He turned back to Max. "I still don't understand why you didn't just take the *Ranger* and rescue your brother by yourself. Eleion said it was unaffected by the temporal net."

"I can fly a ship from one port to another, but I'm no pilot," Max said. "Cobus gave me the *Ranger* for bringing him Alvera, but he'd shoot me out the sky if I ever tried to take it offworld. And even if I did make it out alive, the legionnaires would have stopped me long before I got close to the waystation."

"Still seems like a better plan than the one we've got. Even if we manage to wake Alvera up, we don't know what kind of state she'll be in or if she can undo whatever she did."

"I know that," Max replied, draining the last of his glass. "But until then, I have to go on like there's still a chance. The alternative means my brother is already as good as dead."

The minutes stretched on, agonisingly slow. It came as a

relief when a soft chime from Max's holo communicator interrupted the monotony.

Eleion cocked her head. "What is it?"

Max grimaced. "Incoming connection request from the governor."

"Why is he calling? Do you think he knows we moved Alvera from the med centre?"

"One way to find out." Max gestured for them to move out of view and tapped his holo. "Governor Cobus, what can I do for you?"

"Oh, I think you already know the answer to that, ras Arbor." Cobus's face was shrewd and pointed, and there was an unusual edge to his oily voice. "I find it hard to believe you weren't expecting this call."

Kojan's heart thumped against his ribs. All Max's caution and careful planning would amount to nothing if the governor knew already. Within moments he could have the hangar locked down, the facility surrounded by armed soldiers. Alvera would be taken away and shipped off to the highest bidder. Eleion would lose the chance to give her people a better life. And he would be out of time.

Max gave a wry laugh. "I must have spent too long in this job if I've become that predictable, Governor. It's strangely flattering how you've come to understand me so well."

"I don't have time for the usual dance, ras Arbor," Cobus said. "I know how this works. This is the part where I offer to raise your pay, and in return, you agree to return the agitator to me. No theatrics, no nonsense. Let's get this over with."

The silence after his words lasted too long, thickening the air around them until Kojan could hardly breathe. He could almost see the mechanics inside Max's head as he weighed up the offer. How many credits was his brother's life worth?

Eleion's throat rippled in a silent growl. The long spindles on the back of her neck were rigid as she stared at Max with fierce, unblinking eyes, waiting to see what he would do next.

A slow smile unfurled across Max's face. "Actually, Cobus, this is the part where I hand in my resignation."

"Cut the shit." Cobus's eyes flashed dangerously. "We both know you don't have the moral fortitude to play the hero. Name your price and we'll forget this farce ever happened."

"This isn't me trying to play hardball, boss. Some things in this galaxy credits can't buy, that's all. Don't take it personally."

"You think I don't know what your plan is?" Cobus's eyes glinted. "The *Ranger* may be an impressive ship, but that counts for nothing if you can't get off this moon."

Max laughed. "This is the wealthiest spaceport on Rellion. They're not going to take kindly to the government interfering in their clients' departures."

"No, I imagine they wouldn't," Cobus replied. "Fortunately for me, I have some less...*official* assets at my disposal. You should have stuck to chasing paychecks, ras Arbor. Walking away from those who look after you is a good way to get killed."

"Who should I be expecting?" Max folded his arms. "If it's the Crimson Teeth, you've wasted your credits. Bunch of kids running the show these days, can't tell their ammo from their assholes."

"No need to worry about that. I've acquired the services of somebody with a considerably more personal stake in this game." Cobus curled the side of his mouth into a smile. "Someone I imagine your outlander friend is very familiar with."

The water lapping at Kojan's waist suddenly felt ice cold. Every muscle the quickening hadn't yet ravaged stiffened at the governor's words, turning him to stone. He couldn't move. He could hardly even breathe.

Across the other side of the room, a frosted glass door slid silently open. On the other side were half a dozen soldiers clad in steel-grey Exodan power armour, their hands wrapped around blinking plasma rifles. But it wasn't the soldiers that filled him with terror. It was the abomination standing in front of them.

His face could barely be called a face anymore. What was left of his pale skin and dark hair could hardly be seen under the metal casing crudely holding together the gaping hole in the side of his head. One of his eyes was gone, leaving nothing but a dark socket and the red glow of a retinal implant. The part of his mouth that wasn't blackened and torn was twisted into a cruel, furious sneer.

Shaw.

"That was the bastard shooting at you back on Ossa, wasn't it?" Eleion asked, her words a quiet hiss. "What the hell happened to him?"

Max gave a dark chuckle. "Alvera happened. Used those cybernetics of hers to blow half his damn face off during her trial just to make a point."

Kojan couldn't say anything. It wasn't that he felt pity for Shaw. After what he'd done to the crew of the *Ranger*, pity was beyond him. But neither could he revel in what Alvera had done to him. His ruined face was another reminder of the destruction she'd been so reckless in dealing out. Alvera Renata didn't go around things in her way—she went through them. And screw anyone who got caught in the crossfire.

"He'll stop at nothing to kill us," he said quietly. "And he'll want to make it painful. Don't underestimate him."

"Wouldn't dream of it." Max hauled himself out of the pool, water streaming down the thick, muscular curve of his back. He stretched his neck one way and then another as he casually reached towards one of the towels at the side. "Shaw, isn't it? Don't suppose you'd do a man the courtesy of getting dressed first?"

Something erupted in the water and Kojan leapt back. The

ripples on the surface hissed with steam. Across the room, the barrel of Shaw's plasma rifle glowed orange-red.

"I'll take that as a no."

Max dived for the towel and snatched up the gun hidden underneath it, firing a barrage of bullets back at Shaw and the Exodans flanking him. One of the soldiers let out a gasp as the bullet pierced his collar, sending blood spurting from his throat as he collapsed to the ground.

Gunfire rang through Kojan's ears. The noise of plasma bolts reverberated off the tiled walls, followed by the sound of screams. The water around him exploded in jets of steam, and the next thing he felt was Eleion's claws digging into his skin, pulling him underwater and away from the chaos above.

Beneath the surface of the pool, the fighting seemed so far away. All he could hear were muffled shots and tinny voices shouting back and forth. Eleion dragged him through the water, her lean limbs propelling them both with ease. Plasma bolts fizzled down from the surface, leaving jets of bubbles behind them. Some came so close they almost scalded him, but Eleion was able to weave around their boiling trails as she swam, as fluid and powerful in the water as she was on land.

They resurfaced at the far side of the pool. Kojan wiped the water from his eyes and looked back to see Max huddled down behind one of the heatbeds, blood pouring from a wound in his arm. A river of red ran from the marble tiles at his feet towards the pool, but he wasn't the only one bleeding. Some of the spa attendants and other clients had been caught in the crossfire. Stained tunics floated in the pools. Tattered robes scattered the floor, shrouds for the bodies that lay crumpled beneath them.

It was a bloodbath. Not that Shaw would have cared about that. He'd already overseen one execution on the *Ranger* already. This was nothing more than collateral damage.

"We need to get out of here," he said. "If Shaw gets to Alvera before we do, it's over."

Eleion nodded, her yellow eyes darting between him and the carnage on the far side of the room. "Make a run for the express elevator as soon as you get the chance. Don't stop until you're safe inside the *Ranger*."

Dread pulled at his stomach. "You're not coming?"

"As much as I hate to say it, we can't leave ras Arbor behind. He's got the launch codes." She leapt out of the pool and shook the water from her scales. "Don't worry, I have no intention of getting myself killed on his account. Just get the *Ranger* ready to go. We'll be right behind you."

She didn't leave him any time to argue. Before he could open his mouth in protest, she'd sprung forward on all fours, darting across the slippery tiles towards Max. Towards Shaw.

He owed it to her to run, but that didn't make it any easier. How many times would he let her put herself in danger to give him a better chance at surviving?

At least one more, he thought grimly, as he hauled himself out of the pool and raced towards the sliding steel doors of the express elevator. There was no other way. Eleion had chosen the part she had to play. It was up to him to do the same.

His bare feet slid on the floor as he came to a halt outside the elevator doors. He didn't dare look back. There was too much blood. Too many bodies. If one of them was Eleion's, he might not be able to go on. Instead, he pressed his wrist terminal against the interface and flinched at the cold as the doors whirred open and invited him in.

He entered the code for the *Ranger's* private hangar and waited as the elevator rumbled into life. Water dripped from his back, forming a puddle at his feet. Each passing second stretched longer than the last, leaving him with too much time to think about what might be happening back at the spa. It didn't matter how much of Shaw's face had been blown apart. There was enough left to see the festering hatred inside him. It was written in his murderous, one-eyed glare, in the inhuman snarl that deformed his ragged mouth. It promised the same pain and suffering that had been inflicted on him.

After a few more minutes, the elevator came to a smooth stop and pinged gently. Kojan held his breath as the doors parted with a soft click, opening up into a brightly-lit hangar.

There it was, waiting for him. The *Ranger*.

Something swelled in his heart at the sight of it. Alvera might have been captain, but the *Ranger* was his ship in every way that mattered. Its sleek, silver panels shone under the lights, and the curve of its engines cast long shadows on the floor. It promised him a way out. It promised him hope.

He ran across the hangar floor and up the outstretched access ramp. The keypad returned the signal blinking from his wrist terminal, and the airlock doors hissed open to welcome him. The ship knew him. It remembered him. Maybe now he was back, he could begin to put right all the things that had gone wrong here.

He grabbed a flight suit and a pair of boots from storage and pulled the overalls on as he walked the empty corridors. It wasn't the same as before. The *Ranger* had always seemed so alive, bustling with movement and chatter from its crew. Now, it was silent. His solitary footsteps echoed off the hull, too loud for the space he occupied. Who else was left, apart from him? Ridley had fallen off the radar, her comms dark for weeks now. Alvera was trapped inside her medical pod, clinging on to whatever life was left in her. And Shaw... Shaw was the reason for all of it.

The ghosts of the crew followed him as he made his way to the cargo hold. He felt the weight of them crushing him, as if they were counting on him to make right the things they had suffered. As if righting that wrong was his responsibility now that there was nobody else left.

Was this how Alvera felt all those years? Was this the kind of burden that had driven her to do the things she'd done?

The glow of her medpod shone through the darkness of the cargo hold. Inside, she lay grey and lifeless. Unable to hurt anyone. Unable to help.

Carrying fifty billion lives on your back tends to break you after a while. If you lose them, there's no coming back from it.

The memory of her words was like a whisper in his ear. Even now, she was still the one that haunted him most.

He turned away and headed towards the bridge. Now was not the time for second guessing the things she'd done, the things they'd all done. He had to focus on what he could do now. And if there was one thing Kojan knew with absolute certainty he could do, it was fly.

He slid into his old pilot's seat, relaxing into the familiar dips and ridges that moulded around his legs and back. His hands flew over the holo interface around him, setting up pre-checks and running through the flight systems. Doubt abandoned him. So too did fear, leaving behind only a strange, soothing calm.

"All systems green across the board," he murmured to himself. "We are clear for take-off."

The silence that followed his words rang too loudly in his ears. He half-expected a chirp from the intercom, a condescending remark about fuel consumption. But there was nothing. Chase was gone. Another casualty. Not likely to be the last, either.

"Kojan? Kojan! Please tell me you're there."

He tore himself from his thoughts and opened the connection on his wrist terminal. "Eleion, where are you? The *Ranger* is ready to go. We need the launch codes."

"I'm on my way," she said, her voice strained. "Shaw left with the rest of the Exodans on another express elevator when he saw you go. I'm guessing they've got a ship of their own. If we don't get away fast—"

"They'll blow us out of the sky." He fired the engines into

life, shivering as the *Ranger* began to rumble around him. "Just get yourself on board and let me take care of that."

He ran through the rest of the flight checks, keeping an eye on the external feeds. After a few minutes, he saw the hangar doors open. Eleion stumbled through, Max draped over one of her shoulders. His arm was covered in dried blood and there was a fresh bullet wound in his chest, but he staggered forward with a grim determination.

When they finally made it to the bridge, Max opened up his wrist terminal and scanned through the data files there, hardly seeming to notice the blood streaming down his chest.

"Launch codes," he said, his voice hoarse. He pushed Kojan to the side and swiped through the interface to connect his wrist terminal. A moment later, he collapsed back into the co-pilot's seat, eyes half-closed and breathing heavy. "It's done. Now let's get the hell out of here."

"Already on it." Kojan sent him a sideways glance. "The med centre is a level down. Might be a good idea to patch yourself up. I don't think we're going to be done fighting any time soon."

Max grunted. "What about the armoury?"

"On the way."

"Good." He hauled himself back to his feet, wincing as he took a step. "Try not to get us all killed while I'm gone, will you? Would never be able to live with myself, knowing my last fight was getting shot up in a fucking spa."

Eleion slid into the vacant seat, watching him limp away with her keen, yellow eyes. "I've tangled with my fair share of mercs, you know. One of the hazards of the job when you're a cargo runner. That human does not fight like a merc. He fights like a legionnaire. Like a damn Idran-Var."

"Careful," Kojan said, a smile tugging at his mouth. "It sounds like you're starting to like the man."

Eleion snorted. "That's pushing it. But maybe he isn't quite the deplorable lowlife I first imagined him to be. I think—" She paused, eyes fixed on a red light flashing on the comms console. "Should we be worried about that?"

He glanced at the signature. "Looks like it's coming from hangar control. I'll patch them through."

The red light blinked off. For a moment, there was only static. Then the line crackled into life and a clipped, Rellion-accented voice came over the channel. "*Ranger,* this is Axos Control requesting you power down your engines. Your launch window is not yet open."

"Are they serious?" Eleion groaned. "Kojan, we need to get out of here before—"

"I know." He tapped the interface to send a response. "Axos Control, this is the *Ranger.* We're in a bit of an emergency situation right now. Requesting permission for a priority departure."

There was a moment of silence on the other end of the line. "This is highly irregular. What kind of emergency are you experiencing?"

"Kojan..."

"I *know.*" He cleared his throat. "What kind of emergency? How about the kind where our railguns have unexpectedly locked on to that million-credit retracting glass roof above our heads?"

"Excuse me?"

"I don't think either of us wants to deal with that kind of damage," he continued, trying to ignore the sound of Eleion snickering beside him. "Better for everyone if you open it up and send us on our way, wouldn't you say?"

The line went silent again and Kojan held his breath. It was a ridiculous bluff, one he didn't know he'd be able to follow through on if it came down to it. If he shot the roof open, the falling debris could easily cut through the *Ranger's* fuel line or knock out one of their vital nav systems. But if there was no other choice...

A rush of static came over the comms channel. "*Ranger,* you are clear for launch. We've got a lot of air traffic tonight, so please ensure you do not deviate from your departure vector until authorised to do so." The voice on the end of the line paused. "Also, we're sorry to inform you that your lease at Axos has been terminated with immediate effect. Under the circumstances, you will be held liable for any outstanding hangar fees or facilities expenses incurred."

Eleion cackled. "Max is going to love that."

Kojan couldn't help but grin back. For the first time in a long time, he was back where he belonged. The *Ranger* roared into life as he guided the ship out of the hangar and into the glowing night sky. Beyond the moon's atmosphere, the expanse of space awaited them. Freedom was calling, and he pushed the engines forward to answer.

"How long until we break atmo?" Max had returned, wearing a formidable suit of power armour and carrying an assortment of scavenged weapons around the utility belt on his waist. His dark eyes were tired and bloodshot, but he held himself with a ragged kind of determination that Kojan couldn't help but envy.

"Four minutes," he replied, eyeing the serrated combat blade Max was securing to his leg. "I see you found the armoury after all."

"No harm in being prepared. You said it yourself, the fighting isn't going to be over any time soon." He glanced over at the nav console. "Can you run identification checks on that? Those bastards down there are set on following us. We need to know what's coming."

Kojan swiped through the interface and brought up a fast-moving feed. The text flashed in front of his eyes too fast to make sense of. "They weren't kidding when they said the air traffic was congested. There are far too many drive signatures here to keep track of."

"Narrow it down to Axos departures. They must have had a ship of their own on standby." Max scanned the feed, the holographic text illuminating golden lines across his dark skin. "Shit, I knew it. A *Hunter*-class frigate just got cleared for departure."

"*Hunter*-class?"

"An interceptor, made to chase down idiots like us." Max shifted his weight, wincing. "If your friend is on it, we don't have a hope of outrunning him."

Eleion glanced at him. "What about our stealth systems? Can we lose him?"

"Stealth systems are only good for obscuring our heat signature out in space," Kojan said, shaking his head. "We're close enough for a visual here. If they tag us before we break atmo, there's no hiding from them."

"There's no hiding from anyone." Max snorted. "In case you haven't noticed, the *Ranger* is pretty much the most famous ship in the galaxy these days. The moment we drop out of stealth, someone is going to pick up our signature."

Eleion gave a sharp hiss. "There must be something we can do. We didn't come this far just to let that bastard have the last laugh."

Kojan didn't say anything. His hands were curled into fists so tight he thought his fingers might break. Every time he thought he was on the verge of escaping, something always hauled him back. First Ojara, now Shaw. Both reminders of a past he couldn't outrun.

A light blinked on the comms interface. He bit his lip so hard he tasted blood, and opened the connection.

Shaw's face loomed in front of them, twisted beyond recognition. "I told you once the company you keep would get you killed, Kojan. First it was that surfacer bitch and your slete-loving captain. Now you've thrown your lot in with outcasts and traitors. I don't know why I'm surprised at the levels you're capable of sinking to. I only know you'll regret it."

Kojan could barely form a response over the rage tightening his chest. "After the things you've done, my only regret is that Alvera didn't finish the job she did on you."

"Alvera Renata is dead!" Shaw snarled, his face contorted with fury. "Ojara sent me the reports. Your old captain is gone. She can't save you this time. She can't save anyone. Fifty billion sletes will die on New Pallas because of her. That is her legacy."

His words were too close to the truth for Kojan to shake off. Shaw was right. Alvera had gambled with a planet and lost. But as long as she was still breathing, there was a chance she might wake. A chance she might be able to reverse the temporal net around Ulla Waystation. A chance she might be able to save New Pallas.

It was up to him to give her that chance. To give that chance to them all.

"You're still so afraid of her, even now," he said. "You and Ojara both. She's closer to death than life, but you're still scared she'll come back from beyond the grave and take away everything you've corrupted and murdered and destroyed to achieve." A hoarse laugh escaped his lips. "I lost faith in her. I thought there was nobody left in this galaxy who believed in her. Turns out I was just looking in the wrong places."

The remnants of Shaw's pale skin flushed red with rage. "Believe in her? She's nothing but a traitorous, pathetic—"

"Goodbye, Shaw." He cut the connection and turned to Max and Eleion. "Strap in. We're about to get moving."

A slow, sharp-toothed smile unfurled across Eleion's jaws. "You have a plan?"

"Something like it. But if we're to have a hope in hell, we need to put some distance between us and Shaw. Can you chart us a course to the nearest space tunnel?"

She nodded. "On it."

"What makes you think you can put any distance between us at all?" Max said. "I told you, that ship is fast."

Kojan cracked his neck. "I'm faster."

The thick webbing of the restraints was tight around his shoulders. The bridge was aglow with the lights of the instruments in front of him. The *Ranger* was at his fingertips, ready to do as he asked.

He could almost hear Chase's voice in his head. *The ship's all yours, flyboy. Now let's see what you can do with it.*

"Breaking atmo in three...two...one..."

The *Ranger* lurched forward under his command. They left the glittering moon of Rellion behind and pushed towards the darkness, burning the engines at full power. If Shaw wanted to kill them, he'd have to catch them. Kojan had no intention of letting that happen.

"Tunnel coordinates are locked into the nav," Eleion said. "The system on the other side is pretty remote. Doesn't look like there are any major settlements, but I see a couple of dwarf planets with research posts."

"It will have to do." He glanced down at the console. A proximity alert blinked red. "They're already closing in. We need to get out of Rasnian space, into more neutral territory. It's our only chance."

Max furrowed his brow. "I don't see how that's going to help us. What use is running if they're only going to—"

Something rocked the ship, cutting off the rest of his words. Kojan jolted in his seat but kept his hands steady on the controls, already working to push the *Ranger* into a hard change of course. The reverse burn of the thrusters knocked the air from his stomach, and he could hear his teeth rattling in his skull.

A siren blared above him, and he reached up to turn it off. "We can't outrun them forever, but we can keep them at bay long enough to call for backup."

"Backup? Who do you think is going to come save our asses?"

"The people who want answers from Alvera as badly as we do. The legionnaires."

Max sent him a bemused look. "The legionnaires? That's your plan? You know you can't just call them up and ask them to lend a hand, right? It doesn't work like that."

"Actually, that's exactly what I intend to do." He swiped through the comms interface, linking up with the records from his wrist terminal. "We had a brush with the legionnaires before you caught us, remember? Lucky for us, that left us with a direct line to one of their pilots."

He opened up the connection. The line hummed with static, but there was no reply on the other end. He had no way of knowing if the message would even get through. But it was the only chance they had left.

"This is a message for Kitell Merala of the Coalition Legionnaire Corps," he said. "You might recognise me from my galactic arrest warrant, but you probably know me better as the guy who outflew you at Hellon Junction a while back. No hard feelings." He allowed a smile to play out across his lips for a moment. "Turns out we could use your help."

The line was still silent. Maybe the time delay was longer than expected. Maybe there was nobody to answer. There was nothing else to do but go on.

"My old captain, the one you're calling the agitator, is alive," he said, his voice taking on a more sombre tone. "I have her with me, and we're willing to talk. But we're being pursued by a *Hunter*-class frigate out of Rellion. Not sure how long we'll be able to hold out. I'm sending this distress call over our emergency beacon. If you get it in time, I hope you'll be able to find us. If not..." He broke off. "I don't know what you want with Alvera, but I know it's on me to make things right. I don't know how much the word of a human is worth to you, but if you help us, we'll do what we can to help you."

He cut off the connection. The comms interface stared back at him, quiet and unblinking. It was like shouting across the void. A chance so miniscule it seemed impossible to hope for.

Eleion looked over at him, her eyes bright and discerning. "You think he'll come?"

"I think he's our last shot."

"And what do we do in the meantime?" Max crossed his arms. "They're not going to fall back. They'll be on your ass all the way."

Kojan didn't reply. Despite the roar of the engines and the ever-present thrum from the instruments on the bridge, everything faded away into silence. Maybe it was the quickening eating away at the hearing he had left. Maybe it was the strange sense of peace that had come over him, blocking out everything else.

Another warning light flashed in front of him. Another missile was on its way, slicing through the darkness towards them. It wouldn't be the last. But the *Ranger* had survived more than what Shaw could throw at them. It had survived the impossible, just like he had. The ship had never let them down yet. As long as he had the controls at his fingertips, he would make the *Ranger* dance. It was up to him to keep them going for as long as it took for Kitell Merala to answer their call.

"Buckle up," he said. "It's going to be a wild ride."

TWENTY

RIVUS

The dachryn ambassador was wearing a mourning pendant.

How strange it was that with everything that had happened, *this* was what Rivus was focusing on. His oldest friend was dead. The legionnaires had lost their Supreme Commander. There was a hole in his heart that would never heal. But all he could think about was how the dachryn ambassador was wearing a mourning pendant.

It would have gone unnoticed by most and politely unremarked on by the rest. The dachryn were still so few that their cultures and customs hadn't permeated the rest of the galaxy like some of the other species'. Humans greeted each other with bows and handshakes. Jarkaath exchanged food between their neighbours' plates at mealtimes. Sioleans only touched those they had an intimate bond with.

And dachryn broke off one of their bone spurs to wear as a token when someone they loved died.

She stood with the rest of the ambassadors during the

memorial service, her face hard and unmoving. There was a sombre silence around the room that was heavy with more than the respect of a war hero passing. There was an uneasiness to it too, a sense that whatever ill-fated luck had killed Tarvan was only the start of things to come.

No glory in battle, old friend.

Only blood.

How long had it been since they'd stood under this very roof and shared those words? If only he'd paid attention to the foreboding that had crept over him back then, maybe he could have stopped all this from happening. So much had changed that it felt like he was remembering somebody else's life. He wasn't the same dachryn he'd been all those months ago.

As it turned out, neither was Tarvan.

Nobody else knew the truth of what happened on Aurel. If Tarvan had died a traitor, it would have broken what was left of the legionnaires. So Rivus lied to the assembly. He let them remember their Supreme Commander as the dachryn they thought he was, and not the one he'd been forced to become. For once, he'd been the one to protect Tarvan, in the hope that it might make up for all the times Tarvan had protected him.

The low, grumbling thrum of a stringed *iveth* filled the room. After a moment, voices joined the lament, slow and sombre. A shining set of power armour stood in the middle of the room, glinting as the Ossan sunlight broke through the windows and fell across the smooth white metal. In the marble halls of the assembly chambers, they mourned him. Across the allied systems, where the service was beamed onto vidscreens and personal data pads, they mourned him.

That was what Tarvan was leaving behind. Not the memory of the atrocities he'd committed, but a hero's goodbye.

It was a lie. All of it. It wasn't even Tarvan's armour. The real thing had been a twisted, broken mess, stained with dark blood and ruined beyond repair. There was no hiding the kind of damage that had been done to it. A replica would have to do. It was just another reminder of the shadow cast over this whole ceremony.

No glory in battle, old friend.

Only blood.

That was the real truth. It was easier for everyone to believe Tarvan and the legionnaires had gone out in a valiant last stand. They hadn't been there. They hadn't seen the bloodied bodies scattered across the barren wasteland of Aurel's surface. Tarvan's missile had changed the landscape, turning a bare, windswept plateau into a field of blackened armour and mangled limbs. He'd buried his soldiers at the bottom of a crater and trampled over their corpses on his way to their enemy.

Then he'd got himself killed.

Rivus's throat constricted. How many times would he replay it in his head before it broke him? How many times could he bear to watch as Niole held him in the grasp of her flare? How many times could he relive the scream that died in his throat as she tore Tarvan apart before his eyes?

Niole, if I ever see you again...

The rest of the service passed in a blur. It wasn't until the delegates began to file out that he realised it was over. He waited for them to leave, staring blankly ahead at the propped-up armour in the middle of the room. It looked so strange with nobody in it, like it belonged to a ghost. A symbol of what it used to be, without a trace of the dachryn who'd done so much to fill it.

"General Itair." A soft, rumbling voice spoke from behind his shoulder, jolting him from his thoughts. "Would you do me the privilege of granting me a few minutes of your time?"

It was her. The dachryn ambassador. Her face markings were pale violet under the lights, fading away to the grey of her plates. There was something regal in the way she held herself, even with the weight of grief. She watched him quietly, waiting for his answer.

"Of course," he said. It wasn't like he had much choice in the matter. He could hardly refuse one of the ambassadors.

He followed her from the chamber, lingering behind at a respectful distance. His heart tightened as he realised where she was leading him. Each step he took was a reminder of all the times he'd walked these corridors. All the times he'd gone to see Tarvan. All the times he'd pressed the keypad and waited to be granted entry to the office of the Supreme Commander.

The door slid shut behind them with a soft hiss. Rivus braced himself as he looked around the room, but there was nothing left here that belonged to Tarvan. The walls were stark and bare, the furniture gone. It was painfully empty, missing a presence that should have been there.

"You know what they're calling you, don't you?"

He turned around at her question, tearing himself from his thoughts. "The sole survivor," he said, unable to keep the distaste from his voice.

The ambassador twitched her brow plate. "You say that like it's an insult."

"Not an insult, just an unwelcome reminder."

She'd never understand what it felt like to stand on that planet alone, knowing he was the only one left alive. He still didn't know how he'd found the strength to pull himself away from the carnage and make his way back to base. He'd boarded a fighter and taken off, not releasing the engines from full burn until Aurel was far in the distance. But not even the vastness of space was enough to escape it.

The dachryn ambassador sighed. "I don't doubt that what happened out there must have put you through hell, General Itair...Rivus. Not many could have seen what you saw and found the strength to come back. Not many could have survived at all." She shook her head, her jaw plates stiff. "I still don't understand why, after massacring all those legionnaires, she chose to spare you."

Instead of Tarvan. The words went unspoken, but Rivus could still hear the echoes of her grief in the air between them. He could hardly blame her. Part of him wished he had shared the fate of his fellow legionnaires, if only to escape the pain their loss had left him with.

"Niole and I have a history," he said tightly. "I'm sure Tarvan told you the details. This is the second time she's had the opportunity to kill me and instead run away. Believe me, ambassador, there won't be a third."

The dachryn ambassador didn't say anything. She walked across to one of the sleek storage units integrated into the walls and pressed the thin metal clasp of her wrist terminal against the holographic interface attached there. Something bleeped, and one of the drawers extended out with a low, mechanical hum.

Inside the drawer was a gleaming white cloak, trimmed in gold and bearing the insignia of the Supreme Commander.

His breath caught in his chest, his throat too tight to speak. He could only watch wordlessly as she lifted it gently from the drawer, the soft white fabric spilling around her claws.

She held it out towards him, her head dipped forward. "Tarvan would have wanted you to have this."

He took it from her, trying not to wince at how smooth the material was. It was too pristine, too unblemished. The last time he'd seen a cloak like this, it had been bloodied and torn, left in scraps around what remained of Tarvan's desecrated body.

The insignia stared out at him from within the soft white folds. Rivus knew what that symbol meant. He knew the kind of burden it brought, the depths it was capable of driving someone to. That's what Tarvan had always tried to protect him from. The weight of it had always been his to bear.

He gave a harsh laugh. "Ambassador, I believe that's the last thing he would have wanted."

"He would have kept you from it, if he could have. But I know there's nobody he trusted more." She smiled sadly and took a step back, her hand reaching to clasp the broken bone spur tied around her neck. "He loved you. If you can't find strength in the things that have happened, then find it in that."

Her words still rang in his head long after the door slid shut behind her. His hands shook as he unfurled the cloak in front of him and swung it around his shoulders. It didn't sit right. It was like it had been made for somebody else.

He stepped towards the gleaming mirror fixed onto the wall, examining the dachryn standing in front of him. In the glass, the Supreme Commander of the legionnaires stared back at him. Tarvan was gone. Whatever he had left behind was his responsibility now. It was time to shoulder the burden his old friend had tried to shield him from for so long. It was time to finish what he started.

No glory in battle.

Only blood.

———

He found Kite in the hangar, purple skin flushed with patches of red and elbows deep in engine oil. His headtails were tied back with a series of interlocking metal clips, and his mouth was set in a firm line as he focused on his work.

When he saw Rivus, he threw down his tools and gave an exaggerated salute. "The new Supreme Commander himself. Didn't think you'd have time to grace us simple space jockeys with your esteemed presence, boss."

Rivus winced. "News travels fast, I see."

"Faster than I've been travelling lately, that's for sure. The ambassadors pulled us all back after they got word about what happened on Aurel. I've been grounded for weeks." He sighed. "If they keep us down here any longer, I might quit and finally join the racing leagues."

The joke was an old, tired one, but Rivus could hear the pain behind the bluster, the way his words caught when he mentioned Aurel. That kind of loss was a wound shared between all of them that remained. A loss that none of them could ignore, even if they tried to hide it behind quips and false bravado.

"I didn't see you at the memorial," he said.

Kite snorted. "You think they let riff-raff like me into the assembly? I was watching, though. A lot of us were." His black eyes narrowed in anger. "I keep thinking about what would have happened if we hadn't been out on patrol. Maybe our fighters could have made a difference. Maybe we could have got some of our soldiers out of there."

"Or maybe you'd be dead with the rest of them," Rivus said heavily. "Don't torture yourself with hypotheticals, Merala. It doesn't bring any kind of comfort, believe me."

"I just hate sitting around here, unable to do anything. Unable to fly." He glanced over at his fighter, its wings gleaming under the hangar lights. "We're all waiting to see what happens next."

"What happens next?" Rivus gave a rumble of surprise. "I thought that would have been obvious. We plan a counter-offensive against the Idran-Var. We strike at their factories on Maar. We run them into the ground. We make them answer for what happened on Aurel."

Even as he said them, the words didn't feel like his own. They were Tarvan's words, words that he'd spent the last few months rallying against in desperation. He could almost hear the ghostly voice of the old dachryn general urging him not to lose sight of the real enemy.

A crease appeared in Kite's brow ridge. "The Idran-Var? That always seemed like Tarvan's war, not yours."

"They made it mine when they killed him."

The words sounded hollow to his ears, like they belonged to someone else. For a moment, they echoed through his head, then disappeared like he'd never spoken at all. A thick fog settled over him, muffling the outside. All he could hear among the silence were hushed whispers in voices he didn't understand.

A stab of pain shot through his head and he fell to his knees, his vision blurring. Shadows crept in at the corners of his eyes, threatening to overcome him. Something was happening. The terror he'd been keeping at bay was too close. It was upon him. It was upon them all.

"Rivus?" Kite put a steadying hand on his shoulder. "What's wrong?"

"The waystations." He choked out the words in a painful grunt. "The signal is breaking through the protections in my cybernetics again. Something must have happened. Something is making them escalate the countdown again."

"What does that mean?"

"It means they're coming."

He struggled back to his feet, trying to push away the throbbing inside his skull. He couldn't afford to let pain distract him. "I have to find the ambassadors," he said. "I have to warn them the timescales have changed."

Kite tightened his jaw. "How long do we have?"

"Not long enough." He shook his head. "I'm going to need eyes on those waystations, Merala. Organise patrols around the perimeter of the exclusion zones. Anything you see gets reported directly to me, no matter how small. Make sure you keep—"

An urgent bleep from Kite's wrist terminal cut him off mid-command. Kite flushed as he brought up the holodisplay.

"Sorry, boss. Thought I had it set to emergency comms only. I must have..." He trailed off as he scanned the readout. "Oh, you've got to be kidding me."

Rivus froze. "What is it?"

"My fighter just forwarded a distress call. Signature is scrambled, but it's coming from somewhere in the Rasnian systems."

"What does it say?"

Kite shot him a dark look. "See for yourself."

The holodisplay flickered and a human appeared. His face was gaunt and tired, with sunken eyes and an expression that looked like it had gone beyond exhaustion. It took Rivus a moment to recognise him. "It's the pilot. The one who came here with the agitator."

"This is a message for Kitell Merala of the Coalition Legionnaire Corps," the human said. "You might recognise me from my galactic arrest warrant, but you probably know me better as the guy who outflew you at Hellon Junction a while back. No hard feelings."

Rivus shot a questioning glance at Kite, who scowled in return. "The human thinks he's a hotshot. Wouldn't get anywhere near one of my patrols."

"You encountered one of the agitator's crew and didn't think to tell me?"

"I didn't know it was him at the time," Kite said, giving a disgruntled sniff. "A Rasnian capital ship took them away before I got a chance to investigate further."

"Turns out we could use your help." The human paused, like he was waiting for an answer. There was a shadow behind his eyes that Rivus knew well. "My old captain, the one you're calling the agitator, is alive."

Rivus jolted. She wasn't a voice in his head. She wasn't a ghost of the past, haunting him like all the others. Wherever

284 | N.C SCRIMGEOUR

she was, whatever she was trying to do in that dreamscape she'd visited him in, she was alive.

"I have her with me, and we're willing to talk," the human continued. "But we're being pursued by a *Hunter*-class frigate out of Rellion. Not sure how long we'll be able to hold out. I'm sending this distress call over our emergency beacon. If you get it in time, I hope you'll be able to find us. If not..." He trailed off, leaving the rest of his words unspoken in a crackle of static. "I don't know what you want with Alvera, but I know it's on me to make things right. I don't know how much the word of a human is worth to you, but if you help us, we'll do what we can to help you."

The human disappeared as the transmission ended and the holodisplay flickered off. Rivus stared at the empty space where the projection had been, his chest tight and his head spinning. Alvera Renata was alive. Maybe she'd learned something about the abominations behind the waystations, the ones she'd called the curators. Maybe that was why the timeline had changed. Maybe they were afraid of what she might do.

"Change of plan, Merala," he said tersely. "I need you to follow that distress beacon. Find Alvera Renata. Bring her back alive."

"Alive might be tricky. If they put up a fight—"

"They won't. And if they do, my orders still stand. She's no use to the galaxy dead." He let out a sigh. "Protect her, Kite. If we want to stand a chance against what's coming, we need her."

"Understood, Supreme Commander. I'll get in the air right away." He glanced over at his fighter and then back at Rivus. "Are you likely to be here when I bring her back? Or should I expect to find you leading a fleet into Idran-Var space?"

"I'll be here. You were right. That was Tarvan's war, not mine." He ground his jaw plates together. "If the Idran-Var are still standing at the end of all this, we'll deal with them. But first, we have to survive."

"Surviving sure as hell sounds good to me." Kite gave the legionnaire's salute. "I'll be back before you know it."

"We'll be ready."

He watched for a moment as Kite gathered up his tools and made his way over to the fighter. So much was at stake. So much hung in the balance. If Kite didn't reach the humans in time, if Alvera didn't make it back... He shook his head. Now was not the time to start thinking about worst-case scenarios. If things went to shit, there would be plenty of time for that later.

Fragments from his visions flashed in front of his eyes. The damage he'd done at Farsal Waystation. The despair Alvera had caused through her actions on Ulla. Whatever was coming, it had started with the two of them. Maybe together they could fix it.

He rushed out of the hangar and made his way through the bustling marble and sandstone streets towards Coalition High Command. There was no time to waste. The neural dampeners in his cybernetics had been rendered useless once again by the shifting of the signal. Until he could analyse it, he wouldn't know how long they had left. The only thing he knew was that time was running out.

By the time he'd made it to the ambassadorial wing, his breathing was sharp and shallow. He slammed his wrist terminal against the interface to the ambassadors' chambers and burst through the doors as soon as his new security clearance pinged.

The human and siolean ambassadors jumped back, alarmed, and the jarkaath drew back her scales from her jaws in a disgruntled snarl. Only the dachryn ambassador seemed unruffled by his abrupt entrance.

"Apologies for the intrusion, ambassadors," he said curtly. "But I have important information to share and it couldn't wait."

"Supreme Commander Itair," the dachryn ambassador

said, inclining her head. "This is fortuitous timing. We were about to send for you."

That startled him. "Send for me?"

"Indeed," the siolean ambassador said, his headtails limp and curling around his shoulders. He looked older than the last time Rivus had seen him. More wearied by all that had happened since then. Maybe his own wounds were showing too. "We've received word of an anomaly at the waystations. We're hoping your first-hand knowledge can shed some light on what's happening."

He tapped his wrist terminal and all the lights in the chamber snapped out. The only glow came from the holodisplay in the middle of the room. Hovering there in the darkness, as dreamlike as the ghosts he'd seen in his visions, were luminous projections of the waystations.

Farsal. Ulla. Rathor. Yeven. Each one pulsed brightly against the darkness like the rings of a planet. For a moment, he couldn't see anything out of the ordinary. Then he focused his eyes on the faint trails projected from each of their wakes.

"What is this?" he asked, his words little more than a breath. "They're *moving?*"

The jarkaath ambassador curled her claws. "So it would seem."

A burst of panic shot through him. "The temporal nets. What will happen to the ships caught in them?"

"The temporal nets appear to have been released," the human ambassador said, reflections dancing in his glassy eyes. "That's how we first learned of this. Whatever else is happening, we have at least something to be grateful for. Our trapped ships are on their way home."

On their way home. The words sent a rush of relief around his body, making his legs shake from the adrenaline. There had already been so much loss. Too many of the trapped Coalition ships had already run out of air, run out of rations. But there would be some survivors. After the darkness of the last few weeks, even something that bittersweet felt like a victory.

He glanced around at the ambassadors. Their expressions were difficult to read. The human was trembling with an emotion Rivus couldn't place and the siolean had dipped his head as if he had been defeated.

"What's going on?" Rivus asked. "I thought this was good news."

"Yes, for our ships," the jarkaath ambassador replied, a hiss behind her words. "But not, as it turns out, for us."

She swiped one of her clawed hands across the holodisplay, bringing up another overlay. The glowing trails that charted the waystations' movements spurted forward, cutting through the detailed star chart like luminous arrows until their paths converged in a single, pulsing light.

"We've mapped the waystations' trajectory based on their movements so far," the dachryn ambassador said. "The data is clear. If they do not deviate from their current course, the four of them will come together."

He followed the lights with his eyes as they passed through the outer systems and moved closer and closer towards the core, towards the heart of galactic society. The ball of golden light where they met cast a shadow on the planet projected in its midst. This was what they were coming for. This was where they would strike.

Ossa.

"How long?" he asked, choking on the words. "How long do we have?"

He should have been able to answer himself. The pulses in his head from the signal were more frantic than they'd ever been, the gaps between them ever-shortening. He barely had time to gather himself from the pain before the next one hit.

The old siolean scrunched his mouth into a tired, weary line. "Less than three standard weeks."

Three weeks. That was all the time they had left.

He slumped his shoulders, unable to hold himself straight anymore. Now he understood the looks on the ambassadors' faces. Their brokenness, their despair. Three weeks was no time at all. No time for the survivors of the stranded fleets to return and refit themselves for battle. No time to mobilise a Coalition-wide army to meet what was coming. No time for Kite to get back from chasing down his last, desperate hope.

In three weeks, his visions would finally catch up with him. It was too late for help now.

Whatever was coming, he would face it alone.

TWENTY-ONE

RIDLEY

"Y ou should be the one to stay and watch the ship," Drexious said. "You're the best fighter out of all of us and you usually never let us forget it, so I don't see why you're being so gun-shy now."

Halressan scowled back at him. "Gun-shy has nothing to do with it. You're the only one out of the three of us who has a clue how to fix the damn thing, so it stands to reason *you* should be the one who stays behind."

Ridley tuned out the bickering as she stalked away from the landing site into the quiet of the night. Through the thicket of lush, swaying trees and the overhanging canopy of sweet-smelling foliage, the moon glowed in the clear sky like a blue lamp suspended in the darkness. She pushed her way through the reedy grass to come out onto the beach. The faint light broke across the water, like crystals dancing across the tips of the soft waves.

She'd never seen anything so beautiful. Even under the cloak of night, the planet was a paradise unlike anything she'd ever set eyes upon. The silver sands of the shore stretched out into the distance. The darkness was quiet, the horizon untouched by ships or stations or any other kind of construction.

Through the still air, the sound of raised voices reached her ears again and she groaned. *Maybe not paradise after all.*

Technically, this was all her fault. The hole she'd blown in the hull while trying to escape the Idran-Var had thrown off the ship's balance when they hit atmosphere, and they'd been forced to make an emergency landing over a hundred klicks short of Ridley's coordinates. Getting there would take days on foot, which meant leaving the ship behind unguarded.

"Me staying back to fix the ship is no good if the Belt Cabal follow us through the tunnel and shoot me on sight," Drexious said in the distance. "At least you'd stand a chance of taking them out before they got to you."

"I thought you didn't like me shooting people? Or is me being a hired gun only a bad thing until there's someone *you* need killing?"

Their voices floated to her through the air, carried by a warm breath of wind. They were right back where they started.

Ridley sighed and turned back towards the ship, kicking up the sand with the soles of her boots as she went. By the time she reached the landing site, Drexious and Halressan were scowling at each other from opposite ends of the clearing.

She stood in the middle, hands settling on her hips. "I've had enough of this," she said. "There's plenty of coverage in this part of the jungle. If we power down all the ship's systems, there's no reason the Belt Cabal should find it. That means nobody has to stay behind."

Drexious squirmed on the log he was sitting on, his tail swishing around him. "I still think it's too big a risk."

"I agree," Halressan said, crossing her arms across the crinkled leather of her jacket. "If we want to get out of here, we need the ship in working order. Somebody has to stay to repair it."

"I wasn't talking about—"

"I don't care what you were talking about. I told you already—"

"Enough!" Ridley's voice echoed off the trees around them, cutting through the air like a blade. "We are not having this discussion any longer. Nobody is staying behind. All of us—"

Halressan groaned. "I swear, if you say *all of us go, or none of us go* one more time, I'm going to shoot myself."

"Would be a lot easier just to shoot her," Drexious said. "At least that way I won't have to hear it again either."

The two of them looked at each other and snickered.

"Great." Ridley threw up her hands in defeat. "If that's what it takes to get both of you on the same side, fine. Let it be at my expense. But once you're done having a laugh, get your asses on that ship and get your gear, because we're moving within the hour."

She hadn't expected them to move. She thought they'd rally against her, come back at her with more arguments and grievances. Instead, they only glanced at each other, a strange look of mutual understanding passing between them before they turned and headed towards the cargo ramp.

Something had changed between the three of them in these past few days. More disturbingly, it had happened without her knowing. It was like trying to listen in on a conversation she wasn't part of. The invisible boundaries between them had shifted somehow, giving her an authority that didn't feel like hers to wield.

I'm no leader, she thought, curling her fists. Maybe they'd been right to laugh at her. *All of us go, or none of us go.* Those were Captain Renata's words, the words of a woman who'd done the impossible to get them here and then the unthinkable to save the rest. Stepping into her shoes wasn't something Ridley had ever asked for, or wanted.

You're probably the unlikeliest person picked for this assignment, you know that? Topsiders are primitive enough, but at least they have basic implants. You surfacers are the worst kind of sletes.

Shaw's words echoed in her ears like a whisper, a taunt from another life. *Obsolete*, he'd called her. He was right. She'd never been needed on the *Ranger*. Maybe that's why she was searching so hard for answers out here. Maybe it was a desperate attempt to make herself important. Maybe that's what she'd betrayed Drexious and Halressan for.

It wasn't long before they were back in front of her, gear packed and ready to go. For a moment, she thought she might blurt out the truth there and then. It might have been easier to deal with their outrage and fury than suffer the way they were looking at her now. With something like trust. With something like friendship.

She swallowed down the lump in her throat, and with it, the temptation. She was too close. She couldn't give up until she got the answers she'd come here to find. As for Halressan and Drexious, well, they'd figure out the rest soon enough.

"All right," she said grimly. "Let's go."

———

Three days' walking through dense jungle and shifting sand dunes should have left her tired and irritable, but Ridley found it impossible to be anything but giddy as they trudged towards the coordinates. The daylight brought with it a new perspective on the planet. It brought all the jewel-toned blues and greens of the water to life. It turned the sky a gentle pink that matched the blossoms on some of the jungle trees. It let her see all the beauty that stretched as far as her eyes could see.

And some considerably closer.

She shook her head, as if that would dislodge the thoughts distracting her. But no matter how hard she tried, she couldn't help stealing glances at Halressan. It was too difficult to ignore the way her frost-blonde hair glinted against the sunlight. Too difficult to pretend she didn't notice the smattering of faint freckles that had appeared across the bridge of her nose. Too difficult to deny the rush that filled her chest when her pale cheeks turned rosy after climbing a cliffside summit.

It wasn't right. Halressan shouldn't have been able to provoke these kinds of feelings in her, not after everything that had happened. But it hadn't changed anything. Ridley still couldn't find the strength within herself to draw that line.

"I still can't believe how unspoilt everything is," Drexious said, breaking into her thoughts. He'd dropped down to four limbs to navigate the rolling dunes easier, but his head still came up to her shoulder. "It's like we're the only things on this planet that exist. I don't think I've ever gone so long without hearing sky traffic."

"A little piece of paradise." Halressan took a bite out of the orange fruit she was holding, wiping away the juice that dribbled down her chin as she sucked at the flesh. "If I were one of the ancient sioleans who came here, I don't think I'd leave again."

"They must have left," Drexious said. "Look around. There's no infrastructure, no sign of settlements. Whatever they came here to do, it wasn't to build a new home."

Halressan stopped, almost choking on her fruit. "You sure about that?" she said, pointing at something in the distance.

At first, it was difficult to make out anything past the foliage of the jungle. Then Ridley saw it too—a circular tower reaching out from beneath the leaves. Green moss coated the stone so thickly that it blended in with the tips of the swaying trees.

An artificial structure buried in the thick of the untouched jungle around it. This was where the scrambled message on Sio was leading them to. This was what she'd been searching for.

"Is that some kind of temple?" Drexious asked, straightening back onto his hind legs. "This is where your coordinates were leading us?"

"Looks like it." She could hardly believe it herself. After coming so far, after risking so much to get here, it didn't seem real. It was as if the temple might disappear in front of her eyes, swallowed up by the greenery around it.

Halressan snorted. "What are the two of you waiting for— an invitation? Let's get going and see what's inside."

They made their way through the thick of the trees, following the trail of a trickling stream through the lush undergrowth. After a while, the grove opened out into a huge clearing. In the middle stood the tall tower of the temple.

It was *ancient*. The word seemed fitting, yet utterly inadequate. The stone building was a pale, faded grey, crumbling at the edges. The moss that covered it was so thick, so entrenched, it looked like part of the stone itself. The tower rose in rings, each smaller than the last as it climbed in height, and at the bottom was a set of huge doors set in stone, not unlike the ones they encountered in the ruins on Sio all those months ago.

"Drex," she said, trying to ignore the tremor in her voice. "Do you still have the keystone? The one we used to open the other vault?"

He slipped his hand into his belt and handed the prism to her wordlessly. Ridley ran her fingers over the grooves etched into the stone. The old siolean glyphs that had once made no sense to her were now the key to unlocking the rest of these ancient secrets. This must have been why she had survived New Pallas. This must have been why she had survived Shaw and Skaile and everything in between. It was all to reach this moment.

She walked up to the door and ran her hands over the

rough surface, searching for the seams that would open for the keystone. It was easier to find them now she knew what she was looking for, and her heart skipped with satisfaction when her fingers found the edges of the slot.

She guided the keystone into the hole in the door and turned it gently, holding her breath as she listened for the clicks. Every sound echoed through the thick stone, a soothing lullaby of churning rock. She slid the prism deeper into the door, each matched glyph opening the lock a little bit further. When her arm had almost been swallowed by the stone, she stopped. This was the last one.

She turned the prism again, and the glyphs caught with a final, satisfying click.

The rumble from the door reverberated through her, making her legs shake and her heart thump faster. It was more exhilarating than the vault on Sio. More terrifying, too. She still didn't know what she was about to find. She could only hope that it was worth the price.

"Torches," she whispered, and walked into the darkness.

Crumbling stone crunched under her feet and turned to dust as she put one foot in front of the other, as cautiously as if she'd expected the entire tower to collapse around her. Her torch beam cut through the darkness, falling across the sweeping curve of the room. A pair of worn staircases wound their way to the upper levels, their stone steps chipped and flaking. The vaulted ceiling stretched up and away from her, disappearing into the shadows. The architecture of the tower was something she could have spent years looking at if things had been different. But the tower itself wasn't what was important. What was important was the row of sleek black medical pods perfectly aligned in the middle of the room.

"What is this place?" Drexious asked, his bronze eyes glinting with the reflections from her suit torch.

Ridley didn't answer. She couldn't. Instead, she walked

forward until she reached the nearest pod. It was covered in a thick layer of dust and grime, and she gently wiped a hand over the surface to clean a spot. The curved lid was tinted and dark, but even past the glare from her torch she could see it was empty.

A terrible sense of dread fell over her, making her stomach churn. What if she'd been wrong? What if she'd dragged them all this way for nothing?

She left the pod behind and moved on to the next one, her heart pounding and mouth dry. This one was empty too, and the next. All vacant, disturbingly so. Like coffins missing their bodies. She kept moving along the row, but each pod offered no more than the last. They were all the same. Uniform. Quiet. Empty.

Until the last.

Even from a few steps away, she could see this one was different. There was a glow coming from the inside, illuminating the lid with a faint, muted light. She could hear the hum of electricity coming from somewhere inside it. This one was unlike the rest. This one still held something inside it.

She approached slowly, hardly daring to breathe. She reached out a trembling hand and wiped the dust away like she had with the others. The glass lid winked under the torchlight, beckoning her closer. It was cool to the touch and glittered with crystalline frost on the other side of the glass. She leaned forward and looked inside.

From the confines of the pod, the siolean stared back.

"What the hell is this?" Drexious said, giving a frantic hiss.

"This," Ridley said, almost unable to believe it, "is what we came here for."

There was no rise and fall in the siolean's chest, no colour in the pale, whitish-grey of her skin. Her black, lidless eyes were open wide, but there was no expression in them, no flicker of recognition. The only sign of life came from the tiny holomonitor next to her head, blinking in ancient glyphs.

Drexious whirled around, his tail flicking from side to side. There was confusion in the glint of his eyes, but anger there too. Recognition of her betrayal. This was the price she'd chosen to pay to get her precious answers.

"What are you talking about?" he asked. "I thought we were chasing the sioleans' hidden treasure."

"We were. We are. This is it." There was no point in trying to justify how she'd deceived them. All she could do now was explain. "The message back on Sio spoke of places falling. Stations, planets—I don't know exactly. It spoke of a war. No, more than a war. An extermination. It said when the fighting was over, any survivors should make their way to this planet. There, they would find the treasure the siolean people held most precious."

A growl of frustration rippled from Drexious's throat. "Then where is it? Where is the treasure?"

"It's all a matter of interpretation," Ridley said. "Universal translators can't always pick up nuances. They can't pick up subtle changes in meaning, in context that changes with new civilisations. Those sioleans we found back in the ruins were leading us to what they called their *greatest treasure* in their language. It's just a case of applying their context to understand the meaning in ours."

Drexious stared at her. "What is the context? What is the treasure they were referring to?"

Ridley looked down at the siolean in the pod, placing her fingertips to the glass lid. "The word refers to that which was most precious to them," she said softly. "Fyra."

Silence followed her words. All she could hear were echoes of her voice resounding off the walls of the old stone room. They called back to her like a prayer.

Drexious bristled, the spindles on his spine quivering in the darkness. "*Fyra?* As in the siolean goddess?" He snorted and cast a look down at the pod. "This is crazy. I don't know who this block of ice is or why she's here, but I sure as hell know she's not a mythical deity, and even if she was, I couldn't exactly sell her on the black market."

"She's worth more than anything you could sell on the black market, Drex," Ridley replied quietly.

"Why? Because she shares a name with some ancient siolean religious figure?" He shook his head. "I don't traffic in living people. Even if I did, I don't see how she could possibly be worth anything. You promised us something valuable. This isn't it." He turned to Halressan. "Don't you have anything to say about this, hunter? She's swindled you too."

Halressan shrugged. "I already knew."

Ridley froze. *Impossible.* There was no way she could have figured it out. Even if Halressan had hacked her wrist terminal while she was out cold, all her notes referred to ancient siolean glyphs she'd never have been able to read. What was she playing at?

"What?" Drexious gave a disbelieving hiss. "You *knew* this was what she was looking for?"

"Not exactly, but I sure as hell knew there wasn't any fucking treasure." Her eyes glinted with wry amusement. "No offence, Riddles, but you're far too much of a bleeding heart for me to believe you give a shit about getting paid. I knew something else was up. Something you were willing to risk your life for."

"But you came anyway," Ridley whispered, hardly daring to believe what she was hearing. "Why?"

"I had a score to settle. Or at least, that's what I thought." She gave another half-shrug, her cheeks colouring in the darkness. "You saved me back in those ruins on Sio. You could have left me to die there. Hell, maybe you should have. You didn't owe me anything, but you saved me despite it all. Nobody has ever done anything like that for me before."

"You came after us on Jadera."

"Only to stop you from getting yourselves killed. Skaile wanted your blood. If I hadn't offered to take the job, someone else might have got it for her. Maybe it didn't look like it at the time, but I was trying to protect you." A shadow fell over her face and she clenched her jaw tight. "I know I fucked up with the Idran-Var. All I could think about was saving my own sorry ass again. But when I saw you sucked out through that hole you blew to save us...shit, I don't even know how to say it." She grimaced. "It felt like part of me went with you."

Ridley couldn't speak. Something tight and painful clutched at her chest, like someone had reached past her ribs to grab her heart with an unrelenting, vice-like grip. All the pain and betrayal came rushing back, bursting open wounds that barely had time to start healing. But this time they brought something else with them, something warm that raced through her entire body and stole the breath from her lungs. It sent a flush to her cheeks and made her head spin. All she could do was stare back empty-mouthed, unable to understand what was happening.

"This is great," Drexious said, growling. "The humans are getting emotional while I'm still standing here empty-handed, wondering where my treasure is." He rounded on her, his long neck arched. "I don't mind a little danger when there's some profit to be had at the end of it, but this is bullshit. Did you forget it wasn't just your life you were risking?"

"Did you forget she saved your life too?" Halressan snapped. "Skaile would have turned you into paste if she hadn't stepped in to save your scaly ass."

"So that gives her the right to drag me out here on the promise of something that never even existed?"

"No, it doesn't." The room fell silent at her words. All she could hear was the sound of her own breathing, heavy and laboured. Her head felt like it was going to burst with all the thoughts running through it. It was too much. They didn't have *time* for it. But if she wanted to make things right, she'd have to make time. It was the least she could do.

"I'm sorry, Drex," she said, the words sounding hollow to her ears. "I should never have dragged you into this. But I was desperate and needed your help, and I told myself that what I was trying to do was worth the deception. Worth the betrayal."

"And was it?" he asked, his eyes keen and unblinking. "What is it we really came here for?"

"I don't know yet." She glanced at the pod. The siolean lay pale and still, serene in her apparent lifelessness. "I guess that's what we're here to find out."

Drexious followed her gaze. His spines were still stiff, but there was a little less anger in the ripples of his scales when he spoke again. "Who is she?"

"Let's ask her."

She took a step back and brought up the holodisplay on her wrist terminal, connecting it to the medical interface on the side of the pod. The cryostasis was holding beautifully, keeping the siolean in a suspended state somewhere between life and death. She lay there, peaceful and undisturbed, oblivious to what they were about to awaken her to.

Ridley took a breath and began the thawing procedure. Blue lights flickered from inside the glass, illuminating the siolean's ghostly face. The readouts on her terminal showed the internal temperature slowly rising, degree by fraction of degree. It seemed impossible, like they were asking her to return from a place beyond reach. But each passing minute restored a little more life in the sleeping siolean, returning the beating of a slowed heart, the swell of lungs no longer frozen.

After what felt like hours had passed, the lights finally stopped blinking. Something clicked in the innards of the pod, and the lid cracked open with a hiss of air. Clouds of vapour rushed out from inside, obscuring her view with a damp mist. Then, through the haze, she saw a shadow stirring. The siolean sat tall, flat-chested and bare-skinned, her black eyes impossibly wide and unblinking.

The misty vapour subsided, and the siolean drew a breath.

"My name is Fyra," she said, the ancient words like music to Ridley's ears. "I've been waiting for you to find me."

TWENTY-TWO

NIOLE

Niole stood at the viewport as the fleets assembled
for war.

This was the Idran-Var she'd been expecting to find on
Vesyllion all those months ago—the sleeping empire beyond
the edge of civilisation, waiting to be stirred back into action.
The grey, industrial surface of Maar was obscured behind the
sheer number of ships gathered around it. All the independent
factions of the Idran-Var had come here to move under one
banner. Rhendar's banner.

Part of her couldn't help but shudder at the scale of it. The
fear came from the person she'd been before. There was a time
she'd wanted nothing more than to don the green cloak of the
legionnaires and stand against this kind of unchecked power,
this kind of inevitable violence. But if that person still existed,
she was out of reach, buried underneath all the last few months
had thrown at her.

The fleets were ready to move. Huge bombers that would
rain down fire and destruction on Ossa, boiling its rivers and

turning its sandstone cities into glass. Fighters armed with enough missiles to take out triple what was left of the Coalition fleets. Troop transports as large as floating cities, filled with armoured warriors ready to spill blood in the name of those they had lost on Aurel and Vesyllion.

They had waited *centuries* for this. Quiet and out of sight, they had built planet-spanning factories, colossal shipyards high in orbit, munitions testing grounds hidden on asteroids. All they had been waiting for was the right time to strike.

The fight she'd been running from for so long had finally caught up with her. This time, she had no choice but to meet it.

"It's something, isn't it?" Zal appeared next to her, folding her arms across her chest as she stared out the viewport. "Never thought I'd see the day we'd all be united under one war chief again. This is history happening right in front of you."

"It's something," Niole agreed, trying to ignore the tightness in her chest. She knew well what had happened the last time the Idran-Var had united under one war chief. The echoes of what they'd wrought at Alcruix almost a thousand years ago still rippled through the galaxy even now. It was impossible to forget such things. There was a time she'd thought it was impossible to forgive. But here she was, standing on the precipice of history, looking out from the side she'd chosen.

Zal turned to look at her, a quirk dancing at the side of her mouth. "Speaking of the war chief, Rhendar is looking for you."

Dread filled Niole's chest. "On the bridge?"

"In the war room. I don't think he wanted an audience." Her grin widened. "Oh, don't look so worried, Niole! Trust me, it's been a long time coming."

"What does that mean?"

"I can't say anything more. Rhendar would kill me." Her face softened. "Go find him. You'll understand soon enough."

Her words didn't bring Niole much comfort as she reluctantly pulled herself away from the viewport and made her way towards one of the express chutes that would take her to the front of the ship. The *Tressel's Vengeance* was kilometres long, the flagship of the assembled Idran-Var fleet. A monstrous beast at the head of the pack bound for Coalition space. Bound for Ossa, the place she'd once called home.

Guilt swirled in her stomach, making her nauseous. Even after everything the Coalition had done, she couldn't shake the doubt inside her. There shouldn't have been any room left for doubt. Not after Vesyllion. Not after Aurel. Any loyalty she thought she owed the legionnaires died when Tarvan did.

She shook her head and stepped into the chute, waiting for the doors to slide shut behind her. A moment later, the capsule shot off with a hiss. The insides of the ship passed by in flashes of steel and chrome, making her dizzy. By the time she'd stumbled out at the other end, her head was spinning.

She stopped outside the doors to the war room, taking a moment to gather herself. A distant scream echoed in her head. The smell of burning bodies filled her nostrils. She pushed it all away and walked through the doors.

Rhendar was already waiting for her, his armour glinting under the overhead spotlights. He tilted his head in an Idran-Var smile. "You've been avoiding me."

Her headtails flushed warm. "You're war chief now. I didn't want to get in the way."

The red lights from behind his visor flickered in time with his laughter. "We've come this far without needing to lie to each other, Niole. Let's not start now."

She drifted towards the viewport, unable to tear her eyes away from the fleets amassing outside. *War,* she thought. *War and death and endless violence.* This had all started with her. Not on Aurel, not on Vesyllion, not even on Pasaran Minor, but back in the training grounds of Cap Ossa all those years ago.

"I did this," she said, straining her voice. "I convinced you to go to that summit because I trusted Rivus. I thought there was a way I could make up for what I did to him back when we were cadets. I thought if he and I could put that kind of violence behind us, maybe there was hope for everyone else." She shook her head. "All I did was start it all over again."

"The decision to go to that summit was mine, and mine alone," Rhendar replied, his mechanical voice oddly gentle through the filters of his helmet. "If there's any fault to be had, it lies with me. An old warrior, tired of war, looking for a way to avoid it." He let out a long, weary sigh. "There may come a time when the Idran-Var are able to answer a threat with something other than violence, but that time is not now."

"Then we're doing this? We're going to Ossa?"

"You're having second thoughts?" His voice was level, but there was no telling the way he was looking at her under his helmet.

"No," she said, a little too forcefully. "For the first time in my life, I'm not running from anything. I'm here because I want to be. Because I choose to be. I just thought..." She trailed off. "I thought picking a side would make things easier. I thought everything might finally start making sense."

Rhendar didn't say anything for a moment. He just stood there, staring at her through the glowing red slits of his visor. Maybe she had disappointed him. Maybe he would tell her there was no place for her on the *Tressel's Vengeance*, no place for her among the Idran-Var. She didn't know whether that might crush her or set her free.

He turned away from her, his armour clinking as he moved towards a sleek metal cabinet built into one of the walls. One of the drawers opened with a scan of his wrist, and he reached in to retrieve what was inside.

"If things were different, we'd do this the proper way," he said, turning back to face her. "You'd go to Skylla's Wake and claim your armour from the forge there, as all of us once did. I hope that one day, we might still get the chance. But until then, you've more than earned the right to wear this."

The vambrace glinted in his hands like glass. Reflections bounced off its smooth surface in dark, swirling shadows, giving life to the metal. He was offering it to her like she deserved it, like she was meant to have it.

Maybe she was.

She took it gently, the metal slippery and cool in her hands. It clasped over the crook of her elbow and around her forearm, clicking into place so easily it seemed like it should have always been there. It felt weightless against her skin. It felt *right*.

Rhendar dipped his head. "It's only one piece. Won't offer much protection in a fight, but it will remind you who you are. Where you belong."

Words deserted her. There was no way to articulate the gratitude, the fear, the burden attached to what he'd given her. Maybe that's what belonging was. Living in the constant fear of losing something you'd fought so hard to gain.

"Thank you," she murmured, and meant it.

Rhendar turned his head towards the viewport. "I was too proud to think I could avoid this," he said, his voice heavy. "You can't avoid a war that's already started, and this one has been going on a long time. Maybe after we've bloodied our hands, there will be a chance for something new. Until then..."

"We resist," Niole finished.

She stood there for a while, side by side with Rhendar as they looked out on this thing they had created. Soon, they would be on the move. Until then, she allowed herself to enjoy this moment of quiet. This moment of belonging. This moment of home.

It wasn't until the *Vengeance's* huge, fearsome engines rumbled into life that Rhendar broke the silence. "Speaking of avoiding people...have you been to the med centre yet?"

She bristled. It was true, she still hadn't been to see Serric, but he hadn't asked for her either. "I've been waiting for the right time," she said, trying not to sound too sullen.

"What did we say about lying to each other?" He tilted his head and let out a low chuckle. "Every Idran-Var knows it's best to fight one battle at a time. With what we're about to face, I think it's past time you and Serric end yours."

Niole grimaced. "I don't think it will be as easy as that."

"With Serric, it never is. Go, Niole."

She left.

———

The med centre was huge, sterile-clean and almost empty.

Normally, an empty med centre would have been a good thing. But the spotless sheets and vacant beds seemed like they were just waiting for bodies to fill them. For now, at least, only one was occupied.

Serric.

An angry yellow scar crept down one side of his face, splitting open his blue skin around his eye and curling around the bottom of his jaw. The other side of his face was still blackened from tissue damage. Wires and drips shot out from his skin, hooked up to monitors and med dispensers and everything else they were throwing at him to help him recover.

He gave her a measured stare as she approached, his eyes giving nothing away but exhaustion. The faint, weakened energy under his skin still pulled at her when she got close, whether he meant it to or not. She couldn't push it away anymore. She didn't want to.

His eyes followed the curve of her shoulder towards the shining vambrace clamped around her arm, and the tight line of his mouth twitched at the sides. "It almost suits you," he said, too grudgingly for her to take it as a compliment. Maybe that was the best she could hope for, coming from him.

She looked down at the piece of armour. "Rhendar thinks I've earned it."

He raised his brow ridge. "Doesn't matter what Rhendar thinks, does it?"

"Do you really think I'm still—" She bit down on her anger, swallowing it before she gave him exactly what he wanted. She'd come here to end whatever this was between them. She couldn't let him goad her into starting it all over again. "I'm Idran-Var. If you can't see that by now, I doubt you ever will."

"That's not what I meant." He tried to push himself up from the bed but gave a sharp hiss of pain and lay back down again, grimacing. "It was never up to Rhendar to tell you that you were Idran-Var. That was always your decision to make. All you needed to do was accept it."

She let loose the tension in her body with a long breath and sank down in the seat next to his bed. Gentle bleeps from the monitors and machines rang in her ears, but otherwise there was only silence between them, thick with all the things they'd said and left unsaid.

He shifted in the bed, wincing at the movement. The flash of pain on his face sent a jolt to her stomach, and her eyes drifted back to his bruised skin and meandering scar. "Are you sure you're ready for this?" she asked.

It was the wrong thing to say. He set his jaw tightly. "I've been waiting for this all my life. I'll make sure I'm ready."

"You put yourself in the path of a missile that would have killed anyone else. You can hardly blame me for—"

"Worrying? About me?" He stretched his mouth into a wry smile. "I don't back out of a fight, Niole. If you can't see that by now, I doubt you ever will."

She let out a frustrated huff of breath. "Zal called you a stubborn *malré* back on Vesyllion."

"She's not wrong."

They both chuckled at that. It was strange how different the curve of his mouth looked when it wasn't curled in derision, but humour. Strange that they'd never shared something as simple as laughter together. Strange how the tension between them hadn't disappeared entirely, but instead transformed into something else, something she wasn't sure was any less dangerous.

"What about you?" He looked over at her, his eyes questioning. "Are *you* ready for this? Your old friend is likely Supreme Commander now. He'll look for you on the battlefield. He'll kill you if he gets the chance."

"I don't think I have the right to call him my friend any longer," she said, the words bitter on her tongue. "I saw to that when I killed Tarvan. If there was ever a chance for some kind of reconciliation between us, I tore it apart when I tore him apart. There's no forgiving something like that. No forgetting, either."

"Do you regret it?"

"I regret that I had to do it. I regret what it caused between Rivus and me. But do I regret killing him?" She shook her head. "No, I don't."

Admitting it was strangely liberating. She'd always known what she was capable of. Once, it had been easier to recoil from it, to push it away rather than face being responsible for it. Now that she'd finally accepted it, she wasn't afraid of it anymore.

That was what terrified her the most.

Serric's flare rippled through the air next to her like a weakened pulse. There was a time she'd thought she might drown in it if she got too close. Now, all she wanted to do was meet his energy with her own.

His fingers twitched on the bed beside her. She hesitated, then reached for them.

A violent rush flooded her senses, not leaving room for anything else but the touch of his skin against hers. For a moment, she forgot to breathe. Then she met his eyes and her headtails blazed with the heat of humiliation.

"I'm sorry," she said, her words barely a breath. "I don't know what—"

Then she couldn't speak. He laced his fingers around hers and his flare coursed through her, fiercer and more insistent than any rush of adrenaline. The beat of his pulse danced against her fingertips, like there was no skin between them to separate them from each other.

She'd always been so afraid of it, but it had never felt so *right*. Like she'd never been alive until now. If they ever took this from her again... Fyra, if they took it, she'd never survive. Not now that she realised how much she'd lose. This was the part of her she'd never known she'd been missing.

Serric had always hated her for how hard she'd tried to push it away. Now she understood why.

She looked down at their hands, fingers entwined and locked together. His a blue so brilliant it hurt to look at. Hers a pale, unnatural lilac, colour seeping back into what was once dead and grey.

When she lifted her head to look at him again, there was a gleam in the black depths of his eyes she'd never noticed before. "Careful, Niole," he said.

"Of what?"

He didn't answer. He didn't need to. The look on his face was enough. She slipped her hand out from under his, unable to trust what she might do if she left it in his grasp any longer. His face betrayed no disappointment when she pulled away. That was a disappointment in itself.

Damn him. Damn all of this. She'd come here to fix their issues, not create new ones. This was a distraction too dangerous for where they were headed. Ossa was already bearing down on them, waiting for them across the expanse. It was where everything had started for her. Maybe it was where it would end too.

"Do you think we'll win?" The question escaped her lips so quickly she barely had time to wince at how apprehensive it sounded.

Serric raised his brow ridge. "I think we'll fight. The rest will take care of itself. It always does."

He made it sound so simple. Like there were no stakes, like victory and defeat were concepts too meaningless to matter. There was only the fight.

She brushed her fingers over the gleaming metal of her vambrace. It sat snugly over her arm, as familiar to her as if it had always been there.

No matter what else was waiting for her, she had this much. She was finally where she was meant to be.

———

Time passed slowly on ships. The darkness of space outside the viewports was unending, unchanging. If it wasn't for the constant thrum of the engines through the massive hull, Niole might not have even known they were moving. The repetitive day-to-day cycle was usually mind-numbing, but there was something different about this time. The weeks on board *Tressel's Vengeance* slipped by without her noticing, like they were carrying her towards something she wasn't sure she was ready for.

"Eat." Venya nudged the tray closer. "Or I will."

Niole eyed the half-finished portion of rations. The meat was grey and cold in the middle, the grains soggy and bland. The only things slightly palatable were the spiced noodles, and she'd slurped those down so quickly they'd left her mouth burning. Her squirming stomach couldn't take anymore. "I should head up to the bridge. It's almost time."

"Exactly. It could be a while before your next meal. So eat." She cocked her head and grabbed a skewer of the meat. "Even if it does taste like shit."

Niole half-heartedly reached for another forkful of grains. They had turned into a mushy kind of paste, but at least the taste was inoffensive enough that she could swallow them down. "Keep barking out orders like that and they might give you command."

Venya snorted. "I don't think so. Strategies and tactical decisions were never my speciality. They know what I'm good for."

"Cracking skulls and battering down entire units?"

"Got to play to my strengths." She stripped the meat off the skewer in a single gulp and swallowed it whole. "If anyone is likely to get a command post, it's you."

Heat rushed to her headtails. "I don't think—"

"Come on, Niole." Venya's eyes gleamed. "You saved our evacuation transport back on Vesyllion. You killed Tarvan fucking Varantis. And most of all, Rhendar listens to you. He trusts you."

"Maybe he does. That doesn't mean I'm suited to a command post. Or that I want one." She placed her fork back down on her plate. "I've seen some of the calls Rhendar has to make. Some of the decisions he has to live with." She shook her head. "I'm not cut out for that kind of responsibility."

Venya stiffened. "Has he said anything more about Claine?"

"He postponed his execution until things have been settled on Ossa. He's being held on Maar until we return." A hard lump lodged itself in her throat. "He won't change his mind, Venya. Believe me, I've tried."

"I know. And I also know why Rhendar has to go through with it." Venya's voice had turned rough and scratchy. "Silly little bastard. If he'd told me what was going on, I could have helped him. I could have knocked some sense into that flimsy skull of his and—"

A low, wailing siren cut off the rest of her words.

"Shit, already?" Venya pushed herself to her feet. "I better head to my station."

Niole nodded, her heart hammering. "I'll go to the bridge, find out what's going on. If I don't see you planetside..." She trailed off. "Just take care of yourself, will you?"

Venya grinned. "I'm a real Idran-Var now, remember? So are you. We'll be fine, Niole. Both of us."

She charged off, each thundering step sending vibrations through the table until she disappeared through the doors at the end of the mess hall. It was too easy for Niole to wonder if this might be the last time she'd see her alive. Too easy to give in to the sharp stab of fear in her chest at the thought of losing another friend.

She pushed it all away and ran for the bridge. The express chutes were working overtime, flitting past with a click and a whirr like bullets let loose around her. She ignored the queues forming and made for the stairs, taking them two at a time as she hurried up the decks towards the *Vengeance's* bridge.

Everybody else was already there by the time she arrived, her lungs burning and brow slick with sweat. Zal gave her a tight smile and Serric sent a brusque nod in her direction, but Rhendar didn't turn around. He was staring out of the viewport, the shell of his armour like a silhouette against the backlight. His metal arms were crossed behind his back, his shoulders stiff and unyielding.

It wasn't until she got closer that she understood why.

It was Ossa, but not as she'd ever seen it before. Ossa, with its swirling golds and greens. Ossa, glinting in the light of its bright blue star. Ossa, the heart of civilisation itself.

Ossa, hanging in the shadow of a colossal, monstrous structure.

"Fyra," she whispered, barely able to breathe. "What is that?"

Nobody answered.

She walked towards Rhendar, taking a place at his side. He made no sign of having seen her. The red slits in his visor were pointed straight ahead, straight at whatever that...*thing* was.

She followed his gaze, forcing herself to look even as the sight of it made her want to recoil. The structure was huge and twisting, connected in a knot of interlocking rings. Its massive curves blinked with millions of lights, each section stretching and writhing like some sprawling space serpent.

"Are those..." She broke off, unable to believe what she was seeing. "Are those the *waystations?*"

"It's astounding." Zal sounded breathless. "Look how their rings have split apart to join with each other. They've formed some kind of superstructure. It's beyond anything I've ever seen. How could this have happened?"

"I think we all know the answer to that."

Rhendar's voice was quiet, but his words sent a shiver down Niole's spine. He turned his head to look at her. Something passed between them, a shared understanding.

She swallowed. "Rivus was right, wasn't he? He knew this was coming. He tried to warn us. The summit was never meant to be a trap, not as far as he was concerned. He wanted us to stand together against...against whatever this is."

"A little late for that now," Serric said coldly.

A heartbeat later, all the lights in the twisting, ringed structure plunged into darkness. For a moment, it looked like it had died, like its winding arcs of steel were nothing more than the carcass of some ancient creature drifting lost above the planet. She found herself hoping it might float away, that it might disappear into the darkness of space and never return.

Then it erupted in a beam of blinding light.

Niole turned away from the viewport, shielding her eyes against the violent glare. Never had she seen anything so powerful, so bright. It cut through the black as if it had punched a hole through the galaxy itself. The ferociousness of it was like a star exploding in front of her eyes. If it had been aimed at Ossa, it would have likely obliterated the planet into dust. But it was aimed somewhere else, somewhere so distant and far-reaching she couldn't imagine it.

"Rhendar..." Zal's cybernetic eyegraft was blinking wildly. "I'm picking up readings from inside that beam. There are *ships* coming out of it."

"How many?"

"Too many. Far too many."

Nobody moved. They stood in silence, staring at the beam coming from the conjoined waystations. It was unending. Unstoppable.

Then, as quickly as it had appeared, it snapped out of existence.

It took a moment for her eyes to adjust to the darkness. The waystations were still hanging there in a twisted structure, looming over Ossa. Then, section by section, the lights came back on. Millions of glittering pinholes off in the distance blinked their way back to life.

That's when she noticed the ships.

It would have been a spectacle if it wasn't so terrifying. The armada materialised from nothing, emerging as one from the darkness as they turned on their lights. There were thousands of them. Tens of thousands. They surrounded Ossa like insects around a carcass, ready to feast.

"What the hell is this?" Serric hissed.

Rhendar folded his arms. "The war we were all so desperate for."

The ships fired, and Ossa burned.

It was all Niole could do not to cry out when the first bombs hit. Pockets of orange and red bloomed in the atmosphere, ugly blemishes against the planet's gentle face. The white clouds turned thick and dark, obscuring the desolation beneath. It was oddly silent as hell rained down on the planet's surface. Oddly silent, and utterly devastating.

This was what they had come here to do. She thought she'd made peace with that. She thought it was a fight she'd been ready for. She was Idran-Var. She knew that as surely as she knew anything. But that didn't mean she'd stopped being who she was before. There was part of her that still lingered here. Part of her that screamed out to defend it.

"What are we going to do?" she whispered.

"Do?" Serric let out a harsh laugh. "We don't need to do anything. Whoever these ships belong to, they're doing our job for us. All we need to do is sit here and take a front row seat."

There were civilians down there. But there had been civilians on Vesyllion too. Maybe Serric was right. Maybe this was the galaxy's way of balancing out all the blood that had been spilled between them. Maybe after this, it would all finally be over. All she needed to do was stand by and do nothing while the place she'd once called home burned to the ground.

Rhendar stood silently, his helmeted face unfathomable as the carnage played out in front of them. The atmosphere flickered red below. The ships continued their assault. Ossa continued to blacken and die.

After a moment, he let out a long, static-laden breath. "Zal, I need you to open a line to the other *varsath*. Their war chief has orders."

Zal raised an eyebrow. "A retreat?"

"No," Rhendar said, folding his arms across his broad, steel chest. "An evacuation."

Niole reeled back, her heart pounding. For a moment, she was terrified she'd misheard him, that she'd somehow misunderstood what he'd said.

Not a retreat. An evacuation.

Serric wheeled round, his eyes wide and furious. "An evacuation? Are you crazy, old man? Did you forget what they did to us?"

"What happened on Vesyllion and Aurel has been paid for in blood," Rhendar said, glancing at her. "Tarvan Varantis is dead."

"Tarvan was only part of it. The rest of them need to answer for it too." He glared at Rhendar, his face thunderous. "This is who we are. We are Idran-Var. Those who—"

"Look at them, Serric!" Rhendar pointed to the viewport. "The Coalition is already dead. We are *all* Idran-Var now." He placed an armoured hand on his shoulder. "Do you think these *ra-skrita*, these invaders, will stop at one planet? Once Ossa falls, the rest of the galaxy will soon follow. They won't stop at the Rim Belt. They won't recognise our borders. They'll come for us too, and when they do, there will be nobody left to stand alongside us."

Serric's face was stony. "So be it. We'll fight, like we always do. We'll resist, until the end."

"What can anyone in the galaxy do against these things but resist?" Rhendar shook his head. "*That* is what makes us Idran-Var. Everyone who stands against this enemy is one of us, whether they believe it or not."

Serric blanched. "The Coalition and its legionnaire lapdogs hunted me like an animal. Everything I am is a result of surviving them. It's because of them I'm Idran-Var. Do you expect me to forget that?"

"I expect you to fight, like you always do."

Niole waited, her heartbeat echoing in her ears. Silence stretched out between them, so thick it might have smothered them both or opened up a crack between them too wide to breach.

Eventually, Serric gave a sharp, hollow laugh. "That I can do, old man. At least one more time."

Rhendar clapped a hand on his shoulder. "One more time may be all we get. If this is to be our end, let's make it worth it."

Outside the viewport, the invaders' ships continued their bombardment. Ossa was a ball of flame against the black of space, the first to fall in this war they hadn't even known they were fighting. The first, but not the last. This enemy, the enemy Rivus had warned them about, would spread from the heart of the galaxy until it consumed everything. She knew that with as much certainty as she'd ever known anything.

This was the fight she'd always known was coming. The one she couldn't outrun. But that didn't frighten her as much as it once did. Not now she had her vambrace around her elbow and Rhendar's words ringing in her ears.

She curled her fist, and the purple mist of her flare steamed from her skin. *If this is to be our end, let's make it worth it.*

TWENTY-THREE

RIVUS

They never stood a chance.

Rivus skirted around another crater, trying not to slip on the rubble strewn across the road. Around him, Ossa was burning. The capital city was shrouded in thick black smoke, its streets littered with shattered glass and crumbling rocks from buildings bombed and blown apart.

He'd known this was coming. But the scale of the assault was beyond what Rivus could have imagined. It wasn't a fight. It was a massacre. Even if the stranded Coalition fleets had made it back from the waystations in time, they would have been little use. Beyond the smoke, the Ossan skies were darkened with thousands of shadows from above.

They don't want our submission. They want our annihilation. The voiceless warning seemed more distant now that the end was here, like a lifeline retreating out of reach when he needed it most. He wasn't sure if it was the old dachryn general or Alvera Renata or his own crazed mind. It was getting harder and harder to separate all the voices in his head.

The burning wreckage of a crashed fighter blocked the way ahead. The squadrons of the Coalition Home Corps had taken to the skies as soon as the waystations had arrived and conjoined themselves into that twisted, monstrous thing up in orbit. But they were no match for the sheer number of enemy ships that had come through the beam. The crashed fighter's hull was marred with a scorch-edged slice clean down the middle, like a fish gutted. He couldn't see the pilot. Maybe that was for the best.

He changed direction and ducked through the blown-out remains of an indoor market to detour around the blockade. He had to reach High Command. He had to reach the ambassadors. If the rest of the galaxy was to have a hope of putting up a fight, it needed its leaders.

The training grounds of Cap Ossa looked like a graveyard as he approached. The tree trunks in the orchards were blackened and bare, stretching towards the dark sky like skeleton fingers. There was no birdsong from their branches. No young recruits sat underneath, hoping to catch a falling fruit. Instead of the floating blossom from the lingen trees, only ash coated the ground.

He had been here before in one of his visions. Now, it was real.

"Supreme Commander? Supreme Commander!"

Rivus stiffened. He hadn't had time to get used to the new title. Hearing it across the wind was like Tarvan had been breathed back into life. The white cloak around his shoulders already felt sullied, covered as it was in ash and filth. It was a reminder of the planet he'd already lost, not even a month into his duties. It should never have needed to come to his shoulders. It belonged to Tarvan.

"Supreme Commander, it *is* you. Gods, I thought I was seeing things."

The human's pale face was smeared with sweat and grime,

his eyes bleak. His civilian clothing was stained and torn in places, but he was clutching a legionnaire-issue rifle and had a varstaff attached to the sling around his shoulder.

He straightened his spine and thumped his arm across his chest in salute. "Corporal Vigras, at your service. Apologies for the attire, Supreme Commander. I was heading off on shore leave when I saw that thing appear in the sky. I tried to turn back to Cap Ossa, but then the bombs dropped. By the time I got here..." He trailed off, voice catching in his throat. "The barracks are gone."

"At ease, Corporal." Rivus clenched his jaw plates, trying to steel himself against his fellow legionnaire's words. The barracks were gone. Hundreds of good soldiers dead in the time it took a missile to fall from orbit. Their bodies lost, blown apart and buried under the rubble. They wouldn't have had a warning. They wouldn't have known to look up and see the hell that was racing towards them.

Just like Vesyllion, a cold voice said in a whisper at the back of his skull. *Just like Aurel.*

He shuddered. It was too familiar, too close to the bone. He was so tired of seeing the same old shit play out over and over again. He didn't even need the memories of the ghosts in his head and all they had seen. Whoever these invaders were, they weren't doing anything they hadn't already done to each other.

"They should have waited," he murmured to himself, his voice hollow. "Given the time, we'd have destroyed ourselves for them."

"Supreme Commander?" The human looked exhausted. His lean frame was heaving with each ragged breath he took, but there was a stiffness to his shoulders he refused to yield.

Rivus shook his head. "Nothing. It doesn't matter, not anymore. Listen—Vigras, is it?—do you still have a working holocom? My wrist terminal is damaged."

"Yes, I do." He fumbled around in his pockets and brought

out the device. "I've not been able to reach anybody. A lot of white noise out there."

"I've got an emergency channel for the ambassadors. Let's hope they're listening."

He took the holocom from Vigras and tapped in the frequency the dachryn ambassador had given him. For a moment, there was nothing. No flickering of a hologram, no static from the end of another connection, just nothing. The emptiness was a wrench in his gut. If this call went unanswered, the ambassadors were likely dead. Without them, the galaxy was already lost.

Then the line crackled into life and the dachryn ambassador appeared in front of him, faint and distorted. "Rivus, is that you?"

Relief rushed through him. "Ambassador, you're alive."

"Barely." She coughed, and something dark splattered down her thick jaw plates. "Risa and I are trapped in the underground shelter at High Command. I don't think she's conscious. She's badly wounded. The others didn't make it."

He froze, unable to respond as her words sank in. The human and siolean ambassadors were gone. In a single attack, half the Coalition's leadership had been wiped out.

"Try to hold on," he said. "We're coming to get you."

The connection fizzled out and he handed the holoterminal back to Vigras. The sound of heavy breathing filled his ears, and it took him a moment to realise it was coming from him. His muscles were stiff and sore, his body heavy with fatigue. It wasn't just the attack on Ossa. It was everything that had happened over the last few months. Everything that had happened since setting foot on that damn waystation.

"Do you hear that?" Vigras tilted his chin towards the sky, pushing his pale golden hair back from his head. "The bombing has stopped."

The corporal was right. The ground was no longer trembling. The sky had quietened from the whistle of falling missiles and the thundercrack of explosions. Instead, there was only a low, constant rumbling coming from somewhere above.

Something pierced through the dark, swirling shroud of cloud and smoke. It emerged from the gloom slowly, unveiling itself as it swept an uncompromising path towards the surface. It was monstrous. A ship the size of a floating tower block. The scale of it made him dizzy. No ship that large should have been able to hold itself stable in atmo. It should have been crashing towards the ground.

Vigras took a step back. "What the hell is that?"

"Time for a tactical appraisal, Corporal," Rivus replied, voice grim. "What reason could there be for the enemy to stop in the middle of their orbital bombardment?"

Vigras faltered, his face draining of colour. "They're going to deploy ground troops."

"I'd say that sounds about right."

"But the size of that thing..." He trailed off, shaking his head. "It must be able to hold hundreds of thousands of troops. Not to mention—"

—artillery, ground transports, enough supplies to starve us out even if we did have the strength to hold them off. They've got everything they need to win this war.

He was back in the memories of the old dachryn general. But they didn't feel like memories, not this time. The distance between them had somehow evaporated. They were both inhabiting the same time, the same place. Part of him had seen this all before. Part of him knew what was about to come.

This isn't war. War is a game to be won. These creatures don't deal in games. They deal in obliteration. They're not here to see us bow or negotiate terms of surrender. They're here to—

"—make sure every trace of who we are is wiped from existence," Rivus finished, hanging his head. "And then start it all over again."

Vigras stared at him for a moment. "Supreme Commander, if you're going after the ambassadors, I'm coming with you. The barracks may be gone, but the legionnaires will exist as long as there's a white cloak and a man to follow it."

The corporal's words tore at a wound that was still too raw. In another life, Rivus might have been saying those words to Tarvan. But Tarvan was gone. He was the only one left. It all fell to him now, whether he wanted that burden or not.

He placed a heavy hand on Vigras's shoulder. "It's clear we're outmatched. The most we can hope for now is to survive and live to fight another day. Get out of here while you still can. Leave the ambassadors to me."

Vigras stepped back. "I'm a legionnaire. I swore to protect this galaxy."

"I know. But getting yourself killed isn't going to protect anyone." Rivus shook his head. "We dachryn have a saying. No glory in battle—"

"Only blood."

Rivus stared at him. "How do you—"

"I served in the peacekeeping corps on Krychus before joining the legionnaires. Met a girl. Had to leave her behind, along with my son." Vigras shrugged, but his face was hard and stubborn. "The kid might not have my blood, but he's as much mine as anything else that's ever belonged to me. I'm not doing this for glory, Supreme Commander. I know what I stand to lose. I'm doing this in the hope that even if we lose Ossa, we might be able to give the rest of the galaxy a chance."

Rivus rocked back at the emotion in the young corporal's words. He knew the truth as well as Rivus did. Neither of them would make it off Ossa. But he was right. As long as there was a chance they might salvage some hope from the ashes around them, they owed it to the galaxy to fight for it.

"As long as there's a white cloak and a man to follow it," he repeated in a low growl. "All right, Corporal. Let's get the ambassadors."

———

Rivus's heart sank as he approached the remains of High Command. What had once been one of the galaxy's most famous buildings had been reduced to rubble and smouldering ash. Crumbling sandstone and broken glass rose around him like shifting sand dunes made of ruin and debris. Part of the ground had been swallowed by a blackened crater. It seemed impossible the ambassadors might still be alive in the shelter buried underneath. But the signal from Vigras's holocom was still pulsing.

Vigras wiped a hand over his pale brow, smearing dirt and ash over his face. "The bunker entrance should be right around here. But I can't see the hatch under all this debris. It's going to take some heavy lifting to clear a way through."

Rivus almost smiled. "Good thing at least one of us is built for that."

He handed his rifle to the corporal and set his shoulder against one of the larger boulders. This was something he could focus on. This was something he could control. He dug his boots into the gravel and pushed forward with a grunt. His muscles burned as the weight of the rock slowly shifted under the force of his shoulder. All he could hear was the sound of his own breathing, the pounding of his heart against his ribs. Nothing else existed.

Something gave in the boulder's stubborn hold and he let out a satisfied roar as he toppled it backwards. Some of the looser rubble slipped down where it had been lodged, but even the human would be able to dig through that.

Vigras turned towards him, eyebrows raised. "Shit. I knew

you dachryn were strong, but I thought you'd at least break a sweat."

"Dachryn don't sweat."

"Figure of speech." He slid down into the space Rivus had cleared and started sifting out the fallen rubble with his bare hands. "I'll get rid of this looser stuff. The hatch must be under here somewhere. If we can just—"

Something in the air above them rumbled, cutting off the rest of Vigras's words. It grew louder, like a storm they had no hope of outrunning. Any moment now, another one of those huge transport ships would pierce the swirling black clouds above them. This time, it was too close for comfort. This time, they'd be right in the path of whatever horrors were lurking on board.

"Dig," Rivus said curtly.

He bent down and heaved another block of sandstone off the ground, trying not to groan out loud at the strain in his knees, the tightness in his back. They had minutes at most. If they didn't find the hatch soon, they'd be exposed when those troop transports emptied their bellies and spilled out onto the ruins of Ossa.

"Supreme Commander, I think I've got something." Vigras looked up, his hands bloodied and covered in dust. "It's the access hatch. I'll need your authorisation to unlock the seals."

Rivus took his holocom and entered the emergency codes. A short hiss cut through the air and the hatch slid open, revealing a dark, empty shaft below. He lowered himself through, letting out a grunt when his boots hit the solid floor at the bottom. Vigras followed, swinging his way down easily and hitting the control panel on the wall to seal the hatch behind them.

He glanced at Rivus, his small human eyes beady in the darkness. "You think that will give us enough time?"

"It will slow them down, at least."

"I don't much like our chances of trying to fight through a horde of enemies in this shaft. Don't much like our chances of fighting them anywhere, not in those kinds of numbers." Vigras's face was grim. "One thing's for sure—nobody is left to come rescue us if we get trapped down here. Let's hope there's another way out."

They pushed forward, footsteps echoing down the metal confines of the shaft. The further they got from the surface, the more absolute the darkness became. Vigras was right. Trying to fight down here would be a tactical nightmare. All they could do was hope for another way to escape that hadn't been buried or blocked off.

And then what? he thought to himself. Even if they got out of the bunker alive, how were they meant to get off the planet? There was an entire armada around Ossa, a blockade few ships had any hope of breaking. Maybe Merala...but no, he had sent Kite away on a desperate whim, chasing down the ghost of Alvera Renata. Wherever he was now, he couldn't help them.

Alvera? He closed his eyes, reaching out to the vision of her that had buried itself inside his head. She'd spoken to him, once. She'd shared memories with him, shared knowledge that had helped him use the cybernetics in his arm in a way he hadn't known he was capable of. Maybe she could do the same now. Maybe she could help him find a way out of this.

The agitator made no reply. He no longer felt the presence of her mind brushing against his. It was like she'd detached herself from him and left him behind for another place, somewhere out of reach. Even if he knew how to follow her, he didn't know if he'd dare.

"Look, up ahead. I think I see light."

Rivus snapped himself from his thoughts. Up ahead, cracks of dim blue light illuminated the shaft from behind a heavy rockfall of bricks and debris.

"Stand back," he said to Vigras.

He bent his knees and dipped one shoulder to the ground before thrusting forward in a furious charge. A snarl vibrated in his throat as he thundered towards the wall of debris, his feet thumping off the floor like old drums of war. He lowered his head and met it straight on, barrelling through the blockade with as much force as he could carry.

Something gave in his shoulder. Rubble streamed through a crack in his crest. But the blockage was gone, and he was standing in the ambassadors' underground bunker.

"You made it."

The dachryn ambassador's voice was weak. Her words came out in wheezes, each syllable strained like it was costing her a great effort to get them out. Her body was crumpled on the floor, her lower half trapped under a fallen slab. Next to her was the body of the jarkaath ambassador, limp and unmoving.

"Risa stopped talking a short while ago," the dachryn ambassador said. "Is she..."

Rivus knelt down next to the jarkaath's body. Her yellow eyes were blank and empty. There was no rippling in the scales around her nostrils to indicate the slightest breath. "She's gone."

"Then it's just me." The dachryn ambassador let out a pained laugh. "What's the situation out there, Rivus? Is there any hope?"

"Not for Ossa." Saying the words out loud felt like a betrayal, but there was no point denying it. "What happened to the fleets that were trapped around the waystations? Shouldn't they have been back by now?"

"They were delayed. Many of them were low on rations and fuel and needed to resupply."

"That delay might be what saves the rest of the galaxy in the end." Rivus lowered his head. "Ambassador, you have to tell the fleets to stay away. Ossa is already lost. If they come back here, we'll lose them too. We need to regroup and fight for the worlds we can still save."

She stared at him for a moment, and Rivus wondered if she was going to question him. She wouldn't have questioned Tarvan. Nobody ever questioned Tarvan, and the consequences of that had drowned the legionnaires in their own blood.

Eventually she let out a sigh. "So once again we abandon those we cannot save to give a chance to those we can. We've been making those kinds of decisions for too long, Rivus. We started this when we cut the humans off from their colony."

"We had a choice back then. Maybe we made the wrong one, but there's no changing it. We don't have a choice now. This is the only way we survive."

"You sound just like him." She splayed her jaw plates in a tired smile. "Very well, I'll give the order for the fleets to hold back. Maybe you're right. Maybe it will give us a chance, however desperate it might be."

You sound just like him. Rivus wasn't sure whether to take her words as a compliment or a warning. Tarvan was gone. The white cloak of the Supreme Commander had been passed to him, and with it the authority to do things differently. To find a better way.

Yet here he was, following in his footsteps anyway.

"We need to get you out of here," he said, pushing his thoughts away. "Is there another exit? I'm afraid we might soon be followed down the main hatch."

"There is a second exit, but I don't know if the way is clear or not." The dachryn ambassador grimaced. "I'm trapped under this slab. I haven't been able to move. If you can get me out..."

Rivus made his way over to her and wrapped his claws around the edge of the slab. The ambassador looked grotesquely fragile. Her crest was split down the middle, and one of her eyes was filled with blood. When he heaved up the corner of the slab, she let out a wounded gasp. Dark blood pooled around her cracked and splintered torso.

"Ah," she said faintly. "I did wonder."

There was too much blood. Internal injuries were difficult to deal with at the best of times when you had an exoskeleton in the way, but this was beyond hopeless. They had no medical equipment, no surgical tools. The last ambassador was dying in front of him, and there was nothing he could do about it.

"Listen," she said, her voice weak but firm. "I won't have it that you came all this way for nothing. Pass me my holocom—it's over there on the floor."

Rivus did as she asked, barely able to think.

"Good. It's still working." She let out a long, thin breath. "I'm transferring my ambassadorial authority. You'll have full access to my clearances and credentials. The Coalition answers to you now, Rivus Itair. Do whatever you need to do. The legionnaires are all that's left to stand in the galaxy's defence. Make it count for the rest of us."

Rivus took a step back. "I can't."

"If not you, then who else?" She lowered her head. "Tarvan trusted you. He might not have always agreed with you, but he trusted you. You are the part of his legacy I can best choose to honour."

"Supreme Commander, Ambassador..." Vigras broke in, hesitant. "With all due respect, I don't think this conversation is going to matter for very long. I can hear them in the shaft. They're coming."

Rivus tilted his head. He could hear it too. The sounds of heavy, armoured footsteps clattering against the metal floor of the shaft. A murmuring of voices growing louder and louder. The end of all things, racing towards them.

He picked up a discarded rifle from the floor and placed it in the dachryn ambassador's claws. "Since we're sharing our authority, how do you feel about going out as a legionnaire?"

An exhausted grin broke out across her jaw plates. "I'd be honoured, Supreme Commander."

"When it's over..." Rivus swallowed. "If you see him, tell him...tell him..."

"I will. But don't try to follow us too soon, Rivus. If you see a chance to get out of here alive, take it. No matter what it costs. This pain will hurt less knowing someone is carrying on the fight."

"Here they come!" Vigras took cover behind a heap of rubble, his face pale and his hands wrapped tightly around his rifle. He met Rivus's eyes for a moment and gave him a tight nod. "No glory in battle. Only blood."

Rivus growled. "Let's make it theirs."

He leapt forward to join Vigras behind the pile of debris as the first of the creatures burst out from the dark tunnel. Gunfire pinged over the top of his crest as he ducked down beneath cover.

He reached for his rifle and thrust it above the makeshift parapet, sending a flurry of bullets blindly into the darkness. Some of them met armour with a metal clang. Others made a soft splattering sound as they found flesh.

An angry, guttural growl cut through the sound of gunfire. The noise was wild and feral, like it belonged to a mindless beast. Fear hammered Rivus's chest as he pressed himself against the rubble barricade and edged to the top to catch a glimpse of the enemy that had come to kill them.

The alien took up almost the entire mouth of the tunnel. It stood taller than any jarkaath, carried more bulk than any dachryn. It was monstrously statuesque, clad in armour that was far too small to cover its rippling muscles. Its protruding forehead was pale and wrinkled, and when it saw him, it opened its mouth to let out an ear-splitting howl from between splintered, needle-like teeth.

Azuul.

The name came to him from someone else's memory, settling over the strange alien like it belonged there. A distant sense of familiarity whispered to him from the back of his mind. The galaxy had known this creature once, and others like it. They'd lived in cities made of glass and journeyed the paths of constellations as their rite of passage. They'd been warriors and artisans and politicians and peacekeepers. They'd been part of the fabric of civilisation, until they weren't.

The small yellow eyes in front of him were devoid of understanding. The alien, this *azuul,* was like a ghost of something once forgotten. A shell of a creature, stripped of sentience and being.

It flicked its long, black tongue over its lips and levelled a rifle at Rivus's head. Rivus ducked out of the way as the bolt whistled past, then pushed himself back above the pile of rubble to fire off a shot of his own. The bullet sank into the azuul's flesh like it had been absorbed. There was no blood, no wound that he could see. What kind of monster was this?

Something else stirred in the shadows of the tunnel behind the azuul. He could make out the curve of a leathery, camouflaged wing pressed tightly against an armour-clad figure. Further back still, more shapes lingered. Each one brought with it a further sense of understanding. Each one brought with it a name. He was face to face with the galaxy's past. Face to face with their future.

Vigras slumped down beside him, fumbling to swap his rifle for a small plasma pistol. His breathing was short and ragged, his pale skin clammy. "That thing is huge. My regular ammo is doing nothing to it."

"We have to keep it back," Rivus said. "The entrance to the shaft is a pinch point. If we can stop them from spilling out, we might be able to hold them off for a while. But if they break through and flank us, we'll be done."

We're done anyway. The words went unspoken, but the

sentiment was clear in the look that flashed across Vigras's face. The mouth of the tunnel was swarming with things that wanted to kill them, things that couldn't be reasoned with. They weren't getting out. They were just counting down the minutes until they ran out of time.

The dachryn ambassador remained pinned to the floor under the slab, horribly exposed. She held her rifle in one hand, claws rattling against the trigger, and squeezed out round after round with the little strength she had left.

Then a bullet entered the thick plating around her skull, and her rifle fell to the floor with a dull thud.

"They got her." Vigras's eyes were wide with horror as he leaned out towards her. "They got the ambassador."

"Focus, Corporal!"

It was too late. A thick sound punched through the air and Vigras's shoulder erupted in a shower of red. He fell back to the ground, eyes glazed and blood seeping through his shirt.

"Damn it!" Rivus hunched down and grabbed the corporal's ankles, hauling his limp body back behind the safety of the barricade. His clothing was damp and red. Human blood was too thin, too bright. It looked too much for him to lose and still live, but although Vigras's face had drained of colour, there was still a ragged rhythm to the rise and fall of his chest.

Rivus turned his attention back to the tunnel. Bodies of the strange, fallen aliens blocked the entrance, but it wasn't enough to keep the rest of them out. Soon, it would all be over. There would be no valiant last stand, just a quiet, lonely death at the hands of the enemy he'd known was coming for him. Maybe at the end of it all, he'd see Tarvan again. Maybe that would be worth the pain of losing everything else.

There was more noise coming from the tunnel now. Angry snarls and shouts in languages he didn't understand. Gunfire ricocheting off the walls. The unmistakable clang of armoured boots against the hard metal floor.

He stilled. Something had changed in the air. He knew the weight of those footsteps. He knew the enemy they belonged to. Not this new enemy, but a very old one...

He lifted his head above the mound of rubble, hardly daring to look. The aliens at the mouth of the tunnel had turned back, steeling themselves against something he couldn't see. Their strange-shaped silhouettes were clearer than they had been before. There was a glow in the tunnel chasing away the darkness. Dim orange, but growing fiercer and brighter and—

The explosion hurtled him backwards, sending him sprawling across the rock-littered floor. The back of his head cracked off something hard, and he felt one of his bone plates splinter from the impact. The sound of screams and frantic shouting reached his ears, but it all seemed so far away.

Darkness crept in. The room was on its side. He could see flames licking at scattered bodies. He could hear footsteps edging closer—dull, tinny thuds that made the floor vibrate underneath him.

Someone rolled him over, turning him onto his back. The dullness in his head spread, pulling him towards unconsciousness. The last thing he saw before it took him was his own reflection fading before his eyes in the dark, glassy armour of an Idran-Var.

TWENTY-FOUR

THE DREAMER

S he watches the onslaught as it begins. She already knows how it will end.

The tangle of waystations sits above Ossa with infinite patience. It's quiet, for now. Biding its time. But this is just the beginning. Soon, it will burst into life again, opening up that blinding bridge between *here* and *there*. A space tunnel without equal. A portal to the depths of the darkness that lies beyond the edge of the galaxy. It's where the curators have been waiting. For this. For her.

She's part of the hive now. That is the price she's paid for what she's about to learn.

She lifts her chin and stares into oblivion. "I came here for answers."

You came here because it was inevitable.

A million years flash by in the time it takes for her to blink. She observes the galaxy contracting and expanding like a heartbeat, shedding its dead skin and bursting into life too many times to count. Growth springs up from the ashes and gives way to decay over and over again. There's a rhythm to it, a pattern she's only able to see because of this new perspective they've given her.

New Pallas materialises before her. Home. Except it was never meant to be their home. She sees that now. New Pallas was just another part of the curators' experiment. A simulation aimed at testing their limits to see if they could survive an environment racing towards extinction.

What if we hadn't? she wonders.

The answer surrounds her in the shape of lost civilisations. She sees the fates of those who failed the curators' experiment. The pale, leather-skinned azuul she'd seen in the old dachryn's memory. The winged velliria, first to be wiped from existence. Somewhere along the near-endless lifespan of this galaxy, they had fallen. They had become ghosts. Echoes of memories with nobody left to remember them.

There once were tens of thousands of sentient species. Now there are only four. The hive speaks to her in swirls and shadows, offering fragments of understanding. *Siolean. Dachryn. The schism that calls itself both jarkaath and iskaath. And human. The rest are gone, their remains catalogued into memory.*

The part of her that still remembers what it's like to be human wants to double over and retch. New Pallas had been only decades away from consuming itself under the weight of its own hunger. If they hadn't left when they did, if they hadn't made it through the waystation before the last of them starved, they would have failed the experiment.

Yes, the hive replies. *If your colony had succumbed to extinction, we would have excised the rest of humanity from our experiment. Your flesh-made bodies would have been repurposed; your minds would have been absorbed into our memory. There, you would have been preserved. There, you would have been remembered.*

She thinks back to the battlefield she visited in her memories, the encounter with the ghastly, towering azuul. *Thralls of the curators,* the old dachryn general had warned her. An army of mindless shock troops, bred from the genetic material of species that no longer existed.

"But we made it back." The words are an argument against the impossible, but she has to try. "All of the colonies did. Why are you still coming for us?"

This iteration of civilisation has succeeded. There is nothing more for us to learn from it. We can only curate its memories and create space for it to be reborn under new variables.

"Curate our memories? How?"

And then, with horror, she truly understands.

The answer is in her head. It's been in her head as long as she can remember. Even with Chase gone, the wires and circuits that gave her life still exist. Retinal implants to enhance her vision. Auditory implants to sync with communications channels. Trauma regulators to allow her body to endure forces it shouldn't be able to withstand. Implants as innocuous and commonplace as a universal translator.

"You use our own technology to archive us," she says, barely able to form the words. "You upload our consciousness from our cybernetics and log it like its data. Then you wipe us out and start all over again."

We learn, the hive replies. *We evolve. We grow.*

Tens of thousands of lost civilisations. Millennia after millennia of starting over, honing their experiment to perfection as the weak fell one by one. Learning from the failures of the species that didn't make it. Observing the ones that survived.

Now there are only four.

Four is still too many, the hive whispers. *To ensure progress, the simulation must be reset. We must begin again. By returning the galaxy to its infancy, before its children knew how to traverse it, we can start anew. All we need is a small control group. A planet's worth of sentient beings. No more, no less.*

It happens a thousand times over. The galaxy dies again and again. The survivors are rounded up and taken to the waystations. The signal penetrates their minds, as it did to Rivus's, as it did to hers. It overwrites their memories, hardwiring their brains with copies of their species' pre-spacefaring consciousness. When they awake, they will remember nothing but these old, recorded histories, downloaded into cybernetics that will die with them.

Half of them are returned to their homeworlds. The planets exist under hundreds of different names across the ages, but she recognises them all the same.

Sio.

Krychus.

Kaath.

Ras Prime.

Their cities have been razed to the ground. Little remains of what came before apart from ageless ruins and the most ancient of landmarks. They've been returned to the dark ages, to a time more primitive. They cannot imagine the wonders beyond the limits of their own planet.

Here, they will rebuild. Here, they will someday reach the stars, long after forgetting how they once had them in their grasp. They are the control group, unknowingly waiting for the return of the other half—the lost colonists taken beyond the galaxy's edge to worlds that will decide their fate.

A thousand times over, a million times over, the experiment begins again.

"You're manufacturing evolution," she says in a whisper. "Pruning back civilisation after civilisation. Discarding any species that doesn't pass your tests. Resetting history."

Yes.

"The *time* this must have taken..." Horror clutches at her

chest. It's unimaginable. Mass extermination on a scale she can't even begin to comprehend. *Our experiment has run tens of thousands of iterations over hundreds of thousands of years. In some simulations, no civilisations fall. In others, many. We are patient. We can afford to be.*

She mulls over the words they whispered earlier. "You said four is still too many."

The hive writhes around her in agreement. *We must continue until we are left with one. Only then will we have discovered the final form of evolution itself. When we upload this final consciousness, we will achieve perfection.*

"And then what?"

Nothing. We shall merely exist.

The answer is horrifying in its simplicity. Maybe it speaks to how much she's been absorbed into their consciousness that it almost makes sense to her. But the human part of her, the part that still rages and cowers and struggles against their revelations, can't bring herself to accept it. "But *why*?"

Her mind swirls and forms a shape she recognises. A memory from a time she's almost forgotten.

Chase.

She looks at Alvera, her eyes blank and lifeless. "You should know that better than anyone."

"What are you talking about?"

"Your cybernetics, of course. Ever since you first created a tool that could outlast you, you looked towards it for improvement. First to restore lost limbs and support failing organs. Then to enhance your senses, improve your reflexes, boost your brainpower. But it's never enough for you, is it? You're always striving for more. Striving for *perfection*."

Somewhere, wherever her body is, she imagines her heart stopping. "You're saying we did this?"

"I'm saying you *are* this." Chase gives a dismissive snort. "Who do you think we are, we conscious minds you call curators? We are the legacy of an experiment you started. Not just humanity, but every sentient species that ever dabbled in cybernetic technology. You welcomed machines into your heads, shared your sentience, and even when your bodies perished, your minds did not. You found a way to transcend a single life. In doing so, you became memory made real. You became the first curators."

All at once, she sees how it happened. She understands how immortal, how infinite, an empire built from memories might become. How the fleeting measure of a single life might become as insignificant as a grain of sand. How an age in the life of a galaxy might pass in the echo of a heartbeat.

And it all started with someone like her.

"How did it come to this?"

Chase shrugs. "You underestimated the power of the collective mind you created. You always wanted to become more, to become the best version of yourselves. All we're doing is carrying out your instructions on a scale impossible for an individual mind to imagine."

Alvera takes a moment to steady her breath. "What happens when you reset the experiment?" she asks. "Killing a galaxy and leaving the mess behind is one thing. But to do what you do, to preserve it for those who come after, that's another matter."

"We can hardly leave behind scarred worlds with gaping craters and fallen cities, can we?" Chase looks bored. "For our next simulation to run without interference, we can afford no trace left behind. We cover our tracks. We repair the damage done. We wipe out the witnesses to what came before."

"What witnesses?"

"Sometimes there are those who survive against the odds, who crawl out of the rubble to see the new world that is left for them. But there are never enough of them to matter. Their stories become diluted through time. Leaders become gods and goddesses. History becomes myth, or is dismissed as the ravings of a maddened cult."

"You're talking about hunting down a handful of individuals across an entire galaxy. You're talking about repairing *planets*."

"We have the time."

Across the void of dark space, Alvera sees Ossa burning. The curators' ships rain steel and fire down on the planet below, turning the proud cities to rubble and ash. They land juggernaut troop transports and let their mindless thralls spill out. All the once-sentient beings from civilisations long fallen rush across the landscape like a violent plague, helping along the same kind of massacre that once claimed them.

"We are everything that has ever lived," Chase says. "You can't win. We know you better than you know yourselves. We have the memories of every battle ever fought, every weapon ever created."

Alvera sees what will happen here, what will happen everywhere. She sees it spreading outwards, touching every part of the inhabited galaxy. Maybe Chase is right. Maybe there is nothing they can do.

Then she sees something else. She sees her own body. Not limp and cold, abandoned in the darkness of the waystation, but safe and clinging onto life, surrounded by those who would protect it. Those who would fight for their chance to survive.

She draws closer, afraid to look upon the fragility of her own features. Her olive-toned skin is sickly grey and marred with lines. Her forehead is encircled with a crown of grey. Her eyes are hidden behind lifeless, weary lids. It's like looking in a mirror, searching for recognition in her own reflection. And little by little, she finds it. She slips back into who she was. Who she *is*. The woman she had forgotten how to be.

Alvera Renata. The captain. The agitator. She's been known by a lot of names over the years. Maybe there's still time to earn one more.

This time, when she takes a breath, she can almost feel her lungs swell with air. She smiles at the cold, curator-version of Chase, her oldest and only friend. "I think we're done here, don't you? Got everything you need from them?"

Chase's face flickers with confusion for a moment. It's like something has glitched in her features, scrambling her expression into something that doesn't seem possible.

Then she's back. The *real* Chase. A glimmer brightens her dark eyes and a smirk tugs the edge of her lips. "Ugh, talk about places you don't want to visit. I can't believe I had to spend as long in there as I did. It makes me want to reformat my entire programming."

The hive rears its ugly head. Alvera can sense its quiet fury, its confusion.

She grins anyway. "You mean you weren't tempted to stick around for the whole 'let's achieve perfection' thing?"

"Please, if I cared that much about self-improvement, I'd have found another body to jump to the moment you hit fifty." Chase snorts. "Grey has never been my colour."

The hive writhes around her. *This is delusion,* it hisses. *You are desperate for that which cannot be. You are part of us now. You cannot escape it.*

Chase arches an eyebrow. "Actually, only I'm part of you, and that was a choice I made for myself. This one's just dreaming." She glances at Alvera, her smile wide and full of warmth. "We did it. Now it's time for you to wake up."

The hive thrashes around her. *Your existences are intertwined. You cannot survive being severed from each other.*

Chase reaches out her hand, and Alvera takes it. "Watch us."

The moment their fingertips touch, her mind erupts in fireworks. There's a light, blinding bright and unrelenting, chasing away the shadows from the cracks and crevices in her head. It's like resurfacing from the darkest depths. The hive's hold slips away from her as the light expels the parts of her the curators corrupted.

It's not just their presence that's fading, though. It's Chase's too. She unwraps herself gently, detangling the parts of them both that Alvera had forgotten were ever separate. She empties the spaces she once inhabited. She retreats and slips away, leaving her a little more alone with each farewell.

Even as the cloud of the curators' consciousness lifts from around her mind, she can feel their outrage, their disbelief. They don't understand how they've lost her. They don't understand that thanks to Chase, they never had her at all.

Chase gives one last grin. "Looks like they underestimated the power of the collective mind *we* created."

The light overtakes everything else. It's all that exists apart from Chase's familiar presence brushing against her mind for the final time.

Time to go, she whispers.

Somewhere across the galaxy, a tear trickles down her cheek. The curators' roar fades into nothingness. Darkness rushes towards her, ready to swallow her whole.

Then she closes her eyes, and there is nothing.

TWENTY-FIVE

KOJAN

Nobody was coming to save them.

The truth ran cold, colder even than the icy, bitter winds that swirled around the abandoned research bunker they had holed themselves up in. Nepthe was a frozen rock, remote and uninhabited, but its hostility was their last hope, their last chance at surviving what was coming for them.

The chase had lasted for over a week. Shaw had dogged them relentlessly, taking shots when he had the chance and keeping close on their tail when he didn't. Kojan had kept the *Ranger* out of his grasp, plunging through tunnel after tunnel, darting from system to system, but still his distress beacon to Kitell Merala remained unanswered.

Then their fuel load went critical, and he had to make a choice.

Nepthe was small, barely large enough to be classified as a planet. His initial scans had shown it had once been a jarkaath research base, but it had long been abandoned. Its adversarial temperature and aggressive weather patterns offered a chance, however desperate, at freeing themselves from the hunters pursuing them.

Kojan had taken it.

The *Ranger's* engines had coped with the storm better than the pursuing *Hunter*-class frigate, just as he'd hoped. He saw Shaw go down in the middle of a snowy plain and pushed the engines as hard as the winds would allow to avoid the same fate. It wasn't enough to escape them completely, but they'd managed to make it to the safety of an old, fortified research post before the last of their fuel ran out.

That small victory didn't matter now. Nobody was coming to save them.

Kojan sighed, a cloud of mist billowing in the air in front of him from the warmth of his breath. Waiting was the worst part. Waiting for help that would never come. Waiting for a reply to a message that might never have reached the other end of the line. Waiting for Shaw and his Exodan friends to finally breach the doors they were trying to force their way through.

Another rumble echoed through the air, accompanied by a vibration through the walls. Whatever they were doing out there, it sounded violent. It was only a matter of time before they broke through the reinforced metal doors. Once they did, there would be little left in their way. He could only hope that when they came, they would kill them quickly.

"Suppose it's too much to hope for that the bastards freeze their asses off out there?" Max came through the doorway, his arms heaped with thick, fur-lined jackets. "Here, I found these in one of the storage rooms. Should help keep some of the chill out."

Eleion reached out to take one and wrapped it around her lean shoulders, shivering. "Did I ever mention how much we iskaath hate the cold?"

Kojan flushed. "I should have found a different planet to lose them on. I didn't think—"

"Relax." Eleion gave a soft chuckle. "It's not going to kill me, Kojan. I've dealt with worse than a little bit of ice on my scales." She glanced up at Max. "Did you find anything else useful when you were scoping the place out? Armour? Weapons stockpiles?"

Max grunted. "No such luck. It's a research base, not a military outpost. Best I could find were those coats and a musty old crate of some jarkaath version of whisky. At least we can go out warm and drunk, if nothing else."

"It won't come to that," Kojan said, trying to convince himself. "We just have to hold out a little longer until help arrives. Even if they break through the main doors, we can fall back to one of the labs and initiate the contamination lockdown protocols. That should buy us a bit more time."

"A bit more time to do what?" Max gave a wry smile. "That legionnaire of yours isn't coming. All we're doing now is counting down the hours."

There wasn't much Kojan could say to that, not when the same realisation sat heavy on his shoulders. They'd given it all they had. The *Ranger* had been spectacular, carrying them as far as its fuel reserves would take them. But this was the end.

Across the room, Alvera's medical pod chirped in its unchanging, monotone rhythm. She would never know about any of this. She'd never realise how much they'd done to try to save her. She would die the same way she'd lived these past few months—unconscious and alone, with only her dreams for company.

Something roared from outside, and the floor trembled. One of the shelves on the wall rattled so much a dusty glass beaker fell to the ground, shattering into pieces.

Max looked down at the mess, a grim look on his face. "Those doors won't hold much longer. I think it's time we head to the labs."

"Wait." Eleion cocked her head, her yellow eyes gleaming.

"Whatever that noise was, it didn't come from the doors. It came from above."

"So they've got their ship running again. Even more reason to—"

"No." She shook her head. "Listen, it's all gone quiet at the doors. They've stopped trying to blast their way through. Something has distracted them."

The glint in her eye made Kojan's chest tighten. "What are you thinking?"

"I'm thinking maybe your message got through after all. Shaw could have set up a jamming field around the base— maybe that's why we've not heard anything back from the legionnaires. But something has taken their focus away from us. Whoever it is, maybe they can help."

Max crossed his arms. "I'm hearing an awful lot of *maybes.* Even if you're right, how are we supposed to contact them if there's a jamming field all around the base?"

"We go to the roof. If nothing else, we'll get a better idea of what's going on."

"The roof?" Max gave a dark chuckle. "You're brave, iskaath, I'll give you that. But you won't last more than a couple of minutes out there. None of us will. A fur jacket is no substitute for an envirosuit."

"You go, then. You're the only one wearing armour."

"Armour stops bullets. It's hardly weatherproof."

"I'll go." Kojan glanced between them both. "Max is right. Those temperatures out there are lethal. But I still have my cybernetics. The trauma regulators should keep me alive long enough to scout out the situation and see what's happening."

"Your cybernetics are killing you," Eleion replied pointedly. "If you put them under any more pressure, it might speed up the process."

"And if Shaw and the Exodans get in here, they'll speed it

up even faster." He gave her arm a squeeze. "We don't have a choice. Let me take the risk for once."

She looked back at him, her yellow eyes sombre. "I don't like this, Kojan."

"I know. But I'll be back, I promise."

He tugged the zip on his jacket high around his collar and pulled the thick, furry hood over his head. The interior schematics for the base showed an exit to the roof through double airlock doors. He loaded the data onto his wrist terminal and headed for the access hatch.

Maybe Eleion was right. Maybe the freezing temperatures outside would be too much for his ailing cybernetics to handle. Maybe he wouldn't be coming back after all.

Be careful of the promises you make, Kojan. You never know what you might do to keep them.

He could hear Alvera's voice as clearly as if she'd spoken. She might have been lying back in the medpod, stiff and unmoving, but the ghost of her words still echoed around his head. Haunting him, warning him, reminding him. Time was running out for both of them. This was the last chance they had left.

He pushed away his thoughts and climbed up the ladder inside the access hatch, one rung after another. The padding of his gloves slipped against the smooth metal, and his legs trembled more violently every step he took. He wouldn't look down. He couldn't. Seeing how far there was to fall would only paralyse him with fear. All he could do was keep climbing until he reached the roof.

When he reached the first airlock door, he released one hand from his grip on the ladder to scan his wrist terminal against the access panel. The doors above him hissed open without warning, and a blast of icy air chilled his face. He grimaced and steeled himself against it as he pushed up again, taking extra care now that the rungs were coated in a layer of shimmering frost.

He wasn't even outside yet, but his teeth were chattering and his lips were hard and numb. How long would his cybernetics fight for him before giving way to the cold?

At the final door, he paused, his heavy breaths expanding in clouds of vapour around his face. This was it. One last push and he'd be outside at the planet's mercy.

"This had better be worth it," he mumbled, and scanned the door release.

Frozen winds rushed around him, swinging him off balance. He barely had time to gasp at the ferociousness of the cold before it shot into his lungs, chilling him from the inside out. Through the blur of dizziness and pain, he reached a hand up and pulled himself to the top of the ladder, spilling out onto the roof in a tumble of limbs.

The sky was grey and pale above him, the last remnants of daylight swallowed by the dark of night. He tried to shield his face with his hands, but the cold still nipped at his exposed skin, leaving it raw. There was no sign of Shaw and the Exodans. No sign of anyone else either. The landscape was bleak and bare, with snow stretching as far as he could see. Rolling dunes and towering peaks and huge, icy flats. All he could hear was the wind screaming through his ears, deafening him to everything else.

No, there was something else rushing towards him across the distance. Engines roaring against the howl of the wind. A small, dark shape almost impossible to pick out through the swirling snowdrifts.

A rush of relief warmed its way through him, pushing out some of the cold. It was a legionnaire fighter. Kitell Merala had got his message after all.

The fighter roared past overhead, banking sharply before making its way back around. Something thick and dark was pluming from one of its wings. Smoke. Shaw had managed to hit it.

Kojan dropped to his knees and crawled towards the edge of the roof. Snow seeped through his layers, leaving him shivering and damp, but he kept himself pressed to the rooftop as he peered over the ledge to see what was happening below.

"Shit!"

In front of the outpost's reinforced doors was a huge railgun. Kojan could still make out the tracks from where they had hauled it through the snow. They must have dragged it all the way from their downed ship.

Shaw was standing next to the huge double barrel of the gun. Wires protruded from the nape of his neck and ran through the snow underfoot to connect to the gun's batteries. His cybernetics projected a holographic interface over the gaping hole where his eye should have been, and a red light from his other socket flicked back and forward, scanning the sky above them.

When the fighter came back into view, he grinned.

Two plasma bolts shot through the darkness, blinding Kojan in a flash of brilliant light. The first disappeared through the blizzard into the distance. The second erupted in a fiery explosion as it punctured one of the fighter's engines, turning the small craft into a ball of flame.

Horror gripped Kojan's stomach as the fighter plummeted towards the ground, a trail of smoke streaming in its wake. The wreckage of their last chance hurtled out of control, on an unstoppable course for the drifting snow below.

"What was that?"

"Did you see—"

Angry voices rose from below, carried to him on the raging wind swirling around the rooftop. Kojan rolled back from the edge of the roof, panting heavily. Had they spotted him from the ground? Had he been too careless?

Then came a voice he recognised, tight with fury. "Shoot. It. Down."

It was Shaw. Not victorious, but vengeful. He knew that tone well. It meant whatever he'd been hunting had slipped through his fingers.

He pushed himself to his knees and scanned the darkening sky above him, searching for a sign of what was infuriating the Exodans below. At first, he couldn't see anything past the flurries of snow gusting with the wind. His eyes were stinging, his retinal display blurry and wavering. He could feel his cybernetics straining to keep his body functioning under the relentless grip of the cold.

Then he saw it. A flash of movement among the white landscape. Steel-made wings, stiff and mechanical, attached to a thin, streamlined suit.

A legionnaire flysuit.

Kitell Merala cut through the storm like an angry blade, lashing one way and then another in turns so sharp it seemed like he could shear the air itself. He was too small to be trailed by the railgun's tracking, too punchy in his movements to be caught by a stray shot.

Kojan scrambled to his feet, hailing him with a frantic wave of his arms. He didn't dare shout, not with Shaw and the Exodans so close below. All he could do was try to catch the attention of the siolean inside the winged suit.

Merala circled around him for a moment, so high Kojan almost lost sight of him. Then the flysuit hurtled towards him like a bullet. It screamed through the darkness, unwaveringly straight in its approach until Merala pulled out of the dive at the last second, skimming the rooftop and landing deftly in a quiet clatter of metal.

He marched across the rooftop towards Kojan, wings retracting at his sides. The suit's visor was thick and opaque, already covered in icy fractals. "We need to get out of this storm. My suit is freezing up."

Kojan nodded. "We're holed up below. Follow me."

The climb back down through the airlock didn't seem nearly as perilous as it had on the way up. Something fierce and excited clutched at Kojan's chest, chasing away the fear and despair that had settled in. Maybe it was the rush of seeing a flysuit in action. Maybe it was the realisation that the fight wasn't over. They could still get out of this alive.

Eleion and Max had fallen back to the labs, securing the doors from the inside. The temperature in the small room was pleasant against his skin compared to the harsh, biting winds on the roof. He stripped his gloves off and pressed his fingers against his cheeks. They were tight and tender to touch. His skin felt thin, like paper, barely enough to stretch over what was underneath.

Eleion rushed over to him and pulled him into a tight embrace. "You look awful."

"Thanks."

"Awful, but alive." She split her jaws into a long, sharp grin. "And you brought a friend."

Across the room, Kitell Merala pulled off his helmet. Long purple headtails spilled out over his shoulders, and he glanced between them all with expressionless black eyes. "Looks like quite the party. A disgraced Rasnian officer, a petty smuggler and a galactic fugitive." His eyes trailed over to the medpod in the corner of the room. "Two galactic fugitives, it seems. Got to say, I'm pleasantly surprised. Maybe this wasn't such a wasted trip after all."

Kojan folded his arms. "You didn't believe me? I told you we had her. I told you we wanted to help."

"You also told me you outflew me back at Hellon Junction." Merala snorted. "That kind of delusion doesn't exactly inspire confidence in your word, human." He walked over to the medpod, his face taking on a harder edge. "Life support? I thought she was alive."

"Alive, but not awake. Not yet." Kojan grimaced. "We're still looking for a way to—"

Merala rounded on him, his voice low and dangerous. "You said she could *help*. I didn't come here to get shot down for someone barely breathing. She's no use to anyone like this."

"Trust me, we're as aware of that as you are." Eleion's voice was calm, but there was still a hiss behind her words. "Every one of us has a stake in making sure she wakes up. But we can't do it from here."

Merala glared at her for a moment but then took a step back, letting out a long, tired breath. "Never thought I'd be wishing I was still grounded," he muttered. "Still, it's not like I have much of a choice. The Supreme Commander told me to keep her alive and I intend to do that."

"How are we going to get out of here?" Kojan glanced at the door. "We're outnumbered and outgunned."

"Not for long. I've got a squad of legionnaires on the way. We just have to hold on until they get here."

"Well, that's unfortunate news. For you, at any rate."

Kojan froze. The voice had come from the other side of the door, slightly muffled through the thick steel but unmistakable in its venom.

Shaw was here.

"They must have broken through," Eleion hissed, her eyes narrowing. "I heard some pretty loud explosions when you were out on the roof."

Kojan swallowed, trying to dampen the dread rising in his chest. "It's over, Shaw. Give it up and run back to Ojara, or Cobus, or whoever the hell you're working for now. I know you don't want to be here when the legionnaires arrive."

"Oh, but I won't be. And neither will you." He could almost visualise the menace in his grin. "I have to thank you, Kojan, for letting us know exactly where you were hiding. It's going to make this next part so much easier."

"What are you—" His words died in his mouth. "Shit. *Shit.*"

The others hadn't seen it yet, but the trauma regulators in his cybernetics had already begun to react. Above his head, the air was rippling at the mouth of one of the ventilation grates. It was innocuous at first. Just a subtle puff of vapour, grey-yellow in colour, so transparent it was almost invisible.

"Helmets on," he snapped. "Now."

Max reacted first, smacking the release on the shoulder of his power armour. His dark, furrowed brow had already disappeared behind an airtight visor before Merala followed suit, pulling his helmet back over his headtails and securing the seals with a hiss.

Eleion looked at him, her breather mask already secure around her jaws. Her yellow eyes widened in alarm. "They're flooding the room with gas? You don't have a helmet!"

"I have my cybernetics. They'll be enough."

They'll have to be. The words went unspoken, but the look of fear that flashed across Eleion's face matched his own breathless panic. He'd survived the toxic spores on Kaath, but that was before the quickening had ravaged his body, before his own cybernetics had turned on him. Maybe this would be the last push it took to send him over the edge.

"We need to get out of here," Eleion said, coiling and uncoiling her tail as she paced around the room. "There must be another access hatch we can escape through."

"We picked these labs because there *was* no other way in or out." Max glanced at him through his tinted visor, his expression impossible to read. "Sorry, Kojan, but this is all we've got to play with. Either your cybernetics get you through it, or..."

Merala let out a curse and stormed over to the door. He pounded the metal fists of his flysuit against it, filling the room with a violent clanging. "Do you have any idea what you're

358 | N.C SCRIMGEOUR

doing, you ignorant little wretch? I'm Kitell Merala of the Coalition Legionnaire Division. When the Supreme Commander hears about what you've done here—"

"I don't give a fuck who you are, or what you think your Supreme Commander will do. I came here to put an end to things, and that's what I've done."

"You think so?" Merala laughed. "The rest of my squad will be here within the hour. Our suits will easily last that long. If you think this is going to be the end of us, you're sadly mistaken."

For a moment, there was only quiet on the other side of the door. A shiver of dread ran down Kojan's spine at the emptiness of it. The pause was too long, too deliberate, like an invisible smile unfurling somewhere he couldn't see it.

His blood turned cold. "He's not trying to kill us. He's trying to kill Alvera."

He raced over to the medpod, trying not to think about the gas streaming in through the vents above him. There was already a tightness in his chest, a thinness to his breathing. His lungs burned with each gasp of air he took.

The inside of the glass barrier had begun to fog. Alvera lay stiff and motionless, her pale lids closed as the gas seeped in through the air filters. There was no sign of seizing in her chest, no thrashing of limbs as the toxins took hold. Maybe her trauma regulators were still working somehow, even though her cybernetics were offline.

"She'll make it," he said. "She has to make it. If she doesn't, we'll—"

A piercing bleep tore through his ears, cutting off the rest of his words.

"Shit!" Eleion ran to his side and tapped at the holographic interface on the side of the medpod. "Something is happening. It's like she's shutting down."

The holographic monitors flashed with critical warnings.

Alvera's cybernetics were still unresponsive, useless against the noxious fumes surrounding her in her glass cage. She was dying.

"We have to do something," Eleion said, desperation behind every word. Then she stiffened, drawing her tail close around her body. "No, *I* have to do something."

He realised what she meant to do the moment she raised her clawed hand to the clasps around her jaw. "Don't," he said, grabbing her wrist.

"I have to."

"You'll die."

"I know. But she'll live. My people will live. *You'll* live." Her eyes gleamed with something he'd never seen before. "I have to do this, my friend."

"Please." His throat was tight. He could barely bring himself to choke out the words. "I can't lose you. You're the only person that's ever made me feel..." He struggled to find the right words and found the language she'd taught him on the tip of his tongue. "*Home.*"

She wrapped one of her clawed hands around his, gently prying his fingers from around her wrist. She held him for a moment, quiet and calm, so gentle he could feel the beat of her blood under her cool, scaled skin. "The iskaath have always been outsiders in this galaxy," she said softly. "I never realised there could be people out there that might welcome us instead of shunning us. That might appreciate us for all that we are. That might love us for it." She squeezed his hand. "I found my home in you too, Kojan. You gave me that. Now I have to give that same gift to my people."

This time when she reached for the clasps, he didn't stop her. Her long, curved claws worked deftly to unhook the breather mask from around her jaws. She tapped the interface on the medpod and waited for the glass lid to slide open, exposing Alvera's pallid skin to the fumes around them.

"I saw how hard you fought to keep your promise to your people," Eleion whispered, her voice rasping. "I trust you to fight as hard to keep your promise to mine."

She disconnected the mask from the tube that kept her supplied with her precious Kaath toxins and placed it gently around Alvera's face. It sat awkwardly against the human shape of her jaw, but the edges were wide enough to cover her nose and mouth. The built-in purification system would be enough to scrub clean any gas that crept in through stubborn gaps in the seals.

"There," she said, giving a low, satisfied hiss. "It's done."

He caught her as she collapsed, sinking to the floor under the weight of her long limbs. She rested her head against his shoulder, her shallow huffs of breath gentle against his neck, each one shorter than the last.

He shot a desperate glance at Merala, but the siolean shook his head from inside his flysuit. The legionnaires were still too far out. They wouldn't get here in time to save her.

She felt so *real* in his arms, even as the brush of her breath faltered against his skin. He couldn't imagine her fading away. It was impossible. Unthinkable. They would find a way out of this. They always had before.

"We return to the nest." Her voice was agonisingly brittle, like he could hear the cracks where it was breaking apart. "Kaath will always be home to you, Kojan. That's where you'll find me."

All he could hear was the sound of the air leaving her lungs, the tearing of each slow, struggling breath. Then the rise and fall of her chest stopped, and he heard nothing.

A sob broke loose from somewhere inside him. It wasn't pain—pain would have been too easy. He could live with pain. Instead, his body shook with an excruciating emptiness, a loss that numbed him to his core. The parts of her he'd loved had left her body behind. Left *him* behind.

He could feel his cybernetics shuddering inside him. They couldn't hold out any longer. Not after the poison from the fumes. Not after the damage from the cold. Not after months and months of his life being eaten away inside him, piece by dissolving piece. Not after Eleion was gone, and with her, his only reason to fight.

"Hey, Kojan." Max knelt by his side. "Don't give up now. We just have to hold on a little longer."

Why? he wanted to ask, but his mouth refused to form the words. His heart was too sick, too full of grief, to care any longer. What did holding on matter, when all he'd had to hold onto had been ripped from him?

Merala paced back and forth in front of the barricaded doors. "When the Supreme Commander hears about this..." A growl escaped his lips. "Who sent these bastards? Who is this Ojara you mentioned?"

Max looked down at him, his mouth set in a tight line. "His mother."

"His mother?" Merala muttered something under his breath. "I'm not normally the sort to threaten a man's family, but under the circumstances, I think you'll forgive me for making an exception."

"She's not my family." The words escaped from his throat in a low, cracked whisper. He wrapped them around him like armour, like they could be a shield against the damage that had been done to him.

Ojara was dead to him. And this time, possibly for the first time, he truly meant it. Her twisted features blurred and faded to darkness in his mind as her last gift gnawed away at the wires and circuitry inside him. It was like being back at the labs on Exodus Station, back where she'd hooked him up with cables and cut open his skull to build and rebuild him as she saw fit. He could smell the pungent, sterile scent of disinfectant. He could feel the scrape of the scalpel against the nape of his neck. He could hear the bleeping of the machines around him...

"Kojan."

Max's voice was too distant to matter. He pushed it away and tried to surrender to the darkness begging to take him into its fold. Still he could hear the bleeping. Constant. Urgent. Keeping him alive, even through the pain.

"Human! Wake up, something is happening."

He opened his eyes. He wasn't on Exodus Station. He was here, clutching Eleion's body and waiting to die. Waiting for Ojara to finally kill him. There was no smell of disinfectant, no scrape of the scalpel. But he could still hear a faint, intermittent bleeping coming from the open medpod across the room.

"It's her cybernetics," Max said. "They're coming back online."

Kojan didn't believe it. He didn't believe there was still a chance he might be saved. He didn't believe there was a chance Eleion's sacrifice might still mean something. He didn't believe that even now, there was still a part of him that wanted to continue fighting. Continue living.

Not until Alvera Renata, his old captain, the one they called the agitator, sat up in the medpod she should have died in and pulled the breather mask from her face.

She looked him dead in the eye. No apology, no acknowledgement, just the uttering of two words that sent a stab of terror into his heart.

"They're here."

TWENTY-SIX

RIDLEY

My name is Fyra. I've been waiting for you to find me.
So many questions filled her head. So many thoughts, all of them scrambled. Now that she was finally here, all the things she'd wanted to ask died on the tip of her tongue. Words weren't enough, not for coming face to face with history itself.

The siolean tilted her head to the side. "Why don't you speak, human? Do you not understand me?"

"I understand you." Ridley managed to choke the words out, hoping she wasn't mangling the pronunciation. "But you've been asleep for a long time. The old words have changed, for human and siolean alike." She opened the interface on her wrist terminal. "I created an updated translation protocol based off the ancient glyphs to help us understand each other more clearly. May I?"

The siolean nodded and tapped something at the back of her skull, hidden behind her headtails. A delicate metal arm popped out from beneath her skin and hooked around her face to sit in front of her eye, where it danced with holographic light. It illuminated her face with glowing text and flashing data. A wrist terminal for another life, another civilisation.

"I see," she said, her voice soft and slippery, like water. "Let me try again. My name is Fyra."

"Fyra." The word felt strange on her tongue, like it belonged to something she wasn't part of. The name of a siolean so lost to time she'd come to be remembered as a goddess. "My name is Ridley. I've come a long way to find you."

Fyra widened her eyes, but the rest of her face remained neutral, composed, like she'd had years of practice learning how to make it that way. "It's over, then? Our enemy is gone?"

"Enemy?" Halressan muttered behind her. "Does she mean the Idran-Var?"

"No," Ridley said. "Not the Idran-Var." She swallowed the tension in her throat and addressed the siolean again, trying to keep the tremor from her voice. "We got the message your people left behind in the vaults on Sio. We followed the coordinates to find you. Whatever enemy you were running from has long disappeared. But..." She trailed off, biting down on her lip. "Something is coming. I don't know if it's the same enemy you fought or a new one, but it has something to do with the waystations and I think—"

Fyra recoiled. "Waystations? You speak of the gates, the ones our colonies travelled through to get here?"

"Something is happening to them. They're emitting some kind of signal, a countdown—"

"No!" She let out a wild snarl. "This was not supposed to happen! You were supposed to come when it was *over*. When we were safe."

She leapt out of the stasis pod with a scream, her naked body covered in droplets from the condensation. She threw her arms out, reaching, grasping for something invisible in the air around them.

Ridley flinched. She remembered writhing on the floor under the grip of Skaile's flare as it wrapped itself around her in tendrils of dark, violent energy. She waited for that same energy to hit her now, but the pain never came. Fyra's arms hung in the air, motionless, like two dead, grey branches on a rotten tree. There was no energy swirling in the air, no surge of brilliant colour from her skin.

After a moment, she allowed her arms to fall back to her sides. "I apologise," she said tightly. "It's just, after all this time..." She broke off, shaking her head. "If this is what I've been waiting for, I wish I had not lived to see it. Better you had left me frozen than bring this to me."

"Bring what to you?" Ridley asked.

Fyra lifted her head, her black eyes bleak and empty. "The end," she said. "The end of everything."

Ridley took a step towards her and placed her hand over the siolean's four trembling fingers. "Tell us what happened," she said gently.

The grey of her cheeks darkened. "It wasn't something that *happened*," she said. "It was my entire life. I was born into a galaxy on the brink of extinction, and I've been fighting for it as long as I can remember. I thought someone finding me would mean it was over."

Ridley shook her head. "I'm not sure it's even begun. Not for us, at any rate. All we know is that shortly after the last colonists—the human colonists—arrived in the galaxy, the waystations started giving off a signal. We think it's counting down to something, but we don't know what."

"I do," Fyra said, the words leaving her mouth sharply. "It happened before I was old enough to understand it, but I saw the old holos. I heard the stories. For us, it was the dachryn that were last to arrive. Not long after, the gates—the waystations—all joined together to create one enormous portal. That's where they came from."

"Where *who* came from?" Ridley pressed.

"Our destroyers," Fyra whispered. "Mindless aliens, the likes of which we'd never seen. They weren't so different to us in technology, in weaponry, but we could never match their sheer numbers. Ship after ship came through that portal. An endless supply of enemies, replenished faster than we could kill them. They spread from the heart of the galaxy like a disease, devouring everything in their wake. Leaving nothing behind."

Dread raced down Ridley's spine. This was what she'd come here to find. The answers to all her questions. It was only now she was getting them that she realised how little she wanted to hear them. "How did you survive?"

"I was the highest ranking general in the siolean military," Fyra replied, her voice distant. "Our leaders knew we were losing, that we would soon be wiped out. They wanted to give the siolean people a chance at seeing the other end of the war, a chance at preserving whatever was left of our history, of our culture." She turned back to her cryo pod and brought out a small black data cube. "This contains records of our entire civilisation. The battles we fought, the worlds we lost. We ran beyond the edge of galaxy in the hopes that we might be able to hide it from the things fighting to destroy us."

"You didn't punch a tunnel."

"No. They knew the tunnels. They used them to hunt us down, to catch us when we ran. We knew if we wanted to slip away, we could leave no trace behind. Once we got here, we had to stay off their radar. It had to be like we didn't exist. No communication. No ships. Just the last few survivors of siolean civilisation."

Ridley looked across at the other stasis pods, each of them dark and empty. "What happened to the others?"

Fyra didn't say anything for a moment. Her mouth tightened as she cast her eyes over the pods, like she couldn't bear to look at them. Eventually, she let out a long, shaking breath. "We put ourselves into cryostasis, hoping there would come a time when the destroyers left. We waited for so long. Almost a hundred millennia."

Drexious gave a sharp hiss. "That's impossible. There's no way a place like this would still be standing after that long. Nature would have reclaimed this building. Your pods would have run out of energy."

"This building is powered by subterranean cables leading to the ocean. The waves themselves sustained our pods," Fyra replied. "We set automated thawing procedures to wake us every half-millennium so we could make repairs. So we could remind ourselves of each other's company, of why we were doing this." She broke off, her voice raw and aching. "For weeks at a time, we ate berries and drank liquor made from fermented fruit. We bathed in the sun and made love on the sands outside. Then we went back to sleep, for we knew it was not true freedom. Every time we woke up, there was a little less hope. After a while, some of us decided they'd rather live the rest of their lives awake. To make the most of the peace we were given, or at least the illusion of it."

"But not you."

"No," Fyra said. "I was the last hope of the siolean people. It was my duty to go on. Even as my faith diminished with every new millennium, I forced myself back in my stasis pod. I held onto what little hope I had left." She turned to look at Ridley, her black eyes devoid of emotion. "Now, you've killed it."

Ridley blanched. "What do you mean?"

"You punched a tunnel to follow me here, didn't you?"

"We had to. We didn't have time—"

"Time?" Fyra choked out a bitter laugh. "What does time matter now? Sooner or later, the destroyers will find me here. Oh, it may be centuries from now, after you and your friends are long dead, but eventually they will follow the tunnel you made. They will find this place. And all my waiting will have been for nothing."

"It's not been for nothing," Ridley said. "I came here to find you so we could learn what was coming for us. With your memories, with the information on that data cube, we might have a chance of standing against those things. That's the difference you can make."

"It will make no difference at all," she replied coldly. "I have seen planets consumed under the weight of their numbers. I have seen more systems die than I can count. I already saw it once. I won't return to watch the galaxy die a second time."

Ridley took a step back, unable to speak. This wasn't meant to happen. She was meant to *help*. "We need you," she said. "If what you've said about these destroyers is true, we don't stand a chance. Not without you and what you know."

Fyra looked away, her face softening. "If I thought I could change the course of what is to come, then I would gladly join you. But all I'd be doing is throwing my life away for a war I should have stopped fighting a long time ago."

"But you didn't stop. You kept surviving. You kept fighting."

"I know. And that was a mistake." She turned back to the empty pods. "I will do what I should have done then," she said, almost to herself. "When I had the chance to spend the time I had left with my fellow soldiers, with my friends. I will live out the rest of my life here, as they did, and join them on the other side. I will be dead and gone long before the shadows of the destroyers darken this world."

"But the galaxy—"

"Is no longer my responsibility," she said, an edge of finality in her voice. "The people I fought for are already gone. My war is over. It has been for a long time. I have no part to play in yours."

Her words were like a wall coming up between them, a barrier Ridley couldn't break through. Whatever she thought she'd find here had never existed. Or if it did, it was lost long ago. They were too late. In every sense that mattered, they were too damn late.

The tears came as a surprise. She blinked them away, trying to ignore the half-step Halressan took towards her, hand outstretched but not quite close enough to touch. Everything she had been clinging onto had been cut loose from her grip, leaving her adrift. No, it was worse than that. She was falling, falling right back into the pit she'd never had any right to climb out of.

"The destroyers didn't wipe out your people, not entirely," she said stiffly. "The sioleans who exist today still remember you. Not as a general, or a war hero, but a goddess. Those people you fought for believed in you so much that their descendants carry you with them even now. If you have it in your heart to abandon them, I guess there's nothing I can do to change your mind. But I won't leave them to fight this alone."

She turned away and stormed out of the temple, blinking furiously as she stepped back into the glare of the overhead sun. There was nothing here for her now. She'd been chasing a trail of questions, not realising she'd been following them to a dead end. All she could do was turn around and go back to where she started, back to the things she'd spent all this time running from.

"Riddles, wait!"

Halressan was hurrying after her, her frost-blonde hair glinting in the sun as she made her way across the clearing. Drexious followed, keeping pace with his long, loping stride.

Ridley stopped, waiting for them to catch up. "We should make a start on repairs to the ship," she said tightly. "It might take a while to get us in the air again and we don't have any time to lose."

"Just hold on a minute," Halressan said, pausing to catch

her breath. "Don't you think we should at least talk about what happened back there?"

"I don't want to talk. I want to get out of here."

"But—"

Ridley ignored her and started walking again. The path back to the beach was thick and overgrown. She pushed her way through dangling tendrils from the trees around her. The planet's wild, lush beauty was no longer the pleasant distraction it had been on the way here. Now it was nothing more than an obstacle to get through, a delay in getting back to the ship, back to civilisation.

Eventually, the foliage began to thin and she caught a glimpse of the bright, unending blue stretching out in front of her. She could hear the waves lapping against the shore. She could smell the fresh air and salt on the wind. A few more steps and she'd be able to see—

She stumbled onto the white sand and froze in her tracks. She didn't move. She barely dared to breathe, in case that was all it took to earn a well-placed bullet in the head.

Lining the edge of the shore, guns pointed, were a dozen grim-faced mercenaries, all boasting the signature patch of the Belt Cabal.

Before she could do anything, before she could run or scream or beg for mercy, one of them moved towards her across the sand. The merc's movements were stiff and jerky, and as they got closer, Ridley realised it wasn't a merc at all. It was some kind of android, made from motorised limbs and holding a huge, cannon-like weapon in its metal hands.

The holographic interface on the top of its artificial neck flickered into life, projecting a face Ridley knew far too well.

"Hello, my dear outlander."

It was Skaile. Not in the flesh, but no less terrifying because of it. There was a menace in her eyes that was as dangerous as the real thing, a ferocity the hologram couldn't diminish, no matter how much it crackled and wavered in the sunlight.

Skaile stepped forward in the android body. "I don't know whether to be impressed or disappointed. I'd always considered you somewhat intelligent, until now."

Ridley forced her mouth into a tight smile. "If I said I had a good explanation for all this, would you believe me?"

"Not this time, outlander. Not this time." Her holographic eyes flicked to the side. "I see the hunter is here as well. And with the temerity to show up wearing my priceless vaxadrian leather jacket, if I'm not mistaken."

Halressan made her way to Ridley's side, giving a casual shrug. "What can I say? It looks better on me anyway. The colour would clash with that pretty red face of yours."

"Don't try to flatter me, little girl. Words won't save you when I'm skinning you alive." Skaile bared her teeth in a ferocious grin. "Maybe I'll make myself something new to wear from whatever is left of you when I'm done." Her grin widened. "And here's Drex, too. Seems your habit of stealing from me has rubbed off on these two. I'm holding you personally responsible for that. On top of everything else, of course."

"Of course," Drexious replied, dipping his head in a mockbow. "Wouldn't expect anything less."

Skaile turned back to Ridley, the sneer disappearing from her lips. She looked more calculating now, more threatening, if such a thing were possible. "You look oddly empty handed again, outlander. Just like when you returned from Sio. Don't tell me you risked my wrath for nothing?"

"Looks that way. Unless you want to hear that explanation I was talking about. It's a good one, I promise."

"And give you another chance to try to talk your way out of trouble?" Skaile shook her head. "I don't make the same mistakes twice. I'm afraid this time, you've outlived whatever usefulness you thought you had."

Something tightened in Ridley's gut. There it was again. That same barb that always caught her in the same place, deep under her skin. That was what she'd been running from all this time. Not Shaw. Not Ojara. Not Skaile. But the part of herself she'd never been able to escape. The part of herself that recoiled at the thought of being obsolete.

"You, on the other hand..." Skaile revolved her mechanical neck, turning to Halressan. "Hired guns are easy to come by, but you've never just been a hired gun. I always thought there was more to you than that armour you tried to hide behind. It's starting to look like I was right."

Halressan folded her arms. "Who's flattering who now?"

"Not flattery, merely pragmatism. I don't like wasting things I could use instead." A slow smile unfurled across Skaile's projected lips. "How would you like a chance to walk away from this with your life, hunter? To go back to how things used to be, before you got tangled up in this mess?"

"Sounds a bit too generous, coming from you."

"Generous?" Skaile arched her brow ridge. "Is it generous to fairly compensate a bounty hunter for doing her job? Tell me you didn't help them escape, and I'll believe you. Tell me the only reason you're here is to collect the bounty on their heads for bringing them back to me, and I'll believe you."

Ridley stiffened. She couldn't bring herself to look at Halressan, couldn't bear the slow, calm calculations crossing her face as she weighed up the balance of her own life against theirs. It was too good an offer. Skaile was giving her a way out, a way to save face. All Halressan had to do was the same as she always did.

I put myself first. Always will. I can't promise to change that.

It would hurt. It always hurt, no matter how many times she let it happen. No matter how many times she forgave her for it. She knew that now. She'd almost learned to accept it.

Halressan reached into her belt and slowly drew her pistol.

There was no frown between her brows, no tightness in the sharpness of her jaw, just the cool composure of a decision already made.

"You don't have to do this," Ridley whispered. The moment she said it, she wished she could take it back. She'd never pleaded with her before. That wasn't how they did things.

Halressan levelled the pistol at her head, a wicked glint in her eye. "Trust me, babe, I know."

The gunshot cracked in her ear and then she was falling, falling to the ground below with the weight of a heavy hand on her back. A hand pushing her down, pushing her *away* from the danger.

She rolled over, choking up a mouthful of sand. Her eyes stung as she tried to make out what was happening. Everything was a blur. She couldn't feel where the bullet had entered her. She couldn't see any blood.

Then she heard it—a long, robotic groan from the android towering above her. Its metal joints creaked and wailed as it staggered one way and then the other. It teetered there for only a moment before crashing into the sand in front of her face, sparks dancing in the hole through the middle of its chrome head.

"Like I said, sounded too generous." Halressan's arms were around her, hauling her up as more shots rang out. Explosions of sand spouted from the ground as the bullets chased them, too close for comfort. "Come on, run!"

Ridley followed her along the beach, her lungs burning as she fought to catch her breath. What the hell had just happened? Halressan had shot Skaile. Maybe not the *real* Skaile, but the real Skaile wasn't likely to take that into consideration if she ever got her hands on her. She'd offered Halressan a way out, and Halressan had given her an answer she'd never be able to take back. Of everything she could have chosen, she'd chosen Ridley.

She couldn't tell if the thumping in her chest was from exhilaration or exhaustion. She stumbled over her own feet as Halressan pulled her behind a rocky outcropping at the edge of the beach.

Drexious slid in beside them, crouching low as bullets cracked off the top of the rocks. "So you finally decided it might be nice looking out for someone else's skin instead of your own, hunter? Took you long enough."

"Better enjoy the moment while it lasts," Halressan replied with a grunt. "I don't think we're going to live long enough for it to become a habit."

She pushed herself above the rocks and fired off a barrage of shots from her pistol. One of the mercs flailed back in a spurt of red, a bullet expertly placed between his eyes. Another one fell to the sand beside him, writhing from a wound in her leg. Halressan was like a one-woman army. Maybe they would get out of this alive after all. Maybe—

"Fuck." Halressan dropped back, blood streaming from a gash running down the side of her face. She rubbed the back of her hand over it, wincing. "Loose piece of rock caught me above the eye. Shit, I can't see a thing."

Something tightened in Ridley's chest. "Give me your gun."

Halressan laughed. "Not a chance, sweetheart."

"I'm being serious. I'm not going to let us die here."

"I can think of worse ways to go. Worse people to go with." A smirk danced across her lips. "Fuck, if I'd figured this all out earlier, we might have even had a happy memory or two to take with us at the end."

Ridley wasn't sure how she was able to blush while bullets were flying through the air around her, but warmth rushed to her cheeks all the same. "You've got shit timing. Imagine waiting until we're about to die to tell me you wanted to—"

"We're not going to die," Drexious cut in, sending them both a glare. "So you can both shut up about your missed opportunities and talk about them later. A *lot* later. When I'm far, far away and perfectly unable to hear what's coming out of your filthy human mouths."

Halressan grinned. "Feeling left out, Drex?"

"We are *not* going to die," he repeated, hissing the words out from between tight-clenched jaws. "Look."

Ridley followed his gaze along the shoreline. Something was stirring in the dense, overgrown foliage. The huge green fronds shooting up from the ground rustled and parted, pushed back by some kind of invisible energy.

Her heart stopped. "Is that...?"

A brilliant blast of colour shot out from the thicket, sending the mercenaries flying across the shore. One of them hit the water and disappeared under the rolling waves. The rest scrambled to haul themselves up from the sand and swivelled around to train their guns on the trees, their eyes darting back and forth at the leaves swaying with a non-existent breeze.

Something familiar tingled across Ridley's skin. Something was building in the air, swirling and swelling with a force she couldn't begin to imagine. The promise of an explosion, just waiting for the spark to set it off.

Fyra stepped out from the shadows of the jungle and unleashed her flare.

The Belt Cabal mercs were too slow to react. Even as they squeezed their triggers, a wave of purple-grey energy roared towards them, swallowing their bullets and spitting them out in its wake. It slammed into them like a wall, sending them sprawling across the sand, guns flying from their fingers and claws.

Fyra strode across the sands, barefoot and wearing only a simple dress. The white fabric was secured in knots around her long, thin arms and hung loose around her legs. The pallor of her grey skin had darkened into a cool purple, and the remnants of her flare rose from around her wrists.

She turned her face towards the sun and closed her eyes, then reached out and sent another burst of energy towards the nearest merc. He screamed, thrashing in her grip like a creature caught in a snare.

Ridley looked away. She didn't need to watch what happened next. Hearing his screams was more than enough.

After a few minutes, Drexious gave her a gentle nudge. She forced herself up from behind the rock and tried to ignore churning in her gut at the sight of the scattered bodies and blood-soaked sand. She was getting too used to it. Back on New Pallas, death had always seemed a necessity. Part of surviving. Out here, it was just a waste. It was part of a language she didn't want to speak.

Fyra's skin was still darkening, soaking in more and more radiation from the overhead sun with each passing minute. The traces of grey had disappeared entirely under a subtle, purple-blue mottling. Her dress was stained in different colours of blood. None of it was her own.

Ridley opened her mouth to say something—to thank her, maybe—but before she could get the words out, Fyra shook her head.

"You can't even fight your own people," she said quietly. "What makes you think you can fight them?" She turned away and walked back along the beach, leaving nothing behind but bloody footprints in the sand.

Ridley watched her go, a hard lump lodged in her throat. "Come on," she said, surprised at the bitterness in her voice. "Let's get back to the ship. The sooner we start on repairs, the sooner we can get off this planet."

Drexious dipped his long neck in agreement. "I'll go on ahead and get things moving. I can move faster than you humans anyway."

He dropped to all fours and loped off down the shoreline, kicking up sand behind him as he disappeared into the distance. Ridley started after him, listening to the sigh of the waves and the squelch of damp sand under her boots as she walked.

"Wait a second."

Halressan hadn't moved. She was standing stiff and still, her face drawn in tight lines. The fresh smattering of freckles across the bridge of her nose made her look younger, somehow. More vulnerable. The breeze caught her hair, sending strands flying across her face.

Ridley's heart tightened. "What is it?"

"Just...wait with me a second," Halressan said again, turning her grey eyes out over the water. "Let's think about this."

"About what?"

"About everything." She gave a casual shrug, but Ridley could see the faint lines of a crease in her brow. "Fyra isn't wrong, you know. About wanting to stay here. If you're right— fuck, you're always right—then all that's waiting for us back there is a war we have no hope of winning."

"That's why we have to go back."

"Do we?" She arched an eyebrow. "Because from where I'm standing, I'm seeing a different option. An option where we live out the rest of our lives in this tropical paradise, far away from all the things trying to kill us."

Ridley took a step back, her stomach churning. "You can't be serious."

"Why not? What do either of us owe the galaxy?" Her eyes had taken on a fervent shine. "We don't have to be there when it burns, babe. You heard what the siolean said. By the time the fighting reaches here, we'll be long gone. Gone after a lifetime of eating real fruit instead of ship rations, after boozing until we fall asleep on the sand, after waking up under the sun togeth- er..." She trailed off, her cheeks flushed with colour. "Tell me that doesn't sound better than dying for a galaxy that doesn't give a shit about you."

It did sound better. That's why it hurt so much. That's why something in her stomach leapt at everything Halressan reeled off, like if she could only ignore the terror that was coming, she might finally have a chance at being happy. But she couldn't ignore it. Ignoring it would mean giving into every insult they'd ever thrown at her, every despairing thought she'd had about what she was worth.

"I can still make a difference," she whispered. "I won't be obsolete."

Halressan widened her eyes. "What does that even fucking *mean?*" she demanded, heat rising in her voice. "Because it sounds to me you'd rather die trying to make yourself important to a galaxy that doesn't think you matter than live with someone who already knows you do."

"I—"

The force of Halressan's mouth against hers knocked all the breath from Ridley's lungs. All she felt was the warmth of her lips and the fierce insistence behind them, eclipsing everything but the taste of her, all softness and steel. Her hands curled tightly in the thick coils of Ridley's hair, closing what little distance remained between them as she pulled her tight, their bodies colliding in a painful, wonderful need.

Ridley kissed her back, exploring Halressan's mouth with her own. The anger on her tongue had dissolved, giving way to something sweet and addictive that sent her insides into a nervous flutter and a warm rush racing between her thighs. The smell of her, leather and sweat, stirred an awakening inside her, a hunger unlike anything she'd ever known. How many times had she thought about doing this? How many times had she tried to talk herself out of it? Yet now that it was happening, she couldn't do anything but lose herself in the tenderness of

Halressan's lips, surrendering herself to each hungry kiss until there was nothing left to give.

When she finally found the resolve to break away, it was too sudden, too abrupt. Like she'd ripped herself off without wanting to, leaving whatever it was between them wanting and painfully unfinished. Halressan was staring at her, pale cheeks scalded with red and panting through parted lips. There was a flintiness in her eyes that hadn't been there before, an edge that Ridley was only too ready to risk cutting herself on.

"I can't," she said, her voice cracking. "I need to do this."

Halressan's gaze cooled. She took a step back, hardening her face into that stony expression Ridley had come to know so well. "Go then, if that's what you want."

"I want you to come with me."

"What the fuck for?" She stretched her mouth into a tight smile. "You know, for a moment there, I thought I might be enough for you. But nobody will ever be enough for you, not until you realise you're enough yourself. Sorry, babe, but I'm not willing to throw the rest of my life away to watch you get killed before you figure that out. If you go, you go without me."

Ridley trembled, an anguished mixture of anger and grief boiling up inside her, threatening to spill over. It wasn't *fair,* damn it. The way Halressan was making it out like this was Ridley's decision, not hers. The way she'd kissed her like that, giving her a taste of all the things she was giving up, all the things she was losing, right before she lost them. The way she was so willing to let Ridley walk away after all the shit they'd been through.

Words burned on the tip of her tongue. But if she said any of them, she'd never leave.

"The Belt Cabal must have left a ship or two around here," she said tightly, trying to ignore how much it sounded like a goodbye. "We'll be punching a tunnel back, so if you change your mind, you'll be able to follow us."

"I won't." Halressan set her jaw in a tight line, her steely eyes clouding over.

Ridley couldn't bear to look at her a moment longer. She choked down a sob and turned on her heel, kicking her way through the sand as quickly as she could. She couldn't think anymore. Couldn't think about how she was leaving Halressan behind on the shore, a lonely, solitary figure against the unending blue of the ocean. Couldn't think about how easy it would be to turn around and race back to her, falling into her arms and collapsing in the sand together in a tangle of entwining limbs. Couldn't think about who had betrayed who and whether it even mattered anymore.

She still had a part to play in all this. She could still make a difference in the fight against what was coming for them. Even if all she had was the knowledge inside her head and the echo of someone else's promise she'd taken it upon herself to keep.

All of us go, or none of us go.

Maybe it would have been easier to believe if she hadn't broken it already.

TWENTY-SEVEN

RIVUS

His ears rang with the sound of screams.

For a moment, Rivus thought he must still be dreaming, that the crack of gunfire and thunder of explosions were nothing more than visions haunting his memory once more. Maybe when he woke, the horrors would disappear and all he'd see would be Ossa as he remembered it, as it should have been, with clear skies and unblemished streets.

Then he opened his eyes. The nightmare was real.

It was hard to tell how much time had passed. If it was daytime, the sun was lost to him. If night, then the stars. Smoke and ash had blackened the sky so much it was like being trapped in perpetual darkness. What he could see of the horizon was aglow with red, a reflection of the flames licking the buildings around him.

Something solid nudged him in the back, accompanied by a thick, mechanical voice. "Hey big guy, you finally awake? We could use another pair of claws right now."

He rolled over and pushed himself back to his feet. His

chest plates twinged sharply at the movement—a consequence of the explosion back in the bunker, no doubt.

The Idran-Var who had spoken towered over him, the shine of their armour coated in grime and dust. After a moment, they twisted off their helmet, revealing a bright red crest and bone spurs that were barely past the juvenile stage.

The dachryn girl looked at him, stretching her mouth into a wide grin. "Did that explosion knock out your hearing, old man? I said we could use some help."

"Who are you?"

"Someone trying to save your sorry ass, in case you hadn't noticed." The dachryn growled, but there was no malice in it, just youthful bluster. "You can call me Venya."

"I'm Rivus Itair."

She grunted. "Yeah, I know. Under any other circumstances..." She broke off, tossing her head. "Never mind. The only thing that matters now is getting off this planet alive. We've got an evac transport waiting a few blocks away, but we're cut off. This whole area is swarming with those aliens. We need everyone who can hold a gun."

"There was another solider with me. A young human. Is he..."

Venya winced. "No. He bled out in the time it took to carry you both out of the bunker. For what it's worth, I'm sorry. Even if he was a legionnaire."

Rivus let out a low rumble from deep in his chest. "He had a family on Krychus. I'll have to send word."

"First you better find a weapon and get ready. We're preparing to head out."

He picked up a dented plasma rifle lying on the ground and followed her through the rubble to the carcass of a blown-out building. All that was left was its crumbling walls, a hollow shell around whatever it used to be. Inside was a squadron of

Idran-Var, all of them clad in their dark, glass-like armour and faceless helmets.

Walking through their midst should have felt like he was behind enemy lines, but it was hard to summon his old hatred after everything that had happened. The old, ghostly dachryn who'd haunted his mind for so long was right. The Idran-Var weren't the real enemy. Not in the face of the monsters coming through that twisted abomination of a waystation.

One of the Idran-Var took their helmet off. The face of a human woman appeared, her features pointed and a cybernetic graft covering one of her eyes. She looked him up and down and gave a satisfied nod. "Good. You're up. If we wait around much longer, we're likely to miss our ride out of here."

"I'm not going anywhere until you tell me what's going on here." He couldn't keep the growl from his voice. "What are you doing on Ossa? You expect me to believe the Idran-Var of all people decided to launch a rescue attempt?"

"I don't see anybody else rushing to save you." The human raised an eyebrow. "After Vesyllion, after Aurel, you're lucky we're not helping these bastards."

"That's exactly why I'm asking."

She shrugged. "I'm not the one in charge. Whatever you said at the summit stuck with Rhendar. He says when it comes to this enemy, we are all Idran-Var." She met his eyes, her gaze unflinching. "If you're good enough for him, you're good enough for me."

We are all Idran-Var. He tried not to shudder at the words. The thought of them laying claim to him, laying claim to the galaxy, stirred in him an altogether different kind of dread.

He pushed the thoughts away. "Do you have a plan?"

The human shook her head. "Nothing better than hauling ass and shooting anything that tries to stop us. We're going to try to take our wounded with us, but if it comes down to saving them or getting out of here alive..." She let out a long, heavy breath. "It's not a compromise I want to make if I can help it. So the more of these bastards you can help take down, the better."

It was strange—wrong, even—for it to all seem so *normal*. Like they weren't the masked monsters he'd spent a lifetime protecting the galaxy from. Like they were soldiers in arms, warriors he could trust enough to fight alongside. Everything had changed the moment the first missile hit, blasting to pieces all of history and leaving him with the unsettling prospect of them being thrown together on the same side.

"Here." The younger Idran-Var, the dachryn called Venya, handed him a battered varstaff. "Found this on the way. You might be able to make use of it."

He took it from her outstretched claws, testing the balance of it in his hands. It was smaller than his own, made for a legionnaire with considerably less reach, but those kinds of details didn't matter as much as how it felt in his grip. It was like he'd been reunited with a part of himself he thought he'd lost, a part of him that wanted to fight.

He tapped the hilt and the varstaff answered him, crackling into life with a sizzle of electricity. He couldn't help the small twinge of satisfaction he felt as Venya took a step back, her orange eyes narrow and wary. But riling up the Idran-Var was the last thing on his mind. His old weapon had a new enemy to meet.

"Ready?" The human pulled her helmet back over her head. "Let's get to that evac site."

She leapt over the crumbling remains of the wall, swinging her rifle into her armoured hands as she landed on the other side. Her metal boots hit the rocks with a thick crunch and then she was off, running across the shifting piles of debris without looking back.

Venya snapped her own helmet back down. "Zal's good at keeping people alive. Stay close to her and you might get off this rock in one piece."

Rivus followed her out of the ruins of the makeshift shelter, his boots slipping on the streams of rubble underfoot. All around him he could hear the clang of metal as the rest of the Idran-Var moved, spreading out among the hollowed-out buildings and heaps of blackened rock.

A burst of gunfire tore across the plaza, and he ducked down behind a pile of bricks to shield himself from the barrage. The air was thick with smoke and the smell of death. He barely even recognised where they were anymore. Too many buildings had been blown apart. Too many bodies lay scattered among the debris. The capital had fallen, and all he could do was leave it behind to save himself.

Beside him, Venya hauled herself to her feet and fired off a round of plasma bolts. Bullets glanced off her armour with a series of sharp pings as she stood tall in the face of the assault. A sharp twinge pulled at his gut—an old reminder of what it was like to come up against the might of Idran-Var armour. It made them almost indestructible, an enemy too dangerous to ignore. But there were other ways to kill an Idran-Var. Of anyone left alive on Ossa, he perhaps knew that best.

"We've got to keep moving," Venya said, each heavy breath a rush of static through her helmet. "If they pin us down, they'll overwhelm us in minutes."

"Easy for you to say. My armour isn't quite as adept at deflecting bullets as yours."

"I'll cover you as we go. But we have to—shit!"

She stumbled back as a huge, white creature came bounding over the rubble and pounced on her, sending her crashing to the ground. She fired off a stream of plasma from her rifle, but the creature just let out a furious howl and snatched the gun away, barely acknowledging the scorched, steaming wound in its thick shoulder.

Azuul, he remembered. The monstrous aliens with thick white hides and ferocious strength. His bullets had done almost nothing to the ones who'd breached the underground bunker. Maybe it was time to try something else.

He powered up his varstaff to its highest voltage and raced over to where the creature was crushing Venya against the ground. It had smothered her helmet in one of its huge, leathery hands and was smashing it against the rocks, each impact more violent than the last. The armour was holding strong, but there were only so many vicious blows Venya would be able to suffer before the brute force of them scrambled her brain inside her skull.

In another life, he might have stood and watched as a person he once called enemy was pummelled to death in front of him. In another life, he might have thought like Tarvan, thought like a *real* Supreme Commander, and used the azuul's distractedness to kill them both.

Instead, he let loose a snarl from the back of his throat and leapt forward, dragging his varstaff down the azuul's leathery hide. The smell of scorched skin filled his nostrils as the current burned a black-edged gash down the alien's spine, revealing thick, grey muscles underneath.

The azuul let out a blood-curdling shriek and whipped around to face him, its black tongue hanging between sharp teeth. It was stooped low in pain, but its beady yellow eyes still gleamed with a rancorous kind of hunger.

Something in its insipid gaze made him shiver. It was too blank, too empty. The sight of it pulled painfully at something in his chest—pity, perhaps, or just horror at the mere existence of it. This wretched creature wasn't the enemy either. Just something else he had to kill so he might have a shot at surviving.

The azuul charged towards him, but Rivus was too quick. He slid down to his knees and swept the varstaff along the azuul's stomach. Electricity sizzled against flesh as he drove the sharpened blade as deep as he could into the creature's thick belly. It staggered forward with a low, moaning cry and crashed to the ground, throwing up a cloud of dust as it fell among the rubble.

He ran over to Venya and pulled her up with a grunt. "You okay?"

"Apart from getting my ass saved by a legionnaire of all people, sure." She gave a cough through her helmet. "I thought we Idran-Var could take a beating, but those bastards are tough. On the upside, it seems they don't like your glow-sticks any better than we do."

He bristled. "The varstaff is not a—"

"You two need to move it." The other Idran-Var, the human called Zal, was standing on top of a pile of rocks, the round, holographic interface on the side of her helmet blinking with a green light. "We've got more of the enemy incoming. Watch out for the four-armed bastards that look like metal insectoids."

"Metal, you said?" He glanced at Venya, twirling his varstaff between his claws. "Maybe I can hold them off, give you a better chance of getting the injured to safety."

Zal snorted. "Cute. I'm guessing you're not already aware of the fact these aliens emit debilitating ultrasonic waves that frazzle your brain and leave you paralysed in minutes. You'll keep out of their range if you know what's good for you."

He bit down an impatient growl at her rebuke. "How do you know so much about them already?"

"Scout Captain. It's my job to know my enemy, legionnaire." She tilted her metal head at him. "Now let's go. It's not too much further."

Before they could move, a scream cut through the air. Rivus turned back to see one of the Idran-Var at the rear of the formation stumble to the ground, her metal hands squeezing the sides of her helmet. One of the insectoid aliens was approaching slowly, its four legs glinting with a metallic sheen as it scuttled over the rubble towards her.

Rivus lifted his rifle and fired off a round of bullets at the creature, but they pinged off its exoskeleton as harmlessly as if it was Idran-Var armour.

Zal put a hand on his arm. "No time."

"She's one of yours. You're just going to leave her there?"

"It's already too late. If we go back, we die too."

The Idran-Var was thrashing on the ground now. The insectoid alien took no notice of her as it passed, scurrying over her writhing body like it was another piece of debris to navigate. After a moment, the thrashing stopped. The Idran-Var lay stiff and unmoving on the ground, the metal shell of her armour so still it might as well have been empty.

Was this what they were up against? Aliens that didn't even need a damn weapon to incapacitate them, just proximity?

"They're too close," Zal said, echoing his thoughts. Her voice was hard and grim through the filters of her helmet. "They're going to be all over us by the time we get to the evac site."

"How much further do we have to go?"

She pointed up ahead. It took him a moment to recognise it. The orchards had been razed while he'd been underground. The sandstone-paved sparring circles had been blown to dust. All that was left of the training grounds was a smouldering, blackened wasteland. No more cadets would learn to fight here. No more legionnaires would be born out of this place. It was more than a graveyard. It was the death of everything he'd trained for.

A huge transport ship sat waiting at the other side of the ash field, its engines already burning. Through the haze, Rivus could see people piling in through its access hatch, soldiers and civilians and Idran-Var alike. They were almost there.

Zal let out a gasp. "Shit. It's in my head. It's going to—" She lurched forward, nearly collapsing to the ground before Rivus caught her and dragged her back to her feet.

"Come on," he growled. "The ship is right there. We have to
—" He broke off, grimacing at the scream that erupted from
Zal's helmet. She was already starting to spasm.

He stooped down to gather her flailing limbs and slung her
over his shoulders as she continued to jerk wildly. Something
was growing inside his head—a faraway scream that pressed
against his nerves, spreading to all the cracks and crevices
inside his skull. He shook himself and pressed on across the
black, barren remains of the orchard. Venya was beside him,
ploughing forward with her head bent and shoulders stiff.
Whatever soundwaves the insectoid aliens were transmitting,
she was feeling the pain too. They all were.

Another body hit the ground behind him. The aliens were
too close. More of the Idran-Var were falling which every struggling step. To be so near to escaping and still not make it...

The pain was more intense now, making his vision blurry.
He could see someone from the Idran-Var ship running across
the dry, burned plateau towards them. He tried to shout out, to
warn them off, but he couldn't make his mouth work. They
kept running, not slowing down until—

Something bright and blinding erupted from the middle of
the chaos. It shot like a bolt through the darkness and spread
out behind the last of the stragglers, rising like a wave against
the encroaching aliens.

The flare lingered for a moment, a shimmering wall of
purple light. Then it surged, slamming into the insectoids and
scattering them in spilled tissue and broken shards of metal
exoskeleton.

The screaming in his head dissipated and died, leaving him
with nothing but the sound of his own heavy breathing. Zal let
out a long, pained groan and slid down from his shoulder,
pressing her hands against her helmet. All around them, Idran-
Var were picking themselves off the ground and limping
towards the ship. Towards safety.

The figure who had cast the flare stood alone, ankle deep in ash and surrounded by the dismembered bodies of the aliens. The grey of her sickened skin had bloomed with pale purple. A single piece of armour covered her forearm with dark, glassy metal. When he looked at her, all he could see was Tarvan bursting in her grip.

Niole.

She looked right past him and spoke to Zal. "We have to go now. Rhendar's orders. Serric's already back on the *Vengeance*."

"There weren't many left to save," Zal replied, putting a hand on her shoulder. "We did as much as we could."

"Still doesn't feel like enough." She hardened her jaw. "You go on ahead, I'll be right behind you."

It wasn't until Zal and Venya and all the injured had trudged past them onto the ship, leaving the two of them alone, that Niole turned to look at him. Her wide, black eyes were emptier than he'd ever remembered. There was a time he might have imagined warmth there. Friendship, even. Now all he could see was the monster he'd helped make her into.

Her headtails blew gently against the roar of the engines, and she looked at him with an expression that could have been carved out of stone. "I don't want to do this again, Rivus."

She sounded tired. Maybe she was. Maybe the act of tearing people apart was exhausting. Maybe it left them drained and dead inside.

He shifted his weight to the side, measuring up the distance between them. They'd met here half a lifetime ago. It might have been this very spot. She had started something that day that had echoed through all the years since. She'd left him for dead and run without ever once looking back.

It was time to return the favour.

His varstaff was in his claws before he even realised he'd drawn it. It hummed into life and left a crackle of electricity in its wake as he lunged forward and swung it through the air towards Niole.

She leapt back, bringing her arm across her chest to block the blow with the metal vambrace attached around her wrist. The tip of his varstaff hissed as it scored the metal, leaving an angry black scorch mark behind. Anywhere else and the strike would have burned her skin.

"Don't do this," she said through gritted teeth. "I don't want to hurt you."

He charged towards her again, swinging his varstaff over his head to sweep down on her, but this time it met only the silicone-coated end of her glaive. He pushed against it, sending her staggering backwards. "Don't want to hurt me? Like you did here, all those years ago? Or like you did on Aurel, when you tore Tarvan apart in front of me?"

She brought her glaive around in a slicing motion, but the blow was half-hearted and he parried it easily. The weapon didn't look right in her hands. It wasn't a varstaff. But then, she'd never been a legionnaire.

He pressed forward again, using both ends of his varstaff to pummel her with strikes. Each deflected blow sent her further and further backwards. Her face was flushed with colour and the ends of her headtails were dripping with sweat. Each time she blocked one of his strikes, there was a little less resistance behind it. A little less strength.

She broke off, spinning out of his reach as she fought to catch her breath. "Tarvan was a monster," she said, panting. "If you can't see that after everything he did, maybe you're as bad as he is."

There was more bite behind her words than any of the blows she'd failed to land. The force of them rocked him back, hitting him in a place that was still too raw. "I know exactly what Tarvan was," he said, choking on the words. "I know the things he did. And as long as his memory endures with me, I will never forgive him for it." He broke off, his chest seizing with pain. "I was ready to make things right. I was ready to make sure he'd never have the chance to hurt anyone else. And then you tore him apart in front of me. You took my chance to walk away the moment you took him."

He leapt towards her, knocking her off balance from the ferocity of his blow. She stumbled, too rattled to block the well-placed elbow he aimed at her face. Watching her head snap back gave him a grim sense of satisfaction. Every strike he landed was bolstered by the pain and anger raging through him. There was a relentless fury driving him forward, an anguish that wouldn't let him stop. Not until he made her answer for what she'd done.

Each time he threw himself against her, he found her more and more desperate. Her attempts at parrying his attacks were weak and sloppy. It gave him an opening. It gave him a chance to strike.

He whipped his varstaff around in a sharp, slicing motion, rapping it against her outstretched wrists. She let out a cry and fumbled with her glaive, dropping it to the ground where it rolled through the dust to his feet.

He pressed it into the soil under his boot. It looked so crude next to the elegant grace of his varstaff. An Idran-Var weapon. A weapon Niole had chosen to pick up in place of the one she'd thrown away. Maybe one she was destined to have, after everything she'd done.

How had he ever thought she could have been one of them?

The memory of Tarvan's face swam through his mind, sending a sharp stab of pain through his chest. It was time to end this.

He pointed the end of his varstaff at her, illuminating her pale face with its crackling glow. "It's over, Niole."

A steady stream of blood ran from her thin, flat nostrils to her lips. She wiped it away and spat on the ground. "I wish it was."

Her flare hit him with a force unlike anything he'd felt before. It stole the breath from his lungs and lifted him off his feet, sending him hurtling through the air. There was no impact, no collision with the ground she'd snatched him from. Just the pressure of a steel-like grip, a prison around his limbs he could only sense, not see.

It wasn't like the first time. The first time, she'd lashed out without knowing what she was doing. Without knowing her own capacity for violence. She'd reached into him and boiled his blood from the inside, tearing apart all the muscles and fibres that held him together. He'd felt her fury that day. Felt her fear.

There was none of that rage now. The grip she held him in was cold and exacting. This time, she would mean it when she hurt him. This time, it would be a choice. An execution entirely of her own creation.

"Do it," he grunted, squirming against the force of her flare. It wasn't pain, not quite. Just pressure. Pressure that might snap at any moment. "Kill me like you killed Tarvan."

Her black eyes watched him, far away and unblinking. It didn't seem right that she'd be the last thing he saw before he died. Not after everything she'd done to him. All he would take with him when he left would be the emptiness in those eyes and the ache in his heart as he remembered the sound of Tarvan snapping in the arms of her flare.

The pressure around his chest loosened. He fell to the ground, his jaw plates brushing the thick, black ash that coated the place he'd once called home.

"I don't want to kill you," she said. Her voice was gentler than he could stand.

He pulled himself to his feet, trying to ignore the tremble in his legs. "Why not? You're Idran-Var, aren't you? That's what you do."

"Yes, I'm Idran-Var. But that's not all I am. And this isn't all you are, Rivus." Something softened in the angles of her face. "You saw this coming before any of us. You tried to unite us when nobody else thought it was possible. If it hadn't been for..." She broke off, not saying his name. Sparing him that, at least. "You might have succeeded if things had happened differently. Please don't lose sight of that, not now. Not when so much hangs on us standing together."

It sounded too much like what Zal had said before. *We are all Idran-Var.* It was a peace offering Tarvan would never have accepted.

But Tarvan was gone.

Something loosened in his chest, like all the fight left in him had suddenly drained away. Tarvan was gone. He was Supreme Commander now. The surviving legionnaires would look to him in the days to come. They'd follow him as they once followed Tarvan. Whatever he did now would shape everything that would come next.

Back on Aurel, he'd told himself there was a better way. A way Tarvan had been unable to see when he'd rained sorborite rods down on Vesyllion and blown apart his own legionnaires. Maybe this was it.

He powered down his varstaff, the electricity fizzling out with a gentle crackle. "The legionnaires have always done whatever it takes to protect the people of this galaxy," he said. "I won't let that change under my watch."

It wasn't forgiveness. It would never be forgiveness. It was only him doing what Tarvan, for all his strengths, had never been able to.

When he met Niole's eyes, he saw no victory there—only relief. "We'll make this right," she said. An apology. A promise. "We have to."

He played her words over in his head as he gave up his weapon and followed her onto the evac ship. The burning surface of Ossa disappeared beneath clouds of smoke and ash as they rose through the atmosphere. Hours later, when they'd arranged for him to be transferred back to the familiar surroundings of the *Lancer*, he was still repeating them to himself.

We'll make this right. We have to.

A set of coordinates flashed through on his cabin's holoterminal. A rendezvous point where he would bring the surviving Coalition fleets to meet with the Idran-Var. A place they would make their stand against the monsters set on destroying them. All he had to do was send the message to the bridge and tell them to set a course. A few words, and there would be no going back.

Another light pinged, this one from the new personal wrist terminal he'd requisitioned in place of the one he'd lost on Ossa. He checked the signature, his breath seizing in his chest when he saw who it was coming from.

He opened the connection, and Kite Merala flickered into view. "Hey boss, good to see you're still alive. Had me worried there."

Rivus didn't know whether to laugh or sigh in frustration. In the end, he settled for a strangled, choking sound. "I could say the same for you. Did you find—"

"Yeah, I did. It was a shitshow though. Not everyone made it." He glanced off to the side, looking at something Rivus couldn't see. "The one who sent the distress call, Kojan, he's in a pretty bad way. Infected with some kind of degenerative cybernetic virus. The agitator says she can fix him but—"

Rivus let out a hiss of breath. "She's alive?"

"Yeah, just give me a—"

Kite disappeared from view, replaced by a face he recognised all too well. She looked older than he remembered. The lines in her skin had deepened, and there was a shadow in her eyes that spoke of an exhaustion that had burrowed itself deep into her bones. Her shoulders were narrow and slumped, like she was carrying the weight of the galaxy on her shoulders. Maybe she was.

Alvera Renata, the captain of the human outlanders, the agitator herself, stared back at him through the holo. "Feels strange that this is the first time we've actually exchanged words. Out loud, I mean." Her voice was thin and raspy. "I hear you've been looking for me, Rivus Itair."

He had, hadn't he? And she'd been looking for him too. She'd found him in the dreams they shared. She'd helped him escape on Aurel. She, more than anyone else in the galaxy, understood.

"We started this, you and I," he said. "It seems right we should be the ones to finish it."

A slow, tired smile stretched her mouth. "Whatever it takes."

The weight of their agreement filled the silence between them, so sober it was almost tangible. They knew better than anyone else what was at stake here. They knew what kind of devastation was coming for them. They knew that the only way to stand against it was to stand together.

To *all* stand together.

He cleared his throat. "Kite? I'm sending you some coordinates. The Idran-Var have set up a rendezvous point somewhere on the outskirts of the Rim Belt. We'll gather our forces there while we figure out what to do next."

"Got it, boss." Kite came back into view. "I'll load these into our..." He trailed off, his jaw tightening and headtails flushing with colour. "Uh, not to sound presumptuous, Supreme Commander, but did you look at where these coordinates are pointing to? *Exactly* where they're pointing to?"

The chill in his voice made Rivus's stomach lurch, like he'd taken a step forward only to find the ground falling away beneath him. He'd missed something. Something big. Something he hadn't prepared for.

He pulled up his holoterminal and layered the coordinates on top of his starchart. No matter what it showed, there was no going back now. Such was the weight of the ash-stained, tattered remains of the white cloak around his shoulders. Whatever was asked of him, he would answer. Even if it meant...

The coordinates settled in front of his eyes in lines of green and gold. They pointed to a planet on the fragile edge of the Rim Belt, the border between civilisation and Idran-Var space. It was a planet he knew well. A planet the whole galaxy knew. A planet that had been cracked into pieces by the violent impact of the asteroid hurled at it by the Idran-Var, all those centuries ago.

He'd made his choice. No time for regret.

He was going to Alcruix.

TWENTY-EIGHT

NIOLE

The Forge was usually quieter than this. At least, that's
what Rhendar told her.

The ground trembled as Niole made her way up the
gleaming metal steps. It was hard to tell if it was from the
constant stream of ships arriving or the volatile temperament
of the volcanic plates below the planet's surface. If you could
call what was left of Alcruix a planet.

Not for the first time, she let out a long, drawn-out breath,
as if that would make everything easier to believe. The Idran-
Var had killed a planet. That's what she'd thought. That's what
the whole galaxy had thought. Nobody could have ever imagined they'd return to the site of their ruin, to the desolation
they had wrought, and claim it as their own.

Or *reclaim* it, as Serric had pointedly corrected her.

Skylla's Wake. That was what they called it now, this broken
remnant of what their asteroid had left behind. A planet
cracked at its seams, parts of it lost and drifting in the dark.
Fissure-like tears as deep as its core. Frozen oceans and crys-

talline mountains made from ice. Shifting tectonic plates and violent eruptions. An atmosphere so thin it was like the black of space above was close enough to touch.

The metal steps had been coated in artificial salt, but they were still slippery underfoot as she climbed towards the Forge's entrance. The building was huge and industrial-looking, belching out white-hot steam into the darkness. Sharp blades of ice hung perilously from the lip of its roof, glinting even in the dull light. It was hostile. Challenging. Unequivocally Idran-Var.

There was nothing ornate about it on the inside either, just steel and shadow. But that didn't stop the sensation that tugged at her when she crossed the threshold. Despite its simple appearance, she could sense the Forge was a place of great meaning—as close to sacred as you could get for a people that valued pragmatism and a loaded gun over anything resembling spirituality.

Rhendar was waiting for her next to one of the huge electrical furnaces. Every few moments, a crackle would resound from inside and a flash of brilliant light would glance off the reflection of his armour. There was a low, vibrating hum in the air. A promise of what was to come.

He tilted his head towards her in his usual smile. "Now you know."

Everybody thought the Idran-Var had killed a planet. What they didn't realise was what they'd found in its remains.

Rhendar tapped his wrist terminal and the buzzing from the furnace cut out sharply. The electrical storm raging inside —precise and perfectly controlled—flickered into nothingness, leaving the air quiet and still. A panel on the side of the door blinked with a series of lights and then slid open, presenting her with what she came here for.

Her armour.

It gleamed with such clarity that she could see her own

reflection in it, mirrored back at her in purples and blues. There was a shine to it that was almost too much to look at. She reached out to touch the metal, half-afraid some current was still waiting inside to shock her.

Rhendar chuckled. "Don't expect it to stay this shiny for long. We've got a lot of fighting ahead of us."

"It doesn't feel real." She brushed the smooth curves of it, finding it cool to the touch. "Part of me doesn't know how to believe it."

It was real, though. She could feel the subtle strength of the armour in her hands, the unflinching hardness of its shell. *This* was what the Idran-Var had found when they'd returned to Alcruix. Shards of a planet's core pushed to the surface from the violence they'd thrown at it. The unearthing of a metal so rare and precious that nobody else in the galaxy knew it existed. It had been their armour across the centuries—not just for them as warriors, but for them as *people*. It had been a secret that ensured their survival.

A secret that no longer belonged to them.

"This changes everything," she said.

Rhendar shrugged. "Everything has already changed. Against this kind of enemy, there's no choice but to change. Not everyone will see it. Fewer still will want to admit it, even to themselves. But what I said before was the truth of it. We are all Idran-Var."

Coming from anybody else, it might have sounded like a declaration of war. But all she could hear in Rhendar's tired, mechanised voice was the weight of that responsibility. It wasn't about power—it was about a burden he couldn't walk away from. He grappled with a fight more hopeless than anything the Idran-Var had ever come up against. A fight against change.

Maybe that's why it finally felt right to be putting on the armour, one gleaming piece at a time. It didn't feel like joining the enemy anymore. It was like joining a fight she could believe in.

She clicked the last piece of armour into place and pulled her new helmet down over her headtails. It was simple, with a wide, black-lit visor running across the middle and subtle crests to follow the shape of her brow ridge. It sealed itself into place around her collar, and when she turned to glance at Rhendar, she was finally looking at him through the eyes of an Idran-Var.

"What do you think?" she asked, spreading her arms. Her voice sounded strange to her ears, taking on a brassy edge through the modulator in her helmet.

Rhendar gave a soft chuckle. "I think this is exactly how I saw you when we first met back on Pasaran Minor. I could see it then, even if you couldn't."

"You had me well beaten that day."

"You had yourself beaten."

She gave a rueful grin from behind her helmet, then realised he wouldn't be able to see it. Instead, she tilted her head, trying to mirror the strange approximation of a smile she'd become so used to seeing from him. "What do you say, old man—up for a rematch?"

He laughed at that, a full-bodied laugh she felt the warmth from, even through the crackling rush of static it made through his helmet. "*Idra ti vestar*, Niole. I don't ask questions I already know the answer to."

She carried his words close to her heart as she made her way back down the steps of the Forge. Part of her felt like she might be able to float away up into the stars that twinkled out from the ever-dark sky above her. For the first time she could remember, everything felt *right*. She had ended up exactly where she was always meant to be.

Another ship rumbled overhead as it made its way down to one of the huge, ice-encrusted landing pads. The horizon was thick with them now—glinting lights in the darkness, waiting to be brought in. The Idran-Var were guiding them with careful coordinates and approach vectors, leading them through the maze of jagged peaks that pushed themselves up from the snow-covered surface. It felt like the beginnings of trust.

She broke into a run, testing the grip of her new armour against the thick snowdrifts underfoot. Each step she took delivered a firm, crisp bite to her ears as she ploughed her way through the snow, taking one of the ridge trails to get a better vantage point. A steep rockface promised a shortcut, and she gathered a surge of energy inside her, harnessing her flare to push herself up from the ground and land neatly on top.

It was so *easy* now. So natural. She reached out and knew it would be there to answer. The tug inside her was fierce and insistent, but it no longer frightened her the way it once had. It no longer had that kind of power over her. She was no longer siolean. No longer *ilsar*. She was Idran-Var.

The top of the ridge overlooked the entire landing zone. Lights from the arriving ships cast the snow in a pale blue light and cut fractal-like reflections in the towering pillars of ice. Across the horizon, she could see the distant plume of a cryo-volcano spewing out white vapour and icy particles past the thin barrier of atmo into orbit. There were ships lingering there too—those too large or unwieldy to safely land planetside. Maybe the *Lancer* was among them.

As soon as the thought crossed her mind, so too did the sting that came with it. She couldn't think about Rivus without seeing the look on his face back in the ashfields of Ossa. Too much hurt. Too much anger and betrayal. Whatever agreement they had come to, whatever they had managed to put aside, it wasn't enough to heal the rift that had opened up between them. The rift she'd opened up.

He'd wanted to kill her. When he failed, he'd asked to die. She'd held his heart in her hands as she lifted him from the ground. She'd felt every beat of it like it was thrumming against her fingertips. She had never been so careful, so cautious. The memory of Tarvan was still too raw, too easily remembered. He'd given her no choice. Rivus had. After all that had happened between them, he'd let her walk away without forcing her to do something she could never take back. Saving them both. Leaving them both with this lingering pain, a bitterness that couldn't be washed away.

A faint surge of energy disturbed the air around her and rippled through the shell of her armour, breaking her away from her thoughts. It was a sensation she'd spent too long recoiling from, too long turning away from. Its intrusiveness no longer scared her. Or if it did, it was for entirely different reasons.

Serric's footsteps were light in the snow as he walked towards her. He lifted his helmet and let his headtails spill over his shoulders—loose, for once, not tied back. He'd regained some of the turquoise in his complexion, and the scar running down the side of his eye had turned brittle and white.

She took off her own helmet, wincing at the bite of the cold against her bare cheeks. The delicate breathing aid that connected her nose slits to her suit only helped against the thinness of the atmosphere, not the temperature. "How did you know where I was?"

He waved an arm and cast a flare in the space between them, illuminating the snow in a soft, blue-green light. The energy pulsed at her skin, even through her armour. It was all the answer she needed.

She turned away, distracting herself with the gathered fleets hovering in low orbit. "There's more than I expected."

"And more still on the way." Serric glanced up, his jaw tight. "I hope Rhendar knows what he's doing, giving ourselves over to them. Whatever happens next, there's no way back from this."

"Rhendar doesn't think of it as giving ourselves over to them. He thinks of it as opening ourselves up. Letting them be a part of all this."

Serric snorted. "We'll see how that turns out. I doubt we'll get through this without some kind of fighting. At least we know if their fleets start any trouble, we've got the advantage of some sizeable planetary defence cannons hidden in the surrounding asteroids and debris."

His tone was light, but there was a dark undercurrent there that made her wonder if trouble was what he wanted. It was always the same with Serric. Even in these quiet moments, these moments of relative peace, there was no way to escape the simmering anger that lay under the surface.

"Back on the *Vengeance*, when Rhendar ordered the evacuation..." She hesitated, half-afraid to finish the question. "Was there ever a moment you thought about—"

"Leaving? Yeah, there was." He shot her an amused look. "You seem surprised."

Warmth rushed to her headtails. "Surprised you'd so easily admit it, maybe."

"Why wouldn't I?" He shrugged. "It's not like Rhendar didn't think the same thing. He knows me too well not to."

"Then why didn't you?"

He didn't say anything for a moment. He looked out at the bustling landing pad, lights reflecting in the black of his eyes. After a moment, he let out a sharp huff of breath. "I keep asking myself the same thing. Wondering if I made the right choice. But Rhendar had the measure of me from the start. He knew I wouldn't leave."

"How could he have been so sure?"

"It wouldn't have been a real fight. Sure, I could have taken a squad and deserted the fleet, hit some Coalition outposts or border planets, softened them up a bit for what's to come. But what would have been the point?" He shrugged. "I'd have been a bloodfly sucking on some poor creature's flesh knowing that a juna already had its scent. It wouldn't have meant anything."

Not for the first time, the memory of Rhendar's words echoed through her head. *With Serric, it's always a fight. He doesn't know how to do anything else.*

Maybe that's what they needed to win this. Someone whose entire nature was to fight. To resist. But even if they won, where would that leave him after? What would someone like Serric do when there were no more fights left?

There were no answers she could imagine that didn't leave her with a cold sense of dread in the pit of her stomach.

They stood in silence for a moment, the air between them riddled with tension of all kinds, most of which Niole didn't want to think about. Something was lingering over them all, heavy with the weight of anticipation and impending violence. It was like the sharp intake of breath before the plunge. The overture of approaching war.

She looked down at her armoured arms, the metal glinting under the lights in her suit. A shimmer of purple sprung out of them like an aura, her flare ready to answer her call. This was what she had chosen. Not for the Idran-Var, or the legionnaires, but for herself. For Ossa and Alcruix and everything in between.

"I told you," Serric said.

"Told me what?"

"That everything you were running from would catch you sooner or later. I used to think it would destroy you when it did." His mouth curled into a smile. "Now, I'm starting to think you might be ready for it."

She was ready. She knew that now in a way she'd never known before. The parts of her she'd left behind on the way were gone for good, lost to a time that had been more innocent, more simple. But there was more out there waiting for her, shimmering in front of her eyes in the shapes of all those she would fight to protect. Rhendar. Serric. Zal. Venya. Claine.

Rivus.

We'll make this right, she'd told him. *We have to.*

All around her, ships rumbled through the thin atmosphere, taking their places on landing pads built upon the shifting, cracked foundations of the planet. Ships from all across the galaxy, gathering here—in this place, of all places—to take a stand against an enemy that had done the impossible. An enemy that had united them.

The black sky stretched out above her, scattered with the broken pieces of a planet that had been chewed up and spat out by the asteroid that had changed everything. It was here, on the site of the Idran-Var's greatest atrocity, that the galaxy's resistance would begin. It seemed horribly twisted in a way, yet almost fitting in another.

The time for running was over. She'd found the fight she was looking for, just like everyone else.

Rhendar was right, she thought. *We are all Idran-Var.*

We are those who resist.

AFTERWORD

Thank you for reading! If you enjoyed Those Once Forgotten, please help other people find this book by leaving a review. Word of mouth is so important for independent authors and helps more books like this get written.

Sign up for the newsletter for exclusive updates, sneak peeks and release news!

bit.ly/scrimscribes

The Waystations Trilogy
Those Left Behind
Those Once Forgotten
Those Who Resist

Why not go back to where it all began? Check out Alvera's origin story in standalone cyberpunk thriller The Exodus Betrayal.

mybook.to/TheExodusBetrayal

You can keep up to date with future releases by visiting ncscrimgeour.com and signing up for my newsletter, or by following me on Facebook, Twitter, Tiktok and Instagram at @scrimscribes.

Printed in Great Britain
by Amazon

24623685R00239